Sept 10, 2011

THE LEMON THORN
(La Espina del Limón)

Jess,

Hope you enjoy

Al Giuli

Though some of the places in this story exist geographically, it is not the author's intention to document any specific person, location, or incident. All names are fictitious, with the exception of those followed by trademarks, included by permission of those entities. Also, permission has been granted by the owners in person for use of the name of the non-trademarked restaurant chain, El Pescador. The story is a work of fiction and any resemblance to any actual person, location, or event is completely coincidental.

Edited by Marion Nauman

Cover by Larry Holt

THE LEMON THORN
(La Espina del Limón)

By

Alfonso A. Guilin

Edited by Marion Nauman

Graphic design and typesetting by SketchPad Publications

Dedication:
This brief tale is dedicated to all who labor in the fields to put food on our tables, and to those who pursue truth and justice for their fellow man.

Author's Note:
I thank Carol Cowgill, Marion Nauman, Fr. Jim Rothe and my wife, Jo Ann for their support and encouragement leading to the final draft.
— Al Guilin

Dime con quién andas
y
Te digo quién eres.
(*old Mexican proverb*)

Tell me who your friends are
and
I will tell you who you are.

Chapter 1
Discovery

THE JUNE MORNING was damp and cool. The leaves on the lemon trees glistened with moisture. Although the sun was out, it would take some time for the trees to dry so the pickers could go to work.

Carlos sat, leaning against the front wheel of the bus waiting with the rest of the crew listening to the conversation. As usual it was about women. Then Mario, the foreman walked up and said, "We'll start in an hour if it gets dry." The men were resigned to wait because they knew that if they picked the fruit while it was wet the sensitive skin of the lemons would blotch and the fruit would be unmarketable. So they all waited.

Some of the men smoked. Although it was still morning, a few of the others began eating their lunches. A couple of them fell asleep using their picking bags as pillows. Carlos too dozed off momentarily in the warming sun.

"¡Ya es tiempo!" shouted Mario. Carlos was startled; he scrambled to get his equipment. He grabbed an aluminum ladder from the trailer and started out into the lemon grove. He stopped in front of the set of trees that had been assigned to him and pulled on his leather gloves. They were well worn. Lemon trees' sharp thorns can tear through leather and into flesh if a worker is not careful. That was why most of the men wore khaki shirts with long sleeves, in spite of the heat. The tough fabric helped, at least a bit.

Carlos positioned his ladder, threw the tripod into the tree, and was one step up when he stopped. It felt unstable. He rocked back and forth to settle it in. Again he rocked the ladder but still it would not set. Curious, he removed the ladder and, using both hands, opened the branches to see what the problem was. He was stunned to discover a body leaning up against the trunk!

"Aiee!" he gasped. Suddenly, he felt his stomach churn and his knees shake. It was a few seconds before he felt the thorn that was pricking his cheek. A trickle of blood, mixed with cold sweat dribbled down his face. The body's head and shoulders were slumped over, hiding the man's face. Part of his khaki shirt was torn where the point of the ladder's tripod had rested. The skin was broken as well, but there was no apparent bleeding.

"Que pasa?" yelled Javier, a fellow picker working in the next set of trees.

"Call Mario, *apúrate.*" Carlos had seen his share of dead bodies, but that was during medical training, when he knew what to expect. This time however, he felt nervous.

Javier came over, looked around Carlos's shoulder and saw the body. His eyes widened. *"Hijo!* What the hell?"

"Go get Mario," breathed Carlos.

"Ya voy." Javier hurried away. Carlos did not move except to lean against his ladder. Soon he saw Javier and Mario hurrying down the row toward him. Javier let Mario lead, conscious that the older man would have had trouble keeping up with him.

"What the heck is going on?" asked Mario. Without answering, Carlos opened the branches to reveal the body. "Is he dead or asleep?"

"I don' know. I haven't moved since I found him."

"Well you're the doctor, see if he's drunk or something," urged Mario.

Carlos ducked under the tree and carefully knelt to the left of the body. He grabbed the right wrist. It was cold, as was the neck. He tried to move the head up to see the face, but it wouldn't move. So he backed out and looked at Mario and the rest of the crew that by now had gathered around the tree. "He's dead."

One of the older men made the sign of the cross. Carlos automatically crossed himself, touching his forehead, chest, and shoulders, as did several of the others. Mario turned to a group of the men and said, "Let's go to the road and stop the first foreman who goes by. Let's hope he has a radio!" Turning to Carlos and the others he said, "We'll be back soon." They headed out.

The small group was alone with the body. A few of the men went back to work. They either needed the money, or felt uncomfortable being near the body. Several waited with Carlos and Javier. "How could you touch the guy?" asked one of them.

"I wasn't too keen on touching him because of the circumstances, but I've touched lots of dead bodies in medical school."

"*Chale;* I wouldn't touch him on a bet!" someone said. They kept their voices low, out of respect for the dead man.

At the end of the trees was the paved road. Once they reached it, the men soon stopped a white pickup. Jack, the field boss got out. "What's the problem? Why aren't you men working?"

"There's a dead guy under one of the trees," answered Mario. "We came out to get help because I don't have a radio."

"What do you mean, 'a dead guy?'" asked the field boss, sounding a bit irritated.

"Carlos found a dead man under one of the trees."

"Are you sure he's dead?"

"Yeah, Carlos goes to medical school in Guadalajara. He's seen dead people before." The others nodded and shrugged their shoulders uncomfortably.

"Damn!" Jack reached back into his truck, grabbed the microphone and called, "Harvest One to Base."

A female voice answered, "Base." The radio crackled with static. "Go ahead, Jack."

"Alice, call the sheriff. Tell 'em to send an officer out here, to Block 14. One of the pickers found a dead man under one of the trees."

"Found what?" shrieked the radio.

"A man; one of the workers thinks he's dead," explained Jack impatiently.

"Roger. Base clear!" Alice made the call, then hurried to spread the news to her superiors.

The sheriff's unit and three company pickups arrived at the orchard at the same time. Several ranch supervisors stepped out of the pickups. Other cars slowed and their drivers looked as they passed by. By now, the sun had burned off most of the morning overcast and it was getting hotter. The deputy sheriff walked right through the men, knowing they would open a path for him. He adjusted his belt as he walked.

"Hi, Jack, what's going on? What's this about a dead guy?" asked the deputy.

"Hey, Larry. I really don't know, but one of our pickers says he found a man under a tree. Says he's dead. Figured we'd better get you guys to deal with it."

"Damn! I didn't need this today, but let's take a look." Jack gestured for the deputy and the others to follow as he and Mario led them to where Carlos and the others were waiting.

When they arrived, he asked, "Which one's the guy who found the body?"

"Carlos, com'ere," said Jack, waving him over. "This is Deputy Nelson," he said to Carlos, introducing him.

"Well, Pancho; show me the body," said Nelson with a bit of a sneer.

Carlos straightened a bit. "My name is Carlos," he said deliberately. The deputy stopped, looked at the young man who was taller by several inches than the officer.

"Sure, Pancho," he continued, emphasizing the name. "Did you touch anything?"

"Yes, but not until Mario asked me to see if he was dead. So then I went under tree and checked him over. I only touched the right side."

"How'd you know he's really daid?"

"I checked his pulse at the wrist and neck."

"What are you... some kinda *doctor*?" the deputy asked, not bothering to hide his sarcasm.

"Yes, I am a doctor," replied Carlos evenly.

Nelson stopped again and examined him with suspicion. The tall young man was dressed in clean but stained pants and a shirt with torn canvas sleeves. He wore an old Dodger cap that was frayed from long use. "What do you mean you're a doctor?" asked the deputy.

"I'm a doctor. I graduated from the University of Guadalajara this year."

"Then what the hell are you doin' here pickin' lemons?" asked the disbelieving deputy sheriff.

"It's what I've done for the last several years. I earn enough money so I can return to school every year. I'll start my residency in a couple of months."

Deputy Nelson once again examined Carlos from head to toe and shook his head in disbelief. "Okay, Pancho; let's take a look at yer body over there."

He quickly shoved his hands and his head into the canopy of the tree. "Shit!" he yelped as lemon thorns stuck him in the hands and face. A couple of men pulled on their work gloves and held back the branches for him. He offered no thanks. He stared for several seconds at the body then fell to his knees as he crawled to the body. He looked closely at it and worked his way all around the tree, back to where he started.

"Well, Pancho, looks like he shot hisself," said the deputy, looking up.

"My name is Carlos... What do you mean he shot himself?"

"Well for one thing, he's holdin' a gun in his hand. Why else would the dumb shit be unner a tree like this, stiff as a board?"

"I didn't see a gun," countered Carlos.

"Well 'Doctor,'" sneered Nelson, "there's a gun in his hand. It's up against his left thigh. The gun's a small one, not much bigger than his hand. I saw it when I went around him." Nelson crawled gingerly out of the tree and straightened up. He was sweating. A red welt was noticeable on his cheek, which he touched gingerly. He looked at his finger to see if there was any blood.

Facing Jack and the supervisors, he continued. "I better head back to my car and call the station an' git the rest of the boys out here. Looks like the guy must'a blew his brains out an' now we gotta clean up his mess. Man, I sure didn't need this today." He went to his car, sat down, and made the call. He returned to where Jack and the other company supervisors were waiting. "The big boys'll be here in an hour or so." Rolling his eyes he added, "They're probably having their coffee and doughnuts."

Jack turned to Mario and said, "Okay, Mario. Let's get the men back to work. Let's not waste the rest of the day."

Before Mario had a chance to take a step, the deputy said, "Jack, what the hell you are doing?"

"Getting my men back to work."

"Your guys cain't work here. The place is already thrashed with everyone walkin' all aroun'. This area's going to be off limits for a couple a days," ordered the deputy.

"But we need to pick this block."

"For chrisakes, Jack! Gimme a break! This company has lotsa orchards. Move 'em somewhere else," he said. Unsure, Jack spoke to Mario and the men started to gather their equipment and move quietly back onto the bus. The only sound was the shuffling of feet and the crackling of the radio from the squad car.

Carlos was glad to be getting back to work, and to be leaving the area. He picked up his bag and gloves and headed for the ladder. "Hey, Pancho! Where the hell d'ya think yer goin'? You stay raht here! And leave that ladder alone!" ordered Deputy Nelson.

"I'm going to work. If I don't go with the crew I don't earn any money. I need the money," answered Carlos.

"Well that's jus' tough luck. You stay raht here. I need to talk to you before the boys from downtown get here."

Carlos watched the bus and Jack leave. He wished at least one of his friends could have stayed while he had to be with the tough-talking deputy. When he turned he saw the deputy get a roll of yellow tape from the trunk of his car and begin to string it around the eight trees that surrounded the one where the dead man sat. Next, the officer moved his car in front of the same row to make sure no one entered the area and so the arriving officers could easily find him.

"Come on. Sit in the car while I take some information down."

Carlos dropped his empty picking bag and gloves and reluctantly sat down in the passenger's seat. He scanned the radios, shotgun, and other unfamiliar items in the car. Not knowing what to do, he folded his hands and lowered them to his lap. The car reeked of stale cigarette smoke.

"Name?" asked the deputy.

"What?" Carlos was startled at the question.

"Your name, what the hell is your name?" growled Nelson.

"Oh! Juan Carlos, but everyone calls me Carlos."

"Last name?" The deputy continued down his list.

"Reynoso, R-E-Y-N-O-S-O," he spelled.

"Address?"

"Buena Vista Camp, here on the ranch. I live with my uncle, Francisco Baca in House 30," he replied.

The deputy continued on his questions. When he finished, he took out a cigarette and lit it with a lighter. He offered a cigarette to Carlos. "You sure you're really a doctor?"

It exasperated Carlos that this man couldn't or wouldn't believe him, but he didn't let his voice show it. "Yes, I graduated from medical school, so I have a medical degree. But I won't be a practicing physician until I finish my residency."

"Didja know the dead guy?"

Carlos wondered what Nelson was getting at. "I don't know. I didn't see his face; but there was something familiar about him," said Carlos. "What's going to happen now? I really need to get to work. I know Jack won't pay me for just hanging around with you."

"Well, sorry. It was just your dumb luck to find the body. It'll really be up to the detectives to decide how much of yer time they'll need. If you don' git one of the paper-pushers, it shouldn't take too long."

The car radio continued to make reports and crackle announcements but Carlos had a difficult time understanding what was being said because of the static, especially since much of the communication was done with code numbers. His mind returned to the situation at hand.

Suddenly he started to feel anxious. What if the detectives treated him with as little respect as this deputy had? Would they believe his answers? What if a detective asked about his papers? The cigarette smoke started to make his already nervous stomach feel queasy.

Chapter 2
Tonalá

THE RAINY SEASON STARTED with a vengeance. The rain came down in sheets, washing the streets. Lightning and thunder flashed and boomed. Yet all was seemingly calm; the little Spaniel lay on the Saltillo-tiled floor, seeming to take no notice of the storm. This was the first storm of the season and the town of Tonalá, Jalisco welcomed the rain. It had been hot and the farmers waited for the rains to get their crops in.

Carlos and Licha sat close together on the porch of the second story of her family's home. They breathed in the welcome scent of newly-dampened earth and pavement as it rose to them, but it did not bring them the happiness it did to the rest of the townsfolk. The balcony overlooked a high adobe wall. During the lightning flashes they could see the church steeple and several other tall buildings in the square. Although they were out of the rain, Licha's face was wet. She buried her face in Carlos's shirt to hide and dry her tears.

"When are you leaving?" she asked.

"At midnight. Andrés is taking me to the station."

"Do you really have to go?" She knew the answer to the question, yet she asked it without even thinking.

"*Ay, mi Lichita.* You know that if I don't go to the United States to earn the money I need, I won't be able to start my residency next term." There was no more discussion, as the departure date and the reason for his summer work had been discussed between the two for the last several days. Together, they had gathered his clothes and decided which ones to pack, making sure that he carried only the absolute necessities. He could not afford to carry any excess weight or items he couldn't discard, should he have to in a pinch. The only exceptions were his small prayer book and a rosary his mother had given him. These he would put into his pocket when it came time to make the border crossing.

They held each other tightly without moving. All the movement and passion had been expended the previous night. Tonight they just held on, exhausted, drained of emotion. Carlos had made the trip many times already, starting when he was fourteen. Since the two families had lived next door to each other for many years, Licha was well familiar with this migration. Members of her own family had made similar trips.

Yet this trip was different from the others. During this last school term the two had become very close. They attended the same school, though she was only starting her medical studies and he had just graduated. She knew well his financial needs. However, the logic of this reality did not ease the pain.

Both households were aware of Carlos and Licha's feelings for each other, so each of the family had members made an effort to leave them alone during the last several days. Even the going away meal was subdued. Just after the evening meal they went to San Marcos church for Mass. They took no notice of the gaily-painted store fronts. Their turquoise, red, pink, and blue offered them no happiness.

Even at church they sat apart from the other parishioners who also seemed to be giving them space. The wooden kneeler felt harder than usual. Even the communion host tasted different. The priest chose not to give a homily, making the rest of the Mass seem more poignant. Before leaving, the couple went to the side altar and lit a candle in front of the statue of the Virgin of Guadalupe, then bowed in prayer briefly before going out the massive front doors.

The clouds parted temporarily. They squinted in the bright sunlight as it reflected off the old church's whitewashed walls, then sat for a moment on the steps, holding hands and waiting for their eyes to adjust. Droplets sparkled on the hibiscus leaves in the planter next to them.

"Carlitos," called his father, "Andrés is here."

"*Sí, Papá!* I'm coming," answered Carlos reluctantly.

Licha barely reached his shoulders when they stood up. Her long black hair fell loosely, coming almost to her waist. It tangled in his hand as he embraced her. He kissed her and led her down the steps to where the rest of the family was waiting. They avoided looking at them as they descended. Everyone knew they were struggling to hide their sadness.

Carlos approached his father, "Papá, please give me your blessing."

Everyone bowed their heads. The old man choked back his emotions, and in a firm voice prayed, "Father, we ask for your blessings on our son. We ask you once again to protect him and give him the strength and wisdom to do what is right. We ask you to bring him back to us safely. This we ask in the name of Our Lady and her Son, Amen." The old man looked up to his son, and taking his face in his two hands, pulled him down and kissed him. Then he made the sign of the cross on his forehead.

"Do you have your rosary *mi'jo?*" asked his mother.

"Sí, Mamá."

"Well don't forget to use it," she urged.

"I won't forget; don't worry."

"Do you have the money?"

"Yes, thank you."

Then she added, "Don't forget to eat the empanadas I made for your trip." His mother went on with her reminders as if her words could keep him there a bit longer. "And be sure to say hello to your *tía* for me."

"Yes, yes… I have it all, thank you. As soon as I get my first check I'll send you some money so you can pay the school," he told her. Then he hugged her and gave her a final kiss. He turned to his sweetheart one last time.

"Can I come to the station with you?" asked Licha.

"I think it'd be better if you didn't. It's late and the weather is terrible. Besides, it'd feel better for both of us that way," he said.

"You're probably right." They had another long embrace before parting. She walked quickly back into her house and up to the dark balcony. He knew she was there. He opened his eyes, turned, and looked up… but could not see her.

Carlos turned to his cousin. "Okay, Andrés; let's get going," he said. They piled into his pickup and drove along the cobblestone street that led out to the main highway which would take them to the bus station just outside the city of Guadalajara.

The main bus terminal glistened in the evening rain. All the lights in the terminal were all on and the station was crowded. Buses of all types were parked or idling around the buildings and some were entering or leaving. The roar of their mufflers drowned out the pleasant patter of the light rain. The buses, newly rinsed of dust, were brightly colored and appeared newer than they usually did.

"Are you going on Uncle Tomás' bus?" asked Andrés.

"Yeah, he told me this run wouldn't be full and he's going to let me ride free. If the bus owners complain, he's going to tell them it's good for public relations to have a doctor on board. Anyway, no one has ever said anything before, so I don't expect any trouble. Listen, just drop me off here. It's raining hard now and there's no parking place handy, so I'll just make a run for the terminal."

Andrés did not argue. "Good luck!" he said.

"Thanks, and thanks for the ride."

Carlos held his backpack over his head and ran for the terminal. The Terminal Primera Plus was across the parking lot. He paused to get his bearings. The station was noisy. Over the diesel engines' rumbling, vendors hawked food and drinks, travelers chatted, and families said their farewells. He worked his way over to the bathrooms. He didn't need to go but he knew his uncle would appreciate it if the toilets on his bus didn't get used unless they had to be. The strong smell of urine in the men's room was piercing; he didn't linger long.

He spotted his uncle standing next to the door of the bus talking to his assistant. On these long runs, bus drivers carried an assistant who made announcements and helped with passenger needs. These two had worked together for several years. They were both smoking as they passed the time before departure. "Hello, Uncle Tomás!" he called.

"Carlitos, how the heck are you? Another trip to the north, eh?" answered his uncle. His uniform was fresh, made of a kind of fabric that would look good even after a very long trip.

Tomás was only six years older than Carlos, so he was more like an older brother than an uncle. He'd started driving local buses when he was sixteen and worked his way up to the long routes. For the last eight years he'd been one of the most senior drivers for Primera Plus. Primera was the elite among bus lines and every driver yearned to drive one of theirs. The drive to Tijuana was one of the best routes to have. The route also had the best-equipped service stations along the way.

"You got a new bus?" asked Carlos, eyeing the clean, new paint and unblemished windshield.

"Yeah, it's a new Mercedes, just like the old one, but this one really goes! You'll see!" replied Tomás with pride.

"Carlitos, take the first seat behind me. Both seats are empty now, but we may pick up someone to fill it on the way. Is the backpack all you have?"

"Yep, that's all, travel light as they say. I'll just keep it with me."

"We're almost ready to leave most of the passengers are already aboard." As Carlos set his foot on the first step, he continued. "Did my sister pack any of her famous empanadas? If I know your mother… she did."

"Yeah, she made sure I had something to eat."

"I'll expect you to share some later on," he grinned. "And I suppose she gave you a rosary, too?"

"Yeah, that too," Carlos laughed as he climbed up into the bus. The bus still had the new-carpet and fresh vinyl smell of newness. The passengers were settling in, moving their belongings into the overhead compartments and below the seats to make the long ride ahead more comfortable. He could hear a baby crying in the back. He was glad he was sitting up front.

The bus left the station, its lights reflecting the gentle rain. The well-built Mercedes drowned out the noise of the city and smoothed out the bumps on the worn roadways. Uncle Tomás followed the road that circled Guadalajara to avoid the congestion which plagued drivers even at midnight. Carlos dozed off even before they got onto the main highway heading north.

Chapter 3
A New Friend

JUST AT THE BORDER of Nayarít and Sinaloa states, the bus stopped briefly. The door whooshed open and shortly afterward, exhaled as it closed, bringing in a waft of cool morning air. Carlos felt the seat move as someone sat down next to him. His eyes blinked open and he glanced briefly at the girl. She smiled shyly. He nodded, readjusted himself in his seat, and went back to sleep.

Dawn was well on its way. The bus had left Jalisco's storm behind and was rolling by the sugar cane lowlands of Sinaloa. Carlos stirred and looked over at his neighbor. All he could see was her long, blond hair spilling over a denim jacket. She was asleep with her legs pulled up, making herself into a small ball. He looked up see his uncle's reflection in his rearview mirror. He saw sparkle in his eyes. Uncle Tomás noticed him and winked.

Carlos stretched his stiff limbs. The girl rotated herself around toward him; still in a ball. He could see the top of her head. She was a natural blonde. He noticed there were no dark roots. The sun was now well out and Carlos could tell it was going to be a hot day. The next time he looked toward the girl, her eyes were sleepy but open and she was quietly looking at him. He acknowledged her with a faint smile. Her eyebrows barely moved in some kind of recognition then she slowly closed her eyes again.

The sun was now well out and shone through the tinted windows. People were starting to stir a bit, talking softly among themselves. The baby in the back was starting to whimper. This time his seatmate's eyes were wide open. She uncurled herself and stretched. "Hi, again." He was thankful that her voice wasn't one of those shrill ones, but a soft alto. "Hi," Carlos replied.

"You speak English?"

"Yes."

"Great! I'm Ann; what's your name?"

"Carlos."

"Where are you going, Carlos?" This was followed by a series of rapid questions. It was clear he wasn't going to get back to sleep. However, conversation might help pass the time. "I'm going to Tijuana too. My mother's going to pick me up there, that is, if she got my message." Carlos nodded in acknowledgment. "So, what are you going to do in Tijuana? Do you live there?" she continued.

"No, actually I'll just be there for a day. Then I'm going to another town farther north."

"Oh? Which one? I live farther north, in Encino," answered Ann.

"Santa Paula."

"Really? I know where that is! My parents rent a beach house north of Ventura and we often go to Santa Paula to eat. They have great Mexican food there, did you know that? We'll be going up there again in July." Carlos could only nod as she prattled on. "You do actually speak English, don't you?"

"Yes, I actually speak English," he smiled, gently mocking her.

"Great!"

Tomás looked back at him through the mirror and said, "We'll be arriving at Mazatlán in a few minutes, Carlos."

"Do you know the driver?" she asked.

"Yes, he's my uncle."

"Oh." She paused. "It's nice that you're not traveling all alone. So, will there be something to eat at the bus stop? I'm hungry."

"There are several restaurants and food carts at the next stop. But I have some food my mom sent along, if you would like to share with us. All we have to do is get something to drink."

"Wonderful! I'll bet she's a great cook!"

"Yes, I'll be missing that," mused Carlos. Silently, he added, "among other things."

The houses at the far edge of town began to appear. As they neared the town, they saw people bicycling or walking purposefully, going about their day. Some of them stopped to watch the bus as it sped down the road. The bus station in Mazatlán is also on the edge of town. The bus wheeled into the terminal and came to a stop alongside another Primera Plus bus. "We'll be here for half an hour, announced Tomás' assistant. It's time for breakfast and restrooms. Please be prompt, we'll depart in half an hour."

"Where should we sit to eat?" asked Ann.

"Around the corner is where I always go. It's where the bus drivers eat and hang out."

"Can we do that? Cool!"

They followed Tomás and his assistant to a door posted: **NO ENTRADA**. It opened onto a small dining room. There was a huge coffeepot steaming in the corner. Heavy, earth-colored cups were piled in awkward, leaning stacks. They each got a cup; the men all used several spoonfuls of sugar and lots of milk. Ann filled her cup to the top with the black liquid. Tomás' assistant went off to the dispatch office to check for any messages that might have been left for them.

"Well Carlitos, let's see what my sister sent us," said Tomás. He'd been looking forward to this all night long. Carlos unzipped his backpack and took out a bundle wrapped in aluminum foil. He took out and opened the first packet of carefully-wrapped empanadas. There were six of them, and a small bottle of her special sauce, besides! The empanadas had a delicious-looking brown, blistered crust from the frying. He handed one each to Tomás and Ann. He quickly bit off one end and poured a bit of the sauce into it. Then he downed it in three bites.

Ann tentatively took a bite of the folded tortilla and found the filling was a combination of sweet and hot at the same time. She couldn't identify all the ingredients but there was plenty of meat in them. They were savory and delicious. They were even still a little warm. She waited expectantly as the young man opened another foil package.

"These are really great! What are they called?" asked Ann.

"Empanadas", replied Tomás. "Carlito's mother is famous for them." For a while, the only sounds were the crinkling of paper wrapping, chewing, and the contented, appreciative sounds of the three companions as they ate.

They rode in silence for some time. As the bus pushed north, the landscape became more arid and even though the bus was air-conditioned, the sun that came through the tinted windows felt warm. Finally, Ann asked, "Hey, I noticed your backpack. Where did you get it?"

"At the campus bookstore."

"You went to UCLA Medical School?" She couldn't hide the hint of surprise in her voice.

"I took a night class last summer. I bought it then. It was a class in business administration for doctors. I've taken a couple of night classes there over the last few years, he explained.

"Why did you take classes in medical administration?"

"Well it's something I'm going to need when I set up my practice."

"You're a doctor?" The empanadas weren't the only surprise package to be opened on this trip. Carlos was also proving to be quite a surprise.

"Yes. In fact, I just graduated from medical school at the *Universidad de Guadalajara.*"

"Well I'm impressed!"

"What about you? Are you in college?" asked Carlos.

"I just finished getting my teaching credential at Cal State Northridge. That's why I came to Mexico for a few days to celebrate. Five years was a long time! But then, medical school's a lot longer, isn't it?" she added, turning the focus of the conversation back to him.

As the landscape changed so did the conversation. She kept returning to discussions about college because she was fascinated by how well he spoke English and by the fact that that he was a doctor. Their conversation ranged throughout the day, into the night, and into the morning of the following day.

"So how will you get to Santa Paula?" she asked.

"One of my friends will give me a ride," he responded hesitantly. I'm in no hurry, as long as I get there there by Monday in time to start work."

The bus swallowed more of the desolate landscape. Abruptly, Ann said, "I have a great idea! Why don't you just come with us? I live in Encino, so we can give you a ride that far! Your friend won't have to drive nearly so far to get you. My mother is going to pick me up at the bus station; it'll be a snap!"

Carlos was stunned with the sudden change in conversation. She packed a lot of ideas into a short time. He was thinking of the $1,500 he had in his pocket for paying the *coyote* to help him cross the border. It was what he'd earn in almost three weeks of hard work. He was tempted and was quiet for a long time. He worried; was the possibility of saving that much money worth the risk of embarrassment in front of Ann and her family? "Thanks, but I don't want to bother anyone. It really would be too much of an imposition on your family."

"No, it's really no trouble, and if I know Mom, she'll agree with me. Besides, now that we're friends, I'll be telling her all about you and she'll want to meet you anyway."

He said nothing. She re-coiled herself, leaning up against him this time, and went to sleep. If he didn't have to pay to cross the border, it would be an enormous relief. Picking lemons was hard work and this would pay not only for his tuition, but he'd be able to afford the luxury of going to a movie or concert and buying some clothes. More important, he would not need to take money from his family who were still helping his two younger brothers finish school. Although his father's salary as a teacher was modest, they lived a comfortable life, but Carlos knew there was no extra money.

Yet, if he got caught, he knew that nothing of consequence would happen to him. *La Migra* would just send him back into Tijuana. Then he'd just jump the fence the next day. But he wondered what would happen to Ann's mother. The parched, endless desert usually put him in a dream state, but this new thought gnawed and made him uneasy. He didn't know this girl and he didn't know her family. Perhaps nothing would happen to them. Looking at the dry landscape finally made him doze off, like most of the passengers, including Ann.

The bus now headed west. The irrigated fields of the Mexicali Valley were mostly cotton, interspersed with fields of grain and other crops that Carlos didn't recognize. The Mexicali terminal would be the last stop before they reached Tijuana. He spoke softly to his uncle and briefly outlined the offer Ann had made him. "What do you think I should I do?" he asked.

"Well, I don't think anything would actually happen to them. The customs guys would probably just stop them and chew them out for being so gullible. You could also tell them that the family was unaware of your situation," replied Tomás quietly.

As the bus started over the mountains that would lead them to Tijuana, it swayed around the curves, rousing most of the passengers. Ann said, "I'm sorry, but I couldn't help but hearing you talking over the ride idea with your uncle. So, what did you decide? You will come with us, won't you?"

"I don't know; this was not my plan. It just seems like such a big imposition. I'd rather not… I did really enjoy traveling with you; it made the trip go by much more quickly. It just seems better if I keep to my plans."

"Don't be silly! Tell you what; let me introduce you to my mother at the station and you can decide then, okay?"

"Okay; we'll see what she says." In his mind, he knew her mother would be more sensible and that would end the discussion.

"Mom, Mom!" Ann yelled to a woman standing next to the terminal's gift shop. The station was crowded, so no one paid attention to the reunion. Carlos stood several paces away. With all the noise in the place he could not hear what they were saying. He understood the smiles and hugs, the mother looking at her daughter at arms' length. The mother was an older version of her daughter. Ann turned and pointed to him, then waved, inviting him to join them. He stood, feeling embarrassed and uncertain. He caught the eye of his uncle who smiled and nodded in silent encouragement.

He approached the two women. "Mom, this is Carlos; Carlos this is my mom."

"Good morning, Mrs… he stumbled with the last name.

"Ferranti, Julie Ferranti," she quickly filled in the blank. "This is my son, Mike."

"Good Morning Mrs. Ferranti. It's very nice to meet you. Hi, Mike." The boy, who looked about ten, returned his smile.

"I understand we're traveling the same direction. We'd be glad to give you a lift if you'd like to join us. We'd enjoy the company, if you don't mind lots of talking." She and Ann looked at each other and giggled knowingly.

"Oh, Mrs. Ferranti; I very much appreciate your offer but I really think it would be better if I kept to my plans. I don't want to impose on you."

"Not a problem! As far as I'm concerned, it's all settled. Now we have two girls and two boys; it evens out. It's no imposition." She was as insistent as her daughter, so Carlos went along with the plan despite the worries he kept to himself.

The family Volvo crawled slowly as it neared the U.S. Customs and Border station. The Otay crossing has multiple lanes and their car was in a middle one. Peddlers showed their wares and spoke to Ann's mother. When they spotted a person who seemed to acknowledge their wares, they danced between the cars to reach them, hoping for a sale. He noticed a customs officer with a dog work his way through the cars. The officer could see the passengers looked a little nervous, but the dog seemed unconcerned, so they moved on. When they were just one car from the inspection stop, he saw a Customs Officer turn to look at their car. She made an entry into her computer. He knew she had entered the Volvo's license number. He felt more nervous than ever.

"Good morning, where are you coming from?" asked the officer.

"Just the bus station, I just picked up my children. They were in Mexico for a few days." The officer looked at the Julie Ferranti. She bent over, glanced at Ann in the front passenger seat then quickly looked at the two boys in the back seat. Carlos desperately hoped she wouldn't notice he looked so different from Mrs. Ferranti's other two children.

"Thank you, have a nice day." She waved them through.

Carlos exhaled. What had felt like an eternity to him had actually taken only about thirty seconds. The Volvo sped up. "Welcome to the United States" read the billboard as they passed. Carlos's apprehension disappeared. He now became aware of the car's air conditioner. He leaned back and quietly relaxed.

The red brake lights from the cars ahead and the Volvo's slowing indicated they were approaching the San Clemente Immigration Inspection Station. His apprehension returned. The car slowed to a crawl, but before Mrs. Ferranti could roll the window down, the officer waved them through. He had made it!

"Is anyone hungry?" asked Mrs. Ferranti.

Before either Ann or Carlos could answer, Mike spoke up. "Let's stop at In-N-Out®!" Before she could suggest an alternative he said, "Mom, you promised! You promised, remember?" "Carlos, do you like In-N-Out®?" asked the boy.

Carlos smiled at him and said, "It's my favorite too. There's one in Ventura that I go to sometimes." Mrs. Ferranti chuckled agreeably and soon eased the car over to the right lane, took a freeway exit, and at the familiar yellow arrow, pulled into the burger restaurant's parking lot.

"Mom, did I tell you that Carlos is a doctor? He just graduated from medical school in Guadalajara and he's taken some classes at UCLA, too." Mrs. Ferranti took in Ann's rapid report and looked at Carlos across the table, her eyes showing she was impressed with this information. He'd just taken a bite of his burger, so he just smiled and shrugged his shoulders. "Hey, Mom?" continued Ann, "Can we invite Carlos to stay with us tonight? I could drive him to Santa Paula on Sunday." The surprised young doctor swallowed without completely chewing the bite he had in his mouth.

"Mrs. Ferranti," he protested, gulping. "It's too much to ask; I really don't want to be a bother. I really should get to my aunt's house."

"Does your aunt have a phone?" He nodded, realizing that, after her actions at the border and from this question, that Mrs. Ferranti understood his situation. "You can call her from the house. Tell her you arrived safely and that you'll see her on Sunday. Besides, I'm sure that you would like to meet my husband. You two will have lots to talk about." Again he gulped.

The rest of the freeway drive to Encino was quick; the traffic at midday was moving in good order. Carlos was familiar with the freeway system and had a pretty good idea of where he was. Encino, however, was different. Although, he had been through the area many times, he had never gotten off the freeway in this part of the valley. Mrs. Ferranti crossed Ventura Boulevard and headed up into the foothills. She pulled up into the circular driveway of a neatly kept ranch home. Two Mexican gardeners were raking lawn cuttings and leaves as the family got out of the car.

Although the afternoon was hazy, it was warm. "Mom, we're going to go swimming, but I'm taking a shower first. I feel *so* sticky! I haven't had a shower for two days. Come on Carlos! You can use the shower in the guest room." She pulled him into the house.

"I don't have any clothes to swim in." He shrugged his UCLA backpack off.

"That's not a problem," said Mrs. Ferranti. "Mike, take Carlos to John's room. You can find Carlos some swim trunks that will fit him... and maybe a change of clothes. There should be plenty to choose from in your brother's chest of drawers. That way he can change into some of John's stuff after he swims."

The older brother's room had a single bed and was well-furnished. Mike found some trunks in one of the drawers, "What color do you want: red or lots of flowers?"

"Red is fine," answered Carlos. Where's your brother?"

"Johnny's in the Army. He just got sent to advanced training at Ft. Bliss last month. It's down near El Paso and it's really hot there, so he misses the pool!" He led Carlos to the guest bath and handed him a towel. I'll go get changed. I'll be back in a sec to take you to the pool."

"Thanks!" Carlos showered quickly, and then put on the trunks reluctantly before Mike came running back.

"Let's go!" he said. Following Mike, Carlos hurried down the stairs and into the back yard that rose gently up a slope. Neatly-trimmed flowering shrubs of some kind bordered the yard. A couple of shade trees were positioned to shade a large patio and the several chairs with cushions set haphazardly on it. He crossed a broad lawn to reach the pool, dropped his towel on a lounge chair, and jumped in.

Ann and her mother followed about ten minutes later. They really did look remarkably similar, except that Ann had long hair. They were both very pretty. If Ann wore her hair up under a hat, it would be hard to distinguish the two.

"I understand you're a doctor," John Ferranti began from across the dinner table. Ann's father was tall, with an olive complexion. He spoke with a bit of an accent that Carlos couldn't identify. In fact, it seemed to him that Mr. Ferranti's accent was more pronounced than his own.

"Yes sir," said Carlos.

"Well, we have something in common. I sell malpractice insurance to doctors and hospitals, so I'm around doctors all the time. Oh, and our neighbors on both sides are doctors, too." Ann's dad was friendly to him and he sensed an ease with the rest of the family. Carlos relaxed, ate, and listened to the family conversation.

"Do you kids have any plans for this evening?" he asked after dinner. "And Carlos, is there anything you need to do before you get back to work?"

"Well sir, if it's not too much trouble, I'd like to go to someplace where I can buy a money order to send home."

"We can go down to Gelson's. They sell money orders," suggested Ann.

Mrs. Ferranti said, "Good, you two take care of that. While you're there, why don't you pick up some ice cream and we'll watch a movie when you get back?" She retrieved her purse and handed Ann some money.

"Your parents are nice," said Carlos.

"I know. I told you so! My mom's my best friend and Dad is pretty neat, too. Too bad he works most of the time."

Once inside the store, they debated ice cream flavors, discovering their tastes had several flavors in common. They ended up getting two half gallons, to make sure the rest of the family's tastes were covered.

Carlos bought a money order for $1,000. When he took the money from his backpack, the neatly folded bills still carried the faint smell of his mother's perfume. His mother would be surprised to receive money so quickly. No doubt she would wonder why and then worry how he earned the money so soon.

Chapter 4
Detectives

CARLOS SAW THE GRAY CAR approaching. Even though the car had no official markings, there was 'police' written all over it. The large Crown Victoria's dull color and extra antennas were a clear giveaway.

"Well Pancho, you're in luck. Looks like they sent out Sergeant Teal to look at yer dead man. That means that this'll all be over pretty soon, 'in a jiffy' as they say at the station."

Detective Sergeant Teal was a beefy man. As he stepped out, he stumbled over the orchard's uneven furrows as he got out of the car. He wore a short-sleeved white shirt with a tie that didn't close at the collar and reached only half way to his unseen belt. A tall young woman with very short, deep-black hair emerged from the passenger's side. Her neatly-fitted white shirt and slim build contrasted sharply with the sergeant's appearance.

"Hey, Larry, what's going on here?" asked the sergeant. He addressed the deputy sheriff, ignoring Carlos.

"This fella found a dead guy under one of them trees when he started to work this morning. Looks like he shot hisself. Gun's still in his hand. There was a crew of pickers here so I had the foreman move 'em to another location, but they'd already walked all over the place."

Teal turned to his partner and pretended to take her picture with an imaginary camera. She walked to the gray car and returned with a bag of camera equipment. "Let's take a look."

Not knowing what else to do, Carlos walked with the three into the orchard. He watched as Nelson pulled back some tree branches to reveal the body. The detective and his partner both looked in. As they walked around the tree, Carlos saw Teal motion to his partner to take some photos. She stayed behind to get a few more shots. Back at the car, the deputy handed the older man a clipboard with the information he had taken at the scene and the information he'd gotten from Carlos. The detective read quickly, looking up a couple of times at Carlos as he scanned the paper.

"You understand English?" Carlos nodded silently. "Good. You know this guy?" asked Teal.

"I don't think so, but I didn't look too closely," answered Carlos.

All three of them watched as the woman walked toward them; her white shirt had picked up some stains from the silt-dusted tree leaves. She ran her hand through her hair, trying to get rid of something. "Damn it! I hate spiders!" she growled to no one in particular, as she approached the car.

"Did you get some good shots?" asked Teal.

"Yeah, I took a whole roll." She was still trying to get rid of the spider webs in her hair, glad that she wore it so short.

"I called the people at the lab. They'll be here soon to pick up the body," said Teal. "You and your buddy wait here. Make sure nobody gets near the area, and see if either of you recognize him when they get him out of there."

Detective Sergeant Teal looked at the photographer and bent his head toward the car. She headed back and got in. She was used to his silent treatment. He didn't seem to be comfortable with a female partner, but maybe he'd get used to it…eventually.

The car backed out turned and they left the way they had come.

Chapter 5
A Hint

"CARLOS, WE'RE ALL GOING to church this morning. You're welcome to come with us, of course. We can take two cars, so Ann can give you a ride to Santa Paula after church," said Julie Ferranti.

"That'd be fine," answered Carlos hesitantly, wondering what he'd do if it was a sort of church he'd never been in. As they drove into the parking lot, he was relieved to see the sign: Lady of Grace Catholic Church.

As they walked in from the parking lot, Mrs. Ferranti said, "I think you'll like our priest. He's just out of seminary. His family came to the U.S. from Korea a few years after the war."

The concept of the Holy Trinity always confused Carlos and as he opened the missal, he noticed this Sunday happened to be the Feast of the Holy Trinity. The Korean priest proclaimed the Gospel from the ambo. "I have much to tell you but you cannot bear it now…He will not speak on his own…He will declare what is mine and declare it to you…Everything the Father has is mine…He will take what is mine and declare it to you." The priest finished the Gospel, kissed the book and looked at the congregation for some time before he started to speak.

"Today we celebrate the Holy Trinity, the foundation of all Christianity and of our Catholic faith. But I'll wager to say that many of you do not understand this concept that's so basic to us. Fair enough; fair enough," he repeated with a slight Korean accent. "In a sense we should all be a bit confused because this is one of God's many mysteries, and since we are not God, we are not capable of understanding as He does. So we are perplexed. But we need to remind ourselves that having faith without complete understanding is what faith is all about.

"We can usually understand God even though He Himself is the biggest mystery of all. Jesus was a historical figure so we know about him. But it's the Holy Spirit that leaves us confused at times. How do we account for this aspect of the Trinity? Look at it this way: We know we will never see God in his manifestation, at least not in this world, and certainly not in a way we would recognize him. Jesus we will not see bodily, because we know he died and rose again 2000 years ago, even though he speaks to us through scripture.

"But it is the HOLY SPIRIT," he raised his voice, "whom we deal with all the time. It's my guess that we find this so odd is because the Holy Spirit is here within us. Within us," he repeated slowly. "It's the Holy Spirit that's nagging us from within. The fact is we don't like to be nagged, especially not from within. That's why the Spirit is disturbing." The priest ended his sermon abruptly and continued with the Mass.

Carlos was mesmerized by the surroundings, the Korean priest, the Ferranti family, and the Trinity. He felt his head, mind, and thoughts moving in a circle. He looked at the family. They were quiet, heads bowed. Even Mike was pensive. Ann, who was sitting next to him, glanced his way and smiled. He turned his head and concentrated on the large crucifix behind the altar to focus his thoughts. Somehow, the tortured body on the cross gave him some peace of mind. This seems contradictory, but the image was familiar to Carlos, unlike everything that had happened to him over the last few days.

Carlos enjoyed church. One of the young priests in Tonalá was a good friend and they had once or twice played soccer on the same team. His family was not very religious, but they were good Catholics and he thought of himself in that way. Today, even though the Mass was very familiar to him, as he had taken communion, he felt a new awareness of this mystery of faith that was real, but just beyond the threshold of real understanding.

They drove quietly though the valley as Ann wove her Volkswagen bug expertly through the cars and trucks on the 101 freeway. Even though it was Sunday, the traffic was heavy but moving steadily. It was not until they'd passed over the Conejo Grade and viewed the Oxnard Plain that she spoke.

"Aren't you glad that we met and you came to stay with us?" she asked.

"Yeah," he answered truthfully. Your family's very nice. I just hope I haven't been a bother. I really liked them."

"*Just* my family?" she teased.

At last, the serious mood of the priest's sermon lifted. He laughed, "Yeah, just your family!" he mocked.

Chapter 6
Mario

TWO MEN IN WHITE UNIFORMS were struggling to roll the gurney over the rough ground of the orchard. They were carrying it as much as rolling it. When they reached the roadway where Deputy Larry Nelson and Carlos were standing, they stopped. The body was covered with a blanket and strapped down, secured across the thighs and chest. Carlos noticed the gun which was in a plastic bag lying between the knees.

The man near the head pulled back the blanket for the men to see. There was a pallid gray cast over the dark skin, interrupted by the somewhat darker hint of a mustache and some sparse hairs on the chin. A black knit hat was pulled tightly over the head, with the rolled edge ending midway down the forehead. A worn, khaki shirt was buttoned up to the neck.

"Looks like the poor bastard shot hisself in the head," said the gurney attendant who had pulled down the blanket. He pointed to the left top part of the head, "Din' even bother to take off his cap; shot right through it." He pointed one finger pointing at the head and made a "bang" sound.

Carlos leaned over and saw the slightest of unraveled strands at the bullet's point of entry on the side of the black hat.

"So, do you know the guy?" asked Deputy Nelson.

"No, not really. But I've seen him around town."

"Okay fellas; you can take him now. Make sure you take the gun over to Evidence." Without comment, the men loaded the gurney into their vehicle and left.

"Well Pancho, where do you want to go now?" asked Deputy Nelson.

"Is that it?" answered Carlos.

"That's it fer now. But I have a hunch that'll be all. Teal's not known for digging too hard and anyway, it looks purty straightforward to me. But we may want to talk to you agin. If you come up with any more information, give us a call. Here's my card."

Carlos took the card and put it in his wallet, "Could you give me a ride to where the crew's working? I'd like to at least make up for part of the day."

"Sure, hop in." The deputy started the car and they drove along looking for his crew. It was noon and the men were eating lunch. Carlos could see smoke rising from a fire the men had built to heat their food. As the car stopped, one of the men was brushing away some of the ashes that had stuck to the burrito he'd just warmed.

Carlos got out of the car. He and the others watched the patrol car as it left and turned onto the paved road. Mario was sitting on an overturned bin that was also serving as a table where several men were eating. "Carlitos," he asked, "what happened?"

Carlos opened his lunch pail and set three burritos directly onto the coals.

"Nothing much." Men gathered around to hear what he said. "I answered a bunch of questions for that deputy. Then, a detective and some lady came, took some pictures, and left. I had to wait around with Deputy Nelson until two other guys came in a van to take the body away because they wanted me to look at the guy's face. They asked me if I knew him."

"Did you?" one of the men asked, horrified at the thought of looking at a dead body, and the possibility that they might know the fellow, too.

"Not really, but I've seen him around. He hangs around with some of the guys from San Miguel. I think they're brothers and they bring people up from the border."

"You mean the Melgozas?" Mario asked.

"I think so, but I'm not sure. Anyway, they asked if I knew him. I didn't and I told them so. All I know is that I lost half a day's work sitting in a car."

"Don't worry," Mario smiled reassuringly. "You can make it

up this afternoon."

Although Carlos only picked fruit in the summer, he was very fast. His excellent hand-eye coordination made him nimble and he was able to anticipate the next fruit he was going to pick. Curiously enough, some of the skills that enabled him to be a good picker were the same ones he needed to be a good physician. He chuckled at the irony of that.

He was always willing to dump a bagful in the bin of one of the slower pickers, especially the older ones. They acted if they didn't notice, but it was well known that Carlos enjoyed sharing his skills. He could easily pick five full bins without much exertion, and at $20.00 per bin, he made his daily goal of $100. All the work was done on this piece rate basis. He knew that a few of the older men who had families struggled to make half that amount. Not only that, but getting that paycheck was the only thing they had to look forward to. It put food on the table. He was very aware of how fortunate and blessed he was.

As they worked down the rows through the afternoon, many of the crew members came over to talk to him. They asked about the body and the police. While they talked, each usually emptied his bag into Carlos's bin. There was no acknowledgment on anyone's part, as was their way. Even Mario came over and picked fruit to help him make up for the lost morning.

In addition to being a foreman, Mario was actually a farm labor contractor, so these crew members were really his employees. He paid them and then he billed the ranch owner for what the fruit the pickers harvested, plus his overhead. He was a very simple man. He had been a picker for many years until the company he worked for encouraged him to become a contractor. Jack, already the field boss back then, had helped him get the necessary license and even sold him some of the company's equipment, which consisted mainly of tripod ladders and trailers. It was a mutually satisfactory arrangement. The company no longer had to worry about employment issues since the men were not legally their employees. Yet Mario was actually connected to the company, since he worked only for them. He was well aware that, without the support of Jack, he would still be picking. And he was too old for that.

Mario liked Carlos very much. They were from neighboring towns and he was even a distant cousin to his father. In fact, most of the thirty men who worked for Mario were either related to him, or came from the towns around the village of Tonalá. They were brothers, cousins, in-laws, or friends, so they knew each other well. Only rarely did Mario hire someone he did not know. He felt comfortable with his own, as did the men.

Mario was very nearly illiterate and had trouble with the necessary bookkeeping required by the company and government regulations. In the evenings, Carlos would go to his house to help the old man make out the required daily report, giving his daughter some time off. He would then say, "Carlitos, add another bin to your number." Once, Carlos men-tioned that the count would always be off by one bin and the office might become suspicious.

"Don't worry, Carlitos, just do as I say. The company is so big and has so many crews, the office never checks with the packinghouse. And for that matter, those dummies that work as receivers spill more fruit than is in one bin. So they'll never notice." Carlos had tried to argue, but he knew that it was futile. Besides, he needed the money. With part of every check he got, he always bought some beer and soda for Mario's house.

Carlos was well-liked because of his friendly, open personality. He was not ashamed of picking lemons, but he knew that it was just the best way to reach his goal. Mario and his crew were proud of Carlos's educa-tion and how hard he had studied to become a doctor. In this way, his success was their success and he was willing to share it with them.

Chapter 7

Arrival

ANN TURNED OFF THE MAIN ROAD to a complex of several houses. They were nestled around a lemon orchard. In the front of the houses was a communal vegetable garden, and next to it was a basketball court. Several men and older boys were yelling and cheering as they played. Standing next to the court were a group of boys and girls, watching the game. They too were yelling and cheering. A couple of older men were in the garden tending the plants, but they also were enjoying the game.

Carlos asked Ann to park the Volkswagen under a large pine tree. They watched the game for a moment. "Well we made it," she said. Then she added, "This is a nice place. I had no idea such a place existed! Is this where you live?"

"Yes, this is where I live." He pointed out #30. "I stay with my aunt and uncle most of the people you see are relatives of mine."

"You're kidding!" she said.

"No, I'm very serious. If they're not relatives, then they at least come from the same town or are good friends. I actually went to elementary school up here with most of them."

"That must make you feel not so far from home while you're away from your parents." She paused and looked toward him inquisitively. "Will I see you again?"

"Well, I'll be busy all summer working trying to save money for school." Thinking of Licha, he knew he didn't want to jump quickly into a new relationship. So he was evasive. "I'm sure you'll be busy too."

"Like I told you, my family rents a house on the beach every summer, usually the first week in August. It's not too far from here, a lot closer than Encino at least. If I call, you will you come out to visit, won't you? I would really like to see you and you already know my parents. I'm sure they would be glad to see you again, too!" She spoke so quickly, it seemed she hardly took a breath.

"Sure I'd be glad to come, but I can't promise anything. Sometimes we work on weekends." He might as well be gracious, he thought. He was pretty sure he'd never see her again.

By now most of the players on the court and the onlookers had noticed the Volkswagen. One of the little girls yelled, "It's Carlos!" But no one made a move toward the car. They watched the game and occasionally glanced over their way. The yelling however had diminished.

"Okay, give me a pencil and I'll write down my aunt's phone number. Now don't be surprised if she hangs up. She doesn't speak English, so make sure to say my name." He returned the pencil and the paper with the number. "Ann, thanks so much for the ride; and please give my thanks to your folks. I liked them very much."

"Carlos, I really am serious. I'll call you in a couple of weeks and I expect you to come to the beach. What's the best time to get you?"

"Okay, okay! I'll come," he laughed. He leaned over to kiss her on the cheek, but as she turned, he accidentally brushed her lips. They were both surprised. He felt his face flush and quickly got out, pulled his backpack from the back seat, and closed the door. "Oh! What shall I do with your brother's clothes?" He motioned to the shirt he had on.

"Just bring them to the beach. Now you'll *have* to come or I'll tell Johnny," she laughed as she pulled away and disappeared around the trees.

As soon as the car was out of sight, the game stopped and most of the younger kids ran over to Carlos. The basketball players also came to greet him.

"Nino, Nino!" cried a little girl as she ran to him. He picked her up and swung her around.

"Charlie, how's my little girl?"

"Nino, I'm so glad to see you! We were waiting for you yesterday." The little girl was his niece. Last summer he became her godfather at her baptism.

One of the boys threw Carlos the ball. He dropped his backpack and joined the game. Charlie picked up the backpack and ran to the house to tell her mother.

Chapter 8
Familiar Places

A WEEK HAD PASSED SINCE THE DISCOVERY of the body and things had calmed down. The police hadn't called and, except for a brief notice in the Ventura paper, no one seemed interested in the murder. The body had apparently not been identified and the incident forgotten. Mario's crew was back to normal. Their only interests were in the piece rate being paid and the baseball game standings. Most of the crew members were Dodger fans.

On Sunday morning, Carlos's aunt said to him, "Carlitos, will you take us to church this morning, to the 11:00 a.m. Mass?" As often happened on the weekend, Uncle Francisco was sleeping in. Work was getting more tiring than when he was younger.

"Of course, Tía. I'd be glad to. What time do you want to leave?" he replied.

"Let's go at 10:30. I don't like to be late," said Tía Estrella. They finished their coffee and went to get dressed.

Carlos drove the family car, taking his aunt and his goddaughter to Our Lady of Guadalupe church on the east side of town. Guadalupe was the Mexican church, although there was one Mass in English. The other Catholic Church served the Anglos and the many English-speaking Hispanics. This division was based more on language dominance than belief or ethnicity.

Carlos followed his aunt and goddaughter into the stone building. They worked their way halfway up the aisle of the sanctuary, knelt, and crossed themselves. After a brief prayer, Carlos sat down, leaned back onto the pew and relaxed. He knew this church very well and felt at home, just like he did in Tonalá, where the church was also named Our

Lady of Guadalupe. He also knew the young Franciscan priest who'd baptized Charlie last summer.

He half-closed his eyes and listened to the comforting mixture of sounds: the last few bars of the organist's rehearsal, kneelers banging on the stone floors, and people softly whispering their prayers. The sound of footsteps made him aware that several people had come to sit the pews directly behind him. Someone brushed against his shoulder as they knelt behind him. He moved a bit to one side and hunched over a bit, giving the person room to kneel.

First he noticed the distinctive perfume. It was not overpowering but smelled faintly of citrus flowers, like when the orange trees start to bloom early in May. The woman was so close he could feel her warmth. Curiosity made him want to turn around, but he dared not. Her perfume lingered in his nostrils.

The scent lessened as he, Tía Estrella, and Charlie listened to the readings and the homily. During the sign of peace, he hugged his aunt, his cousin, and the people in front of him. Then he turned toward the source of the perfume. Stunned, he recognized the female detective who'd come to the orchard to investigate and photograph the crime scene. Again she was dressed in white, but this time it was a silk shirt over tan slacks. Her hair seemed even shorter, almost shorter than his, but hers had a shine to it. She was almost as tall as he was.

He said, "La Paz del Señor."

"Peace be with you," she responded, smiling. Then she turned to the people behind her. The rest of the Mass proceeded, but the lingering perfume remained very much apparent to Carlos.

After Mass, they went next door to the parish hall for coffee and Mexican-style sweet bread from a local *panadería*. The detective was talking to two other women. As he approached, she smiled. "Hi, remember me? I'm Connie Alonzo and you're…?"

"Carlos, Carlos Reynoso," he filled in the blank.

"It's nice to meet you in a nicer setting. I came with my mother and sister," indicating the two women she had been talking to. She introduced them.

"Carlos Reynoso at your service," he said, bowing a bit to show respect.

"Connie, we're going to get some coffee. You want some?" asked her sister.

"Yes, black please. Thanks," she said.

"How can you drink black coffee?" he asked. "It's so bitter!"

"I learned to drink it black in college, when we couldn't afford milk or sugar." she answered.

"I know the feeling," he replied, returning her smile. "Would you like to sit down?" He indicated a couple of open spots at one of nearby tables. The two ladies sitting at the other end paid no attention to them. Connie's sister brought back some coffee and some *pan dulce*. She joined her mother who was in conversation with another group.

"Do you come to church here often?" he asked. "I don't think I've ever seen you here before."

"When I do attend church, I usually go to the Old Mission in Ventura; but when I visit Mom I come here. I grew up in this church."

"Oh, that explains why I've never met you before. By the way, did anything ever happen with that guy I found under the tree?" he inquired.

"Well, we did find out who he was. My supervisor said he killed himself and that was that. He closed the case."

"Really?" he said sadly. "Well I'm sorry for the man and his family. I'm glad it was not more complicated." The last part he said slowly and without much certainty in his voice.

"Why did you say it that way?" she asked.

"Well I've been thinking. I assumed the man was right-handed, like most people, but to shoot himself where he did with his right hand would have been very awkward. There would also have been a reaction by his body and arms. The body's position was all wrong."

"What do you mean?" she asked, now regarding him more closely.

"Well, if the bullet went in where I think it did, it would've caused a very strong muscle jerk on the right side. It doesn't make sense," he explained.

"What would cause a body to react like that?"

"The body is controlled by certain areas of the brain, continued Carlos. "For example, if I were to probe a certain part of the brain, the toes might move, or maybe the eyes." He paused. "The region the bullet entered controls the right side of the body. It just seems to me that for him to have shot himself on that side of his head, he'd have to have reached around and almost pointed the gun downward, which is a pretty awkward position to begin with. I didn't see an exit wound to support that theory. And that angle doesn't account for there not being a violent reaction, like I mentioned, or if he was actually right-handed like most people."

He paused to let her consider what he'd said, then continued. "I also think the gun's recoil would have made his firing hand jerk away from the body. The gun wouldn't have been tucked under his leg. Yet the deputy said he found the gun in his hand, tucked under his left thigh." Slowly and almost to himself, he continued, "It just doesn't make sense…"

"How do you know about the brain reaction?"

"Well, I'm a doctor and the brain was part of the curriculum."

"I thought you were a lemon picker," she commented, her surprise evident.

"That too," he smiled.

"I don't understand."

"Simple," explained Carlos. "I just graduated from medical school at the University of Guadalajara. I've picked lemons during the summer, as I have for the last ten years, to pay for school. In September I'll begin my residency. I need money, so I pick lemons."

"Oh!" she exclaimed, understanding dawning on her. He smiled at her confusion.

The parish hall was now very crowded and noisy. Little boys and girls ran about, calling out shrilly to one another. Adults gossiped as they enjoyed the refreshments made by the ladies of the Altar Society.

Carlos then surprised himself by asking, "Would you like to go somewhere and have lunch someplace quieter?"

"Oh!" She too was surprised by the invitation. "Well, I need to visit with mom for a while… but how about a late lunch?"

"Great! I also need to take my aunt home and take care of a few things first. How about we meet at El Pescador?"

"Fine, is 2:00 Okay?"

"Perfect! See you there," he waved as he got up to find his aunt and cousin.

She had changed. She still wore the same silk blouse but now had khaki shorts, white sneakers, and a perky straw hat perched on her head. The new attire made her look a bit taller. Her deep cinnamon skin contrasted with her clothes, making a very pleasing combination. Any makeup she might have had was not apparent, except for a hint of rose on her lips. The same perfume surrounded her like an aurora.

"Hope you don't mind. It was too hot for those clothes so I changed." It was more a statement than a question. She smiled, her brilliantly white teeth adding to the contrast.

He nodded, lifting his eyebrows to indicate his pleasure in her appearance. He was drinking a beer and motioned to the bottle he had. "Like one?" he asked. "They have several kinds."

"Sure, I'll have the same. I'm starving!" she said, as she grabbed a tortilla chip and dipped it into the salsa. "Thank goodness for chips!"

"Here's a menu, but I'm guessing we won't need one," said Carlos. He caught the eye of a waitress across the room and indicated they needed another beer.

"Why?"

"You'll see," he responded mysteriously. "So tell me about yourself. How long have you been a detective?"

"Only about eighteen months." The waitress hurried over with a fresh glass and opened bottle. Connie relaxed back into the seat and drank right from the bottle, ignoring the frosted glass. "But I've been on the force for about five years now."

"Really?" said Carlos, interested.

"What do you mean, *Really?*' Haven't you ever seen a woman cop?" she said with mock amusement.

"Really, really," he repeated, grinning back. "I never have, except on TV."

"Well I'm not a TV cop; I'm a real cop. Now I'm on homicides in the Major Crimes unit, and one of these days I'll be heading up one of the major units in the sheriff's department." She announced this in such a straightforward manner that he had no trouble believing it. For a moment he was overwhelmed. Usually it was the doctor-lemon picker combination that was the center of conversation.

A new voice interrupted their conversation, booming from across the room as a man wearing the company shirt approached. Miguel, one of the restaurant owners came their way, bringing two more cold bottles. "Carlitos!"

"Miguel!" they said simultaneously.

Miguel set down the drinks with one hand and slapped Carlos fondly on the back with the other. "I heard you were in town. I'm pissed that you haven't been here to see us yet. How've you been?"

"Great! It's good to be back up here and see everyone again."

"And how are your parents?"

"They're fine. Complaining about the heat, but glad for the rains," Carlos chuckled softly. Gesturing toward his new friend, Carlos introduced Connie.

"Connie, a pleasure to meet you!" responded Miguel warmly. "What are you two eating today?"

"We haven't decided," smiled Carlos. "We were too busy talking."

"Do you like shrimp soup?" he asked them. Getting an immediate and enthusiastic response, he continued. "Good! Let me bring you some; my brother just made it and it's great. When he hears you're here, he'll probably want to bring it out himself. Are you playing ball with us this season?" As he asked this last question, Miguel started walking away, greeting other customers on his way to the kitchen.

"Probably," called Carlos after him.

"'Carlitos?'" she asked with an impish grin.

"My mother, my relatives, and all my friends call me that." He shrugged and smiled sheepishly.

"Well, Carlitos, it seemed like everyone knows you, except me,"

He did not have time to answer as the chef arrived at their table with two large bowls of steaming soup. He set them down and then sat down next to Carlos. "Carlitos, I've been waiting for you. I'm so glad to see you!" He reached around Carlos and gave him a quick, tight hug. They almost knocked heads. They caught each other up on how their families were doing and Carlos introduced Connie to him.

"Listen, I've got to go back to the kitchen. That bastard brother of mine won't give me a break. Enjoy the shrimp! *Ciao!*" He was up and gone, barely acknowledging Connie's presence.

"Are we supposed to eat *all* of this?" she asked Carlos, looking at the huge bowl of soup in front of her.

"Well, we'd better make a good dent in it or the cook'll be mad," he laughed.

They chatted about their mutual interests and learned more about each other. He learned that Connie had been raised with many brothers, so she was comfortable around men, and athletic, too. She earned a lot of credits at Ventura College and finished her BA on an athletic scholarship at Cal State Northridge, pitching for their very popular and successful women's softball team.

The shrimp soup was delicious but with just half of it eaten, Connie sat back. "This is really good, but I can't eat another bite."

The waitress brought the check and set it next to Carlos. Connie reached over for it, but before she could reach it, Miguel had raced to the table grabbed it, shoving it into his pocket. Carlos knew it was useless to argue and didn't. He offered a smile and nodded in appreciation.

"Listen, you two come next Sunday real early. We can have some *menudo* with a couple of cold ones and we can talk before all the church folks come in. How 'bout it?"

It was more like an order than an invitation.

They looked inquiringly at each other. "I'll have to check my work schedule, but I'd sure like to," answered Connie.

"Great! Then it's set!" grinned Miguel, and with that, he disappeared into the other dining room.

As they headed to the parking lot, Connie said, "Carlitos, thank you for inviting me. It was a great idea; I enjoyed myself. Now I'd better go see Mom before she writes me out of her will. Do you mind if I call you Carlitos?"

"Thank you; I enjoyed myself too," Carlos said with a smile. "Well, you know I only let certain people call me that," he kidded, pausing. "So I guess now you're one of them, but just around my family, ok?"

"Sure! I like the sound of it. Listen, someone offered me some concert tickets, would you like to go? I promise it'll be fun. The only condition is that it will be my treat. There won't be any argument about who will pay. It's my treat," she insisted, smiling. "I'll call you later with the details."

"Okay! Would you like my phone number?" he asked, surprised and delighted at the invitation.

"I already have it," she said winking, and then walked away. He watched her go, but she didn't look back.

Chapter 9
Questions

"Ron, did you know that Juan Melgoza was right-handed?" asked Detective Alonzo.

Detective Sergeant Ron Teal was sitting at his desk. He wore a short-sleeved white shirt and had his hands clasped behind his head. He was looking out the window into the parking lot. "Who the hell is Juan Melgoza and why the hell should I care if he was right-handed?" answered Teal gruffly.

"Melgoza was the guy we found shot to death on the Grady Ranch last week."

"Yeah, I remember. He was the poor bastard that blew his brains out. Nice easy case... open and shut. So what if he was right-handed?" he asked, with only a touch of curiosity.

"Well, you'd think it'd be normal to put the gun in your dominant hand, so since he was right-handed, he would've put the gun against the right side of his head. If he did use his right hand, he'd have had to get his arm way around to the other side of his head." She demonstrated, raising her arm to show what she was talking about. Either way she reached, it was definitely an awkward position. "The coroner's preliminary report says that a bullet from a small caliber gun entered the head high on the *left* side. That would be an impossible reach for a right-hander."

Teal lowered his arms to the desktop and leaned forward, his interest piqued.

"And the position we found him in doesn't account for the arm muscle contraction," she continued. "There would have been a violent muscle reaction from the stimulation caused by the bullet's entry into brain, or the arm would've been moved away from the body when the gun recoiled after it was fired. We never accounted for either of those things." "I get the recoil thing, but what's this about a muscle reaction?" he asked. Teal was having a hard time keeping up. He wasn't used to anyone else offering explanations during an investigation, much less a woman. Especially one he thought he'd wrapped up. He wasn't sure he liked the idea.

"Certain parts of the brain control individual body parts and their actions. For example, when you touch a hot stove, your hand tells a part of your brain that the stove is hot. Then the brain makes you move your hand damned quick. You don't have any time to think about it, thank goodness. It happens really fast, an almost violent reaction. So," continued Alonzo, "if the bullet hit a part of his brain that controlled his arm, he would've jerked it, sort of like touching a hot stove. Yet the gun was found nicely gripped in his left hand and tucked almost entirely under his left thigh."

"Well, said Teal, "if the kid was going to kill himself, it would be normal *not* to act normal; like using his wrong hand or putting his arms around his head to shoot himself, seems to me." To prove his point, he reached his right arm around his head. His stubby arms awkwardly reached only part way around the left side of his head. He tried his left arm, and it too seemed to be far too short. "What angle did they say the bullet entered his head?" he asked.

"The coroner's report is not too specific, it just says suicide."

"So how'd you know that the kid was right-handed?"

"I called the mother; she told me."

"Huh… What else did she tell you?" He asked now very curious.

"She said her son was kind of wild, but never hurt anyone. She also said that he would never kill himself. She was emphatic about that. She also wanted to know when they could have the body for the funeral." Her voice trailed off.

"Shit, Connie! Why'd you have to screw up a good thing?" He smiled.

"Perhaps you better take a closer look; but don't spend too much time. Check with that dumb coroner again. He probably doesn't know anything other than what he wrote down. He's got shit for brains." He chuckled at the thought. "While you talk to that shit-head, I'll nose around at the hospital for a brain doctor." As Connie departed, he continued to himself, "Shit for brains." He chuckled some more.

The coroner's office was in a new, modern building, but it already smelled old and dank. He had combed his wispy hair from one side to the other, hoping to cover his shiny bald dome. The comb-over didn't quite seem to work. He was middle-aged and stocky. He walked with a muscular swagger as he came around his unkempt desk to shake her hand and pull back a chair.

As she settled into the chair, Connie asked, "Doctor Harrison, do you really think Juan Melgoza shot himself?"

"Well, Officer Alonzo, I think so. But it's not an absolutely sure thing. It was an odd place to aim if you're going to blow your brains out. You see, the bullet entered the left side of the head, entering at about a 45 degree angle. Most suicides go for straight in. It's a little awkward, but it looks like he wanted to end it; so he did. People do weird things when things get to be too much for them."

"What about gunpowder residue? I didn't see that mentioned in the report."

"Well, with suicides, you don't have to go into that much detail. I did find some on his hat and on his hand." He paused. "Now that I think about it, the stuff on his hand could have come from the gun itself," he said, silently wishing that he had been more thorough.

"Doctor, when the bullet went through the brain tissue, would there be any bodily reaction caused by the brain?"

"I couldn't tell that much from the brain, because the bullet didn't just go straight through the head. It hit the inside the skull right above his right cheekbone, then bounced around inside, really making a mess of tissue. That part's all in the report I filed." Noticing her steely glare, he continued, "Guess I'll have to add the gunpowder bit to my report."

He set to work on it. She waited for a copy of the updated report, then walked out to the parking lot. She took her time driving back to her office.

"May I speak to Carlos, please?" The phone had been answered by someone who seemed to be a little girl. The patter of small feet slapping along a kitchen floor carried through the line.

"Hello? This is Carlos."

"Carlitos, this is Connie. I just got the tickets for Saturday night. It's going to be in Thousand Oaks. I was thinking that afterward, we could stop and get something to eat. You can still make still it, can't you?" There was a bit of a pause. "Are you still there?"

"Yeah, I just got out of the shower. Sorry. I was drying off."

"Well what do you say; can you make it?" she asked.

"Sure, it sounds like fun! What kind of concert is it?"

"Good, I'll pick you up at 7:00. Be ready!" She hung up without answering his question. He wondered what he had gotten himself into.

Chapter 10
Conflicted Feelings

CARLOS LOOKED AT THE YELLOW PAD for some time. In the upper right corner, he had written the date, but that was all. Only three weeks had passed since he had made the journey north from Tonalá and he had not yet written home. He was especially worried since he had not yet written to Licha. Finally he began. It went much more slowly than any letter he'd ever written.

Dear Licha,

I'm sorry that I haven't written until now, but we have been working hard and little of note has happened here. The one good thing that happened is that I still have the money I was going to pay the coyote to bring me across. A nice family gave me a ride across the border and all the way to Santa Paula. So that is money I won't have to earn. I guess it means I might come home sooner, or maybe earn a little extra if I stay until the end of August.

About the only thing I have done except work is go to church with my aunt. She enjoys going with me because I don't mind if she visits with her friends after church. Usually, I just watch the people.

This will be a short letter because I hope to be home sooner than I expected.

Con Cariño,
Carlos

He sealed the letter and set it aside to mail in the morning.

Charlie burst into the room he shared with her and her little brother, "Carlitos, the lady is here to see you!" she said excitedly.

"Thank you, *mi Charlita*, please tell her I'll be right out." He finally put on a shirt. He had been debating about what to wear, but since he did not know what kind of concert they were going to, he just grabbed what was at hand. It was not a difficult choice since most of the clothes he kept here were for work. He went out into the living room.

"Carlitos, I didn't know you knew Constancia," said his aunt, grinning devilishly. She was enjoying his embarrassment.

"I... We..." he stammered.

Connie wore black high heels with no stockings. She was dressed simply in a close-fitting black dress that reached mid-thigh, and had perhaps little on underneath. The dress was sleeveless and the fabric, while not tight, clung to her body. Again she wore little makeup, although her lips were glossed. She had no jewelry except for tiny gold earrings. The black dress, shoes, and hair set off her brown skin. She was startling in her simplicity.

"Constancia, how is your mother? I see her at church, but it's been a long time since we sat down to talk." She noticed the young man's discomfort and was happy to make him even more so. As Connie responded politely, Carlos hoped the conversation would be short. "And where are you two going tonight?" continued his aunt.

This was too much for Carlos. He finally picked up his niece. "This is Charlie," he announced. "We're partners, aren't we, Charlie?" She nodded shyly. "We even have the same name. She's my goddaughter. She and her brother share their room with me when I come up." The little girl wriggling in his arms lessened his embarrassment.

"How nice of you and your brother to share like that, Charlie!"

"Ready to go?" he asked.

"I didn't know you knew my aunt, 'Constancia,'" he said, stressing her name.

"If you don't call me Constancia, I won't call you Carlitos in public," she countered.

"That's a deal. So where are we going?" he said.

"You'll see." They drove south though Camarillo and up the Conejo Grade. It was just a few days ago, it seemed, that he had just descended the grade and now he was already going up the hill again.

"*Mariachi El Sol de Mexico*" read the marquee as they drove into the parking structure of the Thousand Oaks Civic Auditorium. People walked toward the elevators in pairs and small groups. It took some time to find a parking spot as they spiraled all the way to the top of the parking structure. The elevator was empty when it finally reached the top floor, but it was crowded by the time they reached the ground level exit.

Carlos was relieved to see men informally dressed. He fit right in. Connie too was dressed to fit in, though to his eyes, she was distinctive. She had given him the pair of tickets while they were still in the car; she carried no purse.

The crowd was mostly Hispanic. The noise was loud and festive as the people talked and greeted each other. Carlos did not know anyone, though a few faces were perhaps familiar.

Connie quickly became involved in a conversation with a tall man as Carlos worked his way to the outdoor bar. He mouthed, "What do you want?"

"Beer," she mouthed back. He worked his way back with two bottles and handed one to Connie. "Tom, this is Dr. Carlos Reynoso. Carlos, this is Judge Tom Black. He's one of the judges in our Superior Court." He joined the conversation, learning more about the ways of the justice system.

After the last encore, they headed for the exit. People were in good mood. Some were still singing the verse of the last song, "*Volver, volver...*" He grabbed her hand so they wouldn't get separated as they made their way through the crowd. At last they made it outside. The evening was warm and the sun still had not set.

As they reached her car he asked, "Where to now?"

"You'll see! I hope you'll like the place I chose; but I'm not telling you where we're going just yet."

It took several minutes to get out of the parking lot. As they drove down the freeway Connie asked, "Did you enjoy the concert?"

"Yeah, I really did. But I must admit I have never heard a Mariachi band play something from an opera or a Glenn Miller tune. That was interesting."

"Interesting?"

"Well more like unconventional. Most of their music comes from my home state. We listen to it all the time, but I've never heard anything like that."

She laughed, "Actually, I have never heard the Glenn Miller part either, but the group's leader has a reputation for trying new stuff." They continued north on the freeway, descended the grade to Camarillo, and continued north to Ventura. She took an exit near the coast. They pulled up in front of a restaurant at the Ventura Marina. The summer night was cooler at the beach, but it was still very comfortable.

The restaurant she had chosen was an Italian one and the smell of garlic and the sauces and were strong and pleasant. They ordered and while waiting, enjoyed the late summer sun melt into the Pacific. The colors were magical. A solo piano played traditional Italian tunes, adding to the pleasant ambience.

"Let's dance!" she said, grabbing Carlos's hand. She led him toward the piano where there was a small dance floor. In high heels, she stood a couple of inches taller than him and made no effort to reduce her height. She stood straight and danced comfortably.

Carlos felt her body through the sheer dress, yet just under the smoothness of her skin he was startled at the feel of her well-developed muscles. She certainly felt different from the other girls he knew. They were soft, pliable and pleasant. Connie was not soft or pliable, but she was very pleasant.

After dinner, they danced and talked some more. He was very aware that she drew the attention of many in the restaurant as they danced. "Carlos, it's still early and I live close by; would you like to come by for while? I promise I'll get you home in time for work."

Her body, her perfume, and the music clouded his senses. He was glad he was not looking at her face, but at the piano player over her shoulder. "Yes… I'd like that." He realized that this lady was full of surprises, and he liked that.

Chapter 11
Soul Stripes

EVEN HIS AUNT HAD NOTICED how late he had gotten in. Putting on her most pleasant face, she cheerfully said, "Good morning, Carlitos! Did you sleep well?" Embarrassed, he smiled, hurried through his breakfast and went to change into his work clothes. His aunt and uncle's two grandchildren slept together in a small bed and he slept in Charlie's bed while he stayed at their house. He dressed quickly and in the darkened room, so as not to wake the children. As he grabbed some coffee, his aunt said nothing, because her husband was at the table eating. She hummed along with the radio in a cheerful mood.

"Carlitos, Carlitos, *mi* Carlitos!" a man's voice sang in a loud falsetto. "Where were you last night?" Embarrassed, Carlos tried to ignore the kidding of his crewmate.

"But Officer, I'm innocent. I didn't know what I was doing!" sang out another.

"Father, forgive me for I have sinned..." continued yet another voice.

Carlos buried his face in the tree, picking fruit as fast as he could, shutting out the voices and taunts. He knew that they would last all day and the only way to stop them was not to answer and concentrate on his work. Sweat had already soaked through his shirt and he ignored not only the singing, but the dirt and spiders in the tree. He worked fast. It was obvious the crew knew that he had arrived home just before dawn and that many of the neighbors who were already up saw him as he got out of Connie's car.

Invariably, someone on the crew chose someone to make fun of during the day. Their good-natured kidding made the boring, hard work more tolerable. The day seemed shorter somehow if they had something to divert their attention from the work. Most of the kidding was from the younger members, but even the older members chuckled at their antics. It made their day shorter as well.

At lunch, several of his cousins ruffled his hair, laughing as they walked past him. Again he tried to ignore them. Now the singing had turned to humming and whistling, but he knew it meant the same. There was nothing he could do but wait it out until something else diverted the attention from him.

"I heard that a man who is continuing the work of Cesar Chavez was in Oxnard last night," said one of the men. "I heard he wants to organize the pickers across the river," said one of the older men.

"Well I hope he stays on that side of the river. The last thing we need is something to screw up our work," said another.

"Yeah, but he's well-meaning. The man wants to improve wages and working conditions for us," added another crewman.

"No doubt he wants to improve *his* wages, too!" said the first.

"What do you think, Chalo?" asked one of the men. It was well-known that Chalo Cortez was a strong union supporter. One of the older men, he spoke quietly and was well respected by everyone.

Chalo paused a moment, reflecting. "Chavez isn't perfect, and neither is his union... even today. Some of the people who work for him are idiots. He has faults like all of us, perhaps even more, but he is a simple and sincere man. He came from the fields like all of us. He knows what hard work this is. He knows that we fieldworkers don't have a chance to improve our treatment by the growers unless we band together. Otherwise we'll be under their heels all our lives... our children, too." This last part he said almost under his breath.

The men closest to the soft-spoken man listened quietly. A few men sitting farther away shared their thoughts on this topic with one another, but kept their voices lower, out of deference to the older man. Carlos knew this topic would take their focus off of him; for that he was glad. But he was torn. The last thing he needed was a disruption of the work. He only needed another five or six weeks of work and his personal goal would be met.

He well knew that most of the crew, his relatives, and friends were destined to pick fruit or labor in the fields until their bodies could no longer bend. They had no benefits, no paid retirement to look forward to. Even though the present daily earnings were adequate, there was no hope of earning more per bin or of gaining a position that paid more. Yet, they were better off here than in Mexico which offered even less of a future for them. Carlos thought of the two children who shared their room with him. What would be their future? Would Chavez' effort help them, or would they suffer because of him? At this point, not even the wisest men in the community were sure.

He knew the hard, unrewarding work had provided him the opportunity to get the education required to be called "Doctor." Would he be better off in Mexico, practicing in a small village? He knew he'd actually earn less money there than he did here picking lemons. There was a certain irony in his dilemma.

Although poor and perhaps with little future, this was a proud group of people. They had a dignity that surpassed their lack of education. Their willingness to share even their last bite of food and their good humor were enough for Carlos to have great respect for these men and women. And after all, these were his people. He was proud of them, just as they were proud of him, and proud of their country... even when it failed them.

"What do you think?" one of the men asked Carlos. Before he had a chance to reply, one of his cousins interjected, "Carlitos is only thinking of law and order!" The resulting laughter broke up the lunch period. The men picked up their equipment and headed back to work.

There was no more banter the rest of the afternoon. It was very hot, and the dirt, sweat, and the tense conversation about the union seemed to have wrung the humor out of the day.

Each picker had a diagonal stripe of sweat across his back where the strap of his picking bag hangs around his neck and over his shoulder. It was like the mark of Cain. Even though his clothes were washed every day, even his newest laundered shirts had the distinctive mark on them. It was permanently imprinted.

Also imprinted, especially on the older men who had picked for years, was a slight list. That is, one shoulder was perceptibly lower than the other. A full fruit bag weighs 50 to 60 pounds. Over the years, this weight pulls on one shoulder, right where the strap comes over to hold the bag.

Over time, almost every worker will fall from his ladder. The usual consequence is a hurt back. A doctor's usual prescription would be, "rest and nothing but light work," advice which could not be followed, since the men had to work. There was no light work picking fruit. They could only work until the cumulative effect of the falls or the deforming weight of the bag forced them to quit. The lucky ones would have sons and daughters healthy enough to help them out when they could no longer work.

Carlos had seen these diagonal stripes across the men's backs and he knew there was a stripe of sweat on his back, too. His mark was still superficial. Those on the other men were not only physical, but seemed to mark their very souls as well. They seemed resigned to wear this stripe, knowing the hard work it represented.

The bus dropped them off near at the camp. Carlos was glad to arrive at the large log lying beside the basketball court. One of the men had bought a case of beer. He tossed Carlos a can. The shade of the trees, the cold drink, and the weight removed from his shoulders renewed his spirit.

"I wonder if the law will come and get me tonight..." sang one of the younger men. Everyone relaxed and laughed along with Carlos. He laughed too. He was glad in a way to have been the cause of the humor that enabled them to forget their heavy labor.

Chapter 12
Suspicions

DETECTIVE TEAL WAS ON THE PHONE when Connie came into his cubicle. He waved her to a chair. "Really? Fifteen hundred? That much? Christ! Ten in a van'll bring in nice chunka change!" He listened for a moment. "Yeah, yeah. Thanks; I owe ya."

Connie listened to the one-sided conversation.

"What'd you find out?" he asked as he hung up the phone.

"Not much. There *was* some powder residue, but it doesn't give us anything conclusive. It's really just a theory on my part. I got Doctor Harrison to write up an amended form. What about you?" she asked.

"Well young lady, you figured something was fishy about this. Maybe you're right, but it ain't worth a shit if it's not developed. When I was in high school we used to sneak into a pool hall. I learned to play a pretty decent game of pool as well as some of the talk. One thing a lotta guys'd say was *pool hall talk*. When someone used a sentence with could've, should've or would've, someone'd tell'm right off they was just talking pool hall talk. It meant they were bullshitting and fantasizing. They almost always started off with "If." In police work, we can't afford pool hall talk."

Alonzo smiled and nodded her head in agreement.

Teal continued, "Did you know that the kid was involved in smuggling wetbacks in from the border? Apparently he used his uncle's old van." The term, *wetback* was what some people called Mexicans who came into the U.S. illegally, usually to work in the fields. Some of them arrived wet because they had to swim across a river, or even around the fence that descends into the Pacific Ocean. "At times, the guy would have eight or ten wets in it. He'd pick 'em up on some lonely road, then skirt the inspection station, and then he'd drop them off L.A. The kid'd pocket a thousand or fifteen hundred bucks a head. I heard that sometimes he'd make a couple of trips a week. Not bad for a kid, huh?"

"Well, if that's what he was doing, where did the money go? According to the guys in Property, he had only a few dollars in his pockets," she said.

"Well, 'college girl,' that's what we need to find out. Even if we lowball a number, this kid might've been walking around carrying ten to thirty grand in cash at a time. That might've attracted some of his 'homies,' don't ya think?" He smiled at his use of the word. "And that's not all."

He noticed that she was taking notes on some three-by five-cards she had pulled from her hip pocket. She kept a supply on her at all times, finding the stiff surface easier to write on and easier to carry around than the big yellow pads some of the other officers carried.

"I spoke to Dr. Rossi, the head of Neurology at County Hospital," he continued. "He said your idea about a muscle reaction when the bullet hit a certain part of the brain was 'quite plausible.'" He enjoyed using the Dr. Rossi's fancy words at the end. "In any event, he thought that even if there wasn't a violent movement, it was unlikely that the kid would've nicely tucked the gun under his thigh after the bullet scrambled his brain. There wouldn't a been time before he lost control of his body. Anyway, that was his quick and dirty assessment. He said he'd review the coroner's report in more detail and give us a more specific opinion. Could you get ol' Shithead to send him a copy?"

"I'll do it right away." She started to head out to her car, but turned back when she heard him speak again.

"Hang on! Did you know the guy that found the body, the doctor?" he asked.

"Carlos?"

"Yep, that Carlos guy. Did you know he was wet? I think he might be a good place to start to get us off the pool hall talk shit. We need to get real here."

"Okay, I'll get on it." She had written "Carlos??" on a card, not daring to look up, for fear Teal would see the shock she felt.

Tía Estrella answered the phone, "Constancia! How are you?"

"Fine, fine. Hey, I'm in a hurry and really need to talk with him. It's important. When do you think he'll be back?"

"Not tonight. He said he had some business to do and would be gone over the weekend. Can I give him a message for you?"

"If you see him, would you just tell him I called, please? I'll come to see him Monday, after work. Please ask him to call me if he can't make it."

Chapter 13
Options

Ann had called Friday afternoon. "Carlos? We're at the beach house. You promised you would come to see me. Can you come?" Carlos was surprised at the call. He'd had a couple of beers and felt tired and hungry. He could smell dinner simmering on Tía Estrella's stove. He figured that the only way this was going to be a short conversation was for him to just agree with her. "Oh, Ann. Tomorrow we have to work 'til noon or maybe a little sooner if we finish the place we're working on," he said.

"That'll work out fine, because the mornings have been overcast. It's much nicer in the afternoon and evening."

"Do your parents know that you are inviting me?" he asked.

"Silly! They're the ones who suggested it. Bring your toothbrush so you can stay over. We have plenty of room. Want me to pick you up?"

"I don't know if I can stay overnight. It might be better if I get a ride, since I don't know when we'll finish tomorrow. What's the address?"

His cousin, Alex was at the wheel of the pickup as they drove north through Ventura on the freeway. The road seemed to head right into the Pacific Ocean; then it curved abruptly northward toward Santa Barbara. A bit of the morning haze still hung on and the traffic slowed down a bit as drivers enjoyed the ocean view.

"So what's this all about?" asked his cousin. "Where are you going?"

"It's just a nice family I met who gave me a ride. They're staying out here at the beach. I'm just going to visit with them a while." Carlos looked straight ahead avoiding the driver's eyes. "She said they were staying at the Rincon in the second group of houses."

They passed the group of nice beach homes, took the exit under the freeway, and turned back on the access road. They drove slowly, peering at the house numbers on the rear of the homes, which all faced the ocean. "This is it! Stop here!"

"Want me to come pick you up?" asked Alex.

"I don't know. If I need a ride I'll call, Okay? Thanks!" He jumped lightly onto the driveway and waved. He watched the truck leave, threw his backpack over his shoulder, walked to the back door, and rang the bell.

John Ferranti opened the door; he was dressed just in shorts. His rosy face and shoulders were on the verge of being painfully sunburned, despite his olive skin. He smiled broadly. "Carlos! Good to see you! I'm glad you could join us. Ann told me she had gotten a hold of you. Come on in!" He noticed Carlos looking around for Ann. "Oh, yeah," he continued, "the girls and Mike have gone into town to pick up a few things. They'll be back in a flash. Go ahead and change into your trunks. Then come on out to the balcony with me." He pointed to a bedroom just off the fully-windowed living room. It gave a fantastic view. "You can change in here."

John Ferranti was sitting on the rail of the deck as Carlos walked out. "How about a beer?" asked Ferranti.

"Sure, thanks!" he said with a grin.

Ferranti stepped into the kitchen, pulled out a couple, and opened them. As he walked back, he handed one to Carlos and laughed. "I hope you're more careful than I am. Looks like parts of you haven't seen the sun recently. You'll burn in a hurry if you don't watch out." He pointed at his angry shoulders. "You'd think I'd learn. We've been coming here for years and every time the same thing happens." He grabbed a bottle of sunscreen from the deck's railing and, pouring some into one hand, offered the bottle to his guest.

"Thanks, Mr. Ferranti." Carlos looked at his own body. With the exception of his very brown face and hands, the rest of his body was pale. He took the bottle he'd been offered and sat, looking seaward. The beach was narrow and the stretch he could see was studded with rocks.

"Now I thought I'd told you to call me John, young man. 'Mr. Ferranti' makes me sound old. So how have things been going for you, Carlos?" he asked.

"Very well, thank you. The work's been good and steady. It looks like I'll probably make a bit more money than I'd hoped for. That'll make the first year of my residency easier and I won't have to depend on my family so much."

"Have you ever considered doing your residency here? You know we have some fine programs around the Los Angeles area. Just in case you were interested, I went ahead and made a few inquiries with some of my friends. Several of them attended the same school you did and now have very successful practices in the area. In fact, a couple of them are desperate to get an associate who's bilingual. They could be very helpful to you," he urged.

Surprised, Carlos looked at the man. He saw that he was serious. In fact, it almost seemed as if he'd rehearsed the comments he'd just made. Even though this idea had crossed his mind, he never seriously considered it. He'd pictured himself running a small practice in a little village where he could help his people. He'd thought he would create an ideal rural practice.

"Frankly, John," forcing himself to use the unfamiliar first name, "I have been so busy between college classes and summer work that I haven't given it much thought. It never occurred to me that I might practice in a place other than in my home country." He took a sip of his beer, walked over to the rail and looked out over the ocean. It was easier to talk to Ann's father this way. The ocean's compelling beauty made a good excuse.

"I understand. You know, I also came to this country not knowing what to do; but opportunities opened up. Then I met Julie, and before I knew it, I was a very successful American!" he continued. "But hey, if you ever just want to talk about it, let me know. It never hurts to examine all your options. Opportunities present themselves in the strangest way and at the oddest times."

"You're not an American?" Carlos was surprised at himself for asking such a personal question.

"I am very much an American now, but I wasn't always. I came over from Italy on a student exchange program to study for a year to improve my English and I never left. I worked in a restaurant washing dishes and went to the local college. Still washing dishes, I started taking classes at UCLA. That's where I met Julie. Pretty soon after that, I started to work for her father in his insurance business. When he retired, he sold me the business. Somewhere along the line I became an American citizen, and so here I am. Nothing was planned; it may have just been fate. I just took the opportunities as they presented themselves." He paused, reflecting. "You know, even washing dishes was a good deal. I now own half of that restaurant."

"You were in the country illegally all that time?" asked Carlos, amazed that this was even possible.

"Of course, I was a 'wetback,' as they call them now, until about twenty years ago." He was grinning as he told the story. Turning his head toward the door, he said, "I think I hear the tribe." The two women entered the house carrying bags of groceries and Mike carried a twelve-pack of diet soda.

"Well young man, I see you finally made it!" kidded Julie Ferranti.

"Yes ma'am, thank you for the invitation. You're very kind," answered Carlos.

"Carlos, let's get one thing straight. My name is Julie, not ma'am. Although, the invitation was not entirely my idea, it was a very nice one. We're glad to have you."

She set the bags on the kitchen table. "I do hope that as a doctor, you have more sense than John does and put some lotion on yourself. I don't think I can stand to hear two men moan and cry because they were too manly to protect themselves from the sun. Ann, get this boy that bottle of lotion, I think we left it on the deck."

"Thanks, but we just put some on."

Ann returned swiftly. "Here, let me help you. You missed your whole back." She began spreading the white lotion all over his shoulders and back. Finally, she filled her hand and quickly rubbed it all over his face. "You need to wipe that silly grin from you face."

Amused, he could do nothing but try to wipe the excess lotion off his face. "Uh, thanks, I think," he replied.

"Let's go for a walk," said Ann. "Mom, we're going for a walk... back in a little while!" She took his hand and led him down the steps to the narrow beach.

She wore an oversized T-shirt and underneath it, he could see the faint outline of a colorful bikini. Once they'd gotten to the water's edge, she went on. "I'm really glad you could make it, Carlos. Can you stay overnight? We're going to have a barbecue tonight and some good friends are coming over from the valley."

"Yeah, I guess I can stay. Your family's very nice. I feel very comfortable around them."

"You only like my family?" she teased.

"Of course, why else would I come out here? What else is there?" He ducked skillfully to avoid the blow that was headed for his nose. Then he put his arm around her and, lifting her easily, continued to walk with her under his arm. She wiggled and laughed. He finally put her down. He took her hand and they continued to walk along the water's edge.

As they returned to the house, Carlos was surprised to see a black family arrive. The woman was black, though not particularly dark. She was on the short, thin side and had a contagious smile. She didn't shake hands with Carlos; she hugged him as she did all the others. Their two little girls were identical twins wearing little matching bikinis and sandals. They were about ten years old and had identical puffy Afros.

Their father's skin was almost blue-black. The contrast made his smile especially prominent when the tall man smiled, which he did often. When they were introduced, his huge hands completely swallowed Carlos's own.

"Carlos, this is Don and Clara Goodwin. They're our best friends," said Julie. These two are Mary and Martha." She gestured with an open hand toward the two little girls. "It's up to you to find out which one's which."

They looked up at Carlos momentarily and then at the same time squealed, "Let's go down to the water!" Holding hands, they ran down the steps.

Clara headed for the deck. "They do a pretty good job looking out for each other, but I still watch," she said almost apologetically.

"Well Carlos, I've heard lots about you," said Don.

"Don's the business manager of a large medical center in the Valley," explained John. "It's a very nice facility and they employ many doctors and nurses. More important to me is their need for malpractice insurance." John chuckled at this gentle ribbing and toasted the black man with his beer.

Don laughed gamely.

"Really," continued John, "his medical center is one of the very best in the area. They cover most of the medical disciplines. And they have an outstanding medical reputation. It's also one of the best-run operations, thanks to Don's good business sense."

"Well, John makes me sound pretty good, but I have to agree with John, we do have a very fine facility and an outstanding medical staff. Perhaps you'd like to visit us? I'd be glad to arrange for a tour and maybe have you meet some of our doctors. I think you'll probably find it quite different from the facilities you've seen down south. It might be interesting for you," said Don.

"Thank you very much, I'd like that. But I will be here only a few more weeks and I still have to work," Carlos replied. He knew John Ferranti had plenty to gain by praising Don, one of his clients. But John was clearly trying to help him out too, by giving him access into the medical community. It wouldn't hurt to shake a few hands and make a few contacts.

"You're free on weekends, aren't you? We're open on weekends. In fact, we see many patients on weekends because they can't take time off of work to see us during the week."

"Awww, Don, don't you see? He's so shy he just wants us to plead with him. He doesn't want to be a bother," Ann said. "Well, I'll settle this. I'll pick him up and deliver him to the center next Saturday. Would that be okay with everyone?" Just like that, it was settled.

Carlos woke up early; everyone was still sleeping. He walked out on the deck and looked out to the water. A couple with a black Labrador retriever was walking along the beach. Carlos wore no shirt but had put on his trunks, which were still damp. What had been very clear and simple plans just a few weeks ago were now gray as the morning. He was confused. He always thought that Anglos were cold and selfish, yet the Ferrantis were warm and genuinely nice people. And the Goodwins were black, and just as warm and genuine as the Ferrantis. He'd only seen black people on television news, but they were usually in trouble with the law. The Goodwins sure weren't like them.

He heard soft footsteps and, through the deck's vibration, felt Ann walk up behind him. She put her arms around him and leaned her head up against his back. She held him tight, almost daring him to breathe. He turned slowly, staying within her arms. Her body was warm and the gray morning seemed to tilt. She looked up and kissed him on each side of his face, then gently on the mouth. He tasted the mint from her toothpaste. He kissed her back and hugged her.

"Let's go for a walk," she invited. She led him down the steps to the water.

Chapter 14
Something Else

"I TRIED TO GET AHOLD OF YOU FRIDAY," said Connie.

"I know," said Carlos, my aunt told me. I went to visit some friends."

"Well you must've been out in the sun, because your nose and cheeks are red." They were eating at Bountiful Burritos.

He got up to refill his drink, hoping to avoid any more prying about his weekend. In a few moments, he sat back down.

"You told us you didn't know Juan Melgoza but that you'd seen him around. Do you know anything about what he did, or who he worked for?" asked Connie.

"Not really, but I used to see him once in a while, mostly in town. I just figured he was on another crew, but, come to think of it, he didn't dress like a picker. He didn't live out on the ranch. His family might have lived up the canyon, you know?"

Connie was familiar with the other groups of small houses and the trailer park up in the canyon nearest to the ranch. "Uh huh," she answered. "Did you know that he smuggled men and women across the border? He made a lot of money at it," said the detective.

"Oh, yeah, that's the other place I saw him…at the border!"

"Carlos, tell me what happens when someone wants to come across the border," she asked, prepared to take mental notes. "How does it work?" It would not do to be using three-by-fives in this situation.

"You know, it's really simple. You go to one of the bars near the border, ask anyone, and they'll put you in contact with a *coyote*. You pay the guy and he introduces you to the guide who'll lead you across. He sets a time and place for you meet him at his truck or van during the night. By then he'll have several people to take across. He drives you to a certain spot he thinks is safe and you sneak under the fence." Unconsciously, Connie leaned forward, not wanting to miss a word. "You have to walk most of the night to some place near a road and wait for someone to pick you up. If you're lucky, it's a van and everyone has a seat, but you never know. Then the driver takes only the back roads and eventually you wind up in Santa Ana or Los Angeles. It's really very simple," he said with a smile.

"Is that how you came across?"

"A couple of times. But this time I just rode across in a car with some friends and they never questioned me."

"How much does a ride with a *coyote* cost?"

"With the extra border patrol units down there now, people will pay a thousand to fifteen hundred dollars, U.S., depending on what you have with you. If you don't have all the money, sometimes you can agree to pay it when you go to work. They have collectors that make sure you pay." He grimaced at the thought.

"Do you know any of the collectors around here?" she asked.

"No," he said with a shudder. "I've been lucky and never had to use them. What's this all about? What's your interest in the *pollo* trade?" he asked as he drank his soda.

"Well, you're the one who got me to thinking. First it was that it would've been hard for the Melgoza kid to shoot himself in the head. Well, if he didn't kill himself, then someone else killed him. It made me think about the people-smuggling trade. There could be some connection."

"Do you have any idea about what happened?" asked Carlos.

"We're not sure. We just think there might be a connection between this smuggling business and that boy's death. Frankly, the guys at the office think we're wasting our time that we should just let it go as a suicide. That feels wrong to me, sort of disrespectful."

"I'm glad you're the type who wants justice for everyone, not just the Anglos," he said, appreciating her intentions. They continued nibbling on their fries and burgers, tossing ideas back and forth. "Sometimes I wish I'd taken a closer look at the body. I feel like I'm not getting the whole story. Bodies can tell you a lot, you know."

"Mmm hmm," she agreed through a mouthful. Suddenly she asked, "Carlos, have you ever thought of getting papers and coming to live in the United States?"

"No, I never really have. I've been here so long that in a way, I already consider myself a citizen." He went on. "I graduated from the eighth grade here so I feel at home. I've been so busy trying to finish school that, until this summer, it's never occurred to me." He hoped she wasn't having thoughts about him being here illegally. He'd hate to put her in a bad situation at work.

She finished her burger. Suddenly she said, "Carlos, let's drive to Santa Barbara next weekend. We can have dinner and just walk around. They have lots of new places on State Street and the evenings are very nice now. There're a couple of places where we can dance, too, if you'd like."

As the highway curved around the Rincon, he tried to ignore the homes on the beach, but through the palm trees he did catch a glimpse of the Ferrantis' rented house.

"Why are you so quiet?" Connie asked.

"It's nothing… I was just thinking of the dead guy," he lied.

The lower end of State Street had been cleaned up. The beggars, homeless, and mentally ill were unwanted so they were moved out gradually, away from the prosperous business district. Now an endless sidewalk dotted with coffee shops, art galleries and small clothing stores lined the street. A mix of college students, middle-aged professionals, and the young wealthy in Ralph Lauren shirts walked along the popular street. Laughter and music spilled out onto the sidewalk. A man in rumpled clothes and unkempt hair walked by, wondering aloud softly, as if he were hallucinating again. There was nowhere for him to buy a drink and the people in the fancy shirts not only ignored him. In a way, they actually didn't see him, at least as a person. Even the gentrified dogs ignored him. Sadly, he made his way toward the beachfront. At least he had some friends there.

Carlos noticed the man approaching. Somehow he sensed Carlos wouldn't ignore him and as he got closer he asked, "Man, I'm not going to lie to you. I need a couple of bucks to buy a drink. Can you help me out?" Connie was about to chase him off, but Carlos quickly pulled out two dollars and handed them to him before she could act.

"Carlos, she said in disapproval, "that guy just hustled you for two bucks. You know he'll only buy some liquor with it."

"I know, he said he needed a drink. He was honest and I'll bet he needs a drink in the worst way. How could I say no? Besides, people have been kind to me recently."

"But you're different. You work hard for your money. You're not like him at all."

"No, Connie. I *am* like him, just luckier perhaps. Besides, there've been times when I needed a beer just like him." He took her hand, "Look at it this way: I'm here with a beautiful woman on a pretty summer night. She's going to buy me a beer and dinner… and no telling what else. I'm just sharing my good fortune. What can be wrong with that?"

She looked at his open, kind face for what seemed a long time. Finally she grasped his other hand and, pulling toward her, kissed him lightly on the cheek. "What is this 'else' you're referring to?" she whispered coyly into his ear.

Before he could answer, she led him into a café.

Chapter 15
Angelus Medical Center

H E ONLY HAD TIME FOR A QUICK NOTE, but Carlos figured he'd better send Licha another letter. He realized that it felt like more a responsibility than a need to connect with her.

Dear Licha,

I'm writing this quick letter because in a few minutes, a friend is giving me a ride to Los Angeles for a tour of a medical building. I met a nice man who runs the business and he wants me to see it. I may even get a job there.

The picking work is going fine and I am very well. I hope you are, too.

Please say hello to my parents, and I'll try to write again with more news as soon as I can.

Con Cariño,
CR

"Nino, *la Güera* is here. She wants to know if you're ready," said his goddaughter. He smiled at Charlie calling Ann, *Güera*. It was true that her pale skin and blond hair probably set her apart from most of the people she had ever known.

"Tell her I'll be right there." Charlie scurried off.

"Ann, I'm sorry I'm late, but we worked later than I expected this morning. I just got out of the shower a few minutes ago." Ann was talking to his aunt in the kitchen. She was eating a small burrito over the kitchen sink. Tía Estrella gave her a paper towel to catch the juice that was dripping through her fingers. "I see you met my *tía*."

"Yes! She's also a wonderful cook," said Ann, slurping, "like your mother. Can she make *empanadas* like your mom?"

His aunt replied, "Of course I can! His mother and I learned together when we were still little girls. Do you like them?"

"Oh yes! Carlos gave me some on the bus. They were the greatest!" Ann enthused.

"Then I'll have to make you some sometime," said Tía Estrella. "So, you met on the bus?" she asked, smiling. "What bus?"

"I'll tell you later, Tía. We're late! Ann's taking me to San Fernando to tour a big medical center. We don't want to be late." He waved, pulling Ann to the door. "Bye, Tía!"

Once they were in the car, Ann said, "We had lots of time! I like your aunt and her food's really good. I was actually hoping she'd offer me another burrito."

"She is a good cook, I agree, but if we'd stayed another minute, we'd never have gotten away. If I know my aunt; she will sit you down and tell you about her whole life… and mine as well."

The drive to the San Fernando Valley took less than an hour. The weekend traffic was light and Ann drove fast. The medical center was located near Van Nuys Airport. Ann was her usual confident self and headed toward the area reserved for doctors. Carlos wasn't sure he quite qualified to park there, but it was the only space available, so they took it. As they walked through the automatic doors and into the lobby, Carlos was surprised to see a free-standing sign.

Welcome to Angelus Medical Center
Dr. Carlos Reynoso

Although it was still early, the waiting room was full. There was a toy box and a tiny table and chair set in one corner. Several children who must have become familiar with the room were playing in the area.

"I'm Carlos Reynoso," he told the receptionist.

She rose and led them up a circular stairway which led to a second floor conference room. She knocked on the door and announced, "Dr. Reynoso is here."

"Dr. Reynoso! Come in! We've been just been talking about you," said Don Goodwin as he came over to greet them. He gave Ann a hug and gave Carlos's hand a hearty shake. The black man was wearing a blue and white Nike warm up suit. He went around the table and introduced several doctors and nurses who were enjoying coffee and doughnuts.

"This is Dr. Alex Pilabos, our director," said Goodwin, as he came to a short man with short gray hair.

Pilabos had a strong handshake. "Please sit down, Doctor!" he invited. "Would you and your friend like some coffee? We're just about finished here. Then you and I will visit a bit." Since he noticed the meeting was about over, Carlos declined, but Ann grabbed half of a bear claw. Pilabos looked around the table. "Anything else anyone wants to bring up?" he asked the people around the table. Hearing silence, he continued, "If not, again I'd like to welcome Dr. Reynoso who will be with us a good part of the day. Please make an effort to include him in your patient exams and briefly give him an idea of what your department does and your work specifically. Just go about your work. Let's all make him welcome."

As the employees quietly assembled their papers and prepared to leave, Dr. Pilabos nodded to Don Goodwin, who opened a cupboard and pulled out a white lab coat. He handed it to Carlos so he could see the chest pocket. Carlos was surprised to read his name, neatly embroidered in black above the Angelus logo. The logo had two hands, pressed together in prayer, encircled by a stethoscope. The center's name was written in a wide U, just below the scope's tubing. In the jacket pocket were two pens and a small flashlight. The side pocket held a long box containing brand-new stethoscope! Carlos's eyes were wide as he stammered his thanks. "Th-thank you! Thank you very much, sir. This is very kind of you!"

"Well young man, we're just very glad to meet you, after hearing so much about you from Mr. Goodwin here," replied Dr. Pilabos. "Now Carlos, first you'll spend time with our pediatric unit. I hope you will have time to see as much as you'd like. If you need anything just ask anyone. Don and I have planned a late lunch. It'll be right here around 2:00 p.m. I hope that's not too late for you. Ann, you can go along with him if you'd like."

"No thanks. I have to get a couple of things at the shopping center. But I'll be glad to join you here for lunch, if you don't mind."

"Of course not, we'd love to have your company. See you at two," he replied.

Lunch was served in a smaller room off the conference room. It included a large bowl of shrimp salad and a plate with various types of bread rolls. Another bowl was filled with ice and cans of soft drinks. Lunch seemed formal in its informality.

"Well Carlos, I understand we come from similar backgrounds," began Alex Pilabos. Noting the surprise on Carlos's face, he continued. "I hear you've worked your way through school picking lemons. I did it picking grapes." He spoke in a friendly tone to which his bushy eyebrows added a hint of mirth.

"Yes sir, I hope this will be my last summer having to do that sort of work."

"I can sure understand that, young man," he replied with feeling.

Don Goodwin arrived to join them for lunch. "How was your day? Did you find what we do here interesting?" he asked.

"I am very impressed; I've never seen anything like this. I was particularly impressed with your patients."

"How so?" asked Pilabos. Most visitors were impressed by the building, the equipment, or the staff's warmth or credentials.

"There seems to be a real mix of people. I saw people who seemed to be poor and some who were not so poor," answered Carlos.

Pilabos laughed, "That's very perceptive of you. We found out that good medicine attracts the poor as well as the rich. That's one of the reasons we're located here instead of Beverly Hills. The wealthy can come here but the poor cannot go to Beverly Hills. In addition, our business manager here got us a great deal on this building. On top of that, many of us in the group like to fly, and this location's about as handy as you can get for that."

After the other doctors and nurses had departed, only Don Goodwin, Dr. Pilabos and Carlos remained.

"Carlos," asked Goodwin, "are you aware of the proposed state legislation to permit Mexican physicians to come to the States to practice? They may soon be able to, under certain conditions. As I understand it, the U.S. and the Mexican governments are talking about an agreement that would allow this. The thinking is, we have so many Mexican citizens in this area that it would make sense to have Mexican doctors treat them." Don Goodwin looked at a file as he spoke. "The legislation also would permit an internship with approved facilities such as ours, who have established relations with a local hospital. At the end of the internship program, the doctor could either return to Mexico or continue to practice here. In the meantime, he'd be licensed to practice, as long as he is under close supervision."

Pilabos took up the thread. "At the end of the two years, the license to practice would become permanent. The whole concept makes good sense to us. One of the main tenets of good medicine is that the patient must be able to communicate his symptoms to his doctor, who should be able to understand, ask questions, and advise his patient. How that is supposed to happen when people can't speak the same language is beyond me!" He sighed, his expressive eyebrows reflecting his frustration.

Goodwin continued, "The fly in the ointment is that the California Medical Society opposes the law. Of course, they don't want to provide services to the poor, but they don't want anyone else to do it either. Great logic, eh?"

Carlos listened intently to the black man as he spoke. "What is the doctor supposed to live on while he is here?"

"Good question!" answered Pilabos. "Actually, the doctor and the medical center's directors will just need to agree on a deal and that's it. The legislation is silent on that part. Presumably, the doctor will be generating fees enough to cover his salary. We haven't thought this out completely yet, but if we had someone qualified to take that sort of position with us, he would function as a port of entry to our facility. This doctor would see the patient initially, treat the patient if it's something simple, or refer the patient to one of our other doctors or specialist as needed."

By the tone in his voice and the way Dr. Pilabos looked at him, Carlos could see that they were thinking about possibly taking him on in that position. He felt proud to be considered for the position, but confused.

"There's also another part of the legislation," mentioned Goodwin. "That section of the law requires that the doctor spend sixteen hours each month going to where the poor live and providing treatment there. I suppose this means going to the homeless shelters, the Salvation Army, skid row or somewhere like the clinic we have downtown. When the doctor performs this service, the sponsoring medical center is supposed to provide a nurse and the necessary supplies."

"So, when are you going home Carlos?" asked Pilabos.

"...the end of August. I was hoping to take a few days off before starting my residency. I have been very fortunate this season to have been able to earn the money I need in a shorter time. Thank you very much for inviting me to visit today. It is more that I could have imagined. You have a wonderful medical facility here."

Carlos started to take off the jacket. "No, Doctor," said Dr. Pilabos. "Leave the lab coat on. It's our gift to you. But there is one condition; you must come to see us before you leave. Will you do that?" The older man then pushed a shiny black leather briefcase toward Carlos. He turned it toward him to reveal the writing on one side. Embossed in neat gold letters near the handle was:

Carlos Reynoso, M.D.

"Here, you can put the coat in this. Every doctor needs to have a nice case, especially when he's traveling to different locations to treat his patients. You'll also find a few gadgets that our suppliers provide us; you'll find them handy."

Carlos was overwhelmed. "Thank you again, sir. I do promise to come back and see you again before I leave. Thank you for this visit and for your very generous gifts," he said as he took the case.

Raising one of his eyebrows and inclining his head to one side toward Carlos, Pilabos replied, "It's my pleasure, we fruit pickers need to stick together, you know." He made a friendly chuckle.

Chapter 16
Mysterious Suitcase

"**RON, DO YOU KNOW ANYONE WITH BORDER PATROL?**" asked Connie.

"Yeah, a guy named Johnnie Reyes. He's the officer in change in this area. He's got an office in Camarillo. Why do you want to talk to him?" he asked.

"This thing with the Melgoza kid is getting more complicated. I think he was a small part of something bigger."

"How do you mean?"

"Juan Melgoza's mother called me late last night. I went out to her house and she showed me an old, beat-up suitcase her son had in his closet."

"What'd you find?"

"First there was money: $5,000 in hundreds and three savings account passbooks for banks in Tijuana. Those represent close to a million pesos. That's equivalent to $100,000 U.S.! Then there was a small bag of what looked like cocaine. Last, there were thirty fake i.d. cards. I counted fifteen fake green cards, fourteen social security cards, and one California driver's license. They looked pretty good, too. If I hadn't gone to that presentation we had on recognizing counterfeit documents, I'd never have known they weren't the real thing."

Teal let out a long, slow whistle, "So where's the stuff now?"

"It's getting processed in the Property Room. I told Mrs. Melgoza that we would look into letting her have the cash in a couple of days so she can bury her son... and that maybe we could even give her the passbooks as soon as we looked them over. But I didn't promise anything, of course."

"Have you checked with the banks yet?" Teal asked.

"I made a quick call to one of the banks in Tijuana. They reluctantly verified that the account existed. They wouldn't tell me the exact amount but said it was significant. They verified that Mrs. Melgoza's name was on the account. When I went through the suitcase with Mrs. Melgoza, she told me that about a year ago she signed some documents for her son but she had no idea what they were."

"Wow, that's a lot of cash for a kid with no job!" Teal got up to get some coffee. He offered her a cup, but she declined. She was too pumped up over her discovery to need any caffeine. "You have any ideas?"

"Just the obvious: the kid probably didn't commit suicide. I think he was involved in smuggling wetbacks, drugs or both. Maybe he skimmed some money and someone wanted it back...bad enough to kill him."

"Yeah, that makes sense to me. What do you figure we ought to do now?" Teal was coming to the realization that Alonzo wasn't just the department's way of getting minorities on board, she really did have a good head on her shoulders.

"I was thinking you might be able to use your connections to verify these bank accounts. It'd be nice to know the amount, the dates of deposits, and so on."

"Alonzo, you've done some good work. I think you're on the right track, but if this is anything like it appears to be, it could be more complicated and dangerous. I want you to be very careful chasing this down," he warned.

"Well if you chase down the Mexican bank connection and talk to Reyes at the Border Patrol, I'll keep asking around town to see who else knows what's going on."

Teal was actually worried about her safety, now that he knew the investigation had taken on this new and dangerous turn. "Don't you need some help?"

"No, I think I'm best working alone on this. Too many people might spook someone into not talking."

He knew she was right. "What about the doctor?"

"What doctor?" she asked, misunderstanding his question.

"That lemon picker/doctor, is there any connection there?"

"Oh, I don't think so. He's just a bright guy who's working hard to be a doctor. He just happened to find the body, but will talk to him again.

As I mentioned, he's very bright." She paused. "He may actually know more than he thinks he does. I'll check him out later."

"By the way, do you think he's really a doctor?"

"I haven't checked him out officially, but he's told me he graduated from the University Of Guadalajara School Of Medicine. He was right about the difficulty the kid would've had shooting himself, and also the part about placing the gun neatly under his thigh after the shot was fired."

"As you suggested, I agree that it's possible that he knows more he's telling us. For example, maybe he actually knows who killed the kid or is involved in whatever business he was involved in," said Teal.

The female detective paused for a bit, she ran her fingers through her short hair, "I really think that Reynoso finding the body was coincidental, but I'll keep that in mind." She was careful not to refer to Carlos by his first name. Teal would pick up on that like a flash and know she had become involved with him. That could place Carlos in a dangerous position, especially since he had no papers.

"Anything else?" asked Teal.

"Yeah there is. Do you know anything about counterfeiting green cards, driver's license and other documents?"

"Only what I saw when I went to a seminar in L.A. several months ago. I found out that with some of the new copying machines used in some offices now, a lot of documents can be faked. Mostly, they're just forms with blank lines, so the guy just whites out the information on a form and copies it a bunch of times. So then he has a pile of blanks. Then he just uses a typewriter to fill it in. And there are a whole bunch of guys who make rubber stamps. All he'd need would be one guy to make a fake "official" stamp for the form he's working on. But there may be some new stuff these guys are doing by now. I'll check that out with Reyes when I see him, I'm sure he knows all about this," said Teal as he watched his partner leave the room.

He didn't know about the smile on Connie's face. She knew she had his respect now. He was calling her by her last name!

Chapter 17
Confusion

"THANKS, CONNIE. That was an excellent meal! You're a wonder with all your talents," said Carlos, patting his well-satisfied stomach.

"You've only seen a few of my talents," she kidded.

"I can hardly wait."

"You may just have to," she said as she cleared some of the dishes from the table. Carlos rose to help. She had worked hard to prepare him a nice home-cooked meal. Everyone had their own style, and Connie's salsa wasn't as hot as his *tía's*. Hers had a bit of grated orange rind in it. This made him think of her orange blossom perfume. He playfully sniffed behind her ear.

"Hey! We'll never get this done if you're goofing off!" She turned and snapped a dish towel at him. It made a loud crack.

"Can we blame it on the salsa? The orange in it reminds me of your perfume," he said in his defense. He looked at her with a comically apologetic face.

"What can I do to a man with a face like that?" she laughed.

They finished the dishes talking about the nothings of everyday life, and headed into the living room to visit. As they sat on the sofa drinking coffee she asked, "How was your trip to Los Angeles last week?"

"It was great but confusing…so much that I wish in a way, I hadn't gone."

She raised her eyebrows and pulled her knees onto the sofa, waiting for him to continue.

"Some doctors who own a place near Van Nuys Airport invited me to visit their medical center. They do all kinds of general medical work, and quite a few specialized services, too. It was really very impressive. After I had a chance to see some of the doctors taking care of patients, the director met with me to talk a while." Carlos took a breath and leaned forward as he got to the more serious part. "He mentioned there's a new program being considered in Sacramento that would allow doctors educated in Mexico to apprentice here in California. Essentially, the program is meant to serve the large Mexican population in this area. Part of the deal is that you have to spend several hours a month serving the homeless population as well. After two years you can take the exam to practice here, or return to Mexico. Not only that but they actually pay you, depending on the kind of deal they make with you. They were not too specific about that part of the deal, but it's more than I would make in Mexico, I think."

"Sounds like a pretty great opportunity for you. What part was confusing to you?" asked Connie.

"Well, it's just that my plans were already pretty well laid out. I thought I'd do my residency in Guadalajara, then open a practice in my hometown and live happily ever after," although his manner was jovial, there was a hint of doubt in his voice.

"And now?" she asked.

"Well, it has always been my dream to become a doctor and help people…to help my own people. The interesting thing is that I found out I can do that right here…right here in a foreign country…" His voice slowed and trailed off as the realization of what he was saying dawned on him for the first time.

Connie set her coffee down on the table and moved over to where he was. She put her arms around him and slowly and deliberately found his mouth with hers.

Later on, he said to her, "Now I'm even more confused!" She kissed him gently on the lips.

Chapter 18
Warnings

"COME CARLOS, RIDE WITH ME to the new section." Mario had just bought himself a new pickup truck. The cab still had the smell of a new vehicle mixed with sweat and the cigars that Mario smoked. They followed the road along a *barranca* under the deep shade of eucalyptus trees that lined the creek. The dirt road was smooth but littered with seed buttons from the trees and they popped as the tires rolled over them. Carlos leaned back, closed his eyes enjoying the fresh air created by the shade and the moving truck.

"Nice truck, Mario," said Carlos.

"Thanks. So, Carlitos, how's it been going? You've been busy I hear, too busy to come visit an old friend once in a while." Carlos actually liked the smell of Mario's cigars, as long as the windows were open. The cigar smoke and eucalyptus oil covered the scent of both men's sweat.

"I'm sorry Mario, but it has been hectic, finding the dead guy under my set of trees hasn't helped. And people keep questioning me," he said.

"I understand. But the questioning has not all been unpleasant, eh?" asked the labor contractor with a smile.

Carlos opened his eyes and glanced at Mario, who was keeping his eyes on the winding road. He saw the old man was smiling as he chewed on the cigar. "I don't know what you mean," he replied.

Mario chuckled knowingly. "I may not have much schooling, but I know a pretty woman when I see one. I also have a brother who's a waiter in Santa Barbara. Remember Lalo? He recognized you from back when he lived on the ranch. He tells me you two dance real good. I've been questioned by the police before but never on the dance floor. It must be a new questioning technique, eh?" Carlos started to say something but all he could do was clear his throat. Mario continued. "Of course, your 'questioning' has been the talk of the camp for the last several days. It's the number one topic among the girls, you know… especially at my house."

Again, the younger man cleared his throat.

"*Mi'jo*, you know I love you like the son I don't have. I don't blame you for anything you do, but I will be very disappointed if anything happens that will prevent you from being my personal doctor as I grow older. If you don't become a doctor, I will personally kick your ass," he said.

"You don't have to worry, Mario. Thanks to you and my parents, I can assure you that I will be a doctor. I will take care of you."

"Good! Come over to the house tonight. I need you to help me fill out some government forms and time sheets, okay?"

"Okay.

That evening, Carlos filled out the time sheets on Mario's kitchen table. He knew his wife and daughter had been discussing his social life. Their eyes showed nervousness and curiosity at the same time. "Some more coffee, Carlitos?" asked Mario's wife.

"No thanks," he answered without looking up. He continued to fill out the papers for his boss.

"Nino! There's a lady at the house that wants to see you!" His goddaughter was breathless as she burst through the door. She said she would wait for you by the park. She's the police lady!"

"Thank you, *mi'ja*. Tell her I'll be there in a few minutes." Carlos could feel the women's eyes on him. He avoided looking at them as he excused himself for the evening.

"Good night, Mario. See you in the morning." He walked gratefully into the cool evening air. It was at times like this that he wished he smoked, but although he enjoyed the smell of Mario's cigars, actually smoking them gagged him.

Connie was sitting on a bench, watching some boys shoot baskets.

Carlos sat down next to her and watched silently for a while. "Let's go for a ride," she suggested. "Have you eaten yet?" "Yes, but if you haven't, I'd enjoy having a beer while you eat." This was official business he guessed. Besides that, considering how their last date went, she didn't even offer him a kiss. The car was a blue Ford and, except for the two antennas, it looked like a regular car. They got in and headed out toward town.

"Carlos, this thing with Juan Melgoza is getting more and more complicated. Do you know anything else at all? I mean, do you remember any details other than what you already told me? We're concerned that he may have been involved in something more than we already know."

"Like what?" he asked. But she didn't answer, because they had reached a restaurant and the conversation had to pause a while.

"Hang on a second. If it's okay with you, we'll eat here, where we can sit outside." Carlos agreed and soon they were sitting at a shaded table, well away from the other diners so they could continue their conversation as she ate and he enjoyed a root beer.

"So you were asking about what we think Melgoza was involved in. Actually, we're not sure, but we know there was a lot of money involved. Tell me again Carlos, exactly how everything works when someone wants to cross the border."

"Well," he began, "it's really kind of simple. Right on the border there are lots of bars and restaurants. You just go in and ask someone, anyone at all, and they'll direct you to a *pollero*. You pay the *pollero* money then, or agree to pay at the other end. Then everybody that's going over meets up with him at the place he's picked out. It's always at night, so la *Migra* can't see you doing this. Then this fellow or one or two of his crew will guide you across. If you're lucky, on the other side, someone has been asked to pick you up in a car or van. Before you know it, you're in L.A."

"What happens if you get caught?"

"Nothing really, the Border Patrol takes you to their office. They take your name, even though they know you'll give them a false one. Then they put you on a bus that takes you back to the border. When you get off, there's someone who watches you walk back into Tijuana. Then you try again the next night until you make it."

"Tell me how it works in detail. Why don't you just tell me about the last time you came across with the smugglers?"

"Okay. So after making the contact in the bar, we met at the *pollero's* house. The front looked just like a regular house, but in the back it had a really large room with a few chairs and tables. The night we came across, there were ten of us," he said, recalling the event.

"The people who came with you... what were like? Were they all Mexicans? Were they all men?"

"It's funny you ask, because that time, out of all ten, only two of us were Mexicans. The rest were from Guatemala and Honduras. One was a woman who also came from Central America, Honduras, or maybe Nicaragua," he laughed at the memory of her.

"What's so funny?"

"The lady was..." he smiled, "she was dressed in a shiny blue dress and blue high-heeled shoes, like she was going to a dance. But the fact was, we actually were going for a long hike over some hills and eventually across a river," he chuckled, shaking his head. He stopped for a moment to have a sip of root beer. "Anyway, just before we left the house, two other guys came in. I think maybe they were the *pollero's* cousins. They gave us some instructions about being quiet and spreading out in a long line after we got through the fence."

"Why did they want you to spread out?"

"So if some of the people got caught, maybe most of the others could get away. Anyway, they said we would leave at 10:00 p.m., and that once we crossed the fence, we had to move quickly and quietly, because there were Border Patrol officers all over. They also said if we weren't together at the pickup place, they would not drive back to get us. Then they reminded us we had to move quickly and quietly."

"Where did you climb the fence?" Connie asked.

"Well, we didn't climb over the fence. We actually went under it, and it was only a couple of blocks from the house where we'd met. Getting under the fence was the easy part."

"...then what?" The conversation-interview approach was working out quite naturally, because Carlos talked more than usual because she was eating.

"We walked for about twenty minutes to the base of a small hill where we all gathered under a small tree. At this point the lady was crying. She said she wanted to turn back. Her feet hurt and her dress was torn. One fellow had a pair of rubber thongs to offer her, and someone else gave her a pair of socks. When she put them both on, her feet looked Japanese!" They snickered at the idea. "But she was quiet then, thank goodness! We walked up the hill. Although the hill was not very big, it was rocky, and since it was a very dark night, it was hard to keep to the path. We also stopped several times to listen for noises. But each time it turned out to be other groups of people doing the same thing, but following a different path."

"Did the people carry anything?" she inquired.

"Well, I had a small canvas bag with some clothes, and I think everyone had some kind of a bag, mostly clothes, I think. We all knew not to bring much."

"Did the guides carry anything?"

"Actually, now that you mention it, both of them carried the same kind of bag. They looked like military backpacks."

"How big were those backpacks?" Connie, realizing the information was becoming more specific, began jotting notes on her three-by-five cards as she listened to Carlos. He didn't seem to mind, being happy to help with the investigation.

"They were not big… not big," he repeated, " maybe about the size of three loaves of bread."

"Did you see what was inside them?"

"No, and they didn't offer us a sandwich either," he laughed. "I could've used one!"

"What then?" she urged, forgetting her meal as the story grew more vivid.

"After about two hours we reached the other side of the hill. We came to a creek and waited under a small tree with one of the guides. About ten minutes later, the other one came back. He whispered that there were two Border Patrol officers parked next to the road. So we waited silently." Carlos took another sip and continued. "We waited for about an hour. Then the other guide left and came back. He told us the officers were still there. It was then that they told us we would have to get into the creek and walk downstream past the officers. At first the cool water felt good, but unfortunately the rocks were very slippery. The woman started to make some noise again. She was scared. So two guys got on each side of her to calm her down and help her make her way down the stream. Thank goodness they did that, because we could hear the officers talk as we walked just below their position. We had to move slowly in the water to be as quiet as we could be." His eyes expressed the fear he'd felt that night. "We didn't walk too far," he continued, "but it must've taken an hour or so, because the rocks were slippery and the creek gradually got deeper. Heck, we were about knee-deep when we climbed out. Not too far up from the creek was a large tree that had once burned, hollowing it out like a little tent. There was plenty of room for all twelve of us, though it was tight. We had to crawl in, but it was dry and had a sandy floor. Several of us went to sleep for a little while."

"Were the two guides with you all the time?" she asked.

"Almost all the time, except when the leader checked out the Border Patrol officers near the creek."

"Go on," urged Connie. "This must've been so frightening for all of you!" She had taken out more three-by-fives and continued taking notes.

"The leader took out a radio and told someone that there were ten of us. I couldn't hear the response because he held the radio close up to his ear. The man then told us to relax, and that we would have to wait until there was a shift change at the San Clemente border station. A couple of hours later, the younger guide woke me up. The sun was just coming up. He told us that when he gave us a hand signal, we were to climb the rest of the way up the bank and get into the back of the pickup truck as quickly as possible. He explained that we had to lie down parallel with the truck bed, and that it would be very tight but to just snuggle in, even if someone was on top of you. They would put a canvas cover and other stuff over us. Again he reminded us to be quiet. He even suggested we first take a pee as it would be a long ride."

"That ride must've been awful! Good thing it wasn't hot yet," observed Connie. "Okay, now what happened when you came to the San Clemente checkpoint?"

"Nothing, actually. We started to slow down and the driver yelled back to remind us to be quiet. We slowed down it a bit then we sped up for a long while. Two hours later, we were in Montebello."

"That's it?"

"Pretty much."

"What happened to the guides and their backpacks?" she asked, hoping to fill another card.

"I don't know. Once we got into the pickup, I never saw the bags again. Both of the guides had lunch with us at the house in Montebello, then they left."

"What then?"

"I phoned my uncle and waited a couple of hours for him to come. He brought the three hundred more dollars I needed to pay them off and we left."

"Wow! What an experience! When did this trip happen?" She looked down, prepared to continue writing.

"It was two years ago," Carlos told her. "This year, as I told you, I crossed with some American friends of mine and no questions were asked."

Chapter 19
A Proposal

"CARLOS, WHERE HAVE YOU BEEN? I've been trying to get a hold of you all evening!" said Ann on the phone.

"Sorry, I just got home; I was helping my boss with his paperwork."

"Listen Carlos, my dad's birthday is this weekend. We're having a party Sunday afternoon at the house. We want you to come."

"Gee Ann, this sounds like a family affair," he answered cautiously. "Are you sure it'd be okay?"

"Well it usually is a family affair, but this time it's kind of a surprise. There'll be lots of other people here, too. In fact, Dr. Pilabos asked if you were going to come. He wants to talk to you. There'll be several people from Angelus, too. I can come and pick you up," she offered, not hiding her enthusiasm.

"Okay; sounds good. What time?"

"The party starts at two in the afternoon, but come early so we have some time to visit. I have something to tell you. Oh, and bring some trunks for swimming. What time shall I pick you up?" Ann was talking rapidly again.

"Don't bother; I'll get there. But you may have to bring me home. Is that okay?"

"Of course, Silly!"

Carlos drove up the familiar Conejo Grade that divides Ventura County east from west. The coolness of the coast disappeared as he reached the top of the grade. He closed the window of Mario's new pickup and turned on the air conditioner, which intensified the smell of Mario's cigars. He searched for a radio stations. All the buttons were set to Spanish stations. He shoved in the tape that was already in the slot. It was a familiar one, the *Trios Los Panchos* with Eydie Gormé, one of Mario's favorites. He had been more than willing to lend Carlos his truck. The generous man even gave him a credit card and his PIN number for fuel.

He found the Encino foothills home easily and arrived early, as promised. However, already there were already many extra cars parked nearby. He had to park the truck a block away from the Ferranti's residence. He walked up to the house along with with four other arrivals. One of the couples had two little boys in shorts, with towels around their necks. They didn't bother to knock. They just opened the door and went in. Carlos smiled at them and followed along, as did the others.

Julie Ferranti was in the front room greeting people. She picked up the little boys one by one and kissed them. As she put them down, they ran outside to the pool with their mother hurrying along behind them.

"Carlos, how nice of you to come!" She gave him a hug and kissed him just as she had the little boys. She held him at arm's length, looked at him, "I'm glad you could come. There are several people that want to talk to you," she smiled and hugged him again.

Carlos thought to himself, "…them, and Ann, too." He'd be pretty busy talking, or at least listening.

It was a hot afternoon in the San Fernando Valley. People were gathered under the shade of the umbrellas and trees. Several kids were in the pool. In one corner, a group of men dressed in shorts tended a large barbecue grill, each one sharing his particular method of starting and maintaining the coals.

"Carlos! Carlos!" hollered Ann when she spotted him. She walked up and kissed him hard on the mouth. Her action startled him. Before he could speak she took him by the hand and led him to an older couple sitting under an umbrella. "Carlos, I want you to meet my grandparents."

"Well Carlos, we've certainly heard lots about you! It's nice to finally meet you," the older man got up from the chair and shook Carlos's hand. He was tall and slender, almost thin. His white hair seemed to go in all different directions at once. His face was covered with freckles that also seemed to go in different directions. His lips and nose were covered with a white ointment as sun protection. His face was heavily lined from squint-ing and smiling. He was smiling now. He also had an accent that Carlos could not place.

Ann's grandmother wore beaded sandals and a flowered caftan which fluttered with the breeze. She looked Carlos over, shook his hand and smiled. "Carlos, dear! How wonderful to meet you! It's good to be able to put a face with the name we've heard so often." She winked slyly at her granddaughter.

"Let's go over to the bar and see if my son-in-law has any cold beer." Ann's grandfather grabbed his dapper straw hat, put an arm around the Carlos's shoulders, and led him to a porch next to the house where there were several men drinking various brands of beer.

"He looks like a nice young man, Ann. Where did you meet him?" asked her grandmother, as they watched the two men head across the lawn.

"Oh Grandma, he is very nice! I found him on the bus coming home from Mexico last month. He was just sitting there, waiting for me it seems. We just hit it off."

"We?" Her voice rose, drawing out the word. The elderly lady, know-ing Ann's tendency for dramatic enthusiasm, arched an eyebrow.

"Well I hit it off. But I think he likes me too, although he's way too serious. He thinks he will save all the people in his village."

"Would that be such a bad thing?" the grandmother asked.

"Of course not, Grandma, but he's going to need help!" She sent a self-satisfied smile to her grandmother and walked toward the men.

Next to the house were several large plastic chests filled with ice and drinks. "Boys?" said the grandfather. "Did you leave any cold ones? This young fellow is Carlos and I promised him a cold one." To Carlos he said, "I believe you may have met some of these chaps." Carlos knew then that Ann had probably told her grandfather quite a bit about him, probably too much.

One of them was Don Goodwin, the medical center's business man-ager, who introduced the rest of the men. It appeared that all of them were either employed by or had connections with the facility. "How are things going, Carlos?" asked the business manager. "Enjoying your sum-mer?"

Carlos laughed at the question. "It's been a good summer," he paused. "If I'm lucky, this may be my last summer picking lemons."

Goodwin turned Carlos toward him to focus his attention. He spoke more softly. "Alex will be here soon. We want to talk with you later on, perhaps after we eat." Carlos raised his eyebrows in inquiry. "It's about the legislation we mentioned last time. It passed a few days ago and we'd like to talk some specifics with you. I'll let you know when Alex arrives." The black man's teeth flashed as a huge smile spread across his face. "Now, don't go disappearing with that cute daughter of John's!" he admonished, chuckling softly.

"Ann, this is a nice party. Thanks for inviting me," said Carlos, who was genuinely enjoying himself.

"You're welcome. I'm glad you could come because I have some good news to tell you." Carlos leaned toward her and waited for the news. "I was just hired to teach second grade at Encino Grammar School! It's the same school I went to when I was a little kid. I start this September!" Ann blurted the whole thing out so quickly that Carlos had trouble understanding the significance of what she said. "It's my first job!"

The ice-cold beer, the warm sun, the new job, and the jovial aspect of the party caused Carlos to hug Ann and kiss her on the forehead. She in turn kissed him rather forcefully on the mouth. "That's great! Congratulations!" He took her by the hand, "This deserves a toast. To you: for a wonderful career!" He clinked their bottles together and put his to his mouth, just in time to hold off another kissing assault. They chatted and Ann introduced him to various friends of the family until it was nearly time to eat.

While the women laid out the amazing variety of food they had brought, Carlos asked Ann to explain the ones he'd never seen before. Sometimes, even Ann couldn't tell the difference between a gelatin salad and a gelatin dessert. He hoped he'd have time to sample everything.

Soon, he heard Don Goodwin calling to him. "Carlos! Alex is here. Can we talk with you before he has to leave? We can meet in John's office in a couple of minutes; Ann can show you the way." Goodwin looked odd. He was dressed in shorts and a very colorful shirt, but held a briefcase under one arm. He might have blended into downtown Honolulu, but Carlos wasn't sure. He could hardly keep himself from laughing.

"Carlos, it's good to see you again! Some of us at Angelus have been discussing our future," Pilabos made a big circle with his short arms as he said 'our future.' He then nodded for the black man to continue.

"Carlos, California just passed the law allowing foreign-educated doctors to practice in the state. We're not completely sure how it will work. It will not be effective until the January first, but our attorneys feel confident enough to let us make a proposal to you. Basically we want you to come to work for us, tomorrow, or as soon as you are able to join us. Officially, you won't be practicing medicine, but you will be a 'Medical Intern' until January first. At that time, you may officially join us through the internship program. In the meantime, your job will be to assist where needed in the medical center. We also want you to be the lead man in our outreach program for the needy and homeless. After January first, the job will not change much, but you will be seeing patients on your own as governed by this new law."

Carlos looked from one man to the other but said nothing. He swallowed and felt relieved when Goodwin continued.

Goodwin glanced at Pilabos, smiling. He continued, "In the meantime, the Angelus Medical Center will pay you $40,000 per year, plus benefits that are similar to what we all get. Although, we can't promise anything in the future, if it goes as we envision it, there certainly will be more money when you receive your license. Perhaps even a partnership in AMC, as we call it, assuming both parties want to continue the relationship."

Carlos was still at a loss for words. His eyes were wide, as if he could take it all in more easily that way. He took a sip from the bottle he had in his hand and set it down on the table, buying time. "That's a lot to think about," he said, a grin sneaking across his face.

Alex Pilabos got up and put his hand on the young man's shoulder.

"Carlos, I ask only one thing of you now… that you take a day or two to think about this offer carefully before you answer. Frankly, we at Angelus have thought out this very carefully, had it reviewed by our legal people to make sure we could make this offer correct legally, as well as professionally. We think this may be one way that we can truly benefit our growing Hispanic community. It will meet our moral commitment and be financially rewarding at the same time," he said. "Oh yes! In addition, in the back of the building is a small apartment that you can have until you get settled. It's not being used, and frankly, it'd be good to have someone live in it."

"Gentlemen, I don't know what to say. Yesterday I was picking lemons and tomorrow I have the opportunity to do what I have dreamed all my life. I really don't know what to say," he repeated. "You are so very kind."

"Carlos, we don't want you to say or do anything right now, except to promise us that you will go back home and seriously consider our offer. Will you do that for us?" asked Pilabos.

"Certainly! And thank you for your thoughtfulness. Of course I'll consider it. I am honored by your kind offer."

"Now we'll let you get back to the party or I know a certain young lady who will be thoroughly angry with us for keeping you," said Goodwin, with a wry grin. He opened his briefcase, pulled out a large manila envelope and handed it to Carlos. "This is a written offer for what we just discussed. Look it over carefully. In fact, if you know an attorney, you should have him review it, too. We might be willing to consider some changes. We know that this is plowing new ground, and we want to make sure that it's agreeable and beneficial to us both. You might even want to have John review it. Although he's not an attorney, he is very knowledgeable about these things."

"John...?" asked Carlos, still dazed.

"John Ferranti, our host, the birthday boy! He reads this kind of thing all the time. I trust him and you can trust him, too," said Goodwin.

"Oh, of course!" said Carlos, his thoughts racing. "Thank you; thank you both. I promise I will look at this very carefully and I'll let you know as soon as I can."

"Fair enough," said Goodwin. "Now let's go get another couple of cold ones before they run out!" As Dr. Pilabos made his way toward the front door, the stocky man put one arm around the young doctor's shoulder and they headed out to the patio together.

Before they could get to the beer, Ann grabbed Carlos by the hand

and pulled him away. "Come on! The food is ready. Let's get something to eat!" The couple piled their plates full of food and Ann said, "Come this way; I know a place we can sit."

She led him to the side of the house and opened a wide, sliding glass door that opened into her bedroom. She left the door and curtains wide open so the afternoon sun streamed in. Her room was large. He knew many families who lived in houses no larger than this room. He was startled to see a huge photograph of Mother Teresa leaning over a body lying in the street. The stark black-and-white photo of the humble, but world-beloved nun overwhelmed the room. "Well?" she asked.

"Well, what?"

"Well, what did they want? What did they say? What did Don and Dr. Pilabos want to see you about?"

He took several bites of food, realizing that he was very hungry. Between bites, he smiled as he chewed. Ann didn't eat; she just stared at him, waiting. After some time, Carlos noticed her staring at him. "They offered me a job," he said and continued eating.

"They did what?" she erupted.

"I said they offered me a job at their medical center."

"And what did you tell them?" she asked, frustrated. She still hadn't touched any of her food.

"I thanked them for their kind offer," he replied and continued to eat. He knew she expected more, but he mischievously held back a bit. Besides, he needed time to think.

"Dr. Reynoso! If you don't tell me *everything*, I will kick your butt!" said Ann, exasperated.

He stopped eating and finally replied. "Okay; it's like this. They offered me a job in their medical center as a medical assistant. There's a new law that allows some new kind of residency program." He handed her the envelope which she opened carefully. He resumed eating.

She read the two page letter carefully and started to reread it again. Then she looked up at him. "Carlos, this is fan-TAS-tic! What did you say?"

"Well," he said slowly, "they asked me to consider the offer carefully. They said I should have an attorney look the contract over. Mr. Goodwin even suggested that I ask your Dad to take a look at it."

"Isn't it the most incredible thing ever?!" she blurted, breaking in.

"I told them that I would," continued Carlos.

"Would what?"

"I promised I would consider it carefully and let them know soon, of course."

Now she took a bite. Before she could swallow, a thought crossed her mind. She blurted, "Carlos, do you know what this means?" Without waiting for an answer, she continued. "It means that we'll both be working almost right next to each other! The medical center is only ten or twelve miles away. Oh, Carlos! This is absolutely fan-TAS-tic!"

She noticed he was looking out the doorway. He spoke slowly. "It is a very nice offer. However, I never knew that a nice offer could be so complicated. It's so confusing; I already had the next year planned. I was going to leave in a few weeks. Now this offer makes things so complicated!" He smiled at Ann, "So, do you think your dad would be willing to read this contract over for me?"

"Let's ask him."

Chapter 20
Immigration

"Connie, this is Johnnie Reyes" with Immigration," said Detective Sergeant Teal. "Hector Galindo is with the Inspector's office of the Immigration and Naturalization Service in D.C. I told him briefly about your investigation. Hector's the one who suggested that we meet." Turning toward the others who remained standing during the introductions, he continued, "Gentlemen, this is my sidekick, Detective Connie Alonzo." Also in the conference room were Commander Jenkins of the Sheriff's Department and an attorney from the DA's office whose name Connie didn't remember. No one bothered to introduce him. They shook hands all around and mumbled pleasantries.

"Folks, let's all have a seat," said Connie. She gestured to the conference room's long table which was surrounded by chairs.

"Hector, why don't you tell us what you're looking at and we'll share our information," suggested Teal. "Then we can see if there's a possible connection."

Galindo was a small man with a slicked-back haircut and a narrow moustache. He cleared his throat and opened an official-looking black notebook. The INS seal was imprinted on the cover. "As we all know, for many years Mexican workers have crossed the border to work in the U.S. Everyone is aware of it, and both governments are, too. Since this process was and is beneficial to the workers, their employers and even to a certain extent, both governments, almost everyone has been willing to go along with this and not rock the boat. Once in a while, someone proposes some legislation to set up a more orderly process for this situation. Some people want to make crossing our nation's borders so easy that we might as well not have a border at all. Others want to make so difficult that it'd be like having another Berlin Wall. So in a way, there's a tacit agreement that, as long as no one rocks the boat, we maintain the status quo. Now please understand, this is not our official policy but, lamentably, it is fact." Galindo continued, "As I have said for many years, this has worked just fine. Restaurant dishes were washed, crops were harvested, lawns were cut, and houses were cleaned. And, just as important, especially to these immigrant workers, money was sent to Mexico. So 'no harm, no foul,' as they say."

He was taking a long time to get to the point, and what he'd said so far was old news. People shifted in their seats a bit.

The immigration officer referred to his notebook, "Of course, our government has recently stepped up efforts to stop the flow of drugs into this country. These efforts are aimed at trafficking by car, plane, and even by boat. According to our reports, we've been effective, that is, if the increase in the price of street drugs is any indicator. In order to avoid our current active interdiction program, it seems some bright fellows decided to just walk the stuff across the border. While they're guiding the wetbacks across, it's common for guides to carry six to nine bricks in a light backpack. In some cases, they even put backpacks on the pollos. When you think about it, with thousands of people crossing every year, this trickle of individual backpacks can soon become a river. The irony is that it doesn't cost them anything. In fact, the unsuspecting *pollos* think carrying the stuff is part of the deal they made to get across. If they get caught, the drug runners lose only a few kilos, but the poor folks who carried it are the ones who get busted."

It was quite a story, more complex and interesting than some of them had first thought. Connie, the only woman in the room, spoke up. "So, you think that the Melgoza kid might've been connected with that sort of operation?"

"We're not entirely sure, but we believe the young man got greedy but didn't realize he was playing with the big guys. There is a very powerful group, waaay out of his league that's involved in the drug trade. Your Melgoza must've been pretty far down the line," he concluded. "We've seen this sort of thing happen in Texas several times in the last couple of years, but it's hard to identify the specific people at the top. In fact, a killing like this serves a twofold purpose for them. It gets rid of a specific problem and it becomes a general warning to anyone else who steps out of line."

"Oh, so this has reached other states, then," observed Connie.

Galindo turned to her and replied, "Yes indeed, Detective Alonzo. What has your investigation turned up so far?"

All five men in the room turned toward her expectantly. She laid out some of her three-by-fives. "At this point we don't have much, except that we're sure the boy didn't commit suicide. We also think he was probably murdered. Also, we discovered that he had a whole lot of money in several banks on the border, plus some valuables at his mother's house."

"What kind of valuables?" asked Galindo, leaning forward.

Connie recited the now-familiar list of cash amounts, bank passbooks, and the packet of cocaine. "His mother was quite shocked. She didn't know anything at all about it," she concluded.

"What about this Carlos Reynoso, the fellow that found the body? Anything on him?" asked the immigration officer.

She was mildly startled at the mention of Carlos's name. "I'm sure he has no connection; he just happened to stumble on to the body. He's also the one who tipped me off that Melgoza couldn't have killed himself. That's what prompted us to look into the case a bit further." As Galindo spoke, Connie noticed the attorney taking notes. He seemed to have started doing so right after she spoke.

Galindo flipped his notebook a few pages. "Well we think you're right that the good doctor was just the unlucky guy who found the kid. It doesn't look like he has any connection, so far. Did you know he really is a doctor? Graduated in the top ten of his class at the University of Guadalajara? He went through the eighth grade at Briggs School, near the ranch where Melgoza was found, just outside Santa Paula. Speaks excellent English, too. He has worked picking lemons and oranges for the last seven summers. On several occasions has crossed the border illegally. This last time, he just hitched a ride with a family from Encino and crossed in their car." He continued, "His parents are both educators in Mexico and are well-thought-of in their town. His other relatives in this county are all hard-working fruit pickers or they work in the packinghouse."

"Yes, I met some of them when I was interviewing him as a possible suspect. In fact, I can't remember when I've ever interviewed a more cooperative subject. I've been pretty sure for a while now that Reynoso had nothing to do with this," said Connie. Sure enough, the attorney began writing as soon as she'd finished. She resolved to speak very carefully.

"Yeah, I agree from what she's reported over the last few weeks," added Teal.

Galindo continued. "We understand that Dr. Reynoso has become acquainted with some of the doctors at a very prominent medical facility in the Valley. They are prepared to offer him a deal that would permit him to stay in the country and actually complete his residency here."

Connie, surprised, inhaled quickly and remarked, "You seem to have found out quite a bit about the doctor," she said, using his term.

The federal officer smiled at her and said, "We actually know quite a bit more than that about him, but nothing that pertains to the issue at hand. It has occurred to us however, that perhaps he could be useful to us in this investigation."

"How could he help us? You already said he's not involved and doesn't know anything about this," asked Teal, who was curious about the officer's idea.

"We're really not sure precisely how he can help just yet. We just know that he's bright and, since he's crossed the border illegally many times, he knows the ropes. On top of that, he has the farm labor connection which employs many of the illegals."

"What should we tell him? How is he supposed to help?" Connie asked.

Again Galindo smiled at her. "We don't tell him anything. Except, perhaps give him a little encouragement to take the job offer in Van Nuys. If he does that, we'll fix his immigration status so he can keep his eyes and ears open. He can help us later on, if by some chance we need him. Look at it this way: if he stays, he becomes a permanent, legal resident. He gets a job which pays him very well." He paused, eyeing her and curling his moustache into an almost mischievous grin. "On top of that, he gets to see some very good friends he's made recently..."

Connie immediately looked down into her lap, hiding her blush. Keeping her eyes there, she said, "I guess I could talk to him again... to see what he has in mind. I suppose I could suggest to him that it would be a good idea for him to take advantage of any opportunity to continue his studies here..." Her voice trailed off. She began to worry that they might involve Carlos in something that might interfere with his plans. "Are you absolutely sure there would be no complications for him? The man should be able to continue to pursue his own dream, if that's all he wants to do."

"Of course, this area could always use a good bilingual doctor, so even if he never helps us, he'd be good addition to the country," said Galindo. "If we do use the doctor, we'll be careful with him."

Connie looked directly at the immigration officer, searching for some sign, any sign of how much he knew, but all she saw was a face with the hint of a smile looking back at her. She returned the smile she asked, "How did you say he crossed this last time?"

Galindo gestured to Reyes, the source of this particular information. "It was easy for him this time," reported Reyes. "He met a young lady on the bus he was riding from his home in central Mexico up to Tijuana. Once they reached the bus station in TJ, she offered him a ride across with her family. They got across without him being noticed and soon he was in Encino. I guess he's a lucky young man when it comes to meeting folks."

"Okay," she said. "I'll to talk to him. Maybe I can encourage him to stay in the area. I guess we don't want him returning to Mexico."

"Exactly! I knew we could count on you, Detective Alonzo." Galindo turned to her supervisor. "Thanks, Teal! We all appreciate your help. We'll be in touch." He and the other three men walked out of the office, leaving Connie and her supervisor alone. She stood up and faced the window facing the parking lot, looking at nothing in particular and wondering just how much to tell her boss. At last she turned around, and said, "Ron, can I talk to you?"

"Sure kid, what's up?"

She began slowly. "Ron, you know I've talked to Carlos Reynoso several times. He has been very cooperative and straightforward every time. I doubt very much that he's involved in any of this, except for finding the body."

"I agree with you. Go on."

"Well, in the course of talking to him, I found out he really is a very nice person. We've seen each other...socially...a couple of times."

"I know, Galindo told me. He didn't give me any details, but he let me know that he knew about it. He also let me know that this is much bigger then some dead *cholito* who was found under a lemon tree. I don't want to know any details of your personal life. That's your business, except when it has to do with this investigation. I appreciate you coming forth with this. If this investigation's leading us where I think it is, you and I have to be completely honest and open with each other. Agreed?"

"Agreed." She walked back to her desk and picked up the phone. "Can I speak to Carlos Reynoso? ...When do you expect him to be back? ...Would you please tell him that Connie called, and that I need to see him? ...Thanks so much."

Chapter 21
New Beginnings

H E SAT AT THE OLD KITCHEN TABLE where he'd enjoyed meals with this family over so many summers' time. The time had come to move ahead and develop a new plan for his future. Which of his female friends would be the one? Perhaps Licha would like it up here. He could at least give her the opportunity to see how things were now. He missed the familiarity he had from his long acquaintance with her and her family. It was so very comfortable… and predictable, too.

Dear Licha,

I don't know where to start. By now you have heard that I accepted a position with a big medical group in Los Angeles. It's a wonderful opportunity for me. California recently changed their laws to permit Mexico-educated doctors to do their residency in the state.

I know that you and I talked about having our own clinic to serve our people. In a way, part of that dream will become real here, since many of the group's patients are Mexican and many of those are from Jalisco as well. It may be that our clinic in Tonalá can still become a reality, once I complete the program. It will take two years.

Lots of things have happened this summer, things I could never have imagined. Still, I'm hopeful that they are things that will be good and helpful to all of us.

I will start at Angelus Medical Center next week. I will actually be living there! They are providing me with a nice apartment that the group actually owns. All I need to get for it is a few kitchen things and a bed.

It was my hope that I could come home this year for the holidays, but I doubt that it will happen. My internship and the obligations of the contract I've signed will keep me very busy. That doesn't mean you can't come here during the holidays, of course! How about it? You could stay with my aunt. I'm sure she would just love to have you during Christmas! Would you consider it? I would like so very much to see you.

I hope all is well with you and your family. I will look forward to hearing all about them and you, and everything that's going on in Tonalá.

Affectionately,

Carlos

Carlos reread the letter carefully and sealed it. It was late at his uncle's home. As he was writing, he could hear sounds from the living room where his aunt and uncle were watching television. He went to the refrigerator, took out a bottle and joined them. He sat next to his aunt. Estrella was watching a soap opera on the Spanish station. He knew that was her favorite program. He put an arm around her and squeezed her. She playfully slapped him. The three of them watched the *novella* together. The silent companionship soothed his busy thoughts.

His next step was to call home. He told his aunt and uncle that he was going to make a call home and that he'd pay for it when the next phone bill arrived. They agreed, pleased that Carlos's parents were going to hear his exciting news.

"Mamá, this is Carlos. How are you?"

"Carlitos, is that you? Is something wrong?"

"No Mamá, nothing is wrong. I just wanted to talk to you and Dad. Is he there?

"He just left. He said he was going to get a haircut. We are fine, though it has been pretty hot. What have you been doing, *mi'jo?*"

"Mamá, I wanted to tell you both that I met some very nice people here, some doctors. They have offered me a job at their medical center. I think it will be a great opportunity for me because I will get the same training as I would get during my residency in Mexico, but I'll even be paid while I earn my license!"

"Oh! It sounds wonderful for you... but hadn't you planned to be a doctor in a small town here in Mexico?"

"I know this is a very big change in my plans, but it's an opportunity I could not pass up. I hope you'll be happy for me."

"Carlos, does that mean you won't be coming home?"

"Sí, Mamá, I won't be coming home like I planned, but as soon as I get a chance, I'll come for a visit."

"Have you told Licha?"

"No, not yet. But I've written her a letter and I'll call her as soon as I can." Carlos paused. "Will you tell Dad, please? Ask him to see if he can get my tuition deposit back from the university, too. You two can make some use of it there. And please tell him I'll call him later."

"Carlos, I don't understand all this, but I trust you are doing the right thing. When you talk to your father later, please explain it all to him so he will know exactly what you're doing. We miss you, Carlitos."

"Okay, Mamá, I'll call him." He hung up the phone, knowing his parents would be completely confused just as he had at the sudden turn of events in his life. He hoped that they would be excited for him, and maybe proud. He felt a little steadier about making this decision, now that he had told his mother.

"When will you move to your new apartment, *mi'jito?*" asked Tía Estrella.

"...this weekend. I have to be at work on Monday."

"Oh, *mi'jo!* We're so proud of you, that you will be a doctor! And how wonderful that you'll still be so close! But I will miss you; now I'll only have *mi viejito* with me," she said, looking toward her husband, who was sitting in his favorite rocking chair watching the program.

Uncle Francisco looked their way and smiled. He was used to being called that, but it was said lovingly. "Yes, it's been nice to have another man around here every summer, *mi'jo,*" he said. "I'll miss you, too. Come visit us when you have time, will you?"

"Of course I will! I don't know any of the people at Angelus very well at all yet. I'll be missing you, too!"

The couple had raised Carlos when he was in the States and considered him part of their brood. Their own children were raised and had each left for better jobs some time ago. Only one son still picked fruit. Chuy lived in the same camp, and his wife had a job in town, so their two children stayed with their grandparents most of the time.

Although his uncle had picked fruit all his life, his grandparents were very careful with their money. They had saved enough to buy a small property in town. There were actually two houses on the lot. It was their intention to live in one house and rent out the other for income when he finally retired. In the meantime, they lived in a company house and rented their own home to a family who didn't work on the ranch. They had saved their money judiciously and were actually very well-off. The old man had no reason to keep on working, other than that he enjoyed being with his friends and that it was a familiar habit. He'd worked hard all his life. It seemed like a habit he just couldn't break.

"I told Mario I'd only work until Thursday. I need to get a few things ready to set up my apartment in Van Nuys. I also want to see if I can buy a car to get around," Carlos explained.

"Carlitos, you don't have to buy a car right now! You can use our car or the pickup for a while, at least until you get settled. Take your time; get a good buy. There's no hurry."

"Well, if you're sure…" He knew his uncle was right. He needed to take his time. Too many things were happening at once. Besides, if he took the pickup, he could use it to get some of the things he'd need to buy. After a little more urging by his aunt and uncle, he agreed. "Thank you so very much. I am blessed to have such people in my life as you two."

Carlos looked at his uncle. Although in his mid-sixties, he was still strong and healthy. He ate well, didn't smoke, and drank only a glass of wine with dinner. Only occasionally would he drink anything else. Of course, he did have one shoulder lower than the other, from over thirty years of picking. His only luxury was that he paid a friend ten dollars each Friday to have his back massaged and adjusted. His friend was a *sobador* who took care of many of the pickers who had hurt their backs. The old man had started having this man treat his back before he got hurt. He had told Carlos that it was his preventive medicine. In all the years he worked, he had never once hurt his back. Among pickers, he was the exception.

On occasion, Carlos had gone with his uncle to see the man work. The *sobador* was about the same age as Uncle Francisco. His hair was always perfectly trimmed. He had also picked fruit for many years. In recent years, he had retired from the harvest and devoted himself to working on people's backs and other body parts that caused them pain. He used only two lotions: one was mineral oil in which he soaked fresh eucalyptus buttons. Another bottle contained marijuana leaves soaking in pure cane sugar alcohol. Around his garage he kept several jugs of such liquids, steeping in their respective juices.

Carlos's scientific education made him skeptical of the old man's approach, but on several occasions, he had accompanied his uncle and had a rubdown himself. The truth was, he felt much better after the old guy worked on him. In addition to the treatments, the *sobador* talked constantly. It could be about any subject, but usually he chose something he knew interested his clients. With Carlos, the conversation was often about medicine and anatomy. Although the old man used the wrong names for some parts of the body, he was very knowledgeable about how they functioned.

The *sobador's* jet-black hair had grown a bit gray, but his tee-shirt revealed that his arms and chest remained muscular because of his work. He had fixed up his garage to accommodate his clients. It no longer housed cars but was in fact, a well-equipped office with a used chiropractic table in the center. He had managed to add an old barber's chair where he would cut hair, too. The open room carried a scent familiar to Carlos, eucalyptus and after-shave lotion. There were several chairs for people who were waiting for his services, or just friends who came to talk and watch him work. His regular clients didn't seem to mind the audience or the talk. Often, the clients became part of the audience. There was a TV, but it was rarely on. An old radio was usually on, but it played low enough that it did not interrupt the conversation. Indeed, it had become the men's social club of the camp. It was also frequented by many people who came from town to visit him.

He recalled his first time he got a treatment. The old guy looked over his way and offered an invitation. "How about you, Carlitos?" He switched places with his uncle, and once on the table, Carlos found his back felt much stiffer than he'd realized.

Relaxing into the sofa, Carlos thought to himself, "Life in the fields is simple. People work hard, though it's true that they get little respect from the society they help feed. Yet they find life rich and worthwhile in family, friends, church, beer, and gossip during an occasional *sobada.*" Now, as he recalled those simple days soon to be in his past, he knew that life for him was about to get more complicated, and that a simple back rub would not ease the tension.

Chapter 22
Business and Pleasure

"Connie, it's Carlos. My niece, Charlie told me you called."

"Hi, there! Hey, have you eaten yet?" she asked.

"No, but we're about to in a few minutes, from the good smells coming from my aunt's kitchen."

"Good, I need to talk to you. I haven't eaten and I'm starving. I was hoping we could do both."

After her note-taking and the grilling he experienced the last time they were together, he asked, "Business or pleasure?"

There was a pause on the line, "Actually, a little of both." He could hear the smile in her voice.

"Good! I have something to tell you, too."

"So, want me to pick you up?" she asked.

Carlos paused, "No let's just meet at El Pescador in about half an hour. I have to do a couple of other things while I'm in town."

The restaurant wasn't crowded in the middle of the week. They sat at a table without being formally seated. It saved the waiter a few steps. One of the owners came by. He talked with them briefly and took their order. At first, the two said little and just ate some of the chips a waitress had brought.

"How have you been?" Connie finally asked.

"Fine; but these last few days have been pretty hectic for me." He grabbed another chip and dipped it into the salsa. She said nothing, waiting for him to continue.

"Several weeks ago, I met some doctors who operate a big medical group down in Van Nuys. They invited me to visit their facility. I spent a day with them just observing. They seemed like very nice people. A few weeks later, I saw the managing partners and they offered me a job. From what I understand, there's a new law that will be in effect in January. It will permit foreign-educated doctors to do their internships in the U.S., as long as they do some work with the poor. They handed me a complicated contract that I went over with a friend who knows about such stuff. It looked okay to him, so I signed on."

"Wow!" she replied, feigning surprise. She hated to have to do this with such a nice friend. Their conversation stopped as the waitress came by and took their order. As soon as she left, Connie encouraged him to say more. It was a wonderful opportunity for him, and despite the complications of the investigation, she was happy for him. "Tell me more about it," she urged.

"Starting Monday, I'll be seeing patients under the supervision of the doctors until the law goes into effect in January. On top of that, they will pay me and let me stay in an apartment that's part of the building." He paused to have some more chips. "I'll be moving into the apartment this weekend." He leaned back, looked at her and smiled.

She returned the smile, "Carlos, that's absolutely the best news I've heard in some time! And you start Monday? That's so soon!" she was genuinely pleased for him.

"I'll try to move this weekend, but first I have to go see what this apartment needs for me to get settled in. If I'm not ready to move in that soon, I'll just stay with my aunt a few more days and move during the week. My uncle lent me his old pickup to drive until I can get a car."

"Did you say the medical center had a place for you to live, too?"

"That's what they told me. I haven't seen it yet, but tomorrow after work, I plan to make a quick trip to see it."

"Let me know what you need before you buy anything. I still have stuff in storage that I'd be glad to share with you. I have a bed, some sheets, and some dishes that you can use," Connie offered.

"Thanks, I'm sure I'll need some of that stuff. I'll let you know, once I've seen the place." He paused. "I really have nothing much to move except a few clothes, some books and an old radio."

The food came and they stopped talking for a while as they ate. Some things were a bit mild, to attract the patrons who didn't like the hotter peppers, but there were sauces on the side of many of the dishes for those who preferred the spicier tastes. Connie seemed to like it hot.

After a few minutes, Carlos asked, "So how's the investigation going? Anything new on that poor Melgoza kid?"

"No, not really; except it's gotten more complicated. There seems to be no doubt that he was involved in smuggling people over the border, but there was too way much money involved just for just that. It could be that drugs are involved and no telling what else." She shrugged her shoulders. "Carlos, tell me." she continued. "When you cross the border, how do the guides get paid? Do you think anything else get smuggled at the same time?"

"You pay before you cross, if you're lucky enough to have the money. But most people pay when they get to L.A. or wherever they're going. Usually a relative or a friend comes to pick them up and they bring the money."

"And do the guides carry anything else during the crossing? I know we discussed backpacks the other day. But do you remember them carrying anything more?"

"I've really never paid attention, except that most people travel light. They usually carry their stuff in a little bag, like a backpack or something with a strap. The *polleros* sometimes carry backpacks, but they're not very big."

"Have you ever seen what's in one of them?"

"No. Well, except the last time I crossed, one of the men took out a radio and used it to call someone." They had a few more bites. Carlos realized this was the 'business' part of the date, but he knew he'd brought it on by asking about Melgoza. He did want to be of help, though.

"Do the guides come all the way up to L.A. with the people?" asked Connie.

"Sometimes they do. Other times, one or both of them stay behind. I guess they probably catch a ride back to the border."

"And, thinking back to the last time you crossed at night, did the smugglers go with you or stay behind?"

"Both, actually," he said. "One came with us and one stayed behind for some reason," answered Carlos.

"What happened to their backpacks, do you remember?"

He paused, concentrating for a moment. "You know, I don't remember seeing those things again after we were picked up. I don't think they came with us… I think," he said slowly, "that the guy who stayed behind must've kept them both, but I'm really not too sure." Carlos looked at the detective with curiosity. He asked, "What do you think was in them?"

"Well, I'm not absolutely sure. The obvious thought of course, is that it's drugs…"

"What else could it be?" Carlos shrugged.

"As I said we don't know, but whatever it is, it's small, lightweight, and very valuable." She looked at him, smiled, and took a drink of water. No three-by-five cards tonight.

"What's all this got to do with the Melgoza kid?"

"I wish we knew; but thanks to you, we're sure that he didn't commit suicide. We also know that somehow he was able to deposit quite a bit of money in several Mexican banks up near the border."

"Who has the money now?" he asked.

"Well the banks still have it, of course, but Mrs. Melgoza, his mother, owns it, I suppose. I don't think his poor mother has a clue about what happened, or for that matter, what her son had gotten involved with. Now she's a very sad, but potentially rich woman," said Connie.

"What do you mean by 'potentially'?"

"It's like this. As far as we are concerned, we have no right to the money. Since it's sitting in several Mexican banks where we have no jurisdiction, we don't have access to it. So from our viewpoint, the money belongs to his mother because her name is on each of the accounts as a joint depositor."

"And she didn't wonder about the unusual amount of money?"

"She's a very nice lady who had no idea what she had signed when he set up the accounts. I don't think she'd ever seen the passbooks. She's grieving over the death of her son and it'll be a while before she realizes how much money she really has."

"But won't the people who really own the money want it back?" he asked.

"I'm sure they do, which is probably why Melgoza was killed. Whether they go after his mother to get the money is another thing. For the time being at least, everyone is on the alert and waiting, including the Mexican banks. If anything unusual happens regarding that money, we'll know about it," she added.

"*Hijo,* what a mess!" exclaimed Carlos, shaking his head.

"Well there's one good thing about all this," she said, leaning her head to one side and smiling.

Surprised, he searched his mind for the one good thing. "What good thing?"

She grinned at him, "You got to meet me, didn't you?"

"Oh!" He returned her smile.

Chapter 23
A Farewell

THE LAST DAY OF PICKING LEMONS for Carlos started as usual. The men seemed unusually quiet, not engaging in the normal talk about sports, girls or the piece rate to be paid for the day. Things were quiet this day, except for the radio which was tuned to the local Mexican music station. Carlos too was pensive. He had picked fruit since he was in the eighth grade, and oddly enough, he would miss it. Perhaps he would not miss the hard, dirty work, but he would miss the men, his friends, and all the bantering that went on in the orchards. Although on the whole, they were poor and had little or no education, they were very proud, proud of their heritage, and even proud of their ability to work hard, to do work that others would not. And there was a simple pride that, if they bought a beer, it was with money they had earned. Just as important, they took pride in each other.

Even though their wages were low and hard-earned, the men and women were generous with their money. He had often heard the local priest say that if the rich were as generous as the poor farm workers, the church would have no need to beg for money. Whenever a person got sick or someone in a family died, the guys on the crew would pass the hat, collecting money to give to the ones in need.

Sometimes the priests from their villages in Mexico would send word 'up north' to the men. Someone would act as an agent to collect money to repair a church, buy new bells or whatever the need was at the time.

Life for the farm workers was not very complicated. That part, Carlos knew he would miss. Already his life was becoming more complex and it would still be a few more days before he actually started at the center. A new place to live, forms to complete, and getting a phone of his own were just a few of the things he had to attend to. Picking lemons was hard physical work, but at the end of the day, it ended. There was a lot to be said for the simple life of drinking a cold beer, taking a hot shower, and eating a simple, plentiful meal.

He was also aware that this day would not end simply. Occasions such as a wedding or someone's departure would be the cause of a celebration at someone's house. The party would start with several cases of beer being delivered to the orchard by one of the truck drivers. It would continue later on with food and more beer at someone's home. This particular crew had several good musicians among them, so the guitars would come out of their cases, adding to the festivity.

Today, even field boss Jack the made an excuse to walk into the orchard to talk to Carlos. No mention was made of the departure. It was just simple talk about the day. It was Jack's quiet way of signaling his appreciation. Although the gesture was seemingly empty, Carlos was quite aware of its significance and was touched by it.

"Okay boys, let's finish off! Fill your bins up so we can go home," hollered Mario. Carlos had just started a new bin. As he worked to fill it quickly, some of the other men came up and started to help him fill it. Within a short time, most of the crew was gathering around Carlos's set of trees. The forklift driver brought another bin to the middle of the orchard, but this bin was certainly not empty. In it were several cases of beer and soft drinks, assorted bags of chips, *chicharrones*, and a variety of other snacks.

The men removed their gloves and picking bags. They washed their hands by crushing lemons and using the juice to clean them. Standing near the bin, two of the younger men tossed cans of beer or soda to the others as they arrived. Carlos caught an icy can in midair and eagerly drank a good part of it in one swallow. There was no need to announce the reason for the celebration. It was well understood by everyone, including Carlos. He was not surprised to see some of the other supervisors from the ranch stop by for a beer to acknowledge the occasion.

Apparently the word was out that there was a celebration in the middle of the orchard. Men from other parts of the ranch came and went. The forklift driver who had brought the refreshment bin had a radio. It was tuned to the usual station. Familiar songs competed with the sounds of lively conversation. A couple of school-aged boys arrived, carrying two large pots of pork skins and tortillas. They waited around for a few minutes, until someone gave them each a soda and they reluctantly left.

Speeches were uncommon, but this time Mario waved to a worker standing near the forklift, signaling for him to turn off the radio. Mario stood up, put one foot on the bin and caught everyone's attention. "Boys, it's always sad to lose a good worker, but it's even worse when the good worker is like a son or maybe a son-in-law." This elicited several cheers and whistles from the men. Mario held up his hands for quiet, "But this is not a sad day for me, and it should not be a sad day for anyone here." He continued. "Some of us, because of our lack of education or our inability to speak English, are doing all we can here picking fruit. I guess we should thank God for that. I know that I will always be a fruit picker. But that's okay because it's good, honest work."

The old contractor bent over and grabbed another can and popped it open. The men remained quiet as he sipped. "That doesn't mean that we as a people don't have the capacity to improve or to desire a better life. Perhaps I'll always be here with you, but it's my dream that my children and your children will have better opportunities. I welcome the opportunity to work hard until my shoulders are bent over. On these old bent-over shoulders, I want my children and your children to stand!"

"It has been my honor to have Reynosos working for me for a long time. Our families go back a long ways, and it has been a special honor to have had Carlitos here among us." He gestured to where Carlos was standing and made a slight bow. He continued. "When I look at this in my own simple way, I'm not losing a lemon picker; I'm gaining a new doctor who will look after these old tired bones for me!" The men clapped, whistled and cheered.

Several other men stood up and made similar statements of respect and friendship. The cheers got louder and louder. Finally, Mario looked toward to the forklift operator and nodded. The young driver pulled out a wrapped box and handed it to the foreman. The old man said, "Carlitos, this is a little token of our esteem for you. It's from all of us in this crew and many of your friends from other crews." Mario walked unsteadily toward Carlos, gave him a big hug and kissed him on both cheeks. The cheers and whistles were louder this time.

Carlos took a quick, final swallow from of his beer, squashed the can, and threw it onto the growing pile of empty ones. He took the gift and carefully unwrapped it. In the box was a black leather medical bag, embossed on the side with gold letters which read,

J. Carlos M. Reynoso, M.D.

"Look inside!" yelled one of the men.

Reaching inside, Carlos removed several medical instruments, a tiny, high-intensity flashlight, and a small, mysterious dark box. Puzzlement, then embarrassment crossed his face as he pulled out the box of condoms and finally realized what it was.

"Look at this!" one of the men nearby him yelled to the crowd. "A fine doctor we have here! He doesn't know what these are or what they're for." They roared with laughter, yelling and clapping.

Carlos waited for the cheering to stop and to regain his composure. He held the beautiful leather bag close to his chest. Pointing to the picking bag that was lying on the ground by his feet, he said, "I never thought it would be difficult to leave this bag." Clearing his throat he continued, "It seems I'm trading one bag for another. I know that this new bag would not have been possible without all the help and encouragement of my family and all of you."

He slowly lifted the picking bag. "It's my hope that I will not forget that both bags are just containers; implements to feed or to cure, both of which are very important in this world. The most important thing I will forever cherish is the honor that I have had of working with all of you." He paused for their applause. "This bag," he continued, lifting it high with one hand, "contains not only your gifts, but also the memories of my time among you …which I will never forget." The last few words were muffled. He did not bother to wipe the tears from his face.

One by one, each of the pickers came up to him and hugged him. Some of the younger men actually picked him up with their embrace. Their tears freely falling, mixed with the dirt of the orchard.

After a while, Mario signaled for the forklift driver to blow his horn to get everyone's attention. "All right, boys. Let's go on home and get cleaned up. I want to see you all at my house around 6:00 p.m. Please bring your families with you and we'll continue this celebration."

That night at Mario's, the party went on until late into the night. The food and drink were plentiful. Many of the wives brought special food they had made for the occasion. The people were in a gay mood. Even the children were allowed to stay up late. They played and, like their elders, even danced to the ever-present music.

Carlos sat at a table with Mario and accepted hugs and kisses from the women and *abrazos* from the men. It was a night that would be remembered by everyone, especially by him.

Chapter 24
Needs Fulfilled

THE DAY AFTER THE PARTY, Carlos woke up early, called Don Goodwin at Angelus Medical Center and made an appointment to see him later that morning. He purposely told no one about this appointment. He wanted to be alone to think, then to talk privately and frankly with the business manger. He drove his Uncle Francisco's old pickup and enjoyed the warm air as he traveled over the grade and down into the San Fernando Valley. Though he enjoyed the cooler coastal weather where the lemons grew so well, the warmth of the Valley was more like his hometown of Tonalá. He chose not to use the truck's air conditioner.

His mind raced with questions and concerns. His well-ordered life had changed abruptly by his chance meeting of two people: one a pretty girl who happened to catch a bus in the middle of the night on a Mexican highway, and the other, a dead body found under a lemon tree. What was the meaning of this? Or was it just chance? One day his life was centered around a small village in the highlands of Jalisco and the next, he was moving into the middle of a large metropolitan area. One day he was picking lemons and the next, he would be a doctor in residency at a large medical facility. One day he was living with his aunt, surrounded by a large group of friends and family and the next, he would be living alone in his own apartment. One day his life with Licha was a foregone conclusion, but now other women had entered his life.

"Perhaps a life of picking lemons is not so bad," he mused as he drove into the center's parking lot. He sat in the truck for some time, watching the planes take off and land. He took a deep breath of the warm air, got out of the truck and walked into the air-conditioned building to Don Goodwin's office.

Goodwin looked the consummate businessman, dressed in a crisp white shirt and black tie. Carlos looked at him in amusement, recalling how he looked in his bright tropical shirt, shorts and sandals.

"Carlos, I'll leave you alone so you can review this updated contract we've drawn up for you. If you have any questions, please let me know. The only difference you'll notice from what we discussed earlier is that now the annual salary is $46,000. The reason for the change is that our attorneys suggested that we charge you a fair market rent for the apartment. So we decided to increase your salary to make up for that. In the end, you'll earn the money we agreed on, except that Uncle Sam will now be getting his fair share," he smiled. "I'll be back in a little while," he said, waving as he went out.

Carlos read the two-page contract for yet another time. The repetition did not make it any clearer to him. But Goodwin was right; it was pretty much what had been agreed to. He did take a little more time with the clause that permitted him or the group to sever the contract with a 30-day notice. For some reason, that particular assurance gave him confidence.

Carlos noticed that Don Goodwin and Alex Pilabos had already signed the contract. He signed the document and at that moment, he knew his life had changed. It was done.

He had just walked over and started to read some of the certificates on Goodwin's wall when he returned. Goodwin picked up the document. Noting the third signature, he boomed, "Welcome to the family! Now let's go see what you'll be getting for $600 a month." As he walked out of the office, he handed the contract to his secretary. "Meg, please make a copy of this for Dr. Reynoso. And will you please get us the forms he needs to fill out to get him on the payroll? Thanks. We'll be back in a few minutes so he can have a crack at that paperwork."

"There are only two keys to this door that leads from the apartment into the main building. I'm giving them both to you. This other one is for your front door, which I assume is the one you'll be using most of the time."

They walked inside the apartment. It was empty, except that it did have a small refrigerator and stove. "There's one large bedroom," continued Goodwin, as he led the way around the apartment. There's another small bedroom here, or maybe you can use for an office. The place has never actually been used as an apartment. We just used it to store some supplies; but that's all been moved."

"It's very nice!" said Carlos, surprised at the amount of space that was his alone.

"Frankly," Goodwin continued, "I'm pleased that it'll be used as we intended. It will be handy for you and it will provide some security for us, especially during the time we're not here. Oh, and another thing: Don't buy lots of furniture. We have some things you can probably use in our garage. Ann told me that they have some too, so if you want, we can let you have it if you want."

"Thanks, that's very kind of you and the Ferrantis. I'm sure I'll need some of it. Carlos said this hesitantly since he had never set up a household he had no idea about the process. "I'll get back to you on that."

Goodwin noticed the unsure look on the young man's face. "Carlos, don't worry about all this business. Take your time. How you live here is your own business, although I get the feeling you'll be getting lots of decorating advice." He winked and tossed the keys to Carlos who caught them in midair.

Back at the office, Meg had a stack of papers for Carlos to complete. She'd arranged them on a table next to her desk. "If you have any questions just let me know," she said. She pointed out an unoccupied office desk where he could work.

Carlos examined the several forms briefly and then started to fill in their many blanks. He worked methodically on them until they were all complete and handed them to the secretary. She looked them over briefly. "Everything looks just right," she smiled. "Nothing's missing. Oh, and Carlos, we have our attorneys completing some immigration forms for you. I'll get them to you whenever they send them to me. Welcome to the medical center; I'm sure you'll find it a great place to work," she said with a warm smile. "If you need anything, please ask. I'm here to help you."

"Well there is one thing, actually. Do you know how I can get a phone for the apartment?"

"I can do better than that!" she said brightly. "Let me have an extension put into the apartment. Once you've been here a while, if that's not adequate, then we can put in a separate line. Would that be okay?"

"Sure, that's sound great!" Carlos was grateful that so many people were making things easy for him.

"Oh, that reminds me! You got a call while you were next door. Ann Ferranti phoned and wants you to call her. She said she's home and will be waiting for your call." Meg handed him a pink form on which she had recorded the message and phone number. "You can use the phone over there," she said, pointing to one next to a chair in the waiting area. "After you make your call, Don asked me to introduce you to you to Luz Reyes."

Puzzled, Carlos asked, "Who is she?"

"Luz is our Outreach Worker. She's an R.N.; or rather she will be later this month when she graduates. She coordinates the group's outreach program and is in charge of our weekend clinic downtown. You're scheduled to work with her next Saturday."

"Thanks, I'll be back in a minute," Carlos replied, heading toward the phone. Before he could reach it, Luz came around the corner

"Luz, this is Dr. Reynoso," Meg said as she introduced the nurse to Carlos. She was a slight girl with thick, black hair that flowed down her back in a ponytail. She wore white pants, a brightly-flowered medical smock, and a large smile.

"It's nice to meet you Doctor," said the young lady. "I understand you're from Tonalá?"

"Yes, I was born there and most of my family still lives there."

"I've been to Tonalá; my uncle has a bakery there! I was born in Zapotlanejo," she said with an open-mouthed smile.

"Really?" he said. Then we were neighbors! How long have you lived in L.A.?"

"Actually, most of my life. My parents are from Zapotlanejo. I was born there, but they immigrated to L.A. when I was little. We visit there often, especially during Christmas. Basically I'm a 'valley girl' now," she said.

"I hear we'll be working together this weekend. Tell me what happens at the clinic and what I'm supposed to do."

She led him to a glass-walled conference room so they could speak without interrupting Meg's work. "Well, this is how it works," continued Luz. "Every Saturday morning you'll pick me up at eight. I'll show you how to get there. We open the clinic by nine, and then stay there 'til about one or two, depending on how busy it is. Then you buy me lunch and we drive home," concluded Luz. When she spoke, her pony tail danced behind her head.

"What kind of people do we see?"

"The *Clinica Central* is downtown, right across from the Greyhound Bus Station. There are lots of poor people and homeless folks in that part of town… people with drug and alcohol problems… lots of mental problems. We'll fix up lots of scrapes and bruises from fights. We also see quite a few illegals who are afraid to go to a regular doctor, or can't afford one. And we get some people who just want to use our toilet and wash up." She saw the skepticism on his face at this last remark. "Really, she explained, "finding a bathroom downtown is a serious problem for these people."

"What do I have to do to prepare? Do I need to take certain things?" he asked, feeling helpless in his ignorance.

"Nope, you just have to take yourself. We have some stuff there but most of what we need we take from here in the AMC's van, which you will be driving. I'll take you out back and show it to you. Make sure to get keys to the van and the clinic from Meg before Saturday. Anyway, the van is well-equipped with the supplies we'll need. We have lots of samples, too." Her voice dropped a little. "We also bring some clothes for people that just need a clean shirt or pants, or new underwear."

Carlos looked at Luz curiously to see if she was kidding him. "I'm serious! Some of these people just need some fresh clothes. That part's kind of my mission," she admitted, looking down. "Some ladies at our church gather up donated clothes. They wash them and repair them if needed. They give the clothes to me and I distribute them to the needy. I try to bring more ladies' clothing, because the girls really have a tough time. Clean underwear is a luxury for them. This part has nothing to do with Angelus Medical Center. In fact, I'd just as soon they didn't even know about it."

He smiled at the young woman. He could see that working with her would be an adventure. "Thanks for the information. If you don't mind, I'd like to talk with you again, a day or so before my first visit to review the day."

"Sure, I'd be glad to Doctor," she rose, shook his hand, and left the room. Curiously, although she had departed the room, her presence remained.

He dialed the number. "Ann, this is Carlos. I got your message."

"Carlos are you coming over?"

Surprised, he stumbled, "W-well, I hadn't planned on it. I just came out to the Angelus Medical Center to sign some papers and see where I'm going to live."

"Have you had lunch yet?"

"No…"

"Well, come right over! Mom is making some sandwiches, so we eat and you can tell me about your new place."

"Oh Ann, I don't want to be a bother," Carlos said, unsure of what he wanted to do.

"Don't be silly! Mom is only making sandwiches. I'm sure she'll be mad if I tell her you didn't want to have one of her great bologna sandwiches," Ann kidded, laughing. Bologna wasn't actually anything special.

"Okay, I'll be over in half an hour or so."

"Great, see you then."

Carlos hung up the phone and looked sheepishly at Meg. "Thanks for your help; is there anything else I need to do before I leave?"

"No, but if I need you, I know where I can find you," Meg grinned. Oh, and here's your keys for Saturday!" She handed it to him and pointed out which was to the van and which would open the clinic door. He sheepishly walked toward the exit. She was efficiency itself.

The San Fernando Valley was getting warmer. Carlos avoided the freeway and made his way along the city streets to get a feel for his new surroundings. The dominant feature in the area was the Van Nuys Airport. By now, he was beginning to recognize the mountains in the distance which helped him know which way he was going. The airport served the same function. He noticed several TV news helicopters hovering to one side of the busy runways. The landings and takeoffs of small jets and little planes were continuous.

The drive to Encino wasn't hectic during this time of the day as it would be during the commute hours. Carlos didn't envy Mr. Ferranti and the driving he probably had to do most days, calling on far-flung clients.

Ann was waiting for Carlos at the door. She hugged him and kissed him on the cheek. "I'm glad you could come over."

He raised his brow, smiling. "I didn't think I had any choice. How did you know I was at Angelus?"

"Boy, you have lots to learn about me! I know more about you than you want me to know!" Somehow, Carlos believed her. "Mom! Carlos just got here! Are we going to be eating outside?"

"No," answered Julie Ferranti's voice, "I think it's gotten too hot; we'll eat inside." She gave Carlos a hug as he came into the kitchen. "I understand Ann promised you a bologna sandwich, but we're having a tuna salad instead. I hope you won't be *terribly* disappointed," she joked.

"Thank you, tuna salad sounds delicious."

"How was your meeting at AMC?" asked Julie Ferranti.

"Just fine. I had to fill out lots of forms and I got a tour of where I'm going to live." Carlos answered.

"Good," she said. "That's one reason we wanted you to come over. We have some things in the garage that we should've gotten rid years ago, but I just never got around to it. You're welcome to it. So, what does the apartment have in it now?" she asked.

"Well it has a stove and refrigerator; that's about it," he replied.

"Good! Young man, we can fix you right up, but not until after we eat."

They gathered around the table and dug into the sandwiches, chips, and soda. There were even some cupcakes waiting on the counter for later, Carlos noticed with delight. They ate, chatting about a lot of different things, but mostly Mike's Little League games. He was very enthusiastic about his interests, much like his sister.

"Did you meet Luz?" asked Ann.

"Yes, I did. She seems nice. I guess we're going to spend Saturdays working together downtown, starting next week," replied Carlos.

"Luz is a good friend of mine. Did she tell you that I help at the *Clínica Central* some Saturdays?"

"No, she didn't mention that. We were mainly talking about the clinic work downtown."

"Well, Luz told me about the people she works with, and all the things they need, especially the girls. Clothes, soap and stuff like that… I help at our church, collecting things for her. I'm able to take several boxes of stuff down there every so often. I like giving it out to people who need it so much. I also help with some of the paperwork."

"That's really nice of you, Ann. I'll look forward to having you come along with us," he said politely. He took one last bite and wiped his mouth on a napkin.

"Carlos, grab your drink. Let's go out and see what we can fix you up with." Julie led the way to the garage. "What did you say you already have?"

Carlos answered sheepishly, "Actually I really don't have anything except a few clothes and a radio. I've really never needed anything else, because I've lived with my relatives until now. My aunt and uncle have always had everything I've needed."

"Ah, you helpless boys! You're no different from the ones we have around here," said Julie. She opened the garage door for light, and the San Fernando Valley heat poured in. "Why don't you just pull your pickup around here and we'll throw what you want right in? That way we won't have to handle it twice."

Carlos obeyed without comment. By now he realized that with these two women, he was not in control and he might as well go along with their ideas. Julie and Ann talked to each other, deciding what he'd need, leaving him to move the boxes as instructed, which he did without comment. They knew more about these things than he did anyway. By the time they had finished, the pickup bed was full of boxes, a gray Formica kitchen table and four chairs. Underneath it all was a sofa Don Goodwin had dropped by. It seemed they'd worked almost everything out for him. All three had worked up a sweat.

"Ann, why don't you go fix us all some iced tea while we finish up here?" Her daughter walked into the house, leaving her a few moments alone with Carlos. "So I guess by now you must know that Ann likes you," she said. Carlos smiled sheepishly but mostly avoided the mother's face. "Ann is a fantastic girl, but if you let her, she won't give you a minute to breathe and will run your life for you. You know we love her very much, but John and I both realize she's very strong-minded. She'll bowl over anyone who's not well-anchored, you know what I mean?" She waited for a response.

Carlos faced Julie silently and nodded. "Uh-huh. I'll admit, I've noticed that about her," he replied smiling a bit.

"When she starts teaching, she'll have her hands full. But once she gets her class organized, you'd better look out," she warned. They moved a few things back into place, shut the garage door and headed back inside.

In the kitchen, Ann had three large glasses with iced tea waiting for them. Condensation had formed and it was creeping down their sides. Iced tea was not a familiar drink to Carlos, but, once he'd imitated the others and stirred in some sugar with a long spoon, he welcomed the refreshing drink.

Carlos back-tracked to his apartment and unloaded the truck. The boxes weren't difficult, but the sofa was a bit of a challenge to get through the door. Fortunately, it was a small one and eventually, he maneuvered it into place and sat down on it to catch his breath. He'd have to remember to thank Goodwin for the sofa. He'd be getting a lot of use out of it. He opened each box to find dishes, silverware, pots and pans, kitchen implements, towels, and other things he didn't recognize. Before he opened them all, he began putting things away. It took surprisingly little time, since every cupboard was empty. He sighed and piled the empty boxes neatly on top of each other in the spare bedroom.

Then he noticed a phone on the kitchen counter. He picked it up and noticed the dial tone. It was already connected! He noted the number as well as the extension number typed neatly on the little card that fit under a plastic guard. Mr. Goodwin's secretary was certainly very efficient. He would have to remember that.

Chapter 25
A Revelation

"Carlos? This is Connie. How're things going?"

"Fine; things are fine. Since I'm not really in the program yet, I'm pretty much an observer and translator for the doctors who don't understand Spanish. One interesting thing has been my Saturday visits to the clinic downtown. Since I'm dealing with the homeless, no one seems to mind that I'm just an apprentice." He collected his thoughts.

"That must be quite an experience! You must be helping some very desperate people down there," she observed.

"Well, they seem to appreciate that I say 'Good morning' in a fairly civil way. The fact that I patch them up also makes me a popular fellow. It doesn't hurt our reputation that we let them use the bathroom, either," he chuckled. "On top of that, my sewing ability is getting much better."

"Sewing? I don't understand," Connie said, thoroughly confused.

"These guys fight fall down and all the time, so I sew them up. Most of the time they'll let me sew them up without a painkiller. They just sit there like rocks; they never complain," said Carlos in wonderment. "Let's get back to you, Connie. How's the investigation going?"

"It's slow. The only lead we have at this time is Melgoza's mother, and she has no clue about what was going on. What's worse for us, nobody's contacted her yet about all that money in the bank. Apparently, whoever was going to get it is willing to give it up, instead of risking getting caught. Maybe that's a good thing, because his mom has nothing. She lives out there in a broken-down, ratty old trailer, poor thing."

"Yeah, but I'll bet she'll feel better when she knows the whole thing's over with.

"Oh, we're not questioning her any more, but we are keeping the place under surveillance."

"That's good. I hope it's all over someday soon." Then he remembered how very nice his own place was now, thanks to all his friends, including Connie. "By the way, thanks for the bed and bedding. I really appreciate it."

"Oh? How *much* do you appreciate it?" she asked, the meaning not hidden in her sultry voice.

"Well, I'll tell you," he said, thinking fast. "This weekend I'm coming up to see my aunt and uncle. How about going up to Santa Barbara with me for dinner?"

"Let's just say dinner for starters and you've got a deal!"

He laughed, "Deal!"

He hung up the phone and looked around him. Just a week ago he owned only a small radio some clothes; now his apartment was almost completely furnished. In fact the small apartment was almost too crowded. The people at Angelus, the Ferrantis and Connie all contributed from their excess to make him very comfortable. A few boxes of household goods were still stacked in the corner.

His first week at Angelus Medical Center was hectic. Everyone went out of their way to talk with him and make him feel welcome. The doctors were glad to call him in to see some of their most interesting cases.

The patients didn't seem to mind having an extra doctor in their examining rooms and have their cases discussed. Often, when the patients were Hispanic, he did more than translate the communication; he actually participated in the process. Doctors would usually briefly summarize the case and offer a diagnosis. Once in a while, they actually asked for his opinion. By the end of the week, his feelings of doubt and apprehension were beginning to clear up. He realized that although his medical knowledge and experience were not as extensive as that of his mentors, his foundational education was sound. It felt good enough just to follow and even to anticipate the discussions and diagnoses.

He also found that the doctors seemed to appreciate his questions, which were many. He carried a black notebook in which he made notes in his distinctive handwriting. At the beginning of the week, his notes were mostly in Spanish; now they were mostly in English. In his apartment, he transcribed some of the most interesting cases in more detail in a bound notebook. He also noted on his calendar the future appointments with certain patients that he wanted to follow up.

During the few slow times, he reviewed the extensive files that some of the patients had. He was impressed with the detail and the order of these files. The documentation in this facility's files was certainly different from the patient files he'd seen in the hospitals and clinics he'd seen in Mexico.

Carlos met Luz in the hall and followed her into the employee's coffee room. They both got some coffee and sat at the small table. "Is there anything we have to do to get ready for tomorrow?" he asked.

"Not really, but I was wondering if you could pick me up. My parents have to go to Pomona to visit some relatives and they'll have the car," said the nurse.

"Sure! Where do you live?"

She reached in her pocket and drew out a piece of paper which she unfolded, revealing a hand-drawn map. "Here, I drew this for you. I'll just wait on the corner of San Fernando Road, right there." She pointed to an X on her drawing. "It's just before you get on the freeway."

"That's easy. What time?"

"7:30 okay? That'll give us plenty of time to get down to the clinic."

"Maybe we can get something for breakfast?"

"If you don't mind, I'll bring us both some coffee and something to eat. We can eat on the way south," said Luz.

"Fine, just be sure to put cream and sugar in my coffee." That settled, they drank some of the coffee in front of them. "I understand you know Ann Ferranti," he remarked.

"Yeah, I know her real well. We met in church camp a long time ago. We became good friends. We do lots of stuff through the church." She looked at him closely. "How do you know her?"

"It's a long story. I'll tell you one of these days," he said, evading the subject. "Where do you go to church?"

"Mostly we attend St. Mark's. It's our parish church, but there are several others around here. But you'd probably like St. Mark's; it's a really nice church," she answered.

"The people in the parish are like family to me."

"Do they say the Mass in English or Spanish?"

"Both! And also in Tagalog and Korean," added Luz, watching for his reaction. She knew he'd probably never have imagined that part.

This surprised him, "Really? That's unusual!"

"Really. In fact, you can hear the Mass in just about any language you want to around here. I'll bring you a directory of the churches, but our parish is close. I'm sure you'd like it," she said.

Adding sugar and milk, he refilled his coffee cup and asked, "When will you get your full R.N. certificate?"

"Oh, pretty soon; at the end of the summer," she replied.

"What do you plan to do then?"

She looked at him for some time, hesitating. She stirred her coffee for a moment and then came out with it. "The people here at Angelus have been really good to me. They've offered me a full-time job, which I think I will take in the short run. But I am going to spend all of next month with the Sisters of Social Service."

"Who?" asked Carlos, somewhat surprised.

"The Sisters of Social Service. It's a religious order; they're nuns."

"You're going to join a convent?" asked the wide-eyed young doctor.

"I don't know." Luz paused. "But I've spent a lot of time with some of these sisters and they've invited me to live with them for a few weeks to get a feeling for their community."

"I don't understand why you'd want to become a nun." Before he could stop himself, he blurted, "You're pretty! Don't you want to get married and have kids?" Then he caught himself. "I'm sorry," he continued awkwardly, "I didn't mean to be nosy; it's none of my business."

"It's okay. My parents ask me the same question all the time!" She was smiling, almost enjoying his discomfort. "Even my boyfriend asks me the same question."

"You have a boyfriend?" he asked, this time quite shocked.

"Sure, I have several other admirers as well," she laughed. Luz turned serious. "I have several brothers and sisters. They're all married and have kids. I love the kids and I think the life they have is mostly good. But I wonder if it's for me. That's why I'm going to spend some time living with the Sisters to see what it's all about... to see if it's the life for me," she finished quietly.

Carlos changed the subject. "Okay, I'll pick you up tomorrow at 7:30. You're bringing breakfast, right?" She responded with a smile, nodding. He walked over to refill his coffee cup and left the room. He felt relieved and wondered why the conversation had made him feel so uncomfortable. He'd known nuns all his life. He'd just never imagined one of them as anything but a nun.

Fortunately, one of the doctors invited him along to see a little boy with one leg shorter than the other. Carlos's discomfort disappeared as he jumped into the safer arena of the child's medical problem.

Chapter 26
The Money Trail

CONNIE DROVE HER UNMARKED CAR to the labor camp. The wood-framed houses were small, and very close together. The camp hugged an *arroyo* and the houses followed the natural curve of the stream bed in a single line. The simple houses were almost swallowed up by the natural vegetation, gardens and fruit trees planted by the residents. A narrow strip of paved road ran along them for access. Connie parked at the camp entrance and walked along it. The Melgoza house was nearly halfway down. She had purposely picked mid-morning to visit Mrs. Melgoza. She knew most people would be working and there would be only a few elderly people and kids around.

As she knocked on the door; she could smell food cooking. A small TV was tuned to a Spanish-language station. Mrs. Melgoza reluctantly came to the door. Her hands were still damp, even though she had just wiped them on her apron. Like most of the other women of the camp, she wore an apron over a floral-print dress that hung loosely from her shoulders. These clothes were modest, covering everything, but cool in the summer heat. Most important to the women, they were inexpensive.

"Good morning, Mrs. Melgoza. How are you today?" asked Connie, in her most friendly voice.

The small voice answered, *"Bien."* Mrs. Melgoza took two cups that were drying on the kitchen sink and filled them with coffee and milk without asking. The tiny woman seemed even smaller as she put the coffee on the small table. She put an overflowing spoonful of sugar in her coffee and passed the bowl to Connie. She was nervous. Connie noticed signs that she had been crying.

Connie sat quietly for a short time, sipping her coffee. She asked again, "How are you doing now, Mrs. Melgoza? I know this has been tough on you."

The woman stared into her cup. "I'm fine," she replied. Her eyes welled up with tears which rolled down her wrinkled cheeks. She didn't bother to wipe them.

Connie didn't push her. She went to the stove, poured herself some more coffee and slowly stirred it, but said nothing.

"They want their money," whispered the old lady. She made no eye contact with the detective, who continued to drink her coffee in silence. "They said the money didn't belong to Juan and that it doesn't belong to me, either."

Finally the detective spoke, matching her hushed voice. "Who spoke to you, Mrs. Melgoza?"

"Rogelio."

"Who is Rogelio?"

"One of *mi pobre* Juanito's friends. They live in town." The lady picked up a printed floral handkerchief and wiped the tears from her face. It was a hopeless gesture, as her tears would just continue.

"Do you know Rogelio's last name; where he lives?" Connie gently prodded.

"Sanchez. They live in town, in the camp down by the river."

"What else did he say to you?"

"That's all. He said the money doesn't belong to me." The woman finally looked up at Connie. "What money? I don't have the money! What do they want from me? I don't understand!" The tears rolled again down her cheeks as she hung her head in despair. "He said he would call me later."

"Where's your husband?"

"He's working."

"Does he know anything about this?"

"Ay Consuelito, *mi viejo* knows even less than I do. All he knows is how to pick lemons." The old woman started to cry again.

"Listen, Mrs. Melgoza," said Connie, reaching across the table to take her hands. Don't worry. The next time he calls about this, just tell them what you just told me, that you don't have any money, and that you don't know anything about any money."

"But I don't know anything about that money!" she said, fear evident in her voice.

"That's fine; if he calls again, tell him the truth. Tell him again that you don't know anything about the money. Then tell him that I might know where it is. Have him call me. Here's my number." She handed Mrs. Melgoza her card.

"Are you sure you want me to give him your number?"

"Yes, and tell him I want to talk to him. Will you do that?" Connie's kept her voice calm, trying hard not to further upset the frightened woman.

"Yes, I'll tell him, just like you say. I'll tell him," she repeated. She gently hugged the old woman. It surprised Connie how terribly thin she was. The apron and waistless dress covered a body that was mostly skin and bones. Mrs. Melgoza returned the hug. She clung to Connie for several moments, taking comfort from her strength and confidence.

"Ron, we may have a small break. Rogelio Sanchez, a gang member, contacted Mrs. Melgoza and asked for the money. He's going to contact her again later. The punk scared the shit out of the poor woman. Mrs. Melgoza told him she has no money and that she knows nothing."

"Do you know this Sanchez kid?"

"No, but I called one of my friends at Santa Paula P.D. They told me the kid's a small-time gang member. They know him because of several minor incidents. However, he's got a couple of brothers who are definitely big-time. One of them has done time in prison, and the other one's spent some time at County Jail."

"What else do we know about these brothers?" asked the senior detective.

"There are actually several brothers. Two of them run lunch wagons out to the fields and sell food to farm workers. These two look okay, but two others seem have lots of money. Their girlfriends drive a Cadillac and a Mercedes. They don't seem to have jobs." She looked at her three-by-five cards and continued. "The local cops are suspicious, but don't have any firm evidence about the source of their money. So far they've kept their noses clean in town."

"How'd you leave it with Mrs. Melgoza?" asked Teal.

"I told her to tell the guy that she didn't know anything about the money and to tell him call me about it."

Teal looked at his junior partner and raised an eyebrow. "You think that was wise?"

"I didn't think it would affect the investigation. I feel sorry for the old woman. She was scared to death. If the kid knows I'm in the picture, maybe he'll back off and leave her alone," said Connie, irritated.

He laughed at her, "And here I thought you were a hard-hearted cop," he teased.

"I am, but this could be *my* mother, and nobody messes with my mother," she said, looking determined.

"Okay, okay," he laughed. "What do we want to do about the two brothers?" asked Teal.

"Well I've got one of the girls pulling all the records on them, but in the meantime, it'd be good if we could keep an eye on them from this end."

"How do you want to do it?"

"I thought we'd ask our friends in Santa Paula to keep an extra eye on them for a while."

"What reason will you give them?"

"I'll tell them the truth. That we don't know what we're looking for."

"Okay. They're good guys over there. They owe us a couple of a favors. Make sure you talk to the chief so he doesn't get his feathers ruffled," advised Teal. After a pause, he changed the subject. "So, what's new with your doctor friend? What's he up to?"

She looked closely at the older detective. She hesitated before answering. "I guess he's all right. He started to work at a medical facility in Van Nuys this week and... I'm supposed to see him this weekend."

"Mmm hmm..." The older man had already turned to his computer and started to work the keyboard. He appeared not to be listening to her answer.

Chapter 27
Complications

CARLOS STOPPED AT THE INTERSECTION to pick up Luz at the corner near a mini mart. She held a white paper bag and a briefcase. She wore white pants and a bright maroon shirt with 'Angelus Medical Center' stitched on the pocket.

"Hi, how are you?" she said cheerfully. "Here, I brought you a pick-me-up. My *abuelita* made these just for you." She handed him a roll of bread and gave him a cup of coffee which he set between his legs.

They rode in silence eating, drinking the sweet coffee, and listening to the Mexican radio station. By this time, Carlos knew the way, so the drive was relaxing, since most of the weekend traffic was leaving the city. He turned the AMC van into the Greyhound Bus parking lot, easing around a pothole. This station also handled the Mexican buses that traveled up from the border. The attendant waved at them and moved the orange cone that reserved the closest spot to their little office. Carlos backed the van in and the attendant replaced the cone. He waved again as they crossed the street to the clinic.

The waiting room of the *Clinica Central* was already half full; it smelled strongly of disinfectant and unwashed bodies. The older woman sitting behind the desk wore large gold earrings in her pierced ears and had thin, orange-red hair, carefully styled to cover her scalp. It looked like a home dye job poorly executed. She wore a clinic name tag which identified her as Thelma Watson. Luz introduced him to her.

"Hi, Doc! Glad you made it. You have a few of the regulars waiting for you. She motioned to the ones sitting in the office, but I put a guy in your office. Calls himself José. Looks like he's in pretty bad shape. I thought you'd better see him first. He was already sitting in front of the door this morning when I came in."

"Thanks, Thelma. We'll check him over." He and Luz headed right into the examining room.

The young man was hunched over and leaning to his left. He didn't bother to look up. "Hi, I'm Doctor Reynoso. What's the problem?" The patient answered with a moan. Luz put a thermometer in his mouth. Carlos touched his sweaty forehead which verified the necessity of the thermometer reading. Luz read it a few moments later. She showed it to Carlos with no comment. Between them, they sat the boy on the edge of the examining table and gently removed his shirt which was already soaked with sweat and blood. He gasped at each movement.

Carlos started his routine exam, looking into the boy's face and feeling his throat. As she moved behind the patient, Luz gasped. Her mouth gaped open in shock. Moving around the boy, Carlos too was shocked. On the lower left side of his back was an open wound about five inches long. It was seeping blood and pus. The area surrounding the wound was bright red, angry, and swollen. The smell of the infection was noticeable. The wound had been stitched, though not especially skillfully. Some of the stitches had cut through the flesh, swollen by the infection. Gently they coaxed the boy onto the table face down.

"What happened to you?" asked Carlos, concern evident in his voice.

"I fell and cut myself," he moaned, his words muffled by the paper of the exam table. Carlos and Luz looked at each other, sharing the obvious truth that this wasn't an injury from a fall.

"When did it happen?" he asked.

"Couple of week..." The boy moaned and buried his face on the paper covering the table.

"It looks like you've got a bad infection. You really should be in a hospital. I'm going to clean you up a bit first. Luz, call for an ambulance to take..." The boy cut Carlos off in a panic.

"No! I can't go to the hospital! Just patch me up. I won't bother you anymore." Though he was breathing hard from the effort to talk, he started to get up.

"Listen, *mi'jo,* we're just a small clinic. You really do need to go to the hospital to get this taken care of. It could be serious. It looks like it might be pretty deep." Carlos looked at Luz, searching her face for help.

"Doctor, I heard you help people all the time. Please help me! Please help me!" There was desperation, pain and fear in his voice.

"Okay, okay. Settle down. We'll do what we can, but you have to promise me that if this gets worse, you'll go straight to an emergency room, okay?" Carlos's voice was steady but his face showed his worry.

"Yes, I promise," he answered.

"This is going to hurt..."

"Let's let the kid sleep here. We can see the others in the other treatment room."

When they had taken care of the rest of the patients, Carlos said to the receptionist, "We're going across to the bus station to get a soda. You want anything? I'd take you along, but the kid's still in the back room."

He bought two drinks and found a bench outside, "Carlos, what was that all about?" asked Luz in bewilderment.

"I don't know, but he sure didn't fall and cut himself. I could tell that the wound was too neat and deliberate even with all that infection. It was done with some skill. He even seems to have traces of the disinfection solution we use in surgery."

"You mean someone actually operated on him?" asked Luz.

"I'm just guessing, but it's certainly not the type of wound you get from falling. Only that young man can tell us, but he's scared as hell. I mean, he was ready to walk out when I mentioned the ambulance." They crossed the street and returned to the clinic.

"How's the kid?" he asked the orange-haired receptionist.

"He looks a little better. I checked on him a couple of times. He hasn't budged, poor thing. He's asking for you."

The patient had heard them come in. He had managed to sit up, with his legs hanging over the edge of the examining table. He had a pained smile on his face.

Carlos looked him over. "You really ought to go to a hospital," he repeated. "But if you just won't, you need to take it easy for several days, maybe a week. Also, I want to see you here next Saturday, you understand?"

He nodded, agreeing.

"Now, I cleaned your wound as best I could and re-stitched it. Luz gave you a tetanus shot and another one for the infection. You've been a very brave young man. Here are some pills. I want you to take one every four hours until they're *all* gone. You understand?" Carlos held him by both shoulders, looking him straight in the eyes. "And you'd better be here to see me next Saturday. You promised, remember?"

"I remember," the boy smiled weakly. He shook the doctor's hand and they helped him ease himself off the examining table. He walked slowly out of the clinic.

"Good morning, Carlos! How was your day at the *Clinica Central* Saturday?" asked Alex Pilabos.

"Pretty routine: drunks, mental problems, homeless, and hungry," replied Carlos. "...except for one patient. I saw a boy about sixteen years old who had a severe infection in a cut on the lower left side of his back. He said he fell and cut himself, but Luz and I don't see how that could've happened. Someone had stitched him up, but he got a terrible infection. It was one of the worst infections I've ever seen. I was going to call an ambulance to take him to the ER but the kid panicked. He was ready to run out the clinic. I did my best to clean the wound. I re-stitched it and gave him a tetanus shot and some sample antibiotics. I made him promise to return next Saturday."

"Carlos, exactly where was the wound?" asked Pilabos, his gray eyebrows knit with intense interest.

He turned sideways and indicated the location of the wound on his own back.

"Did the boy say anything else about it?" asked the older doctor.

"He said nothing other than that he fell. But I didn't believe him; neither did Luz." Remembering, Carlos added, "It looked as if he'd had some surgery there."

"What chance is there that he'll return next Saturday?"

"I doubt that we'll see him again. He was one scared kid. If he gets better, he won't return... and if he dies, he won't return," he said slowly.

"Did you write up a report?"

"Yes, all the routine information."

"Well Carlos, you did a good job. Now I want you and Luz to do something important. I'd like you both to take some time today, and even if it takes you a couple of hours, to write a detailed report of exactly what happened. Write down what was said, what you saw, what you did… everything in detail. Will you see that you two get that done today?" asked Pilabos in a hushed tone.

"The routine report's down at the clinic."

"That's fine, but now I want you and Luz to write separate reports about what happened: every detail, even the conversation with the boy. Go beyond the typical medical observations. And bring it to me when you're done."

"Why do you want us to go beyond the usual chart information?" asked Carlos, wondering where this might all lead.

"I've got no idea. I just learned early on that when I saw something different or odd, it was better to document everything, because six months, or a year, or even ten years from now, someone will come along and ask you to remember in detail what you saw and did that day."

It was a lesson that Carlos would remember for the rest of his life.

Chapter 28
A Connection

"Have you been to Ojai recently?" asked Connie as she sat down in the truck next to Carlos. The weekday was warm and relaxing.

"Several times, we picked oranges there a couple of summers ago," answered Carlos.

"I know we talked about going to Santa Barbara, but I think going to Ojai would make a nice drive. I like Ojai. It's a small town and I like its quaintness. I thought we could get something to eat, catch a movie, or just walk around town," said Connie. "There's even a park with a trail going through it, if you want to walk."

"Sure! That sounds good to me. Let's go." He started the truck again and headed out along scenic Highway 150. As he drove, they pointed out the sights to each other. Connie knew the area well.

A stream ran along the east side of the road, and the steep canyon walls provided shade and shelter to plants that couldn't survive in the sunnier areas. They drove through the green tunnel until the narrow road rose and opened onto the high plateau. They passed through a small community which boasted one small school and a single burger stand. Beyond it, there were irrigated farm and ranch properties and a couple of Christmas tree farms. Even this late in the season, a few of the road-side fruit stands offered their wares.

Ojai sits in a bowl surrounded by mountains. The winding road dropped sharply from the summit as it wove into the valley. The temperature increased by several degrees.

They stopped before reaching the edge of town, at an open-air Italian restaurant and ordered a couple of glasses of beer. The place was crowded with customers, but the fresh air, umbrellas, landscaping, and openness made it seem more private.

She looked his way. "How are things going at the medical center?" Connie was genuinely interested in Carlos's new venture.

"Okay, but things get hectic at times. You know, at times I think picking lemons wasn't so bad," he chuckled as he drank from his glass.

"What do you mean?" She paid close attention to him as he answered.

"Well, when we finished picking for the day, we'd have a couple of cold ones, take a shower and that was the end of the day, as far as work is concerned. Now when I finish the day, there's a ton of paper work, making notes, reports... stuff that I don't even understand yet. Last night it was close to midnight before I finished a report about one of the patients we saw at the downtown clinic Saturday."

The waiter arrived with bread sticks. He took their order. Connie had recommended the pizza. They agreed on sausage and extra tomatoes. As their waiter swept back toward the kitchen, she asked, "What was so unusual about this patient that it took so long to write the report? I thought that mostly doctors just add a little something to the medical files."

"The kid himself was not really unusual, early teens, probably illegal. He told me he fell. But the wound on his lower back was infected really badly. It looked so bad that he really should've gone to an ER, but he panicked when I asked the nurse to call an ambulance. He would've walked out the door if he'd had the strength."

Their salads arrived. Between bites, the conversation went on, losing no intensity for the interruption.

"How do you think he was injured?"

"He wouldn't tell us anything more, but it looked like a surgical wound to me."

Connie continued to nibble on her salad. "Tell me exactly where the wound was."

"It was a five or six-inch cut on his lower left back. Why do you ask?" he asked, curious at this line of questioning.

"Hang on. I'll be right back." She took out a few coins and headed over to the nearby pay phone to call her office. She spoke into it for a few moments, and then said, "Read me the last page on the coroner's report." She jotted a few notes on a three-by five. "Okay, thanks. I'll get back to you." She hung up and sat back down at the table.

She looked up from the card, "Was the kid's wound close to his kidney?"

Carlos quickly swallowed the bite of pizza he'd been chewing. He studied Connie's face, puzzled. "Yes, but how did you know what was in my report?"

"What report?"

"...the extra report that Dr. Pilabos asked me to write."

"I don't know anything about your report. What was in it?"

"Well, in it, I mentioned that, although I have not yet seen a kidney operation, the wound he had looked just like my textbook described that surgery."

The pizza arrived at their table. It stood on a little stand above their plates. They exchanged pleasantries with the waiter, who belonged to the family who had started the business years many before. He placed a lighted votive candle under the pizza. Though it was put there to provide warmth, it would have added a romantic ambience, had the couple not been involved in such a serious discussion.

In a lowered voice, Connie asked, "Did you know the Melgoza kid had only one kidney?"

He picked up on her caution and lowered his as he answered. "No, I only saw that guy when he was leaning up against the tree and later, just his face when he was covered up on the gurney. What do you mean he had only one kidney?"

Connie answered, "A few days ago, we finally got the coroner's autopsy report. In it, he wrote that the Melgoza had had his left kidney removed. Although he couldn't tell exactly when it had been removed, he thought it had been removed within the last couple of years or so. I didn't pay much attention to that part of the report then, but now I wonder."

"So how does this connect with the boy I saw in Los Angeles?" asked Carlos.

"It probably doesn't, but wouldn't it be an odd coincidence if both kids'd had a kidney removed?" The detective added some notes to her cards.

"I don't understand. What do these two fellows have to do with one another?" Carlos was confused; he noted the cards as she returned them to her bag. Even on a date, she carried those cards with her.

"Carlos, do you think it's possible for me to see the report you wrote for Dr. Pilabos?" She paused. "Is there any chance you'll see that patient again?"

It was the same thing Pilabos had asked him. "As far as the report, I'll check with Dr. Pilabos. I don't know about seeing the kid. If he gets better, I may not see him again. If he gets worse he'll be in a hospital somewhere or may even be dead."

"Was he that bad off?"

"Yeah, it was a really terrible infection. The only thing going for him is that he's young and he seemed like a tough kid."

"When do you go to this clinic again?"

"We go every Saturday. We're usually there until mid-afternoon, depending on the clients."

"What you think of me going down to the clinic and sort of working with you Saturday? If he comes in, I'd like to ask him a few questions."

"Well," he hesitated, "… our patients come because they know they can trust us. You're going to have to keep it low-key."

"Not a problem."

"And I should check with Dr. Pilabos first."

"Why don't we do it this way? I'll give Dr. Pilabos an official call and ask him if I can see the reports you and the nurse wrote. Also I'll mention wanting to go to the clinic on Saturday."

"Sounds good to me. Would you like another beer?" They didn't discuss the case any further that evening.

After eating, they continued the trip into the little town. They walked along the covered sidewalk and stopped in a shop for ice cream before heading back. The route continued in a ragged circle, curving back southwest. They turned toward the coast. As they left the Ojai Valley and descended into the Ventura area, the weather got noticeably cooler. There was fog bank hugging the coast. Connie's home was up on the hillside that overlooked the old part of downtown Ventura, but during the remainder of their evening visit, they saw neither the view nor the fogbank.

Chapter 29
Progress

ARLOS PICKED UP LUZ AT THE USUAL CORNER. She fastened her seat belt and handed Carlos some coffee and a breakfast roll. "There's another one waiting for you when you're finished with that," she said.

"Thanks! I love your *abuelita's* baking," he said appreciatively. He looked forward to these Saturday treats. He turned the medical center's van onto the ramp leading to the freeway heading south. The early Saturday morning traffic was light.

"Luz," he said, "there's going to be a sheriff's officer at the clinic today. She just wants to observe what we do there. Dr. Pilabos gave her permission to come."

Luz was surprised by this development. "She... um... What do you think she's looking for?"

Carlos kept his eyes on the road. "Apparently she's interested in that kid who came to us in such bad shape last Saturday."

"Oh, Carlos, that boy has been on my mind all week! We should've insisted he go to the hospital. I've been praying for him." Luz was quiet for a minute then asked, "That must be why Dr. Pilabos had us write that second report."

"Well, he did make a point of telling me that any time we see something strange or unusual, we need to document every little detail, no matter how inconsequential it might seem. Apparently it has as much to do with our legal protection as with the practice of medicine. Anyway, as far as I know, she wants just wants to be seen as part of the staff and even help out when she can."

"The cop is a woman?" she asked, puzzled.

"Yeah, actually, Connie's a detective."

"So you've met her?"

"Well, in fact, I met her in Santa Paula, when I found a dead man under a lemon tree," explained Carlos as he balanced his coffee between his legs.

Luz smiled at Carlos. "My, my, my! Don't you lead a mysterious life! And I thought you were just a dedicated young doctor on a mission!"

When they pulled into the downtown transportation center, Connie was already there waiting. "That's her," said Carlos.

"Wow, she doesn't look like any cop I've ever met. Is she wearing a gun?"

"How do I know? Ask her yourself!" Carlos was aware the spritely nurse was still teasing him.

"Hi, Carlos!" said Connie, as she walked over to meet them. "Thanks for letting me tag along. I promise I won't get in the way."

"Good morning! Connie, this is Luz Reyes. She really is the one who runs this clinic. By the way, she wants to know if you're carrying a gun." Carlos ducked skillfully to avoid the playful blow that Luz directed at him.

Luz extended a hand to the detective. "Hi! Glad to meet you. Don't mind our young doctor here; he still has lots to learn."

"It's nice to meet you. Perhaps between us, we can teach the good doctor a thing or two," she said. "...And I *am* carrying a gun." She patted the side of the old sweatshirt she was wearing. "I think it'd be best if nobody knows I'm a detective unless it becomes necessary. I don't want to scare anybody away from the care they need." They agreed it was a good idea. "Now tell me," she asked Luz, "what can I do that's useful but will keep me from getting in the way?"

"One thing that always needs doing is to sweep the place out, uh... if you don't mind," offered Luz somewhat hesitantly.

"That's fine; in fact, I'm *deadly* with a broom!" She laughed at her own cop humor and the two women put an arm on each other's shoulder and walked to the clinic. They left Carlos standing in the middle of the parking lot, wondering what he'd just gotten himself into.

The receptionist was already there, as usual. Thelma made it a point to come early to let in the early arrivals. The waiting room was almost full, and the familiar smell of unwashed bodies and disinfectant hung in the air. They introduced Connie to her as a friend who'd come along to lend a hand. The receptionist welcomed her and said, "We'll sure make good use of you! It's going to be a busy morning; lots of customers." She fiddled with an oversized earring. "By the way, your boy is back. He looks like he's going to make it."

Carlos looked at the orange hair. "You mean the kid with the bad back infection?"

"The very one! He's in room two." She smiled as popped the gum she was chewing.

The three looked at each other. Carlos took charge of the situation. "Luz, why don't you and Connie go in to see the kid? Connie can start to clean up and you can begin examining him. I'll go in after a few minutes." He knew this would give the boy a chance to see Connie as no threat. He busied himself, shaking a few hands in the waiting area and gathering the boy's medical record and some blank forms.

By the time Carlos walked into the room, the boy had taken off his shirt and was already face-down on the exam table. Luz was in the process of gently removing the dressings. Connie was in one corner of the room sweeping the little room. "Well, José," said Carlos, "it's good to see you again. How are you feeling?"

"My real name is Salvador, Doctor. I feel much better. I came back like I promised and to thank you for what you did for me."

"Okay, Salvador. I'm glad you came back. Let's take a look." The redness around the wound had almost disappeared. Though it had not completely healed, it was obvious the infection was under control. He probed the edges of the wound with his fingers and the boy flinched, but said nothing.

Luz removed a thermometer from his mouth, looked at Carlos and mouthed the word, 'normal.' Carlos smiled and nodded.

"Salvador, this looks great. We'll just clean it up and put a new dressing on it. In a few days you'll be back to normal. Have you been taking the pills I gave you?" Carlos asked, raising his eyebrows.

"I took the last one this morning," answered Salvador.

"Luz, would you go see if we have enough samples for one more week? That should do the job. It will take me some time to clean this wound." He winked, and Luz understood that she was to stay out for a while.

"Sure," she said, playing along. "It might take me a while to find it, but I'll do some looking." She headed out.

While the boy lay face down, Carlos started to work on the wound. In a calm and matter-of-fact voice he began, "Salvador, I don't believe this wound was caused by you falling down. If I'm going to take good care of you, I need to know what really happened." The boy flinched again without being touched.

Carlos walked to the front of the exam table and knelt down next to his face. He was crying. "Chava," he said, using the diminutive form of the boy's name, you have to be completely honest with me if I'm to care for you. Medicine is hard enough without having to guess."

The boy said nothing.

Still kneeling next to him, Carlos put his hand on Salvador's shoulder and rubbed it gently. "Did someone operate on you?"

The boy nodded.

"Did someone operate on your kidney?" again the boy nodded.

"What was wrong with your kidney?" Carlos asked gently, still rubbing the boy's back. He felt his patient's breathing ease and his muscles relax a bit.

"Nothing," answered the boy quietly almost to himself.

"Then why did someone operate on you?" He added, more slowly, "Did you donate your kidney to someone?"

"No," the tears in the boy's eyes flowed again, "I sold it."

Carlos pulled a stool next to the boy. He sat down close to him, keeping his hand on the boy's shoulder. "You mean someone gave you money for one of your kidneys?"

The boy nodded yes.

"Where was the operation done?" asked Carlos.

"In Tijuana."

"In a hospital or a clinic?" Carlos noticed that Connie had stopped pretending to sweep and had begun writing on her three-by-fives.

"In a doctor's office," came the shy voice.

Carlos gently patted his shoulder for a moment. "What did the man who operated on you tell you about how you would be after the surgery?" Luz walked back into the room carrying a small bottle of pills. She handed them to Carlos. He motioned for her to stay.

"He didn't talk much to me. He only said that it's okay to live on one kidney and that I would be sore for a couple of days. Is it true? Will I be okay?" The boy seemed to be more comfortable talking even though his head was facing away from Carlos, who continued to pat and rub the boy's shoulder.

"Yes, you can definitely live with one kidney, but you'll need to take good care of the one you've got left. We'll talk about that next time," he promised. "Did they pay you?" asked Carlos.

The boy nodded again.

"How much?"

"They gave me five hundred dollars and a free trip to Los Angeles."

Connie caught Carlos's attention, holding up a card that read, "Dr. Name?" He shook his head. It was not yet time to ask.

"When did you come to Los Angeles?" he asked.

"The same day."

"You mean that someone removed your kidney and the very same day, you walked all the way across the border in Tijuana?" asked Carlos as he raised his voice a bit.

"They operated on me in the morning and later that night, I walked across the border." Salvador cleared his throat. His voice seemed clearer and stronger and his tears had dried.

Carlos straightened up, looked at Connie who was still standing at the counter, writing on her cards. "Let me see if I got this right," he said, "someone, I guess a doctor, removed your kidney in his office in the morning, gave you five hundred dollars. Then later that night, you had to walk across the border where you finally got a ride to Los Angeles."

"Oh, he also gave me some pills," said the boy, in an effort to clear up matters.

"What kind of pills?"

"He said they were for the pain which would go away in a couple of days."

"And you walked across the border the very same day…" Carlos's voice showed his dismay at the thought of such a thing happening. "So, what happened then?" continued Carlos gently.

"They brought me to the hotel where I'm staying now. The next day I was real sick, so I stayed in bed all day. The following day I was even worse. The lady who lived next door heard me and brought me here to see you," he explained.

"Do you know the name of the doctor who took your kidney or any of the people who were involved in this?" asked Carlos.

"No, I met them on the street. One of the *polleros* who was going to bring me across introduced me to him. I don't know if they used their real names, but I don't remember them anyway." Carlos caught Connie's eye and shrugged. They wouldn't be getting a name.

"The doctor told me that he knew a little girl who was going to die if she didn't get a new kidney. He told me how desperate the family was and how much they prayed for God to give them a new kidney that would let the little girl live a normal life. He told me that we all just needed one good kidney; that God gave us two so we could share if we needed to."

Connie had written on another card. She held it up for Carlos to see. "Which Hotel?" Carlos nodded. "So, what hotel have you been staying at?"

"The *¡Pozo del Sueño!* It's not far from here, just a couple of blocks that way." He pointed, wincing a little. Connie recorded this quickly.

"What else did he say to you?" asked Carlos.

"He took me to a restaurant where he introduced me to a woman. She was crying. She kept saying that her little girl was going to die but that she knew the Virgin Mary was somehow going to bring someone who would save the girl's life. She even showed me a picture of her daughter," said Salvador, his voice now steady and strong.

"Had you ever seen this woman before?" asked Carlos.

"No, the doctor and I were already eating when she walked by. She saw us and must have recognized him, because she came over and sat at our table. She kept fingering her rosary the whole time," he said.

"Then what happened?"

"The doctor told me again that we only need one kidney to live a good life. He said it would be a fine gift if someone were to donate a kidney to save the woman's little girl's life, especially since we only needed one." said Salvador.

"What happened next?" Carlos got up from the stool. As the boy continued, he applied an antibiotic to the wound and began to secure it with a generously thick gauze dressing and adhesive tape.

"The lady kept crying and praying. She prayed to the Virgin, saying she knew the Lady would provide a good soul who would save her little girl."

"And then?" He noticed that Luz and Connie were listening intently to Salvador's story.

"I asked if it hurt to give a kidney." The boy's tears now dry, he seemed eager to tell the story. "The doctor said that it wouldn't hurt at all. That I would be sore for a couple of days, but he had pain pills that would make the soreness go away."

"How did the money come into the conversation?" asked Carlos.

The boy thought for a moment. "The woman said that she was willing to pay for everything. She said would also give five hundred dollars to the good person who saved her little girl. She said it was wonderful how God had made us so that we could live very well with just one kidney." The boy seemed proud of how clear his recollection was.

"How did they finally convince you to donate your kidney?" asked Carlos.

"The lady started crying again. She was getting very loud. People in the restaurant were starting to stare at us. Then I just asked if perhaps I could be the donor. The lady stopped crying right away. She thanked God and made the sign of the cross. Even the doctor thanked God for the miracle that had just appeared. The lady got up she told the waitress that I had agreed to donate one of my kidneys to save her little girl's life. Even the waitress fell to her knees to thank God." The boy smiled proudly as he recalled the event.

"What was the doctor doing all this time?" asked Carlos.

"The doctor was actually lots of help. He leaned over and told me to ask the lady if she was really willing to pay for it all, including the five hundred for me. I asked her. She said she would and then she showed me several hundred dollar bills. Then we walked over to the clinic from the restaurant. Then he got me ready and I had the operation. It was dark when I woke up."

"What happened then? Were you alone?" Carlos asked. Salvador sat up on the table and looked at his small, safe audience.

"The doctor gave me a soda and a little bottle of pills to take every two hours for pain. I didn't feel so good, but he said in a couple of days I would feel like new. He took me a couple of blocks away to a house where I stayed with some other people. A couple of hours later the *polleros* took us across. We walked for several hours, to a highway where we were picked up by a van. I fell asleep. The pills were strong. When I woke up again, the driver told me we were in L.A. He suggested I check into the hotel where I am now." The boy's youth seemed to fade as he grew into a young man before their eyes.

Luz picked up the bottle of sample antibiotics and handed them to Carlos. He handed them to Salvador, saying, "Chava, here are some more of the same pills I gave you the last time. Make sure you take them until they're all gone, so you can finish healing without getting infected again. Do you have any questions?"

The boy nodded in agreement. "What will you do now?" asked Carlos.

"I have an uncle in Fresno where I've worked several summers," said the boy. "I'll stay with him."

"Listen, Salvador. I want to make sure that you're okay. Give me your uncle's address and phone number so I can check up on you."

The boy nodded in agreement.

"I'll send you a little booklet they give people who have donated a kidney. There's not much you'll have to do to take care of your remaining kidney, but it has some good information for you. Luz, would you please take Chava's information for me? I want to check on a few things. I'll be right back."

He walked out with Connie. "Did you hear all that?" he whispered.

"Yes; I was writing as fast as I could. Did you believe him?" asked Connie.

"What do you mean, did I believe him? I don't think that kid could've made up such a tale. That cut on his side make sense now. It's got to be true, at least that's how he saw it."

"I believe him too. Thanks for getting that hotel name for me. I thought I might take a walk over there to nose around, maybe talk to some of the people." She continued, "Could you tell him that I might want to talk to him later?"

"Okay, it looks like we still have several hours of work to do here. I'll see you when I get back from the hotel."

Carlos returned to the exam room. Salvador was now dressed and talking to Luz. He took the record from Luz and looked at it briefly. "When do you think you'll be leaving for Fresno?"

"If I can catch a bus in the morning I can be in Fresno in the afternoon. In fact, I'm going to the bus station to buy a ticket right now."

"Chava, I hope everything goes well with you. I want you to do me a favor before you start to do any heavy work. Please see a doctor in Fresno. Tell him what happened to you. I'm sure you'll have no problem, but do this to be sure you're safe. Will you do that for me?" Carlos put his hands on the boy's shoulders as the boy nodded.

"Yes, Doctor Reynoso. I'll do that. How can I thank you doctor? I don't have much money left, but I would like to pay you something," said the boy.

"You don't have to pay us anything, but you can do me a personal favor, if you'd like," said Carlos with a smile.

"Sure; anything! What is it?"

"Sometime in the next several days, a good friend of mine will want to talk to you about this. Talk to her frankly. Tell her everything you told me. In fact, on your trip to Fresno, please try to remember any more details you didn't think of today. You can tell anything new to her when she calls. You can trust her. Will you do that for me?"

"Sure, what's her name?"

"Connie, Constancia Alonzo."

Salvador finished buttoning up his shirt. "Okay, I can remember that name; Constancia is my mother's name. I'll be glad to talk to her." As he walked out the door, he turned and said, "Thank you again. God bless you both."

This time it was Luz who responded, "And may God bless you too, Salvador."

After the boy had gone, Carlos turned to Luz and said, "I guess it'll be another long night writing out another report for Dr. Pilabos." They sighed.

Luz added briskly, "The sooner we get going with the next patients, the sooner we can get to that report!"

The other patients came in with the usual scrapes, cuts and bruises, or suffering from the effects of malnourishment or too much liquor. It was obvious that some just wanted someone to pay attention to them, to tell them they would be all right. It also became quite apparent to Carlos that some just wanted to be touched. It seemed that if the doctor, with his educated, clean hand, would just touch them, then perhaps they weren't so bad off after all.

He quickly discovered that even when touching the person was not a necessary part of the examination, it put them at ease. So now he routinely put his hand on them or just held a patient's hand as they talked, or as he gave instructions. Putting his arm around a person as he walked them to the door seemed to put a bounce in their step as they left.

One of his professors at the university had spoken briefly about the importance of touch, although babies were the focus of his lecture. Carlos very soon became aware that the marginalized needed to be touched, perhaps even more than most people. It was obvious that society generally wanted these people to simply disappear. The last thing they wanted was to have contact; certainly no physical contact. Could medicine be reduced to listening and touching? His brief experience at the Angelus Medical Center's *Clinica Central* downtown was one of ongoing education and discovery.

It was late afternoon before the last of the patients left the waiting room. Their lingering odor was all that was left to indicate they had been there. Thelma Watson had put away her things and said her good-byes before leaving. Luz was straightening the supply cupboard in the back. Connie sat in the corner shuffling through her usual pile of three-by-fives, adding notes and numbers, making connections, and forming theories.

Carlos sat next to her on one of the folding chairs. "And how was your day?" he asked.

"Oh… interesting enough. But first I want to tell you how impressed

I am by what you, Luz and the 'orangehead' do here. Is it like this all the time?" she asked.

"Well, remember I only started coming here a few weeks ago, but I have the impression that this place gets lots of use."

"You know what the people are saying about you, especially the ladies? I couldn't help hearing them talk," said Connie with a grin.

"What do they say?"

"...that you really are a dream, that they feel better just being here," she chuckled. In some way she felt proud.

Carlos shook his head. "Awww, all I do is listen and give out aspirin."

"I guess it must be the way you give them the pills." The detective grinned mischievously. "Could I get you to listen to me tonight? I have a serious body ache!" She snickered.

"If you let me go home and take a shower, and meet me at the door with a beer and something to eat, I'll listen to you all night long."

"You've got yourself a deal, Doctor!" Connie put her note cards away.

Chapter 30
Women!

"Dr. Reynoso, you have a call on line one," Meg called to him as he passed her desk. "You can take it there," she said, pointing to the one he'd used before in the waiting room.

"Hello? … Oh hi, Ann! How've you been?"

"Dr. Reynoso, I'm not very well, I'm upset with you. It's been two weeks and you haven't called or anything!"

"It's been hectic here. I didn't realize I'd be nearly so busy." He sat down next to the phone.

"That's a poor excuse, and not very creative… but I guess it'll have to do." The tone of her voice changed. "Anyway, I'd like to see you," said Ann.

"It would have to be after work. Maybe we can get something to eat?"

"Great! Why don't you come over for dinner? We can talk here."

"I'd like to, but I could be pretty late; sometimes I'm not done until after seven."

"Good; we'll see you then." Ann hung up the phone before he could make any further excuses.

Carlos drove to the Ferranti's along the surface streets. He was getting to know the neighborhood and took his time driving. The summer days were long. It was still early sunset when he arrived at their home. He didn't have to ring the doorbell. Ann had heard him drive up and met him at the door. "Carlos, it's good to see you again!"

"Thanks, for the invitation. I don't think I could have gone to Bountiful Burritos again." He gave her a kiss on the cheek. Ann in turn, kissed him on the mouth.

Ann's parents were already eating, but John Ferranti offered a glass of wine with a gesture and, receiving an appreciative nod, poured him a glass.

"Dad?" asked Mike, "Can I have some, too?"

His father replied, "Not a chance!"

"Carlos, how are things at the medical center?"

"Fine, fine! It's been very interesting. I'm amazed at what I'm learning. The doctors at the medical center are going out of their way to let me look over their shoulders. It's the very best way to learn. On Saturday, I work at our downtown clinic. That's even more interesting," said Carlos as he took the glass of wine.

"I understand Luz goes with you," said Julie.

"Actually, I go with her. If it weren't for her, I'd be lost! She keeps everything organized. She told me she knows you all."

Ann jumped in. "We met at a church camp and became really good friends. In fact I just received the invitation to her graduation. She'll be receiving her B.S.N. degree Are you going?"

"I don't know. I haven't been invited."

"Good, then you can go with me," Ann decided.

"Now that you cornered him Ann, how about getting Carlos some more food? You did invite him to eat didn't you?" said her father.

"Not really, I invited him to chide him for ignoring me the last couple of weeks. But since he's here and truly sorry for his shortcomings, I'll feed him."

John Ferranti couldn't help laughing, "I guess we're responsible for her upbringing, but she reminds me of someone else in the family..." Julie Ferranti gave him a withering look.

He continued, "Are you all settled into your new living quarters?"

"Almost," said Carlos, "It's funny, a short time ago I just owned some clothes and a small radio, now I have an apartment full of stuff. It's amazing! All I need now is a dog and a goldfish!"

John smiled. "I was hoping you would go through our garage again and relieve us of a few more things," he kidded.

Ann brought two plates, gave one to Carlos and sat down next to him. "Daddy, did you ask him?"

"No, I thought I'd let the boy eat first." He paused, sighing and then broached the subject. "Carlos, since neither of us will get any rest or more importantly, dessert… how would you like to spend a few days in the mountains with us? Many years ago," he explained, taking a sip of his wine, "we bought a little shack near Mt. Pinos. There's nothing to do there except read, look at the clouds, and take an occasional walk. It's only a couple of hours away but quite removed from the city lights."

"John, it is not a shack!" protested Julie. "Carlos, it's really very nice. But John is right about one thing, it's a place to look at the clouds or just to do nothing. It's very restful. We'd love to have you to join us."

"It sounds really great, but I'm pretty well committed to the clinic on Saturdays. Somehow, the evenings seem to be filled up with reading and paper work, too."

"Daddy, I told you these Mexican men are just full of excuses!" She turned to Carlos, "Here's how it'll work: Mom and Dad are going up next weekend, on Saturday morning. You will pick me up here after you finish at the clinic, and then we'll join them in the afternoon. We'll spend Sunday there. You can be back at your medical center Monday morning, if you can't get the day off."

"Ann, give the boy a chance to eat," chuckled her father. "At least let him think about it." Her mother laughed, too, and got up to get dessert.

"Oh, Dad! He may be 'Dr. Reynoso' now, but when I found him a couple of months ago, he was a lemon picker. In fact, I'd rather have Carlos the lemon picker join us for the weekend instead of the doctor. That guy was more fun."

"In that case, I'll be glad to come. I'll be sure to bring some lemons." Carlos joined in the laughter.

"Ann. you're just like your mother," chided her father.

"John Ferranti," retorted Julie, "you know darned well that if we waited for you men to make up your minds, nothing would ever get done. So it's easier for us to make up your minds for you!" Mrs. Ferranti set a plate of chocolate cookies on the table.

"Carlos, mark my words. One of these days you'll wonder why God put this girl on the same bus with you in the middle of the night," said John.

"He does do some strange things, doesn't He?" Carlos grinned.

"God does not do strange things! It's you men who do strange things," said Julie.

"John, come on; let's take our walk. We'll let these two clear the table." They rose and headed out.

Carlos watched Ann clear the table. He'd never met a girl so forward and strong-minded. Even though she was brash, he felt very comfortable with her and her family. Licha in Tonalá was a good person; someone he'd known since childhood, but she would never have dared talk to him the way Ann did.

He thought of Connie who carried a gun, who was apparently qualified and quite capable of using it. Luz, his new colleague was attractive and had a boyfriend, but was considering entering a convent. It was enough to confuse a man. He'd never encountered women like this when he was picking lemons.

He picked up his plate and took it over to the kitchen sink. "When do you start teaching?" he asked.

"We actually start in two weeks, with a three-day orientation program. The kids don't come until the first week in September. That'll be the fun part. But I've already been working in my classroom, fixing up the bulletin boards, making lesson plans, duplicating materials… There's just tons of stuff to do!" she said as she rinsed the plates and put them into the dishwasher.

"You sound excited," said Carlos.

"I am. This really is the first job that I got on my own. Working in Dad's office somehow didn't feel like a job."

"Well you should be very proud of yourself. Teaching is a great career for women," he said.

"What do you mean, 'career for women!' There are several men teaching at our school!" Again there was an edge to her voice.

"That's not what I meant…" Carlos knew he was in for trouble and was not exactly sure how to get out of it. "You know what I mean… I mean some jobs women just do better."

"Listen here, Dr. Reynoso. Perhaps you should stop before your Mexican 'macho man' attitude gets you in trouble."

"I would appreciate it very much if you permit me to change the subject. Why don't we talk about picking lemons? At least I know something about that," said Carlos smiling sweetly.

"I don't want to talk about lemons either," she pouted. "I want to talk about us!"

"Are you sure you wouldn't you rather talk about lemons?" This conversation had included a lot of dangerous territory. He hoped her parents would return soon.

Chapter 31
Suits

ONNIE GOT TO HER OFFICE EARLY, filled her coffee cup, and picked up the phone. She called her old friend Nina, an RN who might be able to provide the information she needed. Without referring specifically to the case, Connie asked her about organ transplants, occasionally making notes on more three-by-fives. She thanked Nina and hung up.

Next, she reviewed the report she had written on her visit to the *Clínica Central.* She paid close attention to what Salvador had said, she wished she had recorded it but her notes were very complete; quite adequate at least for the next step.

She had called her supervisor, Ron Teal from home. She briefly told him about the boy selling his kidney. The older detective listened quietly making only an occasional comment. He told her to make several copies of the report and prepare for a meeting at 10:00 the next morning. She reserved the conference room, arranged for coffee, and waited for her partner and whoever else was attending.

Teal was prompt; he had two people with him. One was an older, heavyset man with his tie askew, the knot of the tie hidden beneath one of several chins. The other was a woman not much older than Connie. She wore a cream-colored blouse under a navy Kipling Brothers suit. Its tailoring said *attorney.*

"Connie, this is Agent Susan Moore and Dr. Tom Miller. They're both with the FBI. This is Detective Constancia Alonzo, my partner." Connie noted with pleasure just a hint of pride in his voice. The older detective poured himself a cup of coffee. He offered the two federal agents coffee, which they refused. "Connie will give us a quick summary of what she's found to date." He nodded to her indicating it was her turn to speak.

"Perhaps the best place to start is for you to read this report of a conversation between a young man and his doctor. I witnessed it this weekend at a medical clinic in downtown L.A. I have also included a field report summarizing an ongoing murder investigation we are pursuing." Connie passed them each a copy of the several-page report she had prepared. While they read, she refilled her cup of coffee. She noticed the female agent read quickly, making notes on the report. At one point, Moore opened her briefcase and removed a file to check her own notes, but she did not share them.

Dr. Miller methodically read the reports. Connie noticed that he dog-eared a couple of pages. He then leaned back and tried somewhat unsuccessfully to intertwine his fat fingers over his belly while he waited.

Agent Moore spoke first. "Tell us more about this Dr. Reynoso. How does he fit into the picture?" She looked at the senior agent as if asking for approval.

Connie rattled off the facts. "Dr. Carlos Reynoso, mid-twenties, graduate of the University Of Guadalajara Medical School, home town Tonalá, Jalisco, a small town near Guadalajara. Parents are teachers there. He attended a local grammar school. He has an aunt and uncle in Santa Paula where he has stayed on and off over the last dozen years or so. For the last eight or nine years, he has come up here stayed with them while doing summer work. He's picked lemons with a local labor contractor; using the money he's earned to finance his education."

Connie turned a page in her file and continued. "A few weeks ago, he signed a contract with the Angelus Medical Center in Van Nuys. He will do his residency there under a new state law that permits foreign-educated doctors to do their residency here. In return, he helps in heavily Hispanic communities, in particular with the indigent population. The state law just passed, but does not go into effect until the first of the year. The Angelus Medical Center, through Dr. Alex Pilabos, offered him the contract in anticipation of the new law." She went on. "He was the man who found the body of Juan Melgoza under a lemon tree where he was about to pick. Reynoso was also the one who treated the young man referred to as Salvador, in the Angelus outpatient clinic in downtown L.A. He treated Salvador for a serious infection caused by the removal of one of his kidneys. Dr. Reynoso allowed me be in the exam room during the boy's follow-up visit to the clinic, which was where I heard their conversation. The report includes this conversation almost verbatim."

The older FBI agent unlaced his fingers and said, "What are the chances that… or perhaps a better question is… What is the connection between this doctor's finding the body and his treating the kidney patient in the clinic?"

Connie considered the question. "Actually I've asked myself the same question. I think it's just coincidental. Just like it's coincidental that the one lemon picker who happened to be a doctor found the body."

Agent Moore asked, "Do you know the connection between Reynoso and Angelus Medical Center? What about this Dr. Pilabos mentioned in your report? In other words, how is it that Reynoso and Pilabos got together; was that also a coincidence?" she asked.

On one of her three-by-five cards, Connie jotted, *Carlos – Pilabos, how met? Connection??* She drew a bold black line around the words. "I don't know; but I'll certainly look into it. I'll find out." There was a pause in the room; the silence was noticeable as they pondered the questions.

The quiet was broken by Connie. "I'm curious about FBI's involvement in this issue. What is your interest? Better yet, are you interested in the murder investigation or in the trafficking of human organs? I'm even more curious about what information you might have that might be helpful to our investigation. It seems to me that information should flow in both directions."

Teal was startled to hear such a direct question from his junior partner. He was about to interrupt when the FBI doctor stirred and waved away Teal's expression of embarrassed concern. "Those are fair questions Con…ats…cia." Pronouncing her name was an awkward effort for him. "Can I call you…?"

She quickly finished his query, "Connie; everyone calls me Connie."

"Thanks, Connie. As I said, those are fair questions. First, we're not particularly interested in your murder investigation, except as to how it might relate to the organ issue. That's what brought us here to see you. My colleague here has some general information on the subject, as well as some specific information on individuals we've been watching." Directing his comments at his partner he said, "Sue, give those reports to them to read later." Moore complied silently.

The ample fellow now appeared to be in his element. His voice and gestures were light, continuous and matter-of-fact. He continued, "As transplantation technology has improved over the last several years, we now have the ability to transplant various different organs. You read about these procedures in the newspaper every week or so. The problem is, the supply of available organs and skilled physicians trained to do these procedures has remained quite limited. Therefore, the law of supply and demand has had an impact. Even though criteria have been established through reputable registries to allocate the available organs in an equitable manner, there are some people unwilling to wait their turn. These are the ones who have the money to short-circuit the process."

Connie's pile of filled three-by-fives was building rapidly. She would have to organize them into groups later.

Miller continued, "There is a considerable foreign connection to this. Sue, here is actually connected with our Foreign Service operation. She's been tracking this trade from the supplying countries. For example, some time ago we became aware that at certain times of the year, there's actually a surplus of organs in the system. We finally realized that the Chinese government always executes its prisoners after their New Year. So during that period, their hospitals are full of foreigners who go to China and return with new organs several months later." He interlaced his fingers again and continued. "Of course we've made inquires through our diplomatic channels, asking the Chinese government about this issue; but of course, they said it doesn't happen.

"It seems that most of the Chinese clientele are Asians, but the greatest market is among westerners, where we have a severe supply problem. It is well-documented that in very poor countries such as India, where the poverty rate is so horrendous, selling a kidney or a cornea is not unusual. You can live with one kidney or die with both of them…so you can see for donors it's not a difficult question.

"We have a similar disparity in the Americas. Although poverty may not be as severe in the Americas as in India, for example, the wealth differential between rich Americans or Canadians, and poor Hondurans or Mexicans is just as significant. We know that on this issue, the economic relationship between supply and demand works flawlessly. Organs can be sold for great profit. The fact that this is illegal and immoral only seems to make the profits greater." Dr. Miller paused. "In this country there are some folks so rich and so powerful that they don't have to go to the source. They can have an organ delivered and the surgery done in an American hospital, as long as it's fairly near the border...almost like ordering a pizza."

Looking up from the notes he was taking, Teal asked, "But in a case such as the one with the kidney donor who Connie saw; how does the kidney get from Tijuana to its customer? Where was the customer likely to have had his surgery?"

"That's one of the questions we can't answer yet. That's why we rushed over when we heard about your case," said Miller. Dr. Miller noticed that Connie had been taking notes on the three-by-fives. He noticed that she had just organized the cards in four neat piles in front of her. "Connie, I see you're a card player. Can you tell me what your suits are?"

Connie's face reddened slightly. She felt she had to explain. "The department's great about providing everything we need to do our job, except they have an aversion to providing good note books. For some reason, three-by-five cards are in great abundance, so I use them. I find them very handy."

She pointed to each stack as she answered his actual question. "This pile has to do with transplants; this one with the murder case; this one's for Dr. Reynoso and Angelus Medical Center; and these are the wild cards. The ones I write on the lined side tell me there's a connection to a card or idea in one of the other piles. The ones where I write on the blank side tell me that this is a question, idea, or consideration that might have a link somewhere, but I haven't found one yet. When I start writing a report, or if I'm giving one orally, I first arrange the cards in some kind of logical order. Then I start reporting."

"So, where do we go from here?" asked Teal.

"Well, I like Connie's system. It's telling us, I think, that the common denominators are Dr. Reynoso, the sick kid and the Angelus Medical

Center, or its clinic downtown," said Dr. Miller. "Do you think we could get Reynoso to cooperate with us? For example, would he be willing to take us with him to visit the boy in Fresno to supplement Connie's excellent notes? We'd like to show this fellow, Salvador some photos we have."

The FBI attorney asked, "Connie, I also saw in your report that Mrs. Melgoza has been threatened by someone who wants their money back."

"That's right, Agent Moore. The mom is a very simple lady. She has no idea about what's going on or how much money is involved. All she knows is that her son is dead and some punk threatened her."

"Do you think she would agree to let us to tap her phone calls for a while?" asked Moore.

"Probably so; I've developed a relationship of trust with her. I'll approach her about that and get back to you." Connie turned to Miller and said, "You said you would like to show some photos to Salvador. Can we have copies to see who we're dealing with?"

"Of course, you can; we brought these for you." He passed a set of photos to both Alonzo and Teal. "The man is a doctor in Tijuana; the woman is his wife who also happens to be a nurse. We suspect he is the man who makes the contacts and removes the organs. We just received this information and we'd like to check it out."

"How did you get this information?" asked Teal.

"Well, much of it comes from an order of Catholic priests, brothers and nuns who work with refugees near the border. They've run into people who have sold their organs. They contacted us indirectly through some contacts we have within the church," explained Miller.

Teal looked puzzled. "Let me ask again; how do these organs get across? Do you have any idea?"

The FBI man answered, "As I said we have no proof…yet. You all surely know that all sorts of things: drugs, food, exotic birds and other animals, get smuggled across the border every day. But with organs there's a time element. That is, they have to move quickly or the organ will not be viable. Organs have a short shelf life."

"So what's your best theory about how they're getting across?" Connie prodded. She wasn't sure they were showing their full hand.

"Because of the time element, we believe they're just walking the organs across."

The room fell silent, with the exception of writing on the three-by-five cards. Connie looked at her cards thoughtfully. She rubbed the edge of the card on her cheek. At last, she put it in the first pile. When she looked up, she saw that the other three people in the room were watching her carefully.

Dr. Miller smiled approvingly at Connie. "As you can see Connie, the three of us are curious which suit you played the last card on."

Somewhat embarrassed at the attention she said, "I put it on the Dr. Reynoso pile with reference to transplants."

"Ah, the good Dr. Reynoso again," said the FBI man. "Why did you pick him?"

"Reynoso told me that he has crossed the border several times at night."

Looking at Teal, Miller said, "It seems that we need to get closer to Reynoso. Do you have any suggestions? It seems to me that since you also have a murder investigation going on, perhaps your department should take the lead on this, just so we don't step on each other's toes."

"From our viewpoint it'll be easy. Since Connie has established a rapport with Reynoso, she should continue her murder investigation, but keep her eyes open for any hint of this organ business," suggested Teal.

"I agree with you," said Miller. "We can keep an eye on Mrs. Melgoza to see if she receives any more contacts regarding the money. We might take a closer look at Dr. Pilabos and the Angelus Medical Center, too." Turning to his partner, he said, "Sue, you've been quiet all this time. Do you have any thoughts?"

"I agree with what you said. I must compliment the Sheriff's Office for its excellent work so far, but I wonder if we might take this whole thing one step further."

"What do you have in mind?" asked Miller.

"I wonder what would happen if we put out the word that there is a very wealthy man who needs, say a kidney. That's he's willing to pay top dollar for the service, no questions asked."

"Where would you put out the word?" asked Connie.

"It seems to me that the source would be a good start. We need to put the bait close to the supply end of the business near this doctor and his wife on the border," said Agent Moore.

"Sounds good to me. Since you have the foreign connections, can you set it up?" said Miller.

"Good, I'll cook something up and let you know."

"One more thing," mentioned Teal. "A couple of weeks ago we met with two immigration investigators. The local officer is Johnnie Reyes and the guy from Washington was Hector Galindo. They were also looking into this business, but more from the drug and the illegal immigration angle. You might want to coordinate with them too."

"Excellent, excellent! Thanks for the tip. We'll touch base with our federal brothers," said Dr. Miller. "I'm glad we came to see you. This has been most productive." He turned to Connie, "Young lady, remind me never to get into a poker game with you!" Everyone laughed. They all shook hands and the two FBI agents left.

The two detectives were left alone in the conference room. Connie picked up her cards and put them in her bag. The senior detective looked at her seriously, "Connie, I'm not sure what we're up against. I know plenty about murders, but I have no idea about this transplant business, so you'll have to take the lead on this. And I also want your assurance that if there's any complication with you and Carlos, you'll let me know. This places you into a difficult situation."

"Thanks, Ron. I appreciate your understanding. I'll keep you informed."

He paused then continued. "Also I think it's important to find out how Carlos and Dr. Pilabos of Angelus Medical Center got together. I mean, was their meeting just a coincidence, or is there some connection?"

"I don't know how I'd approach that," mused Connie.

"Okay, let me take a look into that part," said Teal.

Chapter 32
Mt. Pinos

FROM THE SAN FERNANDO VALLEY, HIGHWAY 5 quickly empties into Valencia, provided that there's normal traffic. This Saturday evening was no exception. Carlos and Ann drove out of the city and stopped at an In-N-Out® in Valencia. They got their food to go and ate on the way. Carlos was driving his uncle's pickup and had the windows open. The evening was still warm, but not unpleasant. They could feel the air cooling as they traveled up into the mountains that led toward Bakersfield. The radio station they had been listening to started to fade as they wound up the hill on the crossing lanes which gave this part of the highway its nickname, the Grapevine.

The opposing traffic was predominantly trucks. Many of them had open beds, full of watermelons and other produce from the rich San Joaquin Valley. The old pickup struggled with the ever-increasing grade. Carlos moved over to the right lane and eased along with the slower trucks that were also struggling up the ever-steepening grade. As they moved higher and deeper into the mountains, the shadows extending between glimpses of the sinking sun cooled the air even more.

Just past the little town of Gorman, the road began to descend. They turned left on Highway 33 to enjoy the drive through Frazier Park and to the Mt. Pinos area. The road heading west was almost deserted, but Carlos continued with no rush, enjoying the warm air, the absence of phones, and the frantic pace of the clinic. At Frazier Park they took the right fork toward Mt. Pinos, and soon the road flattened out, leading from meadow to meadow.

"Turn here," said Ann. The sign on the gate read, *Mt. Pinos View Estates.* At the entrance was a small lake. The road skirted the lake toward a small complex of houses. "Just keep following the road; our house is way in the back where it ends."

The road actually did end at the Ferranti's vacation home. It had no formal landscaping, fence, or mailbox and sat among what appeared to be the natural flora...tall grasses and lupine. A wide swath had been mown around the house. The clippings hadn't been removed and were drying where they were cut. This seemed to be the only encroachment on nature. The house sat on the edge of a meadow, and from there the land rose, reaching westward toward a heavily-forested ridge. The ridge was zipped up the middle by the towers and cables of a ski lift, its chairs barely visible in the distance.

"This is it!" said Ann. "This is where my parents come to hide from the city. Mom wants to live up here all the time. Dad is no fan of cold and snow; so it's just their summer place."

They got out of the truck and Carlos removed his backpack and an opaque plastic bag. He raised the bag up to show Ann, "Lemons!" he said, laughing.

"Good! I'd rather spend the weekend with a fun lemon picker not with some dull old doctor."

The house was empty but the kitchen light was on as was the oven. The small kitchen was filled with the aroma of Italian food. A note on a magnetic clip hanging on the hood over the stove read:

Went for a walk, food cooking, beer's cold. J 'n J.

The back of the house had only the natural landscape. It was dotted with a round wooden table and four mismatched chairs. Ann brought out two bottles of beer and turned two chairs so they could enjoy the view. The sun had dropped behind the mountain, which was as yet unable to diminish the bright rays that leaked around it.

"Like my folks said, there's nothing to do here but watch the sun rise and set," said Ann as she handed Carlos a beer and sat next to him.

Carlos leaned back and stretched. "This is nice Ann. I could be tempted to live this kind of life," he whispered as he settled low into the chair, his face transfixed on the mountain backlit by the orange sun.

"It's nice to know that you can be tempted so easily. That will make my job easier. One thing nice about lemon pickers is that they are so transparent and so easily impressed," she said with a smile.

"How many lemon pickers do you know to allow you to make that observation?"

"I only know one but once you know one, you know them all." He reached over and put his hand on hers as they watched the sky redden behind the mountain.

After a long silence, Ann spoke softly, "Carlos I hope you don't mind that I almost forced you to bring me up here, but I truly just want to spend some time with you. Just to sit and talk or just to sit and not talk. I'm afraid that soon we'll both be so busy that we won't have much time to spend together."

Carlos said nothing he continued to look west, fascinated with the fading sun, but still feeling the lingering warmth of its rays. He was also very conscious of the warmth of the young woman at his side. He gave her hand a gentle squeeze. He closed his eyes. He dozed off, only to be almost immediately brought back to reality by the barking of the Ferranti dog that jumped into Ann's lap. Following the dog was Mike, her little brother.

Where are Mom and Dad?" asked Ann.

"They're being pokey," said Mike, as he rushed into the house. The dog leapt off Ann's lap and scrambled after the boy, hoping he'd get his dinner.

Carlos, now fully conscious, took Ann's hand. "Hey, thanks for this great idea and for including me. I didn't realize how much a person could be tied up at work." He paused then continued. "I really enjoyed the ride up here, eating in the truck, and then sitting here, having a beer. But most of all, I enjoy being here with you."

His voice dropped as he finished speaking, and she leaned over to hear him better. While close, she kissed him gently. "Doctor, I am your prescription, the sooner you take your medicine, the sooner you'll feel better."

"You're a quack! Good medicine is supposed to lower your temperature and calm you down!" He laughed heartily.

"Wrong! Good medicine should make your heart race and jump with joy. Joy is what life is all about," she replied with a fake pout.

"In that case, I plan to be a very demanding patient."

"Ah, our wandering children are home!" said John Ferranti, as he and his wife appeared out of the dusk. "How was your trip up?"

Carlos jumped up shook John's hand, and Ann's mother kissed him on the cheek. "The drive was fine… no traffic, no troubles. This is a beautiful place! Thanks for inviting me to come up."

"We're glad to have you here, though we had nothing to do with the invitation," said John. Sit down and let's have another beer. John went into the house and came out with two bottles.

Julie and Ann went inside to finish up with the dinner preparations. When John returned, he sat down next to Carlos. "Well son, how's it going?"

"It's been great; I'm doing what I always wanted to do. Although I'm not officially practicing medicine at the moment, it's as close as it can be. I'm learning a lot." He was thoughtful for a moment, "I'm also earning more money than I ever dreamed about. So everything," he repeated, "everything is working out just fine."

"You must be glad to be out of the orchards," said John.

"I am…I really am. I don't miss the actual work; it's so hard and dirty. It's hard work and it's so simple and honest. But I do miss my friends and family." Carlos drank from his bottle. "I suppose that doesn't make sense does it?"

"Funny, but I think I do understand. One of the best jobs I ever had was washing dishes in a restaurant. It was my first job in this country. Like you, I especially remember the cooks, bartenders, and waitresses. We had some good times," he said wistfully.

"Are you getting along okay with the people at the medical center?" asked Ferranti. "They seem like a good bunch, though I mostly deal with the management."

"Yes, everyone's been great. They're all very nice. The doctors go out of their way to share their most interesting cases with me. I'm also often asked to translate and that gets me involved right away."

"And how are things financially?" asked Ferranti.

"I don't understand, what do you mean?"

"Carlos, I'm going to give you a little bit of advice just this one time. I promise I will not interfere in your life anymore. I want you to know that you need to invest as much money you can spare. Don't just put it in the bank or buy a fancy car; put your money to work for you."

"I haven't really thought much about it yet, but it looks like I will only have few expenses since Angelus is providing my living expenses. I need to return the pickup to my uncle, so I'll be getting a car, but other than that, I don't know anything about investing."

"Then let me offer another suggestion. Even though we're insurance brokers, I have a lady in my office who's a real whiz with money. I'll tell her about you, and then you can deal through her, if you feel comfortable. She takes care of most of my investments. By the way, she recently bought a new car and said the guy who sold it to her gave her a great deal. Maybe she can connect you up with him, once you decide what you want."

"Thanks, I would like to talk to her when you think it's convenient."

"Good I'll arrange a meeting."

They sat quietly and listened to the crickets tuning up for their nightly concert. The stars were beginning to shine and the nip of the cool mountain air finally overpowered the warmth of the day. Reluctantly, they went inside.

Although Carlos had been away from home many times and traveled long distances by himself, he had never been away with people who were not his relatives or his close friends. In his mind the Ferranti's were still neither close friends nor were they relatives, yet he felt very comfortable with them. In a real sense, this was his first time away from home.

After dinner, Ann and Carlos went for a walk. Mr. Ferranti said, "Take a flashlight. There's one by the door." With jackets, the night was cool but very comfortable. Yet, the house and the soil were still radiating the sun's warmth. Being close to each other also offset the cool air.

"Did Dad give you the 'Save Your Money' lecture?" she asked.

"Yes he did. Your dad is amazing! He knows about everything: cars, investments… and even restaurants. I do think I will let him help me buy a car because I don't know anything about car-buying and I need to return my uncle's truck sometime soon."

"My dad's the right guy. And you're right, he does know about lots of things," said Ann proudly.

They walked to the edge of the tree line that circled the meadow. They chose one with a big trunk and plenty of needles under it. They sat down close to each other, looking back at the small grouping of houses without talking.

Chapter 33
Investigation

"Dr. Pilabos, I'm Detective Sergeant Ron Teal from the Ventura County Sheriff's Department. I was wondering if I could speak with you somewhere other than your office." Teal was calling from his vehicle's radio phone. "I'd rather it not be at your office... if that's convenient for you," he said. After a pause he replied, "That's a good meeting place. I should be there in ten minutes or so."

Teal turned off Highway 5 onto the Hollywood Freeway. He finally reached the Sherman Way off ramp. The fast food place was on the corner of Sherman and Bellaire. He walked up to the counter and ordered a soda. He looked around and spotted a small man with graying hair sitting in the corner, drinking coffee and reading a newspaper. At the moment, he was the only man there wearing a suit. Their eyes met; Teal walked over. "Dr. Pilabos?" At the nod, he extended his hand. "I'm Ron Teal. Thanks for taking the time to meet with me."

"Glad to meet you Ron. I must admit, I'm quite curious as to why I'm meeting with somebody from the Ventura County Sheriff's Department."

"I guess it *is* strange, but I'll explain. I'll try not to take too much of your time." He sat down across from the doctor. "Actually we're curious what your connection is with Carlos Reynoso, how you came to know him, who introduced him to you, and how he fits in with your clinic."

"You're talking about Carlos Reynoso, the young Mexican resident doctor who just started to work for us?"

"Yeah, the same fellow."

"That was a curious and lucky story for us. Our business manager,

Don Goodwin met him at a beach party at a house rented by John Ferranti, the man who handles the Angelus Medical Center's insurance concerns. As I recall, his daughter Ann was in Mexico a couple of months ago. She was spending a few days on the beach in Puerto Vallarta after her graduation. As I understand it, she was on her way home and caught a bus in the middle of the night. Her seatmate was Carlos. They got to talking and became friends Then later on, she invited him to the beach party where Don met him." Pilabos took a sip of his coffee. "Apparently this young man had been going up to Santa Paula for years to pick lemons to finance his medical studies in Guadalajara. I understand he has some relatives he stayed with in that area."

"And at what point did you meet him?"

"Anyway, Don Goodwin invited him to visit our facility. That's when I met him. We were both very impressed with this young man. He was just the sort of fellow we were hoping to find. You see, a new law was just been passed in Sacramento, permitting foreign-educated doctors to do their residency in the State, as long as they practice in heavily Hispanic area and do some public service. In anticipation of that law going into effect on the first of the year, we hired him. At present, he's working in our medical center, assisting the doctors. He also works Saturdays in our clinic downtown, helping with the people who live there." Dr. Pilabos looked the detective in the eye. "There's not a problem with Carlos, is there?

"We hope not, but we were very curious about how he met you. We didn't know the story about how Carlos met the girl on the bus by coincidence."

Again Pilabos eyed the detective. "I'm sorry Detective Teal, but I don't think you came so far out of your area to meet me here to just find out how Carlos met Ann Ferranti. If you have anything I should know about Carlos, please tell me about it."

"A few weeks ago we found a dead man under a lemon tree. Actually, it was Carlos who found him. In the subsequent investigation, we discovered the man had only one kidney. One of his had been removed. As the investigation developed, Carlos told my colleague about another young man he had just treated for a serious kidney infection. He permitted Detective Alonzo to work undercover at the clinic on the day he hoped the boy would come for a follow-up visit. She was in the room when the boy told Reynoso that he'd sold his kidney to someone in Tijuana. I understand the kid damned near died from the infection he developed after his surgery." Teal related the story with little emotion.

"I'm familiar with that case. I was so concerned about it that I made sure that both Carlos and Luz, our clinic nurse, documented their work in great detail, because the whole thing just didn't sound right. I just read their reports a few days ago," said Pilabos.

"Well it was actually Carlos who mentioned to Detective Alonzo that there could be a kidney connection with our murder victim. He told her about his interesting case of the boy with the infection, and that he suspected might be from a kidney removal. So she invited herself to the *Clinica Central* last Saturday. Damned if the kid didn't show up, mostly to thank Doctor Reynoso, as Alonzo reported it," said Teal.

"So what's the Ventura County Sheriff's Office interest in all this? Is it the murder, the kidney connection, or Reynoso himself?"

"Frankly, our interest is primarily with the murder, but the organ deal is something the Feds are definitely interested in. We're working together, cooperating and sharing information." Teal looked earnestly at Dr. Pilabos and asked, "Do you happen to know anything about transplants, especially unofficial ones?"

"Neither our clinic nor our main medical center is involved in transplants, but in general I know there's a big demand and a low supply. We also know that some people don't want to wait their turn. I've heard stories about people going abroad to get transplants. Frankly I've also heard of some people around here with so much money that do not want to stand in line. I understand they will pay almost anything to short circuit the system."

"Is this general or specific knowledge?"

"General. As I said, we don't deal in that kind of medicine. When we get someone who needs a transplant, we refer them to UCLA."

"Dr. Pilabos, thank you for your time." He rose to leave. "Here's my card. If you hear anything more about this sort of transplant, please let me know." The detective handed a business card to Pilabos, who was still seated.

As he took the card, Pilabos asked, "Before you leave Detective Teal, tell me where does this leave us with Carlos? Does this change anything in the medical center's relationship with him? I mean, do we have some sort of a problem on our hands?"

"Actually sir, I'd say you potentially have a very fine doctor on your hands. From what I hear he's a very nice young man who just happened to be a doctor who, while picking lemons, found a dead man, and who later treated a young man for the results of a botched operation and was bright enough to put these things together." Teal continued, "I've personally only met him in passing, but my partner has talked to him extensively. She tells me he's very nice young man who just happens to have been in interesting places."

"Do you recommend I tell him about this meeting?"

"Certainly! Please tell him everything. Tell him we talked. Be very frank with him and urge him to continue documenting anything he sees that might be related to this. Ask him to keep you informed if he has anymore contacts with any people who might be involved in this whole thing. And us too," added Teal.

Pilabos stood and shook the detective's hand, "Thanks for coming and for reinforcing our opinion of Carlos. We were so impressed with him that we hired him as an assistant even before the new law would go into effect. We didn't want to lose him to someone else. And frankly, the only thing that's bothered me is that we're possibly stealing a fine mind from Mexico, the country that has nurtured and educated this young man. Now we will be the beneficiaries of Mexico's investment. The only thing that eases my mind is that he will be treating a good number of his countrymen who are already here." Pilabos continued, "Yet, I fear for our neighbors. They're losing some of the most skilled and motivated people just because they see an opportunity in this country which is apparently not available to them in their own country. They've lost many of their lemon pickers and now even their doctors. In Carlos, they may lose both."

"I understand what you're saying. You should meet my partner; she the brightest cop I've run across in a long time. She comes from the same people."

"I'd like to meet her one of these days, thanks for the visit." Teal walked out to his county vehicle.

Pilabos downed the last of his coffee and neatly folded the remains of his newspaper. He set it with some others on a counter, leaving it for others to read. As he started his own car, the pensive doctor thought to himself, "Dear Lord! Now they're selling their body parts to us and we're buying them. May God help us!"

Pilabos called Luz and Carlos to his office. He looked at them both with pleasure. They were bright, handsome and good-hearted; his soul found solace in them. He reflected on his own journey and how his parents had left Armenia for a better opportunity. The aspirations of these two young people sitting in front of him were no different from his. "The genius of this country," he thought to himself, "is opportunity."

"Carlos, Luz," he said, nodding to each. "I read your reports on the young kidney patient and I must say, I was very impressed with the detail, especially with the care you apparently spent on writing them." He looked at Carlos, "Of course you're not as familiar with the English language as Luz, but the report is clear and medically well done. Thank you both for your efforts in the matter. Carlos, it would be all right if you want to let Luz or one of the secretaries review your reports before you submit them, just to make sure that your writing is clear," suggested Pilabos.

Carlos smiled uncomfortably. "I know I struggle with the language and I plan to take an English class as soon as I can enroll in one. In the meantime, I'll get help from the staff."

"Great, but mainly I want you to know I appreciate your effort." Pilabos' voice became more serious. "The reason I called both of you in is that I just had a visit with Detective Sergeant Ron Teal from the Ventura County Sheriff's Office." He nodded to Carlos. "He's investigating the murder of the young man you found while you were picking lemons." Carlos returned the nod. "Apparently the man who was killed also happened to be missing a kidney, like the boy you both treated at the clinic." He stirred uncomfortably in his chair, "As I heard from Teal, they're interested in the murder investigation but also the federal government is looking into this kidney transplant business: the selling and buying of organs. It's an awful business. From what he told me, there are some folks on the border who look for poor people, then talk them into selling one of their kidneys. Somehow, they transport it across the border and sell it to some rich person here in the U.S."

"Only kidneys?" asked Carlos.

"Teal only mentioned kidneys, but I suppose there might be other parts as well."

"How can we help?" asked Luz.

"Just continue doing what you're doing but be extra alert, especially at the downtown clinic. Report anything suspicious to me and to the Ventura County Sheriff's Office. Carlos, you apparently have a connection there. We need to be as helpful to the authorities as we can." Pilabos smiled at the two young people in front of him. "You two could well be the key to stopping some of this horrible business."

"Dr. Pilabos, remember that I'll be spending several weeks with the Sisters of Social Service. Carlos will need some help at the clinic," said Luz.

"Thanks for reminding me, I'd forgotten. Can you suggest someone to stand in for you?"

"A couple of the girls are interested in some additional hours. I'll talk to some of them, if you want," offered Luz.

"Please do that, then talk to Carlos. If the three of you agree on it, let me know. Oh, by the way, how will your time with the Sisters affect your work at the clinic?" he asked.

"It really shouldn't, except for these first few weeks I'll spend with them in discernment. These sisters all work on the outside. Most of them live together, but they do their service in the community by working in whatever field they're trained for." She smiled at the older doctor with a hopeful look on her young face. "I was hoping to continue working here on a professional level, at least for the time being."

"That would please me more than anything, young lady." Dr. Pilabos rose. "Thank you both for all your efforts," said Pilabos.

"Good heavens, Doctor Reynoso! You do lead an interesting life!" exclaimed Luz as they left Pilabos' office. "Tell me about the murder; what's that all about?"

"It was just my luck to find this guy with a hole in head. At first, Detective Sergeant Teal thought he'd committed suicide, but I told his partner that it was improbable that he could have shot himself. Then they did an autopsy and found out that he was probably shot by some-one else. It was then they also found out he had only one kidney. Then later on, you and I ran into Salvador."

"So you knew Connie from that incident?"

"Yeah, that's how I met her. I just happen to mention Salvador's case, next thing I know she invited herself to the clinic."

"My, my, Doctor Reynoso! You definitely *do* lead an interesting life," she chuckled, shaking her head as they walked down the hall.

"By the way, do you know where I can take an English class?"

"I have a couple of catalogs at home. I'll bring them in tomorrow, if I can remember. Actually," Luz continued, "how could I not remember, after all that I've learned about you today!"

Chapter 34
The Checkup

CARLOS PICKED UP THE PHONE. It was Connie. "Carlos," she asked, "when was the last time you were in Fresno?"

"I've never been to Fresno."

"Well you're in for a treat! How would you like to go up there with me?"

"What's in Fresno?" Carlos was cautious.

"Two things," she said. "One: I'll be there. Two: We want to talk to Salvador officially. My office has already contacted his uncle and they've agreed to talk to us."

"Who do you mean by 'us'?"

"You and me, silly! I told them you wanted to see how he was healing and I wanted to talk to him about the surgery he had near the border. I'd like show him some photos we have, and see if he recognizes anything," said Connie.

"When do you want to go?"

"This evening. I told the uncle we'd see them very early tomorrow morning before they go to work. We can drive up this evening, stay the night, and be back by tomorrow afternoon," she said.

"Okay; sounds interesting." She had him interested the moment she mentioned Sal. He'd been worrying about the young fellow and welcomed the opportunity to check up on him.

"Good! Give me your address and I'll pick you up in a couple of hours. We'll beat the traffic out of town," said Connie. He dictated his address, then scurried to get himself ready for the trip.

They took Highway 5, up over the Grapevine, a freeway named for its lanes which cross over each other as it winds its way through the mountain passes. Beyond the fact that Carlos was not driving, it was different. The plain police car had air conditioning and there was an almost constant squawking on the radio. Carlos made an effort to pay attention but he finally gave up.

As they descended steeply to the valley floor, Carlos could feel the growing heat through the window glass. The extensive farming in the valley drew Carlos's attention. He saw several crews of men and women working in the late, hot sun. He marveled at the anonymous figures in the field bobbing up and down. Strangely, even now he saw them as faceless workers. The bobbing figures were quickly left behind in the wake of the police car. Small towns nearly hidden by giant billboards dotted their route. Eventually, they neared their destination.

After they checked into the motel located alongside Highway 99, they drove across to the east side of town.

"Have you ever eaten Basque food?" asked Connie.

"No, but it's always fun to try something new," said Carlos.

The Basque restaurant was a converted house. They sat at a small table in what would have been the living room. They ordered a bottle of wine. Right away, the waitress started to bring them food, served family style, without taking an order. The food came in waves, dish after dish, all of it different yet familiar to Carlos. Connie laughed and warned him that the waitress would be bringing more than anyone could eat of each item. He enjoyed it all. Then they ate slowly, drinking the wine and talking about the food. They didn't mention the reason for the trip.

"I like the food very much. It's almost like eating at home," he said.

"I thought you'd like it, that's why I suggested it. I'm afraid I may be getting to know you too well," she smiled.

Salvador lived with his uncle, not in Fresno, but nearby in the small town of Ceres. Actually the family didn't live in Ceres either, but just outside of town. It was still early in the morning. Connie and Carlos knew that if they wanted to talk to Salvador, they would have to catch him before he and his uncle went to work.

They knocked on door of the small wooden house. A small lady answered. She pointed to the back where they would find Salvador. Beneath two large walnut trees were six aluminum tool sheds. The doors of the sheds were open and they could see that each had two small cots inside. There were clothes and other articles hanging from the low ceilings. They found Salvador in the second shed. He was making his bed. His roommate was about the same age. He left when he saw the two strangers appear.

"Hello Chava! How are you? It's good to see you," said Carlos.

"Good morning, Doctor! Thanks to you, I'm doing fine. I'm working every day and feel fine," the young man answered with a ready smile.

"Chava, this is Connie Alonzo. She wants to talk to you about the people you met in Tijuana, the ones who gave you the money for your kidney. You can trust her and tell her everything. In the meantime, I'd like to check you over." The boy looked carefully at Connie, but showed no indication that he recognized her.

The three had to bend down to enter the tool shed. Salvador sat on a wooden box between the two cots. He removed his shirt for Carlos to examine him. Connie sat on the other cot and removed several photographs from her bag. She showed them to him.

"Salvador, thank you for willingness to help," she said. "We appreciate it very much. I'd like you to take a look at these photos and see if you recognize any of these people."

The cramped tool shed was already getting warm, even though it was still early morning. Other than the cots there were some field boxes with suitcases on top. On one side of the shed hung a calendar decorated with an image of the Virgin Mary. On the other side there was a picture cut from a magazine showing a smiling young girl holding a soda in her hand.

Salvador studied the photographs carefully. He spread them out across his bed and looked at each of them several times. Pointing to one, he said, "I think this is the man who operated on me. I'm not real sure, but I think it's him. But this lady," he added, indicating another photo, "she is the one who told me her baby would die. She cried and prayed for me for helping her baby."

"Are you very sure about this woman?" asked Connie.

"Yes I'm sure!" he replied confidently. "In fact, she's wearing the same clothes in the picture as she did when I met her. It's even the same restaurant, although she's not sitting at the same table. Look here," He pointed. "We sat at this table where this man is sitting, right there!"

"Do you recognize any of the other people?" asked Connie.

"Yes, this one is Lalo. He was the one who led us across the border that evening," said Salvador.

"Now think carefully Salvador," said Connie, taking great care not to influence the young men with her tone of voice. Inside, she was excited to get two positive identifications. "Tell me exactly what happened from the time you first met these people until the time you went to see Dr. Reynoso in Los Angeles. The young man dutifully retold his story, in pretty much the same order he had told it at the clinic. Once he flinched a bit as Carlos put pressure on his side.

The infection was gone and the wound had healed, except for the prominent, tender red scar. "Did you take all the medicine like I told you?" inquired Carlos.

"Just like you told me, I took the last pill one week ago. Do I need to take more?" he asked.

"No, you did just fine! But I'm going to give you this ointment. After work, when you've taken a shower, rub this on the scar. Will you do that for me?" The boy nodded his agreement. Carlos handed the young boy the tube. "Remember every day until it's all gone. If you have any trouble, you have to see a doctor right away, do you understand that?"

"Yes, sir. Thank you," said Salvador.

"Now you talk to Connie, Chava. I'm going in to see your uncle." He bent down to walk out of the shed and continued to the house.

He entered without knocking. There were several men, women and children eating in the small kitchen. Some were at the table and several were standing. An older lady handed him a cup of coffee and motioned to a young man to get up so Carlos could have his place. Carlos knew there was no point in objecting. As soon as he sat down, a young girl served him a plate of steaming beans, chorizo and eggs with several corn tortillas. "Gracias," he said to the girl. He wasn't given a fork, so he ate the food with the tortilla, as everyone else was doing.

Salvador's uncle, Felipe Suarez entered and sat across the table. "How is the boy?" he asked.

"Chava's fine, but I told him to be careful. If he has any trouble with that area in the future, he's to see a doctor quickly," replied Carlos.

"Doctor, we're very grateful to you for helping the boy. He needs to work to send money to his mother; my sister," said the uncle.

"No problem; I was glad I could help," replied Carlos. He continued to eat. The food tasted like home. He'd missed it.

"Where are you from, Doctor Reynoso?" asked Felipe.

"From Tonalá," replied Carlos. "This food reminds me of home."

"Really? We're from Tepatitlán; we're neighbors! Thank you again for your help," said the uncle.

He saw Connie enter the room. He looked toward another young man sitting at the table. He'd already started to get up before being asked. Connie sat down and was quickly served. It was assumed that she wanted to eat. The gesture, and automatic inclusion in the group was heart-warming. "Mmmm, gracias!" she murmured appreciatively.

"What kind of work are you doing?" asked Carlos.

"We're picking plums right now, but next week we'll be in grapes. We also do some weeding and other chores that need to be done," said the uncle.

"Where do all these workers come from? Do they all live here?" asked Connie, joining the conversation.

The old man proudly pointed at the crowded room, "They're my sons, my daughter, some relatives and some friends from Tepa. We all work together."

"I noticed the men sleeping in the metal sheds. Don't they get hot?" Connie asked.

The old man looked at Connie, "It's better than sleeping under the trees. We bought these sheds just so the boys wouldn't have to sleep under the trees. Besides," he said, "When it's hot, they're at work. They only sleep at night after it cools off."

The uncle shot a glance at one of the older boys and the people in the kitchen began to drift off. A few stopped at the stove. Each grabbed a tortilla, and filled it with beans, eating as he left. Even the little girl followed. The aunt started to clean up as soon as they left. "We need to get an early start to take advantage of the cool morning," he said as an explanation for the exodus.

One of the younger boys returned to the kitchen and set a lug box of plums, grapes and other fruit on the table. The aunt put a small bundle wrapped in aluminum foil on top of the box.

Felipe nodded approvingly at his wife. He turned to smile at them, "Some fruit for you trip back."

Carlos could see that Connie was about to protest. Quickly he said, "Thank you very much for breakfast and for the fruit. It's beautiful fruit! I'm sure we'll both enjoy it."

Connie, seeing that it was futile to argue, added, "Thank you very much! You have all been very kind and helpful to us. We may want to come back to talk some more with Salvador. Would that be okay?"

Felipe answered, "Of course! We may be poor and in a foreign country, but that doesn't mean we want to sell our bodies. All we want is an opportunity to work, to feed our families and to give our children the opportunities we didn't have." He continued, "We know this place is not ideal, but if we work hard and save our money, we'll soon pay this place off. In fact, right now we're looking to buy the house next door where my older son will live."

Once Connie had finished her meal, the old man picked up the box of fruit and carried it out to their car. He shook their hands and blessed them as they got in.

They drove in silence until they were back on the highway heading south. Then Connie said, "We shouldn't have taken all that fruit from them. And what's in the aluminum?" she asked.

"If we hadn't taken the fruit, we'd still be there arguing, and they would have been insulted. My guess is that Mrs. Suarez packed a lunch for us," Carlos replied.

"Why would she give us lunch?" asked Connie. "Doesn't she know there are lots of places alongside the road to eat? Besides, it didn't look like they could afford to feed strangers."

Carlos laughed, "Connie how quickly you forget! They wanted to share something with us, so they gave us some fruit, beans and tortillas. I for one am touched at their generosity."

"It's not that," she protested."It's that they're so poor. I should be sharing with them." She turned on the air conditioner; it was warming up in the Central Valley.

"If you can prevent some other kid from having to sell his body parts, that will be sharing enough for them," Carlos replied.

"My, but you have lots of wisdom for such a young man, Doctor!" she said, relaxing into her seat.

"It's not wisdom as much as knowing these people. They're people the same as me. My aunt and uncle in Santa Paula are exactly like them. They may be poor, but they have pride, and pride to them means sharing, even if it's just beans and tortillas. It's easy to overlook the poor. In fact, people would just as soon they had no faces. Then it'd be easier to ignore them or buy them or their body parts."

"I see what you mean. It's a sad thing to say, but it's true," agreed Connie.

He paused, reached into the back seat to get two plums, wiped one off on his sleeve, and gave it to Connie."So, how was your interview with Chava?" he asked.

"That's one bright kid. He agreed to let me record everything. More important, he definitely identified the woman and was pretty sure about the doctor, too. The photo of him isn't the greatest, but there's no doubt in my mind that he's the guy who removed the boy's kidney."

"What's next?" he asked, biting into his plum.

"I have to write this up and talk to some folks from the FBI. Since the doctor's in Mexico, the ball will be out of my court. Then I can concentrate of the Melgoza murder." She finished her plum, opened the window, and spit the seed out. "There's no doubt these two events are related, but the jurisdiction issues of the two countries will make things awkward," she said, almost to herself.

"So this was a productive trip for you?" he asked.

She turned to look at him and smiled mischievously. "Very productive. Very, very nice and very productive…"

Carlos reached to the back seat again. He grabbed two more plums, polished one, and gave it to Connie. Highway 99 shimmered in the summer heat.

Chapter 35
A Meeting

"Connie, how was your trip to Fresno? Didja learn anything new?" asked Connie's partner, Ron Teal.

"It was a good meeting. I got two identifications: one a definite, the other a strong possible. I should have Salvador's testimony transcribed by tomorrow," replied Connie.

"Good, because tomorrow we have another meeting with the fed's to trade information. I was afraid we wouldn't have much to offer. Good thing you got something for us to share."

"I'll be ready. I'll make extra copies of the transcript for them."

Connie and Ron sat in his office waiting for the two FBI agents. Connie kept going over her copy of the report, making an occasional note in the margin. Dr. Tom Miller and Susan Moore walked in and sat down. Miller said, "We meet again." Noticing Connie's stack of papers, he smiled approvingly. "Good. Why don't you start?"

"Here is a detailed report. What you have before you is the transcription of a taped interview with Salvador Hinojosa, taken at his home near Fresno. We were able to verify our suspicions and get an ID for two of the photos you provided. The boy did confirm how the deal came down across the border. He was very positive about identifying the woman in the picture, even the restaurant. He was a little less sure about the doctor, because the photo wasn't very clear, but he thinks it him."

"Hmmm… What else?" asked Miller.

"Well the kid seems to be fine. Dr. Reynoso says he should be okay," said Connie.

Then Ron Teal spoke up. "I met with Dr. Pilabos who directs the medical center where Reynoso works. He was very helpful. It seems his meeting with Reynoso was coincidental. They actually met through a young lady who met Reynoso on a bus in Mexico, where they became friends. Pilabos met him at a birthday party at her family's house. You'll find the details in my report."

"Any more thoughts on the situation?" asked Miller.

Connie flipped through her copy of the report to check her margin notes. "I've been thinking about the situation as a whole and I think we're tackling the wrong end of the problem."

"What do you mean?" Miller asked.

"Just thinking out loud..." offered Connie cautiously. "In economic terms we've been focusing on the supply side. That is, we've only been working to locate the source of the problem. That reveals two problems: First, the people supplying the organs are very poor, so they'll do it for the money. Second, we have the international aspect which makes our job difficult if not impossible.

Perhaps we should concentrate on the *demand* side, that is, the recipients. Who is paying this huge amount of money for the organs, and who is performing the transplant? I know these are not easy questions, but at least these two problems are on our side of the border... I think." There was a pause, and then she continued, "Look at the drug problem, for example. The supplying countries tell us that if we didn't consume the drugs there would be no business. We must admit; they have a fair argument."

Connie pulled out some three-by-five cards. Selecting two, she continued. "In short, people are willing to sell their organs. People are willing to surgically remove them. People are willing to somehow transport them. People are willing to surgically implant them. People are apparently willing to pay huge amount of money because they don't want to wait in line as the normal system requires." She looked at the other three people in the room, "It's the *money* that starts the corruption, not some kid having to sell his kidney. That should be our main focus."

Ron Teal looked approvingly at Connie and then asked the others, "Does anyone know what kind of money is involved?"

Moore opened her mouth to speak, but stopped and looked at Miller first. He shrugged his shoulders, giving permission. "We've heard rumors that a very wealthy man in the area paid one million dollars for a kidney transplant, plus the regular medical costs," she said.

There was a silence in the room. Connie realigned her cards on the table. Teal rocked back in his chair and let out a long whistle.

"Shit," he said in a near whisper, "That's quite a markup, buying something for $500 and selling it for a million!" He paused. "Wait a minute! There have to be several people involved in this transaction; obviously the donor or seller, the doctor who removes the organ, the transporters, and the doctor who implants the organ. So, who keeps the bulk of the money?"

"What would be your guess?" asked Miller, raising one eyebrow.

"The implanting doctor!" answered the two detectives, almost in unison.

"Yep, that's our sense of it, too," agreed Miller.

Teal was pensive. "But wait another minute! Shouldn't it be simple to track this down since there are relatively few people needing transplants? There must also be very few doctors who can perform transplants and very few hospitals with the equipment required to do them." Teal felt they were reaching closure on this case. It seemed so obvious now.

"A few years ago you would've been correct," said Miller, "but now, some shady doctors are even performing the removal procedures outside of operating rooms… in their own offices." Ron sighed in frustration.

"But wouldn't they need a hospital to do the surgery?" asked Connie.

"Possibly not, again the technology has advanced so much that many surgeries that were once done in a hospital and required several weeks' hospitalization are now practically outpatient surgeries. A few clinics now have a small operating room for specialized surgeries these days. You enter a clinic in the morning and you're out a few hours later," explained Miller. "So there are operating rooms available where this could possibly be done, outside of a hospital setting."

"What about the technique for properly removing the organ?" asked Teal.

"That's even simpler, especially if you don't have much regard for the donor. Removal can actually be done in any doctor's office with rudimentary equipment, as long as there's anesthetic available. The Tijuana connection has proven that," he added.

"What about the person who paid a million dollars? Do you know who he is? Who his doctor is? I mean, shouldn't this be simple? The man is extremely sick for years, and one day he's suddenly had a miraculous recovery? You must know where he gets his medical attention." Teal was now sitting on the edge of his chair.

"Yes, we know the names of some very important and powerful people... Very important and powerful...." he repeated. That's as far as we've gotten," said Miller.

"Unlike the drug problem, this client is a one-time customer. Whether he lives or dies, we'll never hear from him again. So we're just left with the doctor who performs the surgery. If he did it once, he'll do it again," Teal said.

Susan Moore had listened to the speculation and added, "If *she* did it once, *she* will do it again."

In astonishment, Teal said, "You mean we're talking about a woman doctor doing this?"

"Sure, why not a woman? They have the same capabilities as men to do great things or evil things." The FBI agent appeared satisfied look to have made such a strong though perverse argument for gender equality.

"But why would she do such a thing?" asked Teal, incredulous.

"For the same reason a man would: for the money, the thrill, who knows?" responded Connie.

Satisfied that the point had been made that women were equal, Connie again picked up the economic argument, "But isn't a million dollars an awful lot of money for this procedure?"

Dr. Miller spoke up this time. "Not when you have several billion, you're dying, and this operation will save your life. If you think about it, it's a bargain for that sort of person."

"How often do you think this happens?" asked Connie.

"As you can imagine, it probably doesn't happen often. There are few people who have that kind of money, and doctors wouldn't want to expose themselves too many times," explained Miller.

Teal stood up, walked around, and sat on the edge of his desk. "So if this happens once or twice, why should we be so concerned?"

"Simple, if one doctor sees another one making a ton of money, he'll want to get in on it. And, as Connie suggested, the law of supply and demand works well. With more people willing to perform the procedure, the price will diminish somewhat," said Miller.

"My God!" said the senior detective."You mean we could have a price war on kidneys?"

"We're not there just yet," chuckled Miller, "but we seem to be headed in that direction.

"So, where do we go from here?" asked Teal.

"We've recently baited a few traps, ones that we can't tell you about. So we'll continue to keep our eye on the medical side of it. If you put your emphasis on the Melgoza case, perhaps we can meet in the middle," said Miller.

Susan Moore put one carefully-manicured fingertip to her lower lip and offered an idea. "I wonder if it might be useful if your young gentleman doctor were to meet our lady doctor?"

Miller spoke up, "That doesn't sound practical; they don't move in the same social or professional circles. Anything too obvious would scare away our target."

"That's true," said Moore, "but there's a conference sponsored by UCLA next month. Perhaps we could encourage Reynoso to attend under the auspices of Angelus Medical Center."

The FBI agent smiled, "What could be more natural than a bright young doctor wanting more information on this cutting-edge technology?"

"Wouldn't it be too obvious, for a guy who just finished school to attend such an affair?" asked Connie.

"Perhaps, but it might be worth trying. I think we should at least think about it. We probably have enough time before we have to send in a reservation for him," said Moore. "Besides, perhaps she might not know he's so new to the field."

Teal responded, "I agree it's worth thinking about. But how do we let him know about it? How much should we tell him?"

"I don't see how we could ask him to go into this blindly," said Connie. "He is a very trustworthy guy, and he really doesn't want to see anyone else get hurt by this whole transplant thing."

"Well," said Miller, looking at Connie. "Since you seem to have a cordial relationship with him, why don't you try out the idea on him? See how he reacts. Okay?"

"If you think this is our best shot, then okay," agreed Connie pensively.

The two agents rose, thanked them for their time, and left the office.

Teal looked the report in front of him; Connie stacked her cards. "What are you thinking, Connie?" he asked.

"I'm concerned," she said. "Carlos has gotten the opportunity of a lifetime to work at the Angelus Medical Center. I wonder if there is downside for him in this deal." She looked down blankly, thinking.

"Let's be straight with him, Connie. Tell him enough of what's going on so that he can decide whether he wants to help or not. From what you've said, he's honest and smart enough not to give anything away, so it's not a risk to share a bit with him." Teal continued, "Actually, I get the feeling he'd do anything for you just because it's you who asks." He smiled her way, but she'd looked down again, still thinking.

"I don't think I have *that* much influence on him…" She let her voice drift off.

"Well then play it safe with him. I get the impression he's bright enough to know what's good for him." He paused. "So now, what do we do with our own end of the investigation?"

Connie shook herself out of her thoughts and joined Teal's new idea. "Well, I guess our main hope is the Montoya kid's mother. We're still monitoring her phone. If they contact her again, we should be able to get there in time to help out. Maybe we'll get lucky," she answered.

Chapter 36
Wheels and a Deal

CARLOS HAD JUST PICKED UP THE PHONE after a page. "Carlos? This is John Ferranti. How are you doing?"

"Fine," he answered. "It's nice to hear from you, sir."

"Carlos, are you still looking for transportation?" He continued as if Carlos had said he was. "My office manger's husband said they just got a trade-in on this great pickup. Same make as your uncle's, but practically brand new. The person that bought it can no longer drive. He just wants get rid of it. Are you interested?"

"I really haven't had time to think about it, but I really do have to return my uncle's truck, even though he said I could keep it. So yes, I'd like to see it, thanks."

"Good come on over tonight and take a look at it."

Carlos made the now-familiar trip to the Ferranti's. He parked in front of the house next to a Toyota pickup that was similar to his uncle's except that it looked new. He looked inside before going up to house. Ann met him at the door with a kiss and hug, "Come in! Dad's in the living room."

"Carlos! Good to see you. Did you see the truck?" John Ferranti spoke in his confident way, as though things were already fact. He sensed that Carlos was unsure about what to do and needed some assurance that the deal made sense. He explained the price, financing, and insurance. Then the deal was struck. Simple as that, John Ferranti tossed Carlos the keys. "Great! The truck is yours; take it home!"

Carlos was a bit taken aback at how quickly the deal was made. "Oh!

But now I have to return my uncle's truck." He hesitated, wondering how he would manage to do that.

Ann solved his problem immediately. "Call your uncle and tell him we're coming over this evening. I'll follow you and bring you back. It's a nice evening and we should be back in just a couple of hours. Okay?"

Carlos made the phone call. When he returned he said, "It's all set. They're home and they're expecting us for dinner."

"Sounds good!" chirped Ann, heading off to grab her purse and a sweater.

Carlos drove north to his uncle's house and parked the pickup in its usual place. Right behind him was Ann in the new truck. He waited for her and they walked into the house without knocking. His aunt and uncle were sitting at the small table drinking coffee. The table was set for two. Immediately Tía Estrella was up, warming the food. Carlos hugged his aunt and shook Uncle Francisco's hand.

Carlos said, "You remember Ann Ferranti, I'm sure." Ann reached over shook the old man's hand. Tía Estrella hugged her, and at the same time, almost pushed her into a chair at the table. Within a short time, there were two steaming plates of rice and beans with green chiles on the table, and hot corn tortillas began to pile up on a small plate between them. The two offered no argument; they began to eat. Ann struggled to eat using just a tortilla, so Tía Estrella handed them each forks. Carlos began to use the fork as well.

"Tió, thanks for the use of the pickup. I'm sorry I kept it so long. I guess the time just got away from me," apologized Carlos.

"Don't worry *mijo!* I can't drive two trucks, you know. I really should sell it, except it's paid for and it's very handy," said his uncle.

"So, how's work?" asked Carlos.

"The harvest has begun to wind down, so we have to walk a lot. My legs don't move as quickly as they used to, but I do okay, okay." The old man grinned. His wife gave him a half a cup of coffee. He spooned in some sugar and filled up the rest of the cup with brandy. He smiled at Ann as he was stirring. "It's good for my old bones," he said to her, winking.

"Carlos, your mother called us yesterday. She told me she hasn't heard from you in several days and she's concerned about you."

"I know I haven't called them in several weeks; I need to do that."

"Promise you'll call today or tomorrow," admonished his aunt.

"Tomorrow. It's too late today," replied Carlos.

"She's very pretty," said the aunt as she added more tortillas to the plate.

"Who?" he answered playfully. "Be careful with her Tía; she speaks Spanish."

Carlos's aunt mussed up his hair. "Well, she's pretty in any language."

After eating, they all sat in the tiny living room. It was crowded with furniture. One corner had a large television and the other corner contained a shrine for the Virgin of Guadalupe. It held a lighted candle and a single rose in small vase.

Tió Francisco said, "Let's take a look at your new truck!" Both men walked out and the two women remained inside, sipping their coffee.

"What do you do, Anna?" asked Tía Estrella, adding an extra a to Ann's name.

"I'm a teacher; I just graduated from college. I'll start teaching in September."

"A teacher; how very nice! Both Carlos's parents are teachers in Tonalá," she said. Her voice actually seemed to twinkle.

"Yes, I know. Carlos told me about them. Maybe one of these days I'll get to meet them. I know he misses them very much."

The men returned. "Ann, we need to get going. It's getting late." Carlos hugged his aunt and shook his uncle's hand. Tió Francisco put his free hand on the young man's shoulder and blessed him. Carlos bent down and kissed the old man's hand.

"I like your aunt and uncle. You three look like a family," observed Ann.

"I'm very fortunate that I have two sets of parents."

They rode in silence through the orchards of the Santa Clara Valley. The evening was warm and the scent of the orange tree blossoms was noticeable in the warm air. Ann said, "I like this area, she said, it's so rural and the people are nice."

"There are some very nice people, but like any other place, it has all kinds of people good and bad," replied Carlos, thinking about the murder in the orchard.

"I know that's true, but I like it. Let's come here to live, Carlos." Ann said this in such a matter-of- fact manner that he almost missed it. Finally he said, "I don't understand. What do you mean, let's come here to live?"

"Because I like it here." She paused, "Carlos I know you're undecided, you just got a new job. You're here in a different country than the one you planned to work in. You just met me a few months ago and you're a man. You probably haven't thought of me as 'us' but I have. I don't need years to tell me what's right and years to make up my mind."

They drove in silence, "I don't mean to pressure you, but I do want you to be aware of my feelings for you. I suppose that in a way that is pressure, but I've been taught that when you make up your mind, you act." She continued, "By now you know I'm not a timid mouse. I not going to slink around, you'll always know what I feel because I will tell you."

Carlos said nothing. He had no idea what to say. It would be very easy to say the wrong thing.

Ann continued, "I'll make a deal with you. You concentrate on the clinic and on getting your license to practice, and I will concentrate on being your very best friend. Deal?"

Carlos smiled, much relieved. "Deal…That's the best offer I've had all night."

"No it's not," she said with a sly smile.

Chapter 37
Suitably Attired

WHEN CARLOS ENTERED the medical center's staff room, he reached into his in-box and pulled out an envelope. It was an invitation with a sticky note saying, "Please see me." It had the initials AP at the bottom. The invitation itself read:

Noted transplant surgeon,
Adriana B. Colson
will present a lecture on the
latest surgical techniques and the future
of kidney transplantation.
Cocktail Reception
Dinner

He knocked on the open door of Dr. Pilabos' office and leaned in. "You wanted to see me about this?" he asked, gesturing with the card in his hand.

"Yes, have a seat." Pilabos rose, walked around his desk, and sat in a chair next to Carlos. "Carlos, though you've only been here a short time, I want to tell you how pleased all the partners are with you. I've heard similar comments from the staff as well."

Carlos twiddled his fingers in his embarrassment. Pilabos paused. "We've been thinking about this transplant business for some time, but haven't had the time to investigate it. I'd like you to attend the conference and meet some of the people. Learn all you can about it to see if it might work for Angelus Medical Center to do this sometime in the future."

Carlos ran his fingers along the edge of the invitation; there was nothing for it but to be direct. He asked, "How does this relate to Salvador and of the kidney trafficking?" His matter-of-fact manner left Pilabos no alternative.

"Good question! I'm glad you asked; somehow I *knew* you would." He paused, feeling somewhat relieved. "I don't know," he repeated slowly, "I really don't know, except that we've been asked by the authorities if we would send you just to scout around. At the same time, it will be good experience for you, and," he added frankly, "perhaps there might be role for the center to play in the future."

Carlos smiled. "It sounds like a good idea, but I think it would be good if someone briefed me about what to look for so I don't say the wrong thing. And..."

"Good idea! I agree with you. I'll talk to them and get someone to brief you... Uh...you have another question?" he asked.

Carlos blushed, his self-assurance fading in front of his mentor. "Frankly, if I'm going to a cocktail party and conference, I need to get some clothes. All I have is work clothes."

Alex Pilabos laughed. "You remind me of when I started. I was already practicing before I got a suit that that wasn't a hand-me-down. Well young man, you've just learned one of the down sides of our profession; sometimes you have to wear a suit and tie." Pilabos noticed that Carlos was still tentative. "Let me make this a pleasant suggestion. Why don't you call Ann Ferranti and invite her to dinner? Then ask her to take you to a men's store to buy a suit and whatever else you need. By the way, do you need money?"

"No sir. I have money; I just haven't had the chance to *spend* any," explained Carlos, somewhat embarrassed.

"Well here's your chance. Call Ann. In the meantime, I'll get you an appointment with someone to brief you on the conference."

They took the Topanga off-ramp to the huge shopping center. The evening traffic was very heavy, but at least it was moving. "Do you want to eat first or go shopping?" asked Ann, as he parked his new truck.

"Let's buy the stuff first; then I'll be able to enjoy eating, if that's okay with you. Where are we going?" asked Carlos.

"We're going to Kipling Brothers, where my dad buys his suits. There are also plenty of places to eat at that end of the mall, too. Where are you going, that you need fancy clothes? Some big event?"

"Just to a medical conference in Century City. Dr. Pilabos wants me to look into a couple of things for the medical center."

"What kind of clothes do you need, Carlos?"

Timidly he replied, "You've seen all my clothes. Remember, just a few weeks ago I was picking lemons. I just need to blend in with the crowd, so something sort of professional looking that's not a lab coat."

"Well Doctor, I hope you brought plenty of money, because we have to get you set up with all the basics, and Kipling Brothers is the place to do it. We should be able to buy most everything there." Carlos winced and smiled uncomfortably.

Ann took Carlos by the hand as they entered the store. They walked to the men's department, where the suits were located. She sought out a short man who was folding some trousers. The salesman smiled when he saw her and met them halfway back. "Juan, it's nice to see you. I want you to meet Dr. Carlos Reynoso. He has an important appointment and needs to dress up a bit. You know: a nice dark suit, white shirts, shoes…the works."

Juan had already sized up Carlos. He had him stand in front of a three-way mirror. Ann sat down to the side to view the process. The salesman brought a series of jackets. Quickly, Ann and Juan had settled on a dark, charcoal suit with faint stripes. Next, Juan measured Carlos for the pants. Carlos stood like one of the store mannequins: mute, with a far off look on his face. Shirts, ties, socks, and shoes followed, everything was black or white except for the color in one of the ties. "What do you think?" asked Ann, looking up expectantly.

"I guess they're okay, but isn't all this rather somber?" he asked.

"You're going to a somber business affair and this is what you'll need." She addressed Juan, "Let's see how he looks in some gray slacks and a navy blue blazer. We'll give him some color with his shirts and ties. In no time at all, the salesman rounded up her request and took a moment to take his measurements. Again Ann concurred with the salesman; Carlos was still in a daze.

"Dr. Reynoso, if you agree with these selections, we can have the alterations done by this Saturday, if that's satisfactory sir," said Juan.

"That will be fine. Thank you," responded Carlos quietly. Ann and Carlos left the store with several bags containing everything that did not need alteration to fit. He was surprised at the number of things necessary for dressing up.

They set all the bundles down on one side of the booth and they sat on the other, facing the big pile. "Ann, I just spent almost $1,000!" said Carlos. She could hear the panic in his voice. "You know how many lemons I'd have to pick to make that much money?"

"Don't worry," she said. "You'll look gorgeous! You'll knock 'em dead at the conference. Besides, you're not picking lemons anymore."

"I'll be dead and broke," he said with a smile.

"Don't worry. If you're dead, at least you'll be the best-looking corpse around!" She matched his smile. "Now, let's see what we want to eat," she continued, handing him a menu.

Chapter 38
The Conference

A S HE PASSED HER DESK, THE RECEPTIONIST SPOKE to Carlos. "A Dr. Miller and Agent Moore told me to tell you they will be coming by at noon today. They suggested going to lunch, if that works for you. If not, I can ring them back for you."

Puzzled, he asked, "Do I know them?"

"They said you don't know them yet, but they were referred to you by Dr. Pilabos."

"Oh…" Still puzzled he answered, "Please page me when they arrive."

"Will do!"

"Dr. Reynoso? I'm Tom Miller, and this is my associate, Susan Moore." Carlos greeted the two visitors. "I noticed there's small restaurant across the street; would you mind if we went there to talk?"

"That's fine. We can just walk over." Carlos removed his white jacket and led the way across the street. The hot Santa Ana winds were blowing. Dust, leaves, and plastic bags were swirling in the air. They were all feeling sweaty by the time they were settled in at their table. They welcomed the cool air conditioning inside.

"Dr. Reynoso, first let me thank you for your willingness to help us. As Dr. Pilabos probably told you, we are both with the FBI. We're a local task force looking into the trafficking of human organs. It just happened that you located the body of the young man who was murdered, and then you treated a boy at one of your clinics." Miller smiled pleasantly as he blotted the sweat from his face with a paper napkin.

Next, the female agent spoke. "Frankly Dr. Reynoso, we've lost the trail. We think that someone at this conference might have something to do with it." Charlene noticed Carlos's questioning face. "We're wondering if Dr. Colson might be a part of the puzzle."

Carlos said, "I did a little research on Dr. Colson. She's an internationally renowned surgeon with an impeccable reputation. How can she be involved? It just doesn't make sense."

"That's our sense too," she replied, "but the few leads we do have keep leading to her, or to someone in her medical group. We just need to check them out more closely. That's where you come in."

"What do you need me to do?" asked Carlos.

"We want you to go as who you are, a young doctor who is interested in the idea of transplantation in general. Take notes, move around, listen to people, and enjoy the lectures. Just be alert." Miller continued in a lighter mood, "If there's nothing there, at least you will have attended a very interesting medical conference courtesy of the U.S. Government. If by chance you *do* hear something interesting, this same U.S. Government will be very grateful."

"How will I report back to you?"

Miller explained, "We want you to write a complete, detailed report of everything you see or hear, and any people you meet who seem of interest. We'll arrange to meet with you later on to get your impressions."

"Am I allowed to talk about this to anyone else, maybe Dr. Pilabos, for example?"

"Of course; Dr. Pilabos helped us to arrange this meeting, so you can certainly share the information with him. Also, if you talk to Detectives Teal and Alonzo, you can share the details with them, since they're cooperating with us on the investigation. It would be better, however, if you let us give them the written report because we will no doubt add to it. And beyond those three people, don't speak of this with anyone." His eyes were commanding, but Carlos didn't need the warning.

Valet parking at the hotel was busy. Men in red jackets ran in and out between the cars as they sped off into the bowels of the parking structure. Carlos's pickup made quite a contrast with all the fancy cars in line to be parked. "Take care of it," he said to a young man in Spanish. The boy smiled, nodded, and soon the pickup disappeared.

The hotel lobby was elegant but surprisingly small. He'd arrived early. He noticed a discreet sign announcing "Transplant Conference." He wandered in the direction its arrow pointed and located the room. Then he walked around the hotel to pass some time, impressed with the luxury of the place.

By the time he returned to the conference room, people had begun to gather. He noticed several displays set up by vendors in the hallway. As he waited in line to register, he perused the vendors' offerings. One woman urged him to place an order for a magnifying device designed to be worn on the head or attached to a lamp. He passed on that. Another was a supplier of hypoallergenic items, such as non-latex gloves and probes. He picked up a brochure. The room was small, and as he entered, he could count fifteen round tables with seating for eight. He got in line at the registration table. He was given a name tag, a program, a "goodie bag," and the number of his assigned table. He got a glass of wine and headed for his table. He exchanged pleasantries with a couple of other doctors seated with him. He took a moment to peer inside his goodie bag. It included a variety of items such as pens and paper tablets, most of which were imprinted with the logo of a pharmaceutical manufacturer or equipment supplier. One curious item was a plastic container shaped like a stomach. It popped open to reveal some antacid tablets.

Promptly, a distinguished, tall and slender man stepped up to the microphone on the dais and asked that the attendees take their seats. As the host for the event, he thanked several people for making the arrangements for the conference and made the expected courtesy references to the vendors' displays. Then, without much fanfare, he introduced Dr. Adriana Colson, the speaker.

As she began her presentation, Carlos, like the other attendees, took a pen and writing pad from his goodie bag for note-taking. However, he would probably be writing down different things than they were.

Dr. Colson was a very small, slim lady dressed in a dark suit made of material similar to the new suit Carlos was wearing. She was probably in her late forties, with a touch of gray in her hair, which was very short in back. The front part was long on one side and curved in a half moon, cupping one side of her face. She kept moving the long strands out of her face by tossing her head or flipping them back with her fingers. Carlos wondered why anyone would want such an inconvenient style. As she spoke, her hair seemed to keep rhythm with her speech. It almost seemed to be part of the presentation. She spoke without notes, her voice strong and clear.

Her talk was not technical, but focused on the history of kidney transplantation and what the future held in store for the field. Off to one side, an aide operated a slide projector, presenting images of old techniques and equipment as she spoke. Her slides showed most of the surgical procedures as drawings, and then followed by photographs. This way, the photographs were easier to interpret. She held up a fist-sized, sausage-shaped artificial kidney, which she predicted would eventually replace the need for human donors. As she began discussing the future prospects for organ transplantation, Dr. Colson placed the device on the nearest table and asked the people there to pass it around the room. The mechanical replacement made its way around the room. As she concluded her talk, the conference host took the microphone and urged everyone to head out to the patio where they would have the cocktail hour, so that the conference room could be set up for their dinner.

Carlos followed a couple of nice fellows from his table out to the patio. They got their drinks and exchanged pleasantries with them for a while, then moved around the room, getting to know some of the other people. He wondered who might be involved in the organ trafficking business. He sipped his drink slowly, because he had no idea how long it might be before they ate dinner. He knew he wouldn't make a good spy, but he was determined to meet as many people as he could and get to know as much about them as possible, given the short time he had.

At last, the emcee called them back to their tables. As they reached their seats, scurrying servers set their meals in front of them. While they ate, Dr. Colson went around the tables. She introduced herself to everyone. She didn't have to bend over to speak to anyone, since she was so tiny. She spoke briefly with nearly everyone. While she shook hands with one hand, the other one tamed her hair. Carlos was eating his dessert, mixed fruit with a whipped cream swirl, when she reached his table.

Cocking her head to read his name tag, she said, "Dr. Reynoso, it's so nice to have such a young man interested in this area of medicine. What school did you attend?"

"The University of Guadalajara. Dr. Pilabos of the Angelus Medical Center asked me to attend your lecture to see if we might be interested in becoming more involved in the transplant field."

"Excellent!" she said. "I know my talk was very general tonight, but as you go out, you will be given a binder with much more detailed information about transplants. If you're not in a hurry, perhaps we can sit and talk after dinner," she suggested.

"I'd like that very much, I look forward to it."

"As do I." She pointed toward the lounge, to indicate she'd look for him there, then she turned to greet the people at the next table.

The hall leading to the lounge was lined with floor-to-ceiling mirrors. Carlos tried hard not to look at himself as he walked, yet he was mesmerized by the image he saw. It was almost an out-of-body experience. Fortunately, the reflection did not seem to radiate the nervousness he felt. His walk had purpose and confidence as he strode to the bar.

"A beer," he ordered in Spanish. The bartender appeared to be about his age. He smiled at Carlos quickly and brought him his drink and a bowl of nuts. Carlos sat quietly, took a sip and began to relax. The bar was elegant and understated. The quiet music somehow made the customers speak in low voices, so that people leaned toward each other to hear.

Carlos opened the binder he'd picked up as he left the conference room. The front page featured a sepia-toned photograph of Colson with her hair framing one side of her face. The face showed a bemusement that some might mistake for a smile. The opposite page listed her numerous accomplishments. That went on for two more pages. Carlos read the resume, but his attention kept returning to the face that was partly shaded by the hair and the photographer's lighting. He wondered what other knowledge and ideas were hiding behind that face.

A few minutes later, Dr. Colson slipped onto the stool next to him.

She gestured to the bartender, two fingers pointing to Carlos's beer. He quickly brought two more. She paid the tab, waving Carlos's hand away. "In the final analysis, beer is my favorite drink, especially after a talk," she said.

"I enjoyed your presentation, Doctor Colson, but I must admit I also enjoy the quiet and a cold beer."

"That's a perception many men don't have." She paused. "So tell me again about your interest in transplants," she asked.

"I just graduated from school and the whole idea of medicine is exciting for me. But to be honest, in school we talked about transplants only in passing." He took a sip and collected his thoughts. "This whole idea of organ replacement is fascinating. I am also interested in the mechanical kidney. Have you actually used them?"

"We have placed several in pigs and they seem to work fine for a while, but there is still more work to do. You know," she said, "it's really is not such a big leap. After all, the kidney is just a filter. Industry has been using filters effectively for many years. It's the power source that tends to complicate things, but we're getting there, too. I think we're about eighteen months from implanting one in a human being."

"Do you think it will replace the need for human kidneys?"

"Not in the short term. Right now, dialysis helps for a while. But when available, human kidneys are the best thing we have to offer, especially since we've overcome the rejection problem. It's the supply problem that leads us to the mechanical route," she said calmly. They sat in companionable silence for a moment. "Say, would you like to observe a transplant surgery?"

Colson had asked this in such a matter-of-fact voice that it didn't surprise him. Still, he hesitated to answer. Finally he blurted, "Of course I would! It's more than I could even have imagined coming from this conference!"

She reached over to his shirt pocket, removed his pen, and wrote a phone number on her photograph in the binder Carlos had been reading, as if the numbers were a necklace. "This is the number of the nurse who keeps tabs on all my surgeries. Call her and give her a number where we can reach you. As you know, these things come up rather suddenly, so don't be shocked if we call in the middle of the night." She slowly, deliberately replaced the pen in his shirt pocket and slipped off the stool. She walked away without looking back.

Carlos finished off his beer and walked out of the lounge. He tried very hard not to look at the reflection in the mirrored hall but when no one was looking, he waved at the stranger in the suit as he walked out to the valet parking area to reclaim his new truck.

It was close to midnight before Carlos finished writing his report. It was five pages of factual observations of what he saw and did. The last page he entitled "Personal Opinion and Observations." He wrote:

> *Dr. Colson appears to be a warm, friendly and very confident person. She speaks openly and easily about medical and non-medical issues. She has invited me to observe a kidney transplant. She asked me to call her nurse to give her my phone number so they could call me next time she's performing a transplant surgery. Should I do this? Could she possibly have a feeling that I might be looking for more than just a chance to see an unusual operation?*

Chapter 39
Sunday Morning

IT WAS SUNDAY. Carlos remembered Luz' invitation to attend Mass with her. Santa Marta was a small parish located several blocks west of the *Clínica Central*. The Santa Ana winds had cleared the valley air of its usual yellowish layer of pollution. He could see the two mountain ranges that bordered the San Fernando Valley very clearly. It had the effect of making the valley seem smaller.

Carlos found the church and parked his truck on the street. He joined the stream of people as they made their way into the church. The priest and procession party had already gathered near the front door. He followed them in. Spotting Luz, he sat next to her. The Mass was in Spanish and with his eyes closed, it could have been in his hometown of Tonalá.

After the Mass, Luz introduced him to her parents and two sisters. "We're having breakfast at the parish hall. Would you like to join us?"

"Sure! Thanks."

Carlos fell in step with Luz' father. They talked as they, and the rest of the crowd, worked their way to the hall, next door to the church. The family sat at a wooden table. Luz and her mother brought over a couple of large bowls of menudo, a plate of tortillas, and condiments. The hall was noisy, children ran about, adults talked, and teenagers in small groups whispered quietly among themselves.

"Did you enjoy the Mass, Doctor?" asked Luz.

"Yes, I did. But call me Carlos, please," he pleaded. "You know, this church is just like the one in Tonalá or even the one in Santa Paula. The people are the same; there's little difference."

"That's the way it's supposed to be," explained Luz. "That's why it's called the *universal* church." Luz caught the eye of a woman with short red hair who was twirling a little girl about. The woman picked up the child and walked over to the table. "Sister," said Luz, "I'd like you to meet Doctor Carlos Reynoso. Carlos, this is Sister Liz."

"Ah... the famous Doctor Carlos Reynoso! I finally get to meet you! Luz has told us a lot about you." The red-headed nun sat at the table and the little girl wiggled out of her arms. She ran off to join some other children in the middle of the hall. Carlos couldn't help but stare at the nun. She was obviously used to being looked over. She wore glasses with darkened lenses, so Carlos could not see her eyes, but somehow he could feel she was laughing at his discomfort.

"I'm sorry, Sister. I've never seen a Sister who didn't look like a... Sister," he said, embarrassed to have been noticed.

"What is a Sister supposed to look like?" she asked, laughing gently.

"Oh, you know: a long black habit and um..." His hand rose to his head. He didn't know the name of the usual head coverings he'd usually seen nuns wear.

Sister Liz nodded, understanding. "We have Sisters who dress like that. If you want, I'll introduce you to one of them, but we're all servants of the Lord. Our order allows us to wear a wide variety of clothing. Actually," she continued with a sparkle in her eye, "you don't look like a doctor, now that I think of it. If I were to guess, I'd take you for, say...a lemon picker!" Sister Liz laughed. Luz chuckled, too.

Carlos laughed along with them. "Well Sister, you're right on both counts! You are looking at a lemon picker who, if he can keep his mouth shut, might be a doctor one of these days."

"Seriously, we're tickled that you're working with Luz at the *Clinica Central.* We're thinking of letting Luz continue working there on weekends when she joins us for her discernment period. In fact, one of the other Sisters might even join you, if that's all right."

"I really enjoy working at the clinic. I don't particularly like getting up early to drive down there, but once I'm there, I enjoy the people. The day goes by quickly. I even like going across to the bus station to eat. You meet all sorts of interesting people there." Remembering her request, he added, "Oh, Luz and I can ask the director for permission to bring another person along to the clinic. We can always use more help."

"Thank you, Dr. Reynoso. It was good to finally meet you." The red-headed nun got up and just as she did, the little girl jumped into her arms again.

"That's some nun," said Carlos, as they both watched Sr. Liz play with the children.

"She is. She's wonderful," agreed Luz.

"She has quite a personality."

"Speaking of personalities, how is Ann? I haven't seen her for some time."

Suddenly weary, Carlos replied, "Fine, I guess. She's excited about starting to teach in a few weeks."

Carlos drove back to his apartment. He realized he was tired. He lay down and went to sleep... until the phone rang.

Chapter 40
At the Hospital

"CARLOS? CAN YOU COME OVER RIGHT AWAY? Your uncle's had an accident." His aunt's voice seemed calm, but Carlos noticed the concern in her tone. "Where is he now?" he asked.

"He's here at the house. He wants you to see him," urged Tía Estrella.

"Is it serious?" asked Carlos, his mind racing.

"He says it's not, but he really wants to see you. Please can you hurry?"

The old man was half sitting on the couch, balanced carefully to ease his pain. He smiled weakly as Carlos entered. Mario was with him, his brow lined with worry.

"What happened, Tío?"

To save the injured man the effort, Mario responded. "One of the company cars drove down the row and hit your uncle's ladder. It knocked him off and he hit the ground. We think he hit a bin when he fell." The concerned he felt showed in his voice. Carlos examined his uncle carefully. He was in a great deal of pain. There was a gash on the side of his head but it was his hip that was the most painful.

"We need to get him to the hospital." Turning to his uncle, he asked, "Do you think you can make it to the truck or should we call an ambulance?" He looked at Mario and Chuy, his uncle's oldest son.

"I can make it in the truck," Tío Francisco answered weakly.

"Mario," he said, "you call the hospital tell them to have a gurney waiting. I should be there in fifteen minutes. Chuy, you can give me a hand."

214 Alfonso A. Guilin

Chuy and Carlos laid a mattress and some blankets in the back of the truck and eased Tió Francisco out as carefully as they could. The old man said nothing, though he gritted his teeth at the slightest movement.

The hospital personnel moved him from the truck to a gurney, and rolled him into an examining room. The emergency room doctor took a look at the head wound but quickly ignored it. He focused his attention on the hip injury.

"Let's get him into X-ray for some pictures of his right hip." He ordered. "Let's call one of the ortho guys in. If it's what I think it is, he's going to need one."

Carlos went to the waiting room. His aunt was sitting in a corner, her lips moving, a rosary in her hands. He sat next to her and joined her in the prayers. The barely audible, repetitive prayers calmed her as it did him. He could feel his breathing melt into the prayers' rhythm. His aunt seemed to shrink into a slumber, yet she continued to finger the black beads

Mario and his wife walked in. Carlos walked over to them. "Tell me what really happened," Carlos said quietly.

Mario's face showed frustration. "It was the boss's son again. That son-of-a-bitch was racing up and down the road all morning. I told Jack about it, but he just shrugged it off. He couldn't do anything. That damned kid is crazy!" growled Mario.

"Did anyone report it to the police?" asked Carlos.

"What good would it do? Even the cops are afraid of that kid and his father," said Chuy who'd been very quiet up to now.

Carlos excused himself a moment and phoned Connie. "Hi, Connie. Sorry to bother you, but I'm at the hospital here in Santa Paula. My uncle has been in an accident. I wonder if you could come down... Thanks." He hung up the phone and headed back to the contractor and his son.

Connie arrived with Deputy Sheriff Larry Nelson in tow. "I asked Larry to take the report, because he's on duty in this sector. So, how's your uncle?"

"We don't know. They're taking x-rays; we should know in a few minutes."

By this time, several crewmembers had arrived, their hair still wet from showering. Connie directed them to the deputy who had moved outside in the shade to take his notes. They could see the angry men surrounding him, all talking at once. It took Deputy Nelson several minutes to calm them so he could take down the information.

Not long after this, the deputy's supervisor, Sergeant Teal drove up. He listened to the men tell give their accounts of the event to Deputy Nelson. Once he had the gist of the situation, he walked back towards the ER waiting room. Through the window, he gestured for Connie to join them.

As she arrived at the table, Connie asked, "What's the deal?"

"These guys are pretty much in agreement that the Grady kid was racin' up and down the road," answered the deputy. Apparently, he clipped the ladder the man was standing on and knocked him down. Several of the men saw it. They said they hollered at the kid but that he just took off."

"I know that kid; he's nuts. I wouldn't put it past him to do such a thing," added the supervisor.

"What we gonna do now?" asked Nelson.

"What would be your normal next step?" Connie asked Nelson.

"Go talk to the kid; get his side of the story. Then I'd take a gander at his vehicle," Larry said.

"Do you know who this boy's father is?" asked Teal, implying the man's power and influence.

"Yep, I know," responded Connie. "It means the Grady kid has rights, so we'll be fair with him and hear his side. Don't worry; we'll be careful not to offend, and we'll be especially careful to take plenty of notes," she smiled, unconsciously giving a pat to her hip pocket and the three-by-fives it contained. Then she turned around and walked back into the waiting room.

Tía Estrella seemed to shrink. Carlos took her to a chair and sat down with his arm around her. Eventually, the ER doctor appeared. "The x-rays indicate a broken hip. The best thing to do is to replace it. They'll be doing it as soon as they can prepare him for the procedure. It's fortunate he hadn't eaten anything since very early this morning. We'd like you to explain this to him and his wife, sir."

Carlos and his aunt followed immediately to see Tío Francisco. Carlos carefully explained to his aunt and uncle what each of the doctors said. He answered their questions and reassured both of them as best he could. Then he helped Tía Estrella understand and sign the permission forms. The doctor left with forms in hand.

Carlos stood, waiting patiently while his aunt spoke a few words of loving encouragement to her husband. Tío Francisco was getting groggy from the anesthetic and was just about to drop off to sleep. Then the two of them walked out into the hallway toward the waiting room.

As they arrived, a young aide came up to them. "We have a chapel down the hall. It's quiet and you can wait there, if you'd like." Carlos motioned for Mario to take his aunt to the chapel. "I'll join you in the chapel soon, *Tía,* he said. Several others followed Mario and the elderly woman as they disappeared down the hall toward the chapel.

Carlos walked over to the vending machine, dropped in some coins and retrieved a soda. He swallowed some and offered the can to Connie who also took a drink. They walked outside and sat on a bench on the nearby patio.

"What's the deal?" he asked.

"Apparently the owner's kid, who is a pain in the ass," she said with obvious disgust, "hit your uncle's ladder and knocked him down."

"What do you think will happen to him?"

She took another drink of the soda. "Oh, I don't know. The old man is a powerful guy in the county *and* he's a good friend of the DA. At best we may be able to scare the shit out of the kid."

"You mean nothing will happen to the kid because of who his father is?" asked Carlos incredulously.

"Actually Carlos, the father is a pretty nice guy. He just happens to have a rotten son. My hunch is that the dad will do the right thing, but," said Connie with a sigh, "I'm afraid nothing much will happen to the kid in the end."

Carlos snorted and finished the soda in one long swallow.

"Does that surprise you?" she asked.

"In Mexico it would not have surprised me. *Here* it does."

Connie sensed his frustration. Things were not always fair when you were dealing with powerful people. It was a hard fact, but sometimes people just had to accept it or suffer the consequences of angering them. Changing the subject, she said, "I read your report on the Dr. Colson's conference. It was a good report but it didn't have any new information."

Carlos looked at her for a brief moment and then smiled, knowing why she'd changed the subject. There really wasn't much either of them could do. So he answered gamely, "Well she didn't tell me she had a sale on kidneys this week!" He squashed the can and tossed into a trash can. "But she *did* invite me to a surgery, so we'll see if she does."

They laughed for a moment, and Carlos was relieved to get his mind off his uncle for a few minutes. Then he remembered something. He looked at Connie seriously and asked, "Incidentally, who's going to reimburse me the $1,000 I spent on the conference?"

"What $1,000?"

"The $1,000 it cost me to buy a new suit so I could attend. I couldn't go in my lemon-picking outfit!"

"You paid $1,000 for a suit?" she asked, puzzled.

"Well there were also shoes, a sports jacket, shirts, ties and some other stuff."

"My, my Doctor Reynoso! You must've made quite an appearance all decked out like that! When do I get to see the new outfit?"

"All you have to do is ask."

Without thinking, Connie responded enthusiastically, "How about tonight?"

He became pensive, "No... not tonight. I think I'll stay over at my aunt's house to make sure she's okay. Why don't you come over and we'll have a beer? It would be nice to have your company... and my aunt does like you."

"Good idea! I'm off at six. See you later!" She walked to her car and drove off.

Carlos walked back into the hospital and down the hall to the tiny chapel. A rosary was in progress. He sat down next to his little cousin Charlie and joined the litany.

The quiet was broken by the surgeon's arrival. Carlos and Tía Estrella walked out into the hall.

"Just as we suspected," reported the surgeon. "The fall broke his hip right at the joint. So we replaced the joint with an artificial one. He'll be fine, though it will take some time for him to heal and get used to putting weight on it again. He has excellent muscle tone, which is in his favor. We'll start therapy tomorrow. He'll be sore as the dickens, but he'll be fine. They're closing him up right now. In a couple of hours he'll be in the ICU where you can see him. You folks have time to go have something to eat." The surgeon put his hand on the aunt's shoulder as they thanked him, and quickly walked away.

The doctor wasn't rude, but he seemed to be in a hurry to finish with them. Carlos smiled at his aunt and shrugged his shoulders. He spent a few moments going over what the doctor had said, explaining the words which had flown by so quickly.

They both returned to the chapel and rejoined the prayer. When it was completed, Carlos explained to all the friends and relatives who'd stayed with them the latest news about his uncle.

Connie knocked on the door. As Carlos welcomed her in, she noticed a good smell coming from the kitchen. "I hope your aunt isn't cooking dinner after all this," she said.

"Well as a matter of fact she is; but don't object. She wanted to cook for us. It will keep her busy and keep her mind off my uncle."

"How is he?" asked Connie.

"He's fine. We saw him. He was groggy but he knew we were there. The fall broke his hip and the ortho did a hip replacement. So, what happened to the Grady kid? Did you and Deputy Nelson talk to him?" asked Carlos.

"It had to be Nelson. His jurisdiction, and I was busy on another matter. I haven't seen his report yet, but he told me the father was at the house when he spoke to the boy. I heard Grady went through the roof! No doubt that kid got chewed out something fierce! Mr. Grady said he'd come by tomorrow to see your aunt and try to make things 'right' whatever that means."

"That's it?"

"Frankly, that pretty much *is* it. There's not much we can do that would stick, unless your uncle and aunt want to make a formal complaint. Even then there would be few or no consequences for the kid," she stated flatly.

"And just exactly what would happen if *I* ran down the Grady kid?" asked Carlos, frustrated. Connie said nothing, but smiled crookedly and sighed in resignation.

"I think I'll stay over until tomorrow so I can be here when Grady comes over."

"Good idea," agreed Connie.

Chapter 41
Surgery

THE NEIGHBORHOOD AROUND ST. VINCENT Hospital had changed since the building was constructed. The building itself had two faces: the original building and a recently-built wing. Carlos arrived early, announcing himself at the desk. The receptionist looked at her computer screen then at Carlos, "Dr. Reynoso, you're expected. Take the elevator to the third floor. Check in at the desk and they'll direct you to Surgery."

"This way, Dr. Reynoso," called a young woman. "We've been expecting you." She led him to a small room. The familiar green scrubs hung neatly in an open closet for him to select. The caps and shoe coverings were in boxes on a shelf. "You're just in time." Carlos smiled, unsure of what to do. "You can dress and can scrub here. I'll be back in a couple of minutes to help you with your gloves." She pulled the door shut as she departed.

In a short while the young woman returned. "Is this your first time here?" she asked.

"Yes. It's also my first time to see this kind of surgery," he said honestly.

"You're lucky then. Dr. Colson is a wonderful surgeon. Don't be surprised at what goes on. She talks *all* the time, but if you listen carefully, she will have answered all the questions you could ever ask by the end of the surgery." She helped him with his gloves and mask then led him into the operating room.

"Ladies and gentlemen, this is Dr. Carlos Reynoso, a recent med school grad of the University of Guadalajara. He's shown some interest in the work we do here. I invited him to look over our shoulders. So let's get started," said Dr. Colson.

Carlos looked around; the room was located in the older part of the hospital. The fixtures and equipment were old, the paint faded and peeling in many areas. As if reading his mind, Dr. Colson said, "Don't worry about this old room Doctor; it's quite clean. It's the team's that important, not the room. In fact, I dare say we could do this surgery in my kitchen. Come closer and take a look at what we're doing."

Just then, Bobby Darin's voice came on over the speakers. His familiar crooning of "Mack the Knife," told a woman she'd gotten deep into his heart.

Dr. Colson kept up a running commentary about the female patient, her symptoms, health history, and the procedure that was underway. After nearly three hours, she announced, "Okay! Let's close up." Turning to Carlos, she asked, "Doctor, do you have any questions?"

Carlos noticed the twinkle in the surgeon's eyes. "One thing I don't understand. What is the source of the kidney you used? Where did it come from?"

"Good question, Doctor. This lady was on dialysis for about three years. During most of that time, she was on a recipient list waiting for a kidney. I suppose some poor devil had an accident and, luckily for us, had made arrangements to donate his organs. So here we are." After only the briefest pause, she asked, "How do transplants work in Mexico?"

"Frankly, I'm not sure. That's why I asked."

"We'll check with the lady out at the desk in this unit. I believe she'll have some of the information. We'll be through here in a few minutes." The room grew quiet. Carlos noticed Colson was humming a popular tune as she and her team finished. "Okay," she said, "I'm going out to talk to her family. Thank you all for your good work. Dr. Reynoso, if you have a few minutes, we'll buy you a cup of coffee; my staff will show where. I'll catch up with you in a few minutes."

Carlos sat at the table with the members of the surgical team. They were discussing the challenges of the procedure and reviewing the specific challenges presented by surgery they'd just completed. Carlos managed to ask a question about some special equipment they had used, and one fellow explained that it was a new device that they were trying out. All agreed it had performed its task very well, far better than what they'd used previously.

Soon, Dr. Colson walked in and filled a paper cup with coffee. She sat across the table from Carlos. Her hair had fallen out from under her cap. Speaking to her team she asked, "Well, did you answer all our visitor's questions?"

Smiling broadly, Carlos answered, "Indeed they did, Dr. Colson. I thank you and your team for the invitation. I've spent the last several nights reading over the treatise you gave us at the conference, so the procedure made sense to me. This has been very interesting. Thank you again."

"You're welcome; it was our pleasure. We may be doing some trials trying some of the new artificial units out on pigs later on. If you're interested, we'll give you a call," she offered. He noticed the same bemused look in her eyes that he had seen in her photograph.

Genuinely impressed, Carlos answered, "Yes! Of course; any time. And I'd be very interested in any material you can suggest for me to read."

"Great! We'll put you on the mailing list, but you'll be sorry! We have your address already and I'll ask my secretary to send you some material. Leave your phone number with Susan here, and we'll let you know when we're about to do those artificials." Colson stood up and, coffee in hand, left through the swinging doors of the room. The door continued to swing after she left.

Instead of reporting to Angelus, Carlos went to his apartment to write briefs for Dr. Pilabos and for the investigators. There was nothing unusual about the first brief, about his visit and the surgery he'd seen. He concluded with Observations and Personal Opinion:

> *Dr. Adriana Colson is obviously a very talented, skillful surgeon with an enormous reputation. She performs the surgeries with efficiency and confidence. She accompanied it with a running commentary explaining what she was doing. Although she seemed to be somewhat irreverent, she is very serious about her work. She mentioned in jest*

that someone with her skills could do the surgery in her kitchen. I have no reason to doubt that statement. She is doing some experimental work with mechanical kidneys on pigs and suggested I might be interested in this. If she invites me again, should I accept?

He took the brief to the secretary. "Please type this up for me. It's for Dr. Pilabos. Feel free to correct my grammar and spelling. Please make me look good!" He smiled at the secretary as he walked away.

The brief for the investigators would have to have more detail. He decided to start by making a list so he wouldn't forget anything.

Chapter 42
Mr. Gomez

ONNIE WALKED INTO TEAL'S OFFICE, "We're in luck! Mrs. Melgoza just got a call from the guy who's leaning on her for the money. He told her they found out which bank the money is in. They're going to bring some signature cards for her to sign."

"Did they identify themselves?" asked Teal.

"No, but the woman said it's the voice of the same person who's been calling her all along." She looked at her partner, "What do we do now?"

Teal was pensive. "I think we should be at the house, waiting for this lowlife. Perhaps we should make an arrest. Maybe this will put pressure on these guys. When are they supposed to contact the old lady?"

"Tomorrow afternoon," answered Connie. "I agree. I think we need to make them sweat a bit."

"Can you set it up?"

"I'll see to it." Connie went to her desk and made a series of calls.

The young woman walked tentatively to the door and knocked, "Mrs. Melgoza? I'm Tencha Valenzuela from the notary's office in Oxnard. I've come to get your signature on some cards." The old woman opened the door, hesitated, and then let her into the house. The stranger went over to a table and removed several cards from a large envelope. She began to spread them on the table, "Now if you will sign here…"

Connie stepped out of the shadow of the kitchen, as Mrs. Melgoza rose and backed away from the table. "I'm Detective Alonzo with the Ventura County Sheriff's Department. You're under arrest." She said this calmly as she showed Valenzuela her badge. She looked at Connie in bewilderment.

"I don't understand! What are you doing here?" gasped the notary.

Stepping inside and blocking the exit, Teal spoke. "We're with the Ventura County Sheriff's Department, and as Detective Alonzo said, you're under arrest, ma'am." Teal showed her his badge. Turning to Connie, he gave the order: "Read 'er her rights."

When Valenzuela saw Teal's badge, fear rose in her face. As Connie pulled the Miranda card from her pocket, she spoke again. "I don't understand. What's this all about?"

"We'd like to ask you some questions, but you don't have to answer if you don't want to. We want to make it clear to you that you have a right ask for an attorney." Connie addressed the woman in less threatening voice. Then the detective read her the official statement as required by law.

"I don't understand..." Tears welled up in her eyes and streamed down her cheeks as she began to tremble.

"Miss, you're in lots of trouble! Who sent you here to get these signatures from Mrs. Montoya?" asked Teal sternly.

"My father. He has a notary office in Oxnard. He told me to get Mrs. Melgoza's signature on these bank cards then to notarize them. That's all I know." She was now sobbing quietly.

The two detectives looked at each other. Teal said, "Looks like we need to talk to her father." He got the name and address of the business from Valenzuela. To Connie he said, "You wait here with her. I'm going to Oxnard to talk to her dad." He got the name of the business and its address from the notary, verified it in Mrs. Melgoza's phone book, then left.

Connie called in a plainclothes officer as her backup. She didn't want one of the people who had threatened Mrs. Melgoza to show up while she was here alone, and Connie knew she'd be needing to leave soon.

The squat, heavyset notary looked up from his desk smiled at Teal, "Good afternoon! I'm Andres Valenzuela. What can I do for you?" He extended his hand.

Teal sat down, blocking his exit from behind the desk. He ignored the hand and showed his badge, saying quietly, "I'm Detective Teal with the

Ventura County Sheriff's Department. We have just arrested your daughter."

The color drained from the man's fleshy face. "Why? What has she done?"

"Right now we have her in custody, but we will book her for threatening an old lady and for trafficking drugs. If convicted, she'll spend fifteen to twenty years in state prison is my guess," said Teal.

"I don't know what you mean!" he said. "I sent her to Santa Paula to notarize some papers. What has she done?" The man's jowls began to tremble. Sweat began to bead on his forehead.

"The cards your daughter was to notarize were based on threats made to the lady regarding money held in Mexican banks. The money came from drug deals and other illegal activities." The detective's voice grew more ominous. "Your daughter will not be a young woman when she gets out of prison."

"But she doesn't know anything," spluttered Valenzuela. "I just sent her to sign some papers. She does this for me all the time. That's our business here. That's what we do," he said, fear rising in his face.

"In that case I have to inform you that you're also under arrest." Teal read him the Miranda statement. "Perhaps you should call an attorney, which is what I recommend to you. But we need some answers to some very serious charges, or you and your daughter both just may be in prison for a very long time." Teal's voice was low, cold and calculating. The effect on the notary was chilling.

"I still don't know what you're talking about. What do you want to know?" he asked.

"If you and your daughter are not involved, then tell me, who asked you to get Mrs. Melgoza to sign those cards?"

"Some guy came in earlier today. He asked if we would get the lady's signatures and notarize them at her place. He's supposed to call here later to see if they're ready so he can pick them up," said the man, now somewhat calmer.

Teal picked up the phone. "Connie, scribble some fake signatures on those cards and let the Valenzuela girl go. Tell her to come back to her office and act as if she'd gotten the cards signed. Follow her at a distance; we'll wait for you here."

It had taken Connie some time to calm the young woman down. She just couldn't stop crying. She'd rushed into the bathroom and vomited to the point of dry heaves. Only after Teal's call, when Connie told her what was she was about to do, did she settle down. Connie assured Tencha that her part in pulling this off would look good if she actually did end up having to go to court. Quickly, Connie handed her a washcloth and told her to wash her face and refresh her makeup. Connie quietly told the plainclothes officer to follow Valenzuela. "I want to stay a few minutes here with Mrs. Melgoza to make sure she's okay."

Connie parked her car across from the notary's office. She walked into a convenience store, bought a soda and a newspaper, and waited in her car. Within minutes she saw an obese man walk toward the office. His neck bulged with a huge goiter. Fat made his legs swing slightly out as he walked. Even from across the street she could see the business owner blanch when he saw the man enter.

The big man pulled out his wallet, removed several bills, placed them on the counter, and picked up a large envelope. As he turned to leave, Teal intercepted him ID in hand. Connie took a long drink of her soda before crossing the street. She glanced carefully all around to see if the fat man had company. When she walked in, she heard Teal say, "You have the right to remain silent..."

"Ah, Connie!" he said. "It looks like we finally caught our man. Call in a squad car. Have them take him to jail and book him for murder, drug trafficking, and conspiracy. That should put him away for a while." He paused, then added, "Let's call our two friends from the Feds; they might want to join us when we talk to our friend here."

Connie walked up behind the man and made him lean up against the counter. Then she kicked his feet to make him spread his legs apart. His arms were so short and fat that she had difficulty getting the handcuffs on him. With his full weight leaning against the counter, she pulled one hand behind his back, cuffed it, and then cuffed it to the other. She patted him down. Just inside his pants she found a small handgun in a leather holster. It was wet with sweat. She put it on the counter. She turned him around and continued the search. The goiter on his neck was huge. It grew from his left ear to his shoulder. Connie tried not to look at it. The man said nothing and made no noise except for his labored breathing. The huge growth made his small eyes recede into the fat. Connie could feel the hate radiating from them.

The patrol deputy came in and repeated the search. Connie noticed he had surgical gloves on. She watched the deputy struggle to get the man into the back seat of his patrol car. It was almost comical.

She opened her purse and broke open the seal of a wet wipe packet. She carefully washed her hands with it. Not satisfied, she removed another one and repeated the process.

"Connie, before we leave, why don't you take a statement from the young lady? I'll take one from Mr. Valenzuela." Turning to address him, Teal asked, "Is it okay if we use your office?" The man nodded.

Chapter 43
The Interview

THE **FBI** AGENTS WALKED INTO THE INTERVIEW ROOM at the county jail just as Detective Sergeant Teal was called to the phone. As he listened, Teal's eyes lit up. "Bring it right over," he said, "and thanks!" He put the phone back in its cradle. "It's our lucky day!" he said to the agents and Connie. "We'll be getting some good news before we talk to our buddy."

Teal and Alonzo had brought in a long, slim table for the four of them to sit behind. On it sat a tape recorder and a couple of blank tapes. A single chair sat across the room. The assembled group exchanged the usual greetings and took their seats. They discussed various strategies for the interview to come and decided upon one, agreeing to be flexible as things went along.

Then the lab manager arrived. Without bothering to introduce her, Teal said, "Okay, Sally, what've you got for us?"

"Remember how we had another distinct print that we couldn't ID on the gun that the Melgoza kid had in his hand? Guess what? It matches the guy you booked last night. It's a perfect match, no doubt about it." Smiling, she handed a single page report to Teal and turned to leave.

"Thanks, Sally! Great work… and just in time, too!" he called after her. He then turned to the others. "On a hunch I asked the lab to compare Gomez' prints to anything we'd picked up in this case so far, and so here we are." He waved the paper at his visitors.

Agent Miller smiled, "Good! That will certainly make questioning this fellow more interesting."

While they waited for the fat man Miller asked, "Have you both read Dr. Reynoso's reports about his two meetings with Colson?" Teal and Connie both acknowledged seeing them. "It seems that our boy may have struck Colson's fancy."

"What do you mean?" asked Connie.

"Well it's not every day such an important surgeon invites someone just out of med school to observe a procedure." Miller would have continued, but noted a slight commotion in the hall.

"Ah! Here comes our boy," said Teal.

The fat man with the goiter was escorted in and told to sit in the single chair. His escorts left to wait in the break room. The orange prison jumpsuit Gomez now wore made his ugly growth seem even more prominent. The hate of the previous night had turned into fear. He eyed the two FBI agents closely as Teal introduced them to him.

"Mr. Gomez, "For your information and for the record, this session is being tape recorded. Present this morning are: Detective Constancia Alonzo, FBI agents Dr. Thomas Miller and Susan Moore, and myself, Detective Sergeant Ronald Teal and of course you, Mr. Jacinto Gomez. Mr. Gomez, please indicate for the record that the people I named are present at this meeting?"

"Yes," Gomez answered in a heavy accent. It sounded like "djess."

"Mr. Gomez," continued Teal, "I understand you have been informed of your rights. Is that correct?" inquired Teal. When Gomez nodded in the affirmative, Teal continued. "You have the right to have an attorney present. You do not have to answer any questions. You are here voluntarily; you have agreed to cooperate with this investigation. Is that correct?" asked Teal. Though these questions were redundant, there had been cases lost when someone neglected to review the accused rights before interviewing them and Teal wasn't going to allow that to happen.

"You understand, Mr. Gomez," continued Teal, "that you have been charged with first the first degree murder of Juan Melgoza. If you are tried and convicted, it could mean the death penalty."

Head lowered, the man nodded. "Please answer the question Mr. Gomez."

"I understand."

"Mr. Gomez, the FBI agents are also interested in this case but for other reasons which we will explain in a bit. It is possible. I repeat, it's *possible* that the first degree murder charge could be lowered, so that the county would not have to ask for the death penalty if you cooperate with their investigation. If convicted, you would still go to prison, but there would be no death penalty. Do you understand?"

Beads of sweat glistened on Gomez' face and rivulets of moisture ran down the taut skin of his goiter. Teal nodded to Connie, who had a series of three-by-five cards with a question on each.

"Please state your full name and address." she asked. Connie wrote quickly as he answered and put the first card aside. She continued with a series of questions to establish identity.

Then she asked, "Do you know a person by the name of Juan Melgoza?" Gomez seemed startled; the fat of his face quivered. Connie produced an envelope, and from it, drew out a series of photographs. She fanned them out in front of him. One photo was of a young man with a faint smile. The four others were of the dead youth, taken from various angles. "For the record, I am showing Mr. Gomez a series of photographs of the deceased," said Connie toward the recorder.

To herself, Connie read a question from one of her three-by-five cards. She looked Gomez in the eye as she asked, "Mr. Gomez, did you kill Juan Melgoza?" Though the skin over the goiter was stretched taut, the growth appeared to quiver. Gomez looked around the room, as if looking for some way to escape.

Connie smelled the strong odor of urine. She noticed the orange jumpsuit cloth darken as the dampness spread. The man followed Connie's gaze to his crotch. He realized he had wet himself.

Connie repeated the question slowly. "Mr. Gomez, did you kill Juan Melgoza?"

"Yes," he said meekly.

"Would you speak louder, Mr. Gomez? Did you kill Juan Melgoza?" she asked more forcefully.

"Yes, I killed him! I killed him!" he repeated, this time, much more loudly.

She picked up another card. "And exactly *why* did you kill Juan Melgoza, Mr. Gomez?"

"The sonofabitch stole the money that we were supposed to share!

The dumb bastard took the cash and put it in a Tijuana bank. We had the money in small bills like we planned, and he went and deposited it!"

"So, where did this money come from?" asked Connie.

"I dunno, but it was what we agreed to," said the fat man.

"How much money was it?"

"Fitty grand."

Connie noted the amount on the card. "Why was it paid to you and Juan Melgoza?"

"We were paid $50,000 for the kidney." Gomez now seemed resigned, even relaxed, and spoke more freely. He even smiled, as if divulging the information was humorous in some way. Creepy as it made her feel, Connie realized he was either proud of having "earned" such an amount, or more likely, he was at last realizing that, by divulging this information, he was helping himself.

Connie raised an eyebrow toward Agent Miller, who picked up the questioning, "Mr. Gomez, thank you for your willingness to cooperate with our agency. We will certainly take note of your cooperation. Now, where did the kidney come from?" asked Miller.

"Tijuana."

"How did you transport it and where did you deliver it?"

As if sharing a joke, Gomez said, "We crossed it from Tijuana with the pollos. It was in a Donald Duck t'ermos. Then we drove it to the L.A. Hilton Hotel by the airport and jus' left it in a room."

"You carried it in a child's thermos jug?" asked Miller in astonishment.

"A Donald Duck t'ermos. You know, like little kids carry to school. The ones with the wide mouth?" He made a circle with the two fingers of each hand indicating the large opening. Then he added, "In tomato juice."

Teal now interrupted, "Your mean to tell us that you smuggled the kidney into this country in a thermos of tomato juice?"

"Djess!" The fat man chuckled.

"You actually put the kidney in tomato juice?" asked Teal.

"Well, not me. But firs' they seal the kidney in a plastic bag. They put it in the bottom of the t'ermos and then they fill it up with cold tomato juice and ice cubes."

The agents and detectives exchanged astonished looks. Then Miller pressed on. "You delivered it to the Airport Hilton. Who did you give it to there?"

"We go to the desk, an' they give us a key. We just go to the room, pick up a briefcase with our money in it. We leave Donald Duck and take off. That's it," answered the self-satisfied Gomez.

"Is that exactly what happened the last time you delivered a kidney?" asked Teal.

"No. The last time, I had to deliver some *pollos* to Fresno. Juan delivered the tomato juice and picked up the money. I din't see him for two days. I guess that was when he opened the bank account in Tijuana. What a dumb kid," finished the fat man more quietly.

"Now think carefully, Mr. Gomez," urged Agent Miller, "do you have any idea where the money came from? Do you know who picked up the kidney, or where it went after you delivered it?"

"No. All we were doin' was picking up our money."

"How many times or how often have you transported these thermoses?" Teal asked.

"Once or twice a year, not often. But we didn't always carry tomato juice. We carried other stuff," added Gomez.

"Like what?" asked Connie.

"You know, we did favors for some powerful men in Tijuana. Since we were leading the *pollos* already, we just carried backpacks for these men." Gomez seemed to relax.

"Mr. Gomez, we appreciate your cooperation," said Connie, following notes on one of her cards. "Later on, you will receive a written copy of our conversation today. When you get the transcript, please read it over very carefully. You may ask us to make changes if you think something was copied incorrectly. Then we would like you to sign it. I understand you have an appointment with the attorney who was assigned to you. I suggest you listen carefully to his advice."

Teal headed down the hall to retrieve the prisoner escorts. They transported Gomez back to his jail cell.

The four law enforcement officers sat and looked at each other. The smell of urine lingered heavily in the office. Teal opened a window to let in some fresh air. Teal said, "Dr. Miller, you're in the medical business. Is what he said about transporting the organ in tomato juice actually possible?"

"On the surface it's weird as heck, but it does make sense. If the kidney is sealed well in the plastic, the juice and ice cubes will not only keep it cool, but protect it from being bounced around and bruised," explained Miller. "Hell, even the Donald Duck thermos bottle makes sense. Who would ever dream there was a smuggled kidney inside it?" The FBI agent chuckled.

"But where did the kidney go? Who picked it up and who rented the room at the Hilton?" asked Teal.

"Good questions," said Miller. "And who received a transplant three days before Melgoza was murdered?"

"And, come to think of it, who do you suppose got Melgoza's kidney?" added Agent Moore.

Teal said, "It seems that your agency is in a better position to answer these questions. We'll continue talking to Gomez. Somehow, even though we scared the piss out of him, he may be holding back something he knows, or perhaps something he's not even aware he knows."

"That's a fair summary, Ron. Let's go with these questions 'til something turns up. In the meantime, what should we do with Reynoso?'

"What do you mean, 'What should we do with Reynoso?'" Connie asked, as calmly as she could manage.

"We got a call from the boys at Immigration and Naturalization. They're ready to issue him a permanent residency card or at least a *green card*. They asked if they should... or perhaps we could hold it over him to make him a bit more cooperative?" hinted Miller, raising an eyebrow.

Before Connie could answer, Teal jumped in emphatically, "Reynoso has done everything we've asked him to do. Without his insight, we wouldn't be having this conversation at all. And it's my hunch that he'll continue to be helpful in the future. Yes, I definitely think that the immigration guys should issue the card. He deserves it."

Miller smiled, "That's our sense too, but we wanted to make sure you were in agreement with us."

Teal turned to his partner. "Connie, what do you think? Is it time to reward the good doctor?"

Thoughtfully, Connie flipped her three-by-fives. "Yeah, I agree. It's true; he has been very cooperative and helpful. We shouldn't stand in the way of this opportunity for him." Thinking a moment, she continued, "I also think he will be willing to help in the future."

The FBI agents stood up and gathered their belongings to leave. "Good," said Miller. "We'll pass on the word to the boys at INS. They should have the cards out to him in a few days."

The two detectives remained for a moment without speaking, in the lingering smell of urine. Finally Connie spoke. "Thanks for jumping in before I said something I would have regretted."

"You're welcome," said Teal easily. "You'd have done the same for me. Anyway, I think Miller was toying with you just to get a rise from you. But I agree with you; we're not through with Dr. Reynoso. I'm sure we'll be talking to him soon enough." He continued, "Have you seen him recently?"

"Well, since we made the trip to Fresno, his uncle was hurt in an accident. I saw him briefly then. We were mostly talking about the accident and the kid who caused it. Carlos comes to visit them every weekend. Is there some reason we should talk to him?"

Teal smiled, "I don't think you need a reason, but I do think it's a good idea to keep seeing him to keep up with what he's been up to. Think you can handle that?"

Connie smiled at the prospect. "I can handle that." She gathered her three-by-five cards and the two headed out to their cars.

Chapter 44
Clinic Day

W HEN CARLOS STOPPED TO PICK UP LUZ for their Saturday visit
to the downtown clinic, he was surprised to see Ann. The two
were waiting on the corner, drinking coffee. Ann had an extra
cup in her hand and a sly smile on her face.

Luz said to Carlos, "I brought coffee, some *tamales* for breakfast, and
a friend. I hope you don't mind." The two women climbed into the pickup.
"Of course not; we need the help. After all, *someone* has to sweep up the
place," replied Carlos with a grin.

Although it was only midmorning, it was already hot. The forecast
offered no relief. This time the clinic was full. The line of people flowed
out the door and down the sidewalk. Many of them wore all the clothing
they owned, even though the heat was unbearable. Toddlers ran around
in just their diapers. The crowd parted to let the three friends into the
clinic. Luz addressed the receptionist with orange hair, "What happened?
Where did all these people come from?"

"The word is out that we have a young, handsome doctor with great
hands. It seems they all want to be touched by him." She smiled at Ann
and Luz. Carlos apparently missed her point.

The heat intensified the smell of poverty in the office. Yet the people
were friendly, cordial, and respectful of each other. The parking attendant from across the street brought several boxes of doughnuts and
distributed them to everyone. In a very short time they were all eaten. He
picked up the empty boxes and returned to his post across the street.

Carlos took his time with his patients. He put his arms around them and picked up the babies and played with them as he examined them.

A young man wearing an overcoat and a wool stocking cap despite the heat stood up. Suddenly, he began to yell and scream, frightening everyone. Babies cried and their mothers cowered. He charged at the patients in the waiting room. People retreated into each other like metal filings pulled away by a magnet. Hearing the commotion Carlos, and Luz ran to the reception room. The man turned quickly to confront the two dressed in white coats, "Who are you?" he challenged them loudly.

Carlos responded softly, "My name is Carlos. What's yours?"

"I nuh… know who you are!" he said in fear. "You… you're one of *them!*" The young man's face was flushed and saliva sprayed out as he spoke.

"No, I am not one of them. I am one of *you*," said Carlos calmly.

"You're not li… like me; you can't be," The man retreated slightly.

"Yes, I am one of you and you are one of me. We are brothers and these are your brothers and sisters," Carlos countered, gesturing slowly with an open hand toward those in the room.

"If they are my b… brothers, why do they reject me? Why d… do they hate me?" He looked at the people cowering by the wall.

"They don't reject you. It's just that they too feel rejected. We all feel doubt in some ways. We don't reject you. We just don't know you yet. So, what's your name?" asked Carlos.

"Tuh, tuh, Tommy," the bewildered youth stammered.

"Tommy, you're one of us. We're your family. Families love each other, even sometimes when we don't act like it. But we're still family. I'm your brother." Carlos reached out, slowly took the man's hand, and drew him to himself in a gentle embrace. A young woman holding a baby was standing nearby. She approached the two men. The room was quiet. Even the street noise seemed to lessen. The woman slowly handed her baby to the man. "This is your baby brother," she said.

The man looked at the baby. The child had no shirt on, just some red shorts over his diaper. He was waving his little arms and legs. The baby focused on the man's eyes. Someone brought a chair and the man sat down, the baby in his arms. "His name is Jesús," she said.

"Jesús is muh… my brother?" he asked.

"Yes," said the young mother. "He is your brother and I am your sister." Several people now approached the two. Slowly, someone in the back began to applaud, within seconds the entire room was in an uproar.

"How do you feel now, Tommy?" asked Carlos.

"Better. Th.. this is nice. I'm sorry. I feel fuh… fine, but my legs won't let me sleep at night."

"Well now, let's go take a look at your legs." The baby was still focused on Tommy's eyes. Carlos gently took the baby and returned him to his mother. The two men followed Luz into one of the exam rooms.

Gently but firmly, Luz convinced the man to undress to his shorts. Once the several layers of clothes were removed, they revealed a skinny, pale body with prominent ribs and joints. While Carlos tended the legs, Luz took a wet towel washed the man's face and body. She asked him, "Tommy, when did you last eat?"

"I don't re… re… remember, I don't…, I cuh… can't…" he stammered.

"Okay, Tommy. Those sores on your legs are infected. Now that I've cleaned you up and put some ointment on your sores, I'll put some bandages on for you. That will help you need to keep those areas clean. Put this medicine on them every day. Will you do that for me?" asked Luz.

"Yuh… yes ma'am," replied the young man.

"Hey, Luz. What happened to those tamales?" asked Carlos. She dashed out for a moment and handed three to Carlos.

"Here's the rest of the medicine, he said. Eat one tamale now, then the second one in four hours, and the third one before you go to bed. Do you think you can do that for me?"

The man nodded and smiled for the first time. He immediately began devouring the first tamale with obvious delight.

"Good! We'll be here next Saturday. I want to see you again. I know all your brothers and sisters will want to see you as well, especially now that you have a little brother."

"Thank you Doctor; thank you Nurse," The young man walked out the door licking the corn husk of the first tamale.

It was midafternoon before the waiting room was cleared. All three finally realized how exhausted and hungry they were. "Well, Doctor Reynoso! I have to say, I was very impressed with you today. You have marvelous bedside manner! But you *did* give away our lunch, so now you need to rectify that," said Luz, a twinkle in her eye.

"I'd be glad to! Any suggestions?"

"Let's go to Philippe's! We can get some great sandwiches there," offered Ann.

"...and a cold beer?" queried Carlos.

"And a cold beer!" affirmed Ann.

The popular eatery was full, yet they got their food quickly. They sat in a corner booth. Carlos ate half his sandwich quickly before he sat back and relaxed. He noticed the sawdust on the floor and people eating in small groups. All of these people, sitting only a few blocks from the clinic appeared to be well-nourished.

After several bites Ann said, "I have to tell you two how impressed I am with what you are doing at the clinic. It's so sad that people live in such a terrible conditions. It's just fantastic what you do to help them."

"Medically, we don't do all that much. The reality is that many just want to be reassured that they're okay," said Carlos.

"Actually," added Luz, "these people are not much different from our patients at Angelus Medical Center. A good number of the people we see there don't actually have a medical problem; they just want some reassurance, too."

"It seems to me then," observed Ann, "that the best medicine might be a hot shower, a haircut and some clean clothes."

Luz answered, "Ann, you're right. That and a bowl of oatmeal would solve half their problems."

"You know what's amazing to me? It's that the clinic sits almost in the shadow of the high rise office buildings of the rich, some banks, and a government building. Yet some people, like poor Tommy, don't have enough to eat," observed Carlos. "People have to scrabble and beg just to get a bandage on their leg. That some people don't have the opportunity to use a clean toilet…" he continued. "And this is the richest country in the world… It's amazing."

Chapter 45
The Confrontation

CARLOS DROVE TOWARD THE ENTRANCE to the ranch's housing area. He was surprised to find a large group of men and children bunched in the open space, nearly blocking the roadway. He drove slowly through the crowd. He saw Paco, one of his older cousins. "What's going on, *primo?*" he asked.

"The union is helping us organize a strike because of the way they treated Tió Francisco," replied his cousin.

"What happened to him?"

"Instead of coming himself and talking to our uncle, Grady sent his chicken shit attorney. He said that it was really Tió Francisco's fault that the kid hit him with his car. Then he said that, because wanted to be fair, he would give him $1,000. On top of that, they will have to move out of the house by the end of the month. They want him to sign a paper giving up his right to sue, too" The young man's face was red with anger.

"Did he sign it?" asked Carlos.

"No, he told them, he needed time to to read it and to have someone in the family explain it to him. Tió told the attorney to come back today." Paco was now even angrier. "That little mousy bastard told him if they didn't sign the paper, he would be evicted from the house in just three days!"

"But they've lived in that house for over twenty-five years!" said Carlos, shocked. "How did the union people know to come?"

"I called them. I heard them say that they protect workers, so I'm giving them an opportunity," Paco said wryly. "I think they're the ones who phoned the paper. See that guy over there?" he asked, pointing to a man with a steno pad and camera. "He's from the Examiner."

"Listen, I'm going to the house to see them. Connie Alonzo will be here in a few minutes. Let her through, will you?"

"You mean that lady cop?" asked his cousin.

"Yeah. Tell her I'll wait for her at the house." Carlos waved goodbye and drove carefully through the crowd.

Carlos walked into his uncle's house. The old man was walking back and forth, leaning on a walker. For the first time in his life, the old man looked frail. He seemed smaller in stature. Tió Francisco's face lit up when he saw his nephew. "Carlitos! I'm so glad you're here!" There were tears in his eyes. Carlos gave him a long, gentle hug.

Tía Estrella, who had heard his voice, came out. She, too had been crying. She hugged Carlos without saying a word and immediately returned to the kitchen to prepare lunch. Just at that moment, Connie knocked and Carlos let her in.

"You remember Connie Alonzo? I asked her to meet me here." Carlos said to his uncle.

"Of course we remember her. I knew her when she was a little girl," said his aunt, peering out of the kitchen. Come here both of you, and you too, *Viejo!* I just made some beans." The old woman's voice had suddenly regained its lilt.

"Let me see the papers that attorney wants you to sign," said Carlos. His uncle pointed to them on a table in the living room. Carlos slowly read the two-page document, then passed it to Connie.

After a few moments, she declared, "I wouldn't sign this on a bet! Basically, it says that Grady has no responsibility, and that your uncle was in a place where he shouldn't have been. Of course, out of the goodness of his heart, he wants to give your uncle $1,000. On top of that, they will have to move. If he doesn't sign, he'll get nothing and will have to move out in three days." Connie's indignant voice was a higher pitch than normal.

"My aunt and uncle have lived here for twenty-five years and raised their family here. Two of their sons also live here. My uncle has worked in the company's orchards all that time. Doesn't that count for anything?" asked Carlos.

"Not according to this agreement," she said, "but it should!"

Carlos shook his head. "I didn't think Mr. Grady was that kind of man. He's always been fair with us in the past."

"If that's so, then I'll bet you Grady may not even know about this. He probably told his law firm to take care of this and one of his pea-brained attorneys dreamed this up."

"What do you suggest?"

"First, send word to the crowd to let the lawyer through when he comes. They can yell at him and cuss him out, but there can't be any violence. You'll talk to him here. I'll just listen. Don't introduce me, but I'll make myself obvious," said Connie.

Carlos heard some commotion from the crowd. "He must be here already."

Soon, the attorney knocked at the door. Carlos invited him in. His face was ashen and his hands sweaty. He hurriedly introduced himself as Alvin Johnson, representing the interests of Grady Farms. "What are all those people doing out there at the entrance?" he asked.

"They were waiting for you. They heard about the chicken shit offer you made to these people. They heard that you threatened them to kick them out of the house... this house where they've lived for over twenty-five years, where they raised all their kids!" Carlos said this is a low, steely voice. He knew he'd frightened the attorney.

"I haven't threatened anyone," the attorney said lamely. "Just who are you?" he asked.

"I'm Doctor Juan Carlos Reynoso." The use of his formal title gave him some authority.

"Mr. Grady has authorized me to make this very fair offer to settle this matter. If Mr. Baca will kindly sign this letter, I have a check here that will resolve the issue," pressed the attorney.

"You call this a fair offer! First you blame this man for the accident he suffered and then threaten to kick his family out of their house if he doesn't sign away his rights! You don't call this a threat?" said Carlos, his voice trembling with anger.

"Of course it's not a threat," answered the attorney evenly, recovering his composure somewhat.

"All those people out front don't think it's fair. The union representatives don't think it's fair. The *press* won't think it's fair and I don't think it's fair!" said Carlos sternly. As he noticed the corner of the attorney's eye twitch, he felt calmer and more sure of himself.

"What union? What press? Who called them?" he asked, worry evident in his expression.

"*You* did, with your chicken shit settlement offer, my friend. *You* did," answered Carlos. He made no secret the scorn he felt.

"Well, we have the law on our side. We are well within our rights to demand they move from this property. We also have the right to remove all the people from this unlawful gathering you have in front of it," declared the attorney. He was sweating now and looking uncomfortable.

Connie, who had quietly observed this interchange finally stepped forward a pace. "Mr. Johnson, I'm Detective Constance Alonzo with the Ventura County Sheriff's Department." She handed the attorney a business card. "Sir, it's my understanding that landlords have to give at least thirty days' notice to evict. For your information, the people you met at the entrance live here. They have a right to be here, as do any guests they invited. I suppose they invited the reporters as well."

"Mr. Grady has the right to protect his property and to do as he sees fit to protect it," countered Johnson.

"Of course Mr. Grady has all those rights and we'll make sure that his rights are protected. But you sir, must respect the rights of these folks, too," said Connie.

Johnson eyed Connie suspiciously. "How is it that you just happen to be here?" he asked.

"That's it exactly," she said. "I just happened to be here on some other official business. This family has been very cooperative with our department, something which we appreciate very much."

With a sigh of resignation, the attorney quietly said, "Okay, what will it take to resolve this situation?" He waited while Carlos discussed the situation with his uncle.

Tió Francisco and Carlos spoke softly for several moments, as Tía Estrella listened in, nodding in agreement from time to time. "My uncle just wants to be treated fairly," started Carlos, "and to resolve this thing in a reasonable manner. He would like his medical bills taken care of. In addition, as you must surely realize, he has just undergone a serious orthopedic operation, and, as his doctor will agree, it will be at least a couple of months before it would be reasonable for him to move to a new location. He also wants Mr. Grady to come here personally, so he can thank him publicly."

"Bu... but what about the union and the... and the reporters?" Johnson stumbled over his words. "What hap... happens to them?" he asked.

"Friend," said Carlos, "you brought all that on yourself, so you get to take care of that on your own. My uncle had nothing to do with that business."

"But Mr. Grady will be ticked off at me!" he protested.

"I'm sure he will be, but that's your problem sir," said Connie, opening the door to usher him out.

It was clear that the attorney's car had reached the front entrance. There was an explosion of noise. People shouted raucously and honked their car horns. This was followed by laughter and singing.

Tió Francisco looked sad. "You know, Carlitos, we've lived here since we came to this country. We've been very happy. We don't want to cause so much trouble that people will lose their jobs or homes. We just need a little time to paint our house in town and fix it up a little. That'll take a little while."

"Don't worry about that. You'll have plenty of time, but it's probably a good idea to give your renters notice to give them time to move, too."

"Would you do that for me please, Carlitos?" asked his uncle.

"Of course. I'll give them a call, then send them a nice letter to make sure they understand."

A few moments later, Carlos's cousin Alberto came into the house. With him was a young man whose long hair was tied back with a red bandanna. He wore a shirt with the sleeves cut off. A droopy mustache framed the lower part of his face.

"This is Johnny Cruz, said Alberto. "He's with the Agri Workers of America."

"Nice to meet you," said Carlos, extending a hand.

Cruz smiled. He walked over to Tía Estrella and gave her a hug, as if he had known her for a long time. She accepted the hug and almost pushed Cruz onto a chair. Within seconds she set a plate of food in front of him. He began to eat.

"Nothing like beans and tortillas," he said appreciatively.

Carlos sat down across the table from him. "Johnny," he asked, "how did you hear about our uncle's problem?"

Johnny smiled. "We have been interested in this company for a long time. How it treats our brothers. One of our supporters let us know how unjustly they were treating your uncle. Then your cousin called us. This is exactly what the union is all about, to help in the fight for justice. So here we are."

"My uncle doesn't want to make any trouble. He just wants to get well, move to his home in town, and plant a garden."

The union man's eyes narrowed icily on Carlos, "That's what we want for *all* of our people. We're tired of our brothers and sisters sacrificing their bodies to make these guys rich, only to be put out to pasture with no grass. You're uncle is lucky. We know he owns a home and probably has some money saved, but most farm workers don't. They are forced to depend on charity."

Carlos opened his mouth to speak, but the union man continued. "Farm work is noble work. We think we men and women who work in the field deserve dignity, not a kick in the ass when we are no longer useful." Carlos was surprised at the intensity and the anger in his voice. He remained silent to let him continue, even though there was a long pause. Johnny's head tilted a bit as he appraised Carlos. "You're the doctor, aren't you?" Carlos nodded. "Well, your kind leaves the fields. In a few years you'll forget the field and the people. You'll be just like the rest of them!"

Carlos's face flushed with anger. "Wait a minute! I worked my ass off here in these orchards for more than ten years to put myself through school to better myself. No one cut me any slack. I paid my dues. I know what rotten work it is to pick lemons, that's why I studied to get out."

Johnny smiled and leaned back in his chair, "Good! Then you can help us organize so *all* our brothers can have a shot of bettering themselves. But if some of us *have* to spend our lives in the field, let us work with dignity."

"What do you mean by helping you organize?" asked Carlos, feeling cornered.

"Well you're now a big man around here. Workers here respect you. They think you're some kind of a hero and they need your help," he said. Still smiling, he took a bite of tortilla.

"I'm no hero. I don't even live here anymore. I just came to visit my uncle and aunt. What can I possibly do?" said Carlos meekly.

"Well, we're here to help your uncle and aunt. We'll be here raising hell until your uncle's taken care of. I'm sure we'll scare the shit out of the owner, and eventually, he'll pay dearly to get rid of us. Don't worry, these nice folks will be taken care of. But we want you to remember the next brother who is in need," said Johnny.

"I already help in a free clinic downtown; I spend most of my Saturdays there," explained Carlos defensively.

"Good! Take care of the drunks, the whores, and the nuts! Let your brothers in the fields, be poisoned, disfigured, and treated like animals, not men. Then you can sleep comfortably in your soft bed," replied Cruz.

Angry, Carlos started to get up. He felt Connie's hand on his shoulder. She pressed down hard enough to prevent him from standing. She also squeezed and the pain of it distracted him. He looked up at her with a surprised frown, but he remained seated. Recovering his composure he said, "We appreciate your help, of course. Putting the pressure on will improve my uncle's chances of being treated more fairly. And I'll certainly think about what I can do to help."

Cruz smiled, stood up extended his hand to Carlos. "You're welcome, Dr. Reynoso. It's our pleasure and duty to help where we can. We appreciate the success you have worked so hard for, and we'll also appreciate any help you can give us." With that, Cruz took another tortilla from the plate, rolled it up, took a bite and, nodding his thanks to Tía Estrella, walked out of the house.

He felt Connie's hand rubbing his shoulder gently where just a few seconds ago there had been a sharp pain. She patted his shoulder, "How does it feel to be baited by an expert?"

"What do you mean 'baited?'"

She sat down beside him. "Dr. Reynoso, you were just baited by some-one who does it all the time. First he insulted you. He taunted you with the hero bit; he questioned your efforts to help at the clinic; then finally, he told you how he's helping your uncle. That made you feel like you had to help him. Then he got you to commit to their cause."

"But I didn't commit to anything."

"Yes you did. You told him you would think of how you could help."

"But that doesn't mean I have to *do* anything," Carlos said helplessly.

"He got you to acknowledge that they are helping your uncle, so he will take credit for anything your uncle gets beyond what that weasel offered. You can be sure that he will come back to remind you of that one of these days."

He smiled meekly, "Am I that easy, that naive?"

She put her arm around his shoulder and hugged him, "Yes, you're a babe in the woods, Doctor. That's why you need someone to take care of you."

"Are you baiting me too?"

"Yes, I'm baiting you, but I am no amateur like Cruz. I get *real* com-mitments right away," she said with a mischievous grin.

"What do I have to do for you?" he asked resignedly, fearing what kind of paperwork or investigative adventure this might entail.

"First, you have to buy me dinner tonight… and maybe dance with me. Then you have to be *very* nice to me," flirted the detective.

"That's all?" he said, smiling with relief.

She leaned down to whisper in his ear, "Oh, that's just for starters…"

Chapter 46
An Evening Out

" "DR. REYNOSO, I HAVE A CERTIFIED LETTER FOR YOU. I hope you don't mind that I signed for it," said the receptionist, reaching for it.

As he looked at the envelope, he saw that it was from the Immigration Service. He opened it hurriedly and out dropped a plastic card. He picked it up from the floor. His photograph looked back at him from the card with a serious expression. It was the famous "green card." Curiously, the card was actually blue. He turned it over and flexed it a couple of times. He was pleased to have the much sought-after card. He knew of people who had paid thousands of dollars for one. Others actually risked their lives and some even died to get one. Yet he had applied just a few weeks ago and now suddenly, he had the prized card in his hands. He stayed in the reception area to read the form letter. Replacing it in the envelope, he continued to look at the card.

The receptionist asked, "Is everything okay, Dr. Reynoso?"

He looked up. "Yes, yes, everything is just fine. Thank you for signing for it. Yes, everything is fine." He walked down the hall toward one of the waiting areas, pensively rubbing the smooth card on his cheek.

Sitting there by herself was Ann. She waved at him. "Hi, Carlos!"

"Ann! How nice to see you! What are you doing here? Are you sick?" he asked as his eyebrows furrowed.

"Of course not, silly! I just came to see you. I thought we could go across the street to eat... if you have a little time?"

Carlos looked at his watch and said, "Sure let's go!" He walked back to the receptionist, "We'll be across the street having lunch, in case anyone needs me."

They sat down. "I haven't heard from you for a couple days. I just wanted to see you. So, what's new?" asked Ann.

He showed her the letter and the card. She read the letter carefully then looked the card over. "Carlos, this is wonderful! But why do they call it a "green card" when it's actually blue?"

"I have no idea. Maybe they ran out of green plastic," he chuckled.

She handed the card back to him, "Carlos, this is such marvelous news."

"Even if it's the wrong color? Do you think I should call it my 'blue' card?"

They ordered lunch. "Tell me about your coming-out party," she urged.

"What coming-out party?"

"Well, you spent close to $1,000 at Kipling Brothers just so you could to go to that medical seminar…"

"The clothes were fine. I felt a little strange in them, but no one else seemed to notice. Thanks you for your help."

"Well, it seems like there ought to be some other use for them. After all, I haven't seeing them on you yet!"

"I guess we'll have to change that, won't we?"

"Since you brought it up, the school is having a dinner for new teachers. I need an escort… someone who has a nice new suit," she said hiding her grin by taking a bite of her sandwich.

"When is it going to be?"

"Next Friday evening."

Carlos thought about it. "Sure! It sounds like fun! Do you want me to pick you up?"

"Actually I thought I'd pick you up, since the dinner is in this part of the valley. Is that all right with you?"

"That's fine, but we can't stay out too late. The next day I have to work downtown at the clinic."

"Don't worry. You'll be in the company of a very proper teacher…at least at the dinner." Carlos blushed and smiled at the thought.

Ann knocked on the door of Carlos's apartment next to the medical center. He was putting on his tie, "Hi, come in," he called. "I'll be ready in a minute." When he came out of his bedroom he was wearing gray slacks, a blue striped shirt, and his blue blazer. "What do you think? I won't embarrass you in front of your friends, will I?"

She looked at him appraisingly. "No, you won't embarrass me. You'll do just fine." She walked around him slowly, "I must admit, I have very good taste."

"Ann thanks for the help. I like the clothes too, even though I'm still a bit uncomfortable wearing such fancy things."

"I was not referring to the clothes."

He smiled. "So, where are we going?"

"To a restaurant not far from here. It's kind of a welcoming party, a pep talk kind of dinner for new teachers. I hope it won't last too long."

Carlos was intrigued to be in the presence of mostly women. Most of the few men in attendance were huddled in a corner. The women moved around greeting each other, some with handshakes others with hugs or kisses on the cheek. Ann held onto Carlos's hand tightly. Her nervousness surprised Carlos.

"This is Dr. Reynoso," she said as moved through the room, introducing him. It was obvious that many of those present were also nervous. On the other hand, Carlos was relaxed and enjoyed himself, chatting amiably with those he met.

One lady asked him, "What's your Ph.D. in?"

"I'm sorry; I'm a medical doctor," answered Carlos.

"Oh!" she said, laughing gently. "You don't have to apologize."

Carlos noticed several people with drinks in hand. He asked Ann, "Would you like a drink? I'm going over there for a beer."

"Sure! Please, but just bring me a soda."

Although the meeting had nothing to do with him, Carlos was interested in the proceedings. He was also intrigued that Ann so nervous in this situation. It was quite a contrast to her usual self-confident personality. He was glad to be of some comfort to her, to serve as someone for her to hang on to for a change.

"Whew! I'm glad that's over," she said as they walked out into the parking lot. "Thanks for coming with me. I hope it wasn't too boring for you." She put her arms around him.

"No, actually I enjoyed myself. It was a different experience for me. It's not too often I'm in a room with lots of pretty women teachers."

"I didn't see any pretty women."

"Well, there were many, but one in particularly caught my eye," teased Carlos.

"Anyone I know?"

"I doubt it. Maybe I'll tell you one of these days."

Chapter 47
A Clinic Helper

" "Dr. Reynoso, you're wanted on line one," the receptionist said as he walked by.

He picked up the phone. "Hello? Dr. Reynoso here."

"Carlos, this is Adriana. How are you?"

"I'm fine," he said, trying hard to place the name.

"I was thinking about you and your impression of the kidney transplant we performed the other day," she said.

Recognizing the voice just as she mentioned the transplant procedure, he was relieved, but a bit surprised Dr. Colson had used her first name. "I was impressed, particularly with how straightforward it can be when there's an efficient team working. It almost looked easy, but of course, that was because you are so experienced."

"That's the trick. It's easy when you know what you're doing. It's become second nature to my team. They react and, more importantly, they anticipate. That's what makes them good." She paused. "Anticipation or thinking ahead is crucial; it saves time, and in our case, it saves lives."

"Anticipation," he replied, I'll have to keep that in mind."

"Anticipation is innate in some people, but it can also be learned. When someone has the gift then gets the training, the results can be magical. That's how I pick and train my team." Carlos said nothing, wondering about the purpose of the call. "And you, Dr. Reynoso, how are you at anticipating?"

Cautiously, Carlos said, "At times I seem to have a sense of what's coming, but I've never really thought about it."

"Good! Then it's something we can discuss. I was wondering if you would like to have lunch tomorrow. It's rare that I have a day free."

"That sounds great, but tomorrow I spend a good part of the day in our downtown clinic. It's part of our community service project at Angelus. I'm afraid it would have to be a very late lunch."

"Where is you clinic located?"

"Downtown Los Angeles, right across from the Greyhound Bus terminal."

During the long silence that followed, Carlos heard a few pages being turned. Dr. Colson was checking her schedule. At last she suggested, "How would you like some help? We can have lunch afterwards."

"Dr. Colson, it would be an honor to have you there of course, but it's just a simple clinic for the poor. Much of what we do is just holding hands and listening."

"That's fine! Perhaps it would do me good to see the people before they get to me. It's been a long time since I've done this, but I can assure you Dr. Reynoso, I won't embarrass you." Her voice had a happy lilt to it.

"Great! We're there to open at 8:00 a.m. You can park at the bus station next door. Tell the parking attendant you're with the *Clinica Central* and he'll keep an eye on your car. As an afterthought he added, "We'll have an extra doughnut for you."

Luz went into a panic. "You invited Dr. Adriana Colson, a famous surgeon, to help at the clinic? I can't believe it! What will she think of our poor little *clinic?* What on earth is she going to do?" She'd hardly breathed as she spoke.

Carlos explained. "First, she invited herself. Second, from the looks of the people out front, we're going to need her help, so we'll just put her to work."

"But how can I tell her what to do?"

"Just like you tell me."

"But I know you, you're just a…" she paused in mid sentence.

"A what?" He smiled understandingly at her, laughing comfortably. "Just treat her like good help, and let's thank God for sending us the extra hands." They drove on and Luz calmed down a bit, but she was still anxious as they arrived.

As they entered the parking lot, the attendant removed the plastic cone next to the clinic. As he got out of his truck, Carlos greeted him. "Good morning, Angel! How are you doing?"

"Just fine, sir. I mean, Doctor," he replied shyly.

"There will be a Dr. Colson here in a few minutes. Save her a spot and keep a good eye on her car. She's an important person and we need her help." Carlos put his arm around the young man as he spoke to him. He turned to go into the office. Suddenly he stopped. "Shit! I forgot the doughnuts! I promised her doughnuts!"

Now Luz was in a real panic. "You promised her doughnuts and you *forgot* them? There's no time to get any now; it's too late!" she exclaimed.

The parking attendant smiled. "Wait a moment." He went into his little booth and brought out six boxes of doughnuts. "Day old, but they're good," he grinned.

Carlos took the boxes, "Angel, you're a life saver!" Can I pitch in a few bucks to cover the cost?"

"No problem, Doc," said the attendant. "They're day-old from my mother's shop. It's her way of helping out."

"Well then, please pass on our appreciation to her. She gives everyone a big boost with these," he replied. Carlos and Luz headed toward the clinic's door.

"Carlos," whispered Luz, "you're *not* going to feed her day-old doughnuts, are you?" she protested, as they entered the office.

"Why not? If they're good enough for our clients, they're good enough for her." He took one from the top box and ate it as they brought the boxes to the reception area.

From the reception area, they could see that the sidewalk outside the clinic was cluttered with people and their belongings. Backpacks, grocery carts, wagons, rolled blankets. There was even a small dog, half-asleep on a sleeping bag. He was tied to a corner of it with a thin cotton rope. The clinic's interior was also full. Carlos placed the doughnuts on the desk. The orange-haired receptionist was chewing gum loudly. "Ah, the doughnut man has arrived!"

Carlos opened a box took out another doughnut. "Good morning,

Thelma! Dr. Adriana Colson will be here shortly. Put her to work. Oh, and save a doughnut for her."

The patients began to stream through. Carlos examined them, listened to them and talked with them. Once they were treated, Luz escorted them back out into the waiting room.

"Did Dr. Colson get here yet?" he asked Luz, when she returned.

"She got here right after we did. She's wonderful! She jumped right in and even seems to be having fun."

"It must be the doughnuts!" he laughed. Luz frowned at the joke.

The work continued into the afternoon. Carlos saw Colson as she escorted a woman and her baby back to the reception room. The doctor wore white sneakers and white jeans, topped with a white jacket. Her hair was wrapped in a bright red bandanna so she wouldn't have to flip the long strands back as she worked. Dr. Colson was only about five feet tall, quite slim and almost child-like, yet her persona was much larger. She seemed to tower over people even when she looked up at them.

Everyone in the clinic sensed her power and reacted accordingly. She got respect and deference almost automatically. Colson seemed to sense her impact on people. She used it to put people at ease, but also to command movement without asking for it. Carlos smiled to himself as he observed this phenomenon. She looked up at him from across the room, acknowledged his presence with a lift of her brow, and then turned into the examining room she was using.

It was three o'clock before they finished seeing their last patients. Carlos, Luz and Dr. Colson gathered around the orange-haired receptionist.

"Boy, that was something!" said Adriana Colson. "Is it like this all the time?"

"All the time," answered Thelma, "especially since the word about our new doctor got out," she said, smiling and nodding toward Carlos.

"Where do you get your supplies?" asked Colson.

"Some from our medical center, which is stuff that has expired, and some things are pharmacy samples. The day-old doughnuts come compliments of the parking attendant and his mother," explained Carlos.

"We have some supplies you can use. I'll send them over next Saturday."

"Anything you can spare will be very welcome," said Carlos, smiling.

"Luz, I'm very impressed with your sense of organization here. Where do you work when you're not here?" asked Colson.

"I just got my RN certificate and now I work for Angelus Medical Center. I think I'll probably continue there after my discernment period."

Colson looked at Luz carefully, "What's a discernment period?"

"I'm considering joining the Sisters of Social Services. I'm going to spend part of this summer living with them, so we can check each other out." Luz answered, "But I'll continue to be a nurse regardless, somewhere or other."

Colson looked at Carlos meaningfully. "Well Luz, if people around here don't treat you right, come see me."

Luz made a humorously wicked face at Carlos. "Thank you Dr. Colson. You never know when I might show up on your doorstep."

"Well, Carlos, now that I've put my time in, it's time you kept your end of the bargain." She removed the red bandana and shook out her hair.

Chapter 48
Stella

"Connie, Gomez' attorney wants to meet with us. She's on her way up; says she just wants to touch base with us. You have any idea what she wants?" asked Detective Sergeant Teal.

"No I don't. I didn't know he had an attorney yet. Who'd he get hooked up with?" she asked.

"Stella Bright."

Just as he mentioned her name, a very large, white-haired woman slowly ambled into the room. She was breathing heavily. The attorney was fat, very fat. Her huge arms stretched the fabric of the tent-like dress she wore. It looked like a housecoat. The tension on the dress caused the buttons to make a series of scalloped edges down the center of the dress. Her briefcase was a large canvas bag which trailed her, riding on a wheeled luggage dolly. Her makeup has been carefully applied, somewhat shocking in its bold colors. Perched atop her white, tightly-curled hair was a pair of dark glasses that partially disappeared in her hair. She arrived enveloped by a faint smell of a lavender. Her whole persona and scent quickly dominated the room.

"Hello, Ronnie! How the hell are you? Haven't seen you since you guys screwed up the Sanchez case a couple of years ago." The words came out in short segments punctuated by gasps as she caught her breath. She sat down without being offered one. As she sat, the chair groaned and seemed to disappear. She glanced at Connie but seem to ignore her.

Teal's face tensed, but he said, "Doing fine, Stella, doing fine. How about you? Have been keeping busy?"

"I'm *always* busy. I deal with lots of assholes. There's always a big supply of those it seems."

Teal chuckled. "Now, that's not a nice way to refer to your clients," he chided.

"I wasn't referring to my clients… or anyone in this room, heh." The last syllable came with effort, as she'd run nearly out of air. She pulled the cart closer and removed a file from the bag. This time she took a more deliberate look at Connie.

"Stella, this is Detective Connie Alonzo, she's my new partner."

"Speaking of assholes, what happened to your old partner? What a useless twit he was!" Her brash manner certainly did not help Connie to see her as a professional.

"Joe retired a year ago," responded Teal without emotion.

Stella looked at Connie, "Well honey, don't get the wrong idea. This bag of shit and I went to school together. In fact, we even dated a couple of times… had some good times, if I remember well."

"It's nice to finally meet you. I've heard lots about you," said Connie.

"If you heard it from Ronnie, it's probably true. The rest of the assholes around here wouldn't know the truth if it bit them in the ass."

Connie smiled at Teal. He rolled his eyes in return.

"Ronnie, didn't your mommy tell you if you made a face, it would freeze that way?" Stella wheezed.

Somewhat embarrassed, Teal cleared his throat and attempted to change the course of the conversation. "So, what can we do for you today, Stella?" he asked in his best businesslike voice.

"I want to talk about Tomás Gomez. But I first want to make a formal complaint. The poor fellow has a huge growth on his neck and you haven't provided him any medical attention." She pulled out a letter and handed it to Teal. "You know better than that, Ronnie. Gomez may be a prisoner, but you have no right to neglect him. He's still a human being."

"Now come on, Stella. He's had that thing for years. It's nothing he got here."

"How do I know you didn't beat the shit out of him and cause it?" she asked without looking up from her file.

At this point, Connie couldn't help but step in. "Ms. Bright, we *certainly* did not mistreat Mr. Gomez! We have made every effort to treat him with dignity. If you think I would be part of mistreating someone, you have another thing coming." Connie's voice had an edge.

Bright studied Connie briefly. "Well Ronnie, it looks like you don't have a wallflower here. This one seems to have balls." Turning to Connie, she continued, "I know you didn't beat him, but the fat bastard is still one of us. He still requires medical treatment even if he had the problem before he was arrested."

"We'll make sure someone takes a look at Mr. Gomez," said Connie.

"Thank you, Dearie. Now that wasn't all that difficult, was it?" smiled Bright. The smile was that of a satisfied predator, enjoying its kill.

"Ms. Bright, what else can we do for you?" continued Connie, anxious to finish with the woman.

"I'll tell you Dearie. What you can do for me is tell me why you interrogated my client without me being present. You know very well, the man has a right to have his attorney present." Stella's voice now was deeper and serious. As she squinted, her eyes grew smaller as they receded into her face.

"Mr. Gomez was read his rights at the time of his arrest. That, of course, included his right to be provided with an attorney. He was once again notified of his rights when we interviewed him in this office in the presence of two FBI agents. We have his consent in a recording, as well as in writing, a document which I'm sure you have already received." Connie's voice was businesslike, but her tone told the attorney she had crossed the line.

"I understand you threatened him with the death penalty! That's as good as kicking him in the balls." Bright was now wheezing heavily.

"Ms. Bright, we mentioned to Mr. Gomez that one of the possible penalties for a first degree murder conviction is the death penalty. We certainly mentioned that, as you'll note in the record. It was no threat." Connie continued, her voice now especially calm. "As you know, we found a gun on Mr. Gomez. In addition, his fingerprints matched those on the gun we found with Mr. Melgoza. What's more, Gomez told us he killed him because Melgoza wouldn't tell him where to find his half of the money he felt he was due. This was, of course, from a delivery they had made. He made no bones about it." Connie took some three-by-fives out and jotted a few notes on them.

The fat woman turned to Teal and suddenly asked, "Ronnie, what would it take to drop the first degree charge?"

Teal responded quietly. "Stella, there's much more to this than just the Melgoza murder. We're also interested in some drug smuggling and other stuff that we think Gomez knows about. He told us precious little about that, even though he said he would cooperate. If he *were* to cooperate, we'd be willing to talk to the DA, and perhaps the FBI who also have an interest in this, about considering some kind of reduced charge."

"Are you telling me you can get the assholes at the DA's office to reduce the charge?"

"Now Stella, you know damned well I can't tell them what to do. What I said was that I would be willing to talk to them, try to convince them to reduce the charges if Mr. Gomez provides us with some useful information."

"What if he told you everything he knows, but then you didn't think the stuff was useful? Then what?"

"Then we would be back at square one, I guess. Still, I think his cooperation would have some effect on the prosecution."

"I'll make a deal with you two. You get a specialist to see Gomez about the goiter, and I'll *try* to get him to cooperate with you. We can take care of this day after tomorrow." The wheezing now was less pronounced than it had been, though after she spoke, the fat continued to jiggle a bit.

"Stella, you know how these specialists are. It takes forever to get an appointment. What if we can't get one with this guy?" pressed Teal.

Stella smiled smugly as she reached into the file for a card. "Don't worry Ronnie. This guy has a slot open tomorrow. Just call him." She handed over the business card and labored to rise. Connie moved forward to help but was waved off. "Dearie, it was nice to meet you. Do me a favor? Don't let the assholes in this place get to you. You look like a nice girl. I sure would hate to see you turn into a useless twit like Ronnie's old partner." The woman had to turn sideways to get through the door. The little cart bounced against the door jamb.

Even after Stella Bright had left, her presence lingered in the remaining hint of lavender perfume. Teal looked at the business card carefully and handed it over to Connie. "I didn't know you were good friends with a famous attorney!" exclaimed Connie, awed. "Was she always so…"

"Fat?" filled in Teal. "Actually, believe it or not, she was a knockout in school. She was a cheerleader and had a body that women and men would kill for. Only her brashness hasn't changed."

"What happened to her?"

"I'm not sure. She went off to UC Berkeley and I lost track of her. Next time I saw her, she was a defense attorney and was even heavier than she is now."

"Boy, she's quite a package."

"Connie, don't ever let her fool you. She is one of the sharpest attorneys around. Some of the boys at the DA's office always try to avoid her, especially those with political ambitions. She'll make them crawl and look like worms if this gets to trial."

"What about this business about getting Gomez to see a specialist? Is there something here that I don't see?"

"I don't see anything either at the moment, but you can damned well bet she's not pushing this for his looks. This is just her first move. We won't see the reason till much later in the game, if we see it all," replied Teal thoughtfully. "You'd better call the guy to set up the appointment. I'll call Miller and Moore to see if they want to be here for the meeting with Gomez."

Everyone was sitting at the table, with Bright and Gomez at the far end. There was tension in the room. The detectives and FBI agents were alert, and Bright and her client were making every effort to appear calm. Gomez, was surprisingly successful at this.

Ron Teal reached to the tape recorder in the middle of the table and punched a button to start it. Looking around the table he said, "For the purpose of this deposition, the following are present: Detective Constance Alonzo, FBI agents Doctor Thomas Miller and Susan Moore, attorney Ms. Stella Bright, her client, Mr. Tomás Gomez, and myself, Detective Sergeant Ronald Teal."

After a series of preliminary comments, Connie spread several cards from her stack of three-by-fives in front of her and began: "Mr. Gomez, you have already given a statement admitting that you killed Juan Melgoza because he took some money that had been paid to both of you for transporting a human kidney and drugs into this country. Would you explain to us now, in your own words, how this material was transported into this country?"

Gomez wore an orange jumpsuit but seemed very much at ease. Looking at his attorney, he began. "Several times a week we help people cross the border. Sometimes we help carry other stuff at the same time." The orange suit made his goiter even more prominent. It was so large that it stretched the skin, giving it a sheen.

"What kind of stuff?" asked Connie.

"Drugs, I guess. Sometimes kidneys or some other stuff we didn't know about. They din't always tell us what we were carrying."

"So, the things you brought across changed from trip to trip?" she asked.

"Yes, but sometimes we just guide the *pollos.*"

"What are *pollos?*"

"*Pollos* are what we call the illegals that we bring across."

"Mr. Gomez, the last time you transported a kidney, how did you do it and where did you take it?" she continued.

"I tol' you already. The kidney was in a Donald Duck thermos jug. One of our guides carried it in a backpack. After the crossing, we took it to the Hilton over by the airport in L.A."

"Mr. Gomez, who was it that supplied you with the kidney in the Donald Duck thermos jugs?"

"A doctor."

"Was it the same doctor every time?"

"Yes."

"What is the doctor's name?" Connie asked.

"I don' know."

"Mr. Gomez, I'm going to show you two photographs. Tell us if you recognize anyone in the pictures." Connie handed him the two photos. Stella intercepted the photos. She looked at them for a moment; then whispered something in her client's ear.

"Yes, that's the doctor, and that woman is his wife, but I don' know their names," said Gomez.

Connie continued to the tape recorder. "For the record, Mr. Gomez has recognized and identified the individuals in the photographs numbered 20 and 21 as the doctor and his wife, who we believe currently reside in Tijuana, as the persons who gave them the thermos jug containing the kidney to transport across the border." Turning to the prisoner, she continued. "Mr. Gomez, please tell us what happens when you deliver the thermos jug to the Hilton."

"It's simple. We go to the desk, ask for the key to Mr. Willard Smith's room. It really isn't a key. It's plastic thing that looks like a credit card with holes in it. We go into the room, leave the backpack on the bed, and then pick up another backpack that has our money in it. That's it. Then we just leave." As she listened to his response, Connie pulled up several new three-by-five cards.

"And why would a hotel concierge give you a key to another man's room?" asked Connie.

"I dunno. Maybe Mr. Smith just tells them to."

"Do you know the name of the man who employs you to make these deliveries?" asked Connie.

"It's the same guy. He said his name was Willard Smith."

"Have you ever seen this Willard Smith in person?" she asked.

"Yes, once about a year ago when we had a similar deal."

"Do you think you could recognize this Mr. Smith if you saw him again?"

"I think so." Gomez smiled and relaxed back into his chair.

"Mr. Gomez, now we're going to show you a video from the security cameras at the Hilton. We want you to look at it carefully. If you want, we can stop or rewind it. Please look at it carefully and tell us if you recognize anyone."

Gomez' face blanched and sweat began to glisten on his forehead. He looked at his attorney for guidance. "Can you give us a couple of minutes alone?" asked Stella.

"Sure, we'll just step out into the hall," said Teal, rising. The others followed.

"Don't go far; it'll only take a minute," said Stella.

At Stella's signal, everyone returned to the room and took their seats. Her face was scowling. "Ronnie, you didn't tell us about any video tape!" she said angrily.

Teal replied, "Actually I didn't know about the tape until an hour ago. I understand it was provided by Mr. Miller, with the cooperation of the Hilton Hotel."

Stella looked coldly at the FBI agents. "I'm going to let this proceed because of my client's willingness to cooperate in this matter in spite of my misgivings about this unethical treatment by authorities. I want to say for the record that if there are any more surprises, we will no longer be so cooperative and I will file a complaint with the courts."

"Mr. Gomez, you will see many people, but we have already identified Juan Melgoza picking up the key at the front desk. We want you to pay particular attention to what happens shortly after that," continued Connie.

Connie laid out several three-by-fives, picked up a remote control, and turned on the television. It was located in the corner of the room. The tape was clear and had apparently been made up of videos taken by several different cameras at various locations. The date and time was imprinted in the lower right hand corner.

The first several minutes of the tape showed the lobby, the staff, and other people moving in and out. "I think that's Mr. Smith," said Gomez, leaning forward.

Connie stopped the tape rewound it to the point when a tall man in a checkered sport coat appeared. He had white hair cut very short. Connie noted the frame number in the corner of the screen. "Is this the man you believe is Willard Smith?" she asked.

"I think so," answered Gomez.

"Okay, let's continue with the tape. It's not much longer," she said.

The next scenes showed a frontal view of the man in the hallway entering a room, then the same man in a hallway with a small, green backpack. Next they saw the same man in an elevator with several people. The last segment showed the man walking out the door and beyond the range of the cameras.

"That was Mr. Smith. He's a very tall man and always wears the same checkered jacket," said Gomez.

Stella Bright's face quivered even before she spoke. "This is bullshit! Anyone can tell this tape has been cut up and pieced together. It's worthless as the balls on some people I know." Her voice was sharp, her eyes reduced to slits in her face.

Tom Miller broke the quiet, "You're absolutely correct, Ms. Bright. You are very observant. We *did* do a cut-and-paste job on this copy… because we didn't want to be here twenty-four hours watching tapes. We took it upon ourselves to make a condensed version."

Stella started to speak, but before she could, Agent Moore broke in. "For your benefit, these are copies of the entire tapes. As you can see, they take up four cassettes. When you review them you will see where we found the parts you just saw." Moore placed the four tapes in front of Stella.

Stella looked away from the FBI man, then at Connie. "Will there be anything else? My client wants to be as cooperative as he can be."

Connie replied, "No, that's it for now. We appreciate Mr. Gomez' cooperation. We especially appreciate your cooperation Ms. Bright."

"We'll see, we'll see," she said. She followed her client out, deliberately leaving the tapes on the table.

For a few moments, no one spoke. Teal finally broke the silence. "That was an impressive tape! How were you able to put it together and then focus on this guy Smith?"

Miller spoke, "It really wasn't too hard. Gomez told you that he demanded the money from Melgoza a couple of days after he returned from Fresno. We just sat and watched the hotel's tapes of the two days before he was killed. We spotted Melgoza getting the room key within an hour or so. Then we knew we had the right day. Then our Mr. Smith appeared. As you know Ron, the kidney is time sensitive. It had to be picked up quickly. It's my hunch that it was implanted by the afternoon of the same day."

Connie asked, "Tom, by now you've identified Smith, haven't you?"

"Well, yes and no."

"What do you mean, 'yes and no?'" asked Teal.

We don't know his real name, but we do know who he works for," answered Miller.

Teal and Connie exchanged glances. Then they both looked at Miller who was obviously somewhat uncomfortable. Finally reached back to pull the door all the way shut and said, "What I am going to tell you is very confidential. It can't leave this room until we know what we're dealing with. This fellow we're calling Smith, because we really don't know his name, works for the CIA!"

There was an intake of breath and a long pause. Finally Connie spoke. "You've got to be kidding, Tom! What is he a crooked agent or something?" Connie took one of her cards and wrote in large letters, *SMITH/ CIA/ KIDNEY!!??*

"No. We understand he's one of the best foreign operatives the Agency has. He's normally stationed abroad," said Miller.

"Then what the hell is he doing at the L.A. Hilton picking up a human kidney drenched in tomato juice and leaving that kind of money to scum like Gomez and Melgoza?" asked the bewildered Teal.

"We really don't know, so we've put in an inquiry with our folks in D.C. I understand some of the big boys from both our agency and theirs are coming out in a couple of days. Perhaps we'll find out... or perhaps we'll never know..." mused Miller.

"Good Lord!" said Teal. "In the meantime, what the hell do we tell Stella? If she finds out, she'll shred us to pieces!"

With a sigh Moore answered, "I believe the best course of action is to say nothing at all to her for a couple of days. In fact, let's just all avoid her if we can."

Chapter 49
Grady Visits

THE TWO GRADY MEN were obviously cut from the same cloth. The older Grady was short, with a definite middle. He was dressed in slacks, an open-necked shirt with no tie, and a brown sports jacket. His son was a younger version of him, and both walked with a similar, loping gait. The two walked down the street and knocked before entering the little house. Carlos had been waiting with his aunt and uncle for the ranch owner. Grady Sr. had called the previous day and made an appointment.

The older Grady greeted Tió Francisco. "Francisco, it's good to see you! I hope you're feeling much better now. My son would like to say something to you and your family."

There was a hint of fear and hesitation in the young man's eyes. "Please accept my apology for the accident. It was my fault," he said, his head hanging down. "I feel very badly that I caused you so much pain."

The well-rehearsed statement was stilted, but Carlos's uncle accepted it as it was meant. He smiled, "Thank you, young man."

The older Grady continued. He nodded to Carlos's aunt. "Now Estrella and Francisco, I also owe you an apology for sending that attorney the other day. I should have come myself. I'm here to assure you that we will take care of all the medical expenses necessary to get you back on your feet. I understand you're planning to move to your house in town. Please take all the time you need to make the arrangements. We are in no hurry to move someone else into this house until the next picking season, and that's a good way off.

"I also spoke to our insurance carrier. One of their representatives will come by to see you soon. They will provide you some compensation while you're off work. They will make some kind of settlement as required by law for workers that are hurt on the job. I know that this would normally be taken care of by Mario's insurance, but I'll put it on mine so that Mario's insurance won't be affected."

The old uncle smiled again. "Thank you, Mr. Grady. This is good news for Estrella and me."

Grady Sr. turned to Carlos, who had been listening to the conversation. "You must be Manuel's nephew. I've heard a lot about you. I understand you're now a physician?"

"Yes, I'm Carlos Reynoso, sir."

"I understand you've worked on the ranch for several summers," said Grady.

"Almost ten. Picking lemons and oranges helped me pay my way through medical school in Guadalajara."

"Congratulations!" He reached over to clap Carlos on the back. "It's very nice to hear we were of some help with your education." Grady continued, "Say, do you know about this union business? What's that all about?"

"Well, I don't really know much about it. I live down in the L.A. Basin now. What I do know is that your attorney actually threatened to kick my uncle out of this house. And this was just after he'd come home from the hospital! Then he asked him to sign away all his rights. Somehow the union got wind of it. The guy who came here said they were going to help my uncle."

Irritated, Grady said, "Well he's certainly not my attorney anymore! Carlos, perhaps I can rely on you to make sure your uncle gets the best treatment. If you think he needs something, will you let me know?"

"Of course."

He passed Carlos a business card. "You can reach me at either of these numbers."

After a few more pleasantries, the two Gradys left. They passed a man wearing a distinctive red bandana, but neither Grady recognized him.

Only minutes after the Gradys' departure, Johnny Cruz knocked on the door. He wore the same red bandanna on his head. He wore a huge smile. "So, how'd it go Doc?"

"Great! The old man and the kid apologized. Grady he said he would take care of everything. My uncle will be okay now. Thanks for your help, Johnny."

"You're welcome. Now it's on to help the rest of these poor bastards," replied the union organizer.

"What do you mean? Who else needs help?" asked Carlos.

"Do you think it's only your uncle who's getting screwed? Hell no! This happens every day, especially to workers like your uncle who are easily intimidated. We need to organize all these guys so we can protect them. They need better wages and more benefits for their hard work. More than anything, they deserve some respect and dignity, don't you agree?" asked Cruz.

"Of course I agree!"

"Good! Then you'll help us?"

"What do you mean help you? What do you expect me to do?" asked Carlos guardedly.

Johnny laughed. "Aw, don't worry, Doc! We won't ask you to sacrifice your new cushy job. But one of these days when I'll need some stitches or a broken bone set, will you help me then?" He raised his eyebrows and met Carlos's eyes, pressing for an answer.

At this point, Carlos remembered Connie's comment about "being manipulated by an expert." Johnny apparently knew what buttons to push to get a reaction from him. He answered, "Well, if someone breaks your arm or leg, you can count on me."

Johnny laughed, "I don't know Doc; you sound a bit too eager to work on me. If you don't mind, I'll postpone taking you up on your offer as long as I can." The union organizer was still laughing as he sauntered out.

The phone rang. It was Connie. "Carlos, how are you? I heard you were visiting your uncle; how's he doing?"

"He's fine. Mr. Grady and his son were just here. The kid apologized and the old man said he would take care of everything. It looks like things are turning out okay."

"How about dinner later?"

Carlos answered, "Would you mind coming over here? I need to talk with my uncle for a while." Catching Tía Estrella's eye and winking, he continued. "I'm sure we can eat here. You know how my aunt loves to cook."

Estrella beamed with pleasure at the news.

The tiny living room was crowded with visitors, including a physical therapist who was giving instructions to Tío Francisco. Everyone seemed to be enjoying watching the young woman work as she pushed and pulled with surprising force on his leg. Of course, the pain made the uncle wince a bit, but he did not complain.

The therapist said, "Mr. Baca, you are certainly in great shape for a man your age! You'll be ready to get rid of that walker in a few days. Just keep doing your exercises. I'll see you day after tomorrow."

The therapist packed up her equipment and left. The spectators followed her out.

As soon as the doorway cleared, Connie arrived. She was carrying a two-pound box of chocolates. She walked over to Tío Francisco and handed it to him. His face lit up and he reached up to give her a hug. Then he opened the box, chose a piece and passed the box around.

"You've made a big hit with my uncle. He just *loves* chocolate, especially Lucy's Nuggets," said Carlos.

Tía Estrella cautioned, "Now just one piece before dinner! It's almost ready." She disappeared around the corner. Carlos, Connie and Tío Francisco chatted about how tough physical therapy can be, and how wonderful it was to be rewarded with chocolate after such a hard workout.

Soon, out came Tía Estrella, who led everyone to the table. She served them large bowls of soup. The bowls were steaming, filled with vegetables and chunks of meat. Tía Estrella began to pile heated corn tortillas onto a warmed plate the middle of the table.

"This soup is fantastic!" said Connie, slurping appreciatively.

Chapter 50
A Fairy Tale

"Good morning! I'm Kelli Givens-Amam." She looked around the room. "Let me guess... You must be Detective Connie Alonzo and this is your partner, Ron Teal." Connie and Ron smiled and nodded silently. "And you two are my colleagues from the FBI: Agents Miller and Moore, right?" They also nodded in agreement. The woman was the complete opposite of someone who might wish to be inconspicuous. The CIA agent was slim and very tall, well over six feet. Despite her height, she wore high heels. Her colorful and elegant turban made her appear even taller. Her black face and Asian features melded to make the fortyish woman very attractive indeed.

She had a ready smile and, knowing the effect of her striking appearance, she explained: "My dad was a black officer serving in Korea and my mother was a young native he met. I never knew her. My dad brought me back while I was still in diapers. I grew up in Kansas City. I graduated from West Point. After a stint in the Army, I was recruited by the CIA. I've spent a good part of my professional life wandering around the world for the Agency."

Satisfied that she had answered the questions she knew that were on their minds. She continued, smiling pleasantly. "First, let's agree that this is just an informal, off-the-record chat to see if we have any common areas of interest. Would one of you could give me a brief outline of where you are?"

There was silence. Ron Teal finally began, if only to pass it off to his partner. "Connie is our lead investigator on this case. She can give us a quick run down."

Connie had already arranged her cards, so she began easily. "This investigation started several weeks ago with what we originally thought was a simple suicide. That quickly turned into a murder investigation. That led to threatening phone calls to a poor widow. That led us to finding out about international drugs trafficking associated with an organization which helps illegal aliens enter the U.S. That in turn led us to discover trafficking in human organs, specifically kidneys. That is what led us to Willard Smith, who we believe is one of your agents." Connie paused. She looked straight at the woman. "And at this point, we don't know what to think."

Kelli Givens-Aman smiled at everyone around the table, "Let me share an Arabian fairy tale." Surprised and curious, the agents and detectives settled back into their chairs to hear her story.

"Once upon a time, there was a good king who ruled a tiny country which occupied a key strategic area in its part of the world. Several countries' leaders vied to become an ally of this little kingdom. The land was also the source of a very valuable mineral greatly prized by the king's neighbors, friends, and even his enemies. Now the kindly king had only one son who would be the next king. The prince was the light of the king's life. One day, the boy got very sick. The illness made his immune system attack his kidneys. The only thing that could save him was a skillful surgery. He appealed to one of his friends to help save his son."

She paused, smiled knowingly, and looked around the room. "Now to his friends, arranging the surgery was a rather simple matter and they very much wanted to be helpful. The one problem was that a kidney is a valuable commodity and it can be difficult to obtain one that matches the recipient, as you are probably aware. Yet this same organ is uncomplicated; most people can live very well indeed with just one. So it was just a matter of somehow finding a donor." Her listeners exchanged glances.

She took a deep breath and continued. "Arrangements were made to obtain an organ and the surgery was performed successfully. The prince has recovered and is expected to live happily ever after. He has returned to his important country. We hope the king and his eventual successor will remain eternally grateful to their helpful friends." She paused again, looking out the window to gather a final thought. "It was also agreed that this would be done with little fanfare. Things were kept quiet because any adverse publicity would embarrass not only the kindly king but his good friends."

There was absolute silence in the room, except for the quiet shuffle of Connie's cards as she jotted a few notes and located others. The others looked to her for comment. At length she spoke up. "The only problem with this fairy tale is that there is a dead man, his frightened mother who has no idea what has happened, a murder suspect in custody, plus no telling how many other laws were broken and rights compromised. Of course, that doesn't even cover the morality of this fairy tale. Fairy tales usually have a moral, don't they?" she challenged Givens-Amam.

The CIA agent sighed. "In my business, unintended consequences seem to be the norm. But still, you have a valid point, my dear."

"So, where do we go from here?" asked Teal. "If Stella gets wind of this, it will wreck our case against Gomez."

"Who is Stella?" asked Kelli.

"She's Gomez' attorney. You can damned well bet she'll light up the night skies with this information when she gets wind of it," answered Teal.

"Make a deal with her. Have him plead to a lesser charge," she offered.

"That will just make her more suspicious. She knows we've got him dead to rights," countered Connie.

"Kelli," began Tom Miller, "you said this was just an 'informal chat.' We talked about fairy tales and unintended consequences. But how are we to proceed officially? And now that some people have learned that organ trafficking is a lucrative business, what do we do about that?"

"Good questions, Tom. I would request that at this point, you proceed with your normal process, but don't be in too much of a hurry. In fact, taking a vacation would be a good idea. I can only tell you that this is a matter of great importance to our country. You will be hearing from us, probably indirectly, with suggestions for how this might be handled."

"One more thing," asked Miller, "we've had our eye on a Dr. Adriana Colson. Is she the one who implanted the kidney?"

The CIA agent adjusted her turban for a moment and stood, looking taller than ever. Her smile was mysteriously aloof. "I have to catch a flight. It was a pleasure to meet you all. I only ask that you keep an open mind about this. Oh, one more thing. I can tell you that Dr. Colson and I were at The Point together." She went around the table, shook hands with each person and left.

Ron Teal shook his head and said, "Now what the hell do we do?" He looked at Miller, "What do you suppose she meant by that comment about Colson?"

"Hell, I don't know. I can't read smiles," answered Miller.

The meeting broke up, the attendees lost in their own thoughts.

Chapter 51
A Boyfriend

WHEN LUZ WALKED IN, CARLOS WAS READING an article about transplant procedures, written by Dr. Colson. "Got a couple of minutes?" she asked.

"Sure, what's up?"

"This Saturday my parents are giving a party to celebrate my graduation. I was wondering if you and Ann would like to come." She sat across the table from Carlos. "It's just family, very informal, but the food will be good and the beer cold."

"Sounds great! I don't know about Ann, but I'll ask her. Even if she can't come, I'll be there. What time?"

"Good! Come about five. If I know my dad, the party will be going on most of the evening."

"Sounds like my kind of party. I'm looking forward to meeting your father." Carlos paused, "When do you join the Sisters of...?"

"Sisters of Social Service, and I'm not joining now. They've invited me to live with them this summer just for me to get a feel of their community," said Luz.

"What's in the box?" asked Carlos as Ann climbed into his pickup.

"A present for Luz... for her graduation."

"Damn! I should have gotten her something, too. What do I do now?"

"Well for one thing, you can thank me, plus you owe me $50, because this present is from both of us," laughed Ann.

"Thanks! Getting a present never occurred to me."

"Somehow that doesn't surprise me. Now Luz and her family will know how very thoughtful you are," said Ann mockingly.

Ignoring the sarcasm, Carlos asked, "What did we get her?"

"You'll see."

The party was well underway when they arrived. There were cars parked on both sides of the street for at least a block on each side of the house. People were approaching the house with either presents or pans of food in hand. Fragrant smoke from the open barbecue drifted out to greet them. Carlos immediately felt hungry. He and Ann followed the stream of people, going directly into the back yard through the open gate at the side of the house. There was already a large gathering of men and women, with many children running about. A radio was playing Mexican music. Next to the radio, there were several tubs filled with iced soft drinks and beer.

Luz saw them arrive. "Thanks for coming!" she greeted them. "Come, let me introduce you to my parents." Luz' father was a very tall man. His western straw hat just made him look taller. He was sweating profusely as he added wood to the fire. On top of several concrete blocks, he had a large copper pot with a long, wooden paddle to stir the carnitas he was cooking in melted lard. The aroma was already wonderful.

Mr. Reyes passed the paddle to another man. "It's nice to meet you, Carlos! I've heard so much about you." He shook Carlos's hand firmly. "I understand you come from Tonalá?"

"Yes, sir, I do. My parents still live there and I hope to visit them soon."

Reyes turned to Ann. "Anita, how are you? We haven't seen you around for some time!" He gave her a hug. How are your parents?"

They exchanged pleasantries, and then Mr. Reyes led them to the tubs and dug out three beers. "These okay for you?" he asked. They nodded appreciatively, so he popped the caps and handed them over. "Hey, thanks for coming over and rescuing me! That fire was getting too hot. Luz' boyfriend can stir the meat for a while." As he walked away he said, "Now that you know where the beer is, help yourself."

"That's Luz' boyfriend?" asked Carlos, somewhat confused.

"His name is Felipe. They've known each other since they were kids. Everyone expects them to get married."

"Everyone except the Sisters of Social Service! How does Felipe feel about them?"

"That's the strange thing. He actually likes the sisters and they like him. He's a carpenter and he's helped the sisters fix up their home." Ann was thoughtful, "But I don't know how he really feels about Luz at this point."

Carlos felt very much at home even though most of the people were strangers. The food, the music, and the friendliness of the people were all very familiar to him. Even Ann blended in; she obviously knew many of the people.

Chapter 52
Who's Got Who?

CONNIE AND RON SAT AT THEIR DESKS, both leafing through papers, but not actually reading them. They were waiting for Stella Bright to arrive to discuss the Gomez case. He had no idea how they were going to be able to delay the investigation. He and Connie had discussed various stories they could tell her but they were sure she would crucify them. At last, they had decided to play to her reaction.

Even though the building was air-conditioned, Stella was sweating when she arrived. The luggage cart carrying her briefcase once again bounced against the door jamb as she entered the office. "You got any damn water in this place?" she demanded. Connie got up and removed a water bottle from a small refrigerator.

"Thanks." Stella opened the plastic bottle and drank half of it in one take. She replaced the cap and then rolled the cold bottle against her neck. "Ahhh, that's better!" she sighed. "Now, what's this all about?"

"Ms. Bright, we appreciate your coming to confer with us. Detective Sergeant Teal and I wanted to talk about Mr. Gomez…"

The attorney cut Connie short. "Cut the crap, Honey! Call me Stella… at least while we're alone. By the way, what happened to the medical exam my client was going to get?"

"Stella," began Teal, "one of our county doctors took a look at Gomez. He and the specialist you recommended are conferring on the case. The specialist took some blood samples and did some other some other tests. The county doc will be providing us a report of all the results in the next day or so."

"Thanks, Ronnie. At the least the asshole doctors the county uses have enough brains to appreciate the help of a specialist." Stella looked at each of them with a bit of suspicion. "Okay, now will you two tell me what the hell is going on?"

Connie let her breath out slowly. "Stella, we've run into some complications, so our investigation of Mr. Gomez will be delayed a bit. We know you're concerned with your client." The junior detective paused. "It's just that we've got a few loose ends and we want to make sure we have them all tied up before we make the formal indictment."

Stella took a blue cotton handkerchief from her purse and began to blot the sweat that had accumulated on her neck, never taking her eyes off Connie. Her fat began to jiggle before the laugh came. She used her cloth to blot her tears as they rolled into the sweat running down her face. "You guys just can't get it together, can you? Either you've screwed up the case, or you weenie-brained DA can't decide what to do. In the meantime, you want my client to sit on his fat ass in your stinking jail while you assholes figure it out? Give me a break!" she finished, rolling her eyes in derision.

"Now Stella," said Teal, "Mr. Gomez has some serious problems that go beyond just killing Melgoza. But you're right; there are some complications, international in nature, that are causing the delay."

"Ronnie, you and I go back a long way. We knew each other in very intimate ways that I'll never forget. But just because you screwed me once doesn't mean you can screw with me on this issue!" Stella fixed her eyes on Teal. A brief tenderness was quickly replaced with a hard glare.

Connie could feel the tension between the two, so she wisely said nothing. Meanwhile, Teal dropped his gaze and looked at the floor, seemingly embarrassed by Stella's reference to their earlier relationship. Then he took a deep breath. His eyes were cold as they met and held those of the woman before him. Very quietly and deliberately he said, "Stella, we've got Gomez dead to rights. If we charge him now, he'll either go to prison for life or he'll be on a gurney with a needle in his arm. But as I said, there are some further complications we'd like to clear up." Both women noted Teal's steel-cold voice as he spoke.

Stella blotted more sweat from her neck. B...but my client..."

Teal cut her off. "Bear in mind that it could actually work in your client's favor." Stella's brows raised with interest. "There's also an international connection that other jurisdictions are working on. That will require some time to work out."

"Are you referring to organ transplant scam?" Her comment caught both detectives by surprise. She chuckled, breaking the tension. "Gomez hasn't told me all the details, but enough that I could guess what your 'complications' were."

"All we can tell you is that the Feds are involved and they want some time," pressed Teal.

"Ron, you know very well that my client has a right to a speedy trial. I can't have him sitting in jail while the FBI, the CIA, and no telling who else are scratching their butts. On the other hand, my client wants to be cooperative, and he will be, if we can assure him of some consideration."

"What kind of consideration are you referring to?" inquired Connie.

"To begin with, the elimination of the death penalty. If there's any jail time, perhaps my client can serve it in his country. And for damned sure, he should get some good medical attention in the meantime."

Teal's manner was now back to normal, "We can assure you that he's getting the medical attention he needs. As I told you, your specialist saw him and he's to make a recommendation for treatment soon. As to the rest, we can't make any firm promises, except to say that we'll bring your requests up to the boys in charge. Let's see what they have to say."

Stella said, "I'm going to assume that you two will make every effort to make my point of view well known to those peckerheads, okay? Also, I want you to send me a copy of the doctor's report and his recommendation for treatment as soon as possible. You can do that without getting permission from the Feds, can't you?"

"We've already specified that he's to send you a copy of the report when they send us one," said Teal.

"Fair enough Ronnie. We've got a deal." Turning to Connie, she said, "Thanks for the water. You know, Honey, you should come to work for me. We'd make a good team, and then you wouldn't have to deal with all those pricks." She gathered herself up and left, her cart denting the door jamb as she yanked it into the hall.

Connie started to laugh, at first somewhat softly, then she got the giggles. "What's so funny?" asked Teal.

"That woman is a piece of work! We know we have a solid case against Gomez, yet she thinks she's got us by the throat in a bind!" she answered, chuckling. "Who's got who?"

Teal frowned at his partner; it took him a few seconds to join in the laughter. "She *was* a piece of work and *is* a piece of work. I sure don't want to be the attorney who tangles with her in court."

Chapter 53
Spencers

CARLOS WALKED INTO THE EXAMINATION ROOM to find a middle-aged man who eyed him suspiciously. "Good morning Mr. Spencer," said Carlos. "How are you today?"

"Who are you?" asked the man. He was sitting on the edge of the exam table dressed only in his undershorts.

"I'm Dr. Reynoso. Dr. Pilabos asked me to see you before he comes in." Carlos made an effort to check his wrist, but the man jerked his hand away. Carlos was startled.

"Don't touch me!" growled the man.

"What is the matter?" asked Carlos, confused.

"You can cut my lawn, but you sure as hell aren't going to touch me!" The man's voice dripped in hatred.

"I don't understand," said Carlos.

"No goddamned filthy Mexican is going to examine me. You can get the hell out of here. Tell Pilabos to come in here." The man shook with revulsion. Spit sprayed from his trembling mouth.

At that moment, Alex Pilabos tapped on the door and entered the room. "Did I hear my name?" He looked at the file. "Mr. Spencer?"

"I came here to see an American doctor. I'm paying with good U.S. money and no damned Mexican is going to examine me," declared the patient.

Pilabos noted Carlos's astonished face, then looked sternly at Spencer. "You may get dressed now, Mr. Spencer."

"Why? You haven't even seen me yet!"

"Yes we have, and we don't see your kind here. Pleased get dressed and leave our office. I'm sure you can find your kind of doctor, but not here at Angelus Medical Center. Perhaps a doctor somewhere else will be glad to treat you." Pilabos' voice was cold and his gaze piercing. His icy tone surprised Carlos.

Spencer didn't budge, so Pilabos continued. "Mr. Spencer, if you don't leave quickly and quietly, I will call the police. They have a substation here at the airport. They can be here in five minutes and I will have you arrested for trespassing." He turned to Carlos. "Dr. Reynoso, may I see you in my office?"

When they reached his office, Pilabos offered him a soda.

"Sure; thanks!" The older gentleman went to a small refrigerator, pulled out a couple of cans, and gave one to Carlos.

"Well, what do you think?" asked Pilabos.

"I don't know what to think. That's never happened to me before. That man was angry for some reason. I... I don't even know him! Why was he so upset at me?"

"Tell me Carlos, where have you lived in your young life?" inquired the older fellow gently.

"Except for the last few months here, I've only lived in my home town of Tonalá and on the ranch with my uncle. I've never really had an opportunity to live anywhere else."

"Well Carlos, you've been lucky. Let me share something with you. My parents had to leave Armenia because the Turks killed off half of our people. We were lucky to survive. When my parents arrived here in the U.S., they spoke no English and people treated them like dirt. My father worked in the fields. My mother washed clothes and cleaned toilets for the rich people in Fresno. My parents worked hard, saved money and bought a little store. They made enough to send my sister and me to school. The other kids called us 'Armenian Indians.'

"In medical school, even though I was short, I was always pushed to the back of the room because I was dark-skinned like you. I was certainly never invited to parties. So I just thought to myself, 'Screw you!' and then worked harder than they did. Here I am doing pretty well, but I'll admit, I still carry those scars. There will always be assholes like Spencer. We just need to work around them. Today was a rare exception: I was able to put one in his place," said Pilabos with satisfaction. "I can only hope that he learned something from this little encounter."

"Yes, I'm glad you came in when you did!" said Carlos. He sipped his soda and smiled admiringly at the older doctor, who continued.

"Somehow, guys like Spencer need to put others down because of their own inadequacies. Yet, this is still a great country. It gives everyone an opportunity to succeed if he has the balls to overcome the Spencers of this world."

Carlos spoke quietly. "We have people like that in Mexico. They who look down on those who are poor, like the Indians. In fact they don't just look down on them; they act like they don't even see them."

"Here's a piece of advice that my father passed on to me. It's an old Armenian saying. 'Forgive them, but never forget them.' I know the translation is awkward, but I'm sure you get the meaning," said Pilabos.

Carlos nodded, appreciating the sentiment. He laughed self-consciously as he left the office. He finished his drink, crumpled the can between his hands and tossed it into a trash can.

The young receptionist called him as he passed by her desk. "Dr. Reynoso, you have a call on line three." She pointed to the phone on the corner of the counter.

Chapter 54
A Shock

"CARLOS, THIS IS CHUY. CAN YOU COME QUICK? They just took father back to the hospital. He passed out at the house. We don't know what happened." Carlos sank into a chair as he listened to his cousin.

"Where are you now, Chuy?"

"I'm at the house, but I'm going to the hospital right now. Mom wanted me to call you. Can you come?"

"Yes, of course! How is Tía; is she okay?" asked Carlos, his voice quiet but quavering. The news worried him. He thought his uncle had been recovering well.

"She's seems all right. She's praying, but she really wants you to come. We'll meet you at the hospital, okay?"

"Sure, please tell her I'll be there as soon as I can." Carlos hung up the phone quietly, stared at the tile floor a moment, then turned to the receptionist. "Please tell Dr. Pilabos I had to leave. There's an emergency at home, I have to get up there right away. I'll call later to let you know what's going on."

He walked quickly down the hall to his apartment, removed his white jacket, grabbed a blue Dodger hat and was about to head out when the phone rang. It was Ann.

"Hi, Carlos! The receptionist said you were at home. I just wanted to call. I thought I might come over this evening."

"Sorry, Ann," said Carlos. "I'm just going out the door. My cousin just called to tell me that my uncle was taken back to the hospital. My aunt wants me there. I have no idea what's happened or how long I'll be gone."

"Oh dear! Is it serious?"

"I don't know. I'll call you later, okay?" Carlos hung up. The phone immediately rang again but he hurried out the door without answering it.

Carlos drove west but didn't speed; somehow he felt calm. Yet his mind was playing snippets of conversations and pictures of his uncle. There was no particular order to these memories. He was able to replay some several times, lingering on a few. He smiled and had a silent conversation with his uncle as he drove west on the freeway. He descended the grade through Grimes Canyon toward Fillmore. The orange trees brought even more memories of his uncle. He turned west toward Santa Paula.

It was already noon when he reached the parking lot across from the hospital. Beneath one of the trees he saw a couple of his cousins and several family friends sitting in the back of a pickup talking. Two little boys were playing in the truck bed. The youngest cousin's eyes were red; he'd been crying.

"What happened?" asked Carlos.

"Dad is dead! We don't know what happened. Mario came to orchard to get us. He told us that Dad had a relapse. By the time we got to the house, the ambulance had already taken him to the hospital." The young man pointed to the buildings across the road. "We never got to say goodbye…"

"Dios mio," breathed Carlos, closing his eyes briefly to sending a silent prayer. As Carlos listened to the cousins' account of the past couple of hours, another carload of family members pulled up. One of his cousins held a baby in her arms. She was crying. Carlos hugged her, the baby sandwiched between them.

"Where's my aunt? Is she okay?" Carlos asked the others.

"She's inside; she's been asking for you. You'd better go see her," said a cousin.

In a corner of the emergency waiting room sat his aunt. Two women were with her. They were quietly praying the rosary. Nearby, several men stood watching a muted television mounted high in another corner.

The praying stopped when Carlos approached the women. Carlos knelt in front of Tía Estrella and hugged her.

"Mi viejito is gone; he left me," she wailed softly. "I was supposed to die first. He left me, Carlitos; he left me." Carlos held her a while as she sobbed. Then he stood and hugged the other women and men who had been staying with his aunt.

"What happened, Chuy?" he asked the oldest son. Chuy was twice as old as Carlos. His face was lined with dust from the orchard and his shirt was sweat-stained but dry.

"We don't know. Mario called us from the orchard. He brought us here, but they won't tell us anything, except that he's dead. Mom went in to see him, as did the priest, but that's it. Carlos you go in; see if you can find out anything. Please?" Carlos nodded and mumbled in agreement.

He went to the reception desk. "I'm Doctor Carlos Reynoso. I'd like to see the ER doctor who treated my uncle, Francisco Baca. He was brought in just a couple of hours ago."

The receptionist looked a bit surprised. "Just a moment please," she said. She spoke briefly on the phone, and then pointed to her right. "Go to the side door. Dr. Simms will see you." By the time Carlos reached the door, a young woman had opened it, letting Carlos in.

"I'm Dr. Simms," she said, motioning for him to follow her.

"Hello. I'm Dr. Reynoso. Francisco Baca is my uncle. Would you please explain to me what exactly happened to him?"

"I really don't know. He had passed on before he got here. The EMT said that there were no vital signs when they reached the house. They used a defibrillator and tried to revive him, but it was too late." She continued, "The only damage to his body that I have noticed was the bruise on his right cheek, and a bump on his head, but that probably happened when he collapsed. We haven't done anything except to cover him up. Would you like to see him?"

Carlos nodded and followed her. She led him to a curtained-off examination area and pulled aside the curtain surrounding the gurney. She gently pulled back the sheet. Tió Francisco lay there peacefully. There was the hint of a smile on the old man's face as Carlos looked at his face. As Carlos touched him, he felt the rasp of his uncle's unshaven face. He gently moved strands of his white hair aside and put them back in place. With one finger, Carlos drew a cross on the old man's forehead. Then he gently kissed the trace of the cross he had made. He then made the sign of the cross himself.

It was comforting to have these things to do for his uncle, particularly since it was too late for him to do anything else for him. Carlos didn't bother to wipe the tears that ran down his face.

Dr. Simms noticed Carlos had finished. "I've checked your uncle's record. Apparently he had an accident recently. He had a hip replaced several weeks ago, and according to what's in here, that seemed to go fine. His rehab indicated no problem. To all appearances, he looked to be in pretty good shape."

"Yes, he *was* in good shape. He worked hard all his life and never had a serious illness." Gently, Carlos replaced the sheet over the old man. "So, what happens next?"

"I suppose your family should make funeral arrangements. Also, because of the recent accident and surgery, the family might consider requesting an autopsy. That might be a good idea, since he was in such good health. It's up your family. It would, however, delay burial plans," said Dr. Simms.

"Let me check with them. I'll be right back." Carlos walked back to the waiting room, put his arm around his aunt's shoulder, but then addressed himself to her older son, Chuy and explained the situation to him.

Carlos returned to the ER and found Dr. Simms. "My family would like to have some peace of mind by knowing why he died," he said. "Besides, it will take some of our family members several days to get here for the funeral. So the wait won't be so bad."

"Where can we get hold of you if we have to contact you Dr. Reynoso," asked the female doctor.

"What?" Carlos was somewhat confused by the question.

"If we have to talk to you, where can we find you?" she repeated.

"Oh! Of course." He pulled out a business card. "Let me put down my aunt's number, you can reach me there when I'm in town." Carlos handed her the card. "By the way, would it be possible for some family members to come in to see my uncle before they leave? I'm sure they would appreciate it."

"Sure, we're not busy for the moment. Bring them on in."

Chapter 55
A Farewell

THE PEOPLE FROM THE FUNERAL HOME struggled to maneuver the coffin into the little house. The funeral director had argued strongly that the vigil should be held either in the church, or at the funeral home, where there was more room. Tía Estrella would not hear of it. She told them that the two of them had lived in this very house most of their adult lives, and she wanted to spend the last night there with her husband. There was no further discussion. At last, they succeeded in positioning it properly inside according to Estrella's instructions.

All of their neighbors helped with the preparations. The neighbors on both sides of the house opened their homes. Food and drinks were available to the all the mourners. Children ran around playing tag, tossing balls, and taking turns swinging on a rope that dangled from a tree. To them it was just another big party.

Several of the men had built a fire in the back yard and above it sat the familiar copper pot, cooking carnitas. There were two kegs of beer in large, ice-filled tubs. On an adjacent table were several bottles of hard liquor, cut lemons, and a large bowl of fresh garbanzo beans. In one corner of the yard, five men were playing poker and several others watched over their shoulders.

In the tiny living room the women had gathered. They filled the sofa and chairs, and many sat on the floor. Most wore dark dresses and had scarves covering their heads. Some of the younger ones wore jeans. Women walked in and out, changing places with newcomers as they murmured the Rosary. Carlos's aunt sat in a straight-backed wooden chair beside the open coffin which allowed her to look at her husband as she prayed. She was dressed all in black with a *rebozo* that covered her head and wrapped around her body, which seemed smaller than usual in the crowd. Now and then, women or children would come up to hug her. She would kiss the children on the cheek, smile, and rejoin the continuous prayer.

A baby girl walked by holding onto the people seated on the floor. She grabbed at their rosaries. When that happened, that woman would drop out of the prayer to play with the baby until she wandered off to find another rosary.

Several women were in the kitchen chopping vegetables and talking quietly. One of them brought Estrella a cup of tea. The old woman stopped praying and drank from the cup as she looked around the room filled with loving friends, and then at her husband. She seemed content.

While she drank her tea, Estrella heard the music begin just outside the door. A guitar trio had started to play. They were dressed in dark *guayaberas* and played softly. The rosary stopped. It was well-known that Francisco and his wife enjoyed music and loved to dance. Even the men behind the house stopped to listen.

The little girl crawled over to Estrella. She rose, picked her up, and slowly started to sway with the music. With tentative steps she began to dance with the baby in her arms. The women sitting on the floor scooted back to give her room. Her steps fell into rhythm with the guitars. The little girl buried her head next to her grandmother and went to sleep in her arms. She started to sing quietly along with the trio. Then she turned to face her husband as she continued to sing and dance. The musicians lowered their voices, but Estrella sang louder, carrying the song of love and devotion in a clear voice:

> *Solamente una vez amé en la vida.*
> *Solamente una vez y nada más.*
> *Una vez nada más en me huerto brilló la esperanza,*
> *La esperanza que alumbra el camino de mi soledad.*
> *Una vez nada más se entrega el alma*
> *Con la dulce y total renunciación.*
> *Y cuando ese milagro realize el prodigio de amarse*

Hay campanas de fiesta que cantan en el corazón.

Outside the front door, Carlos stood watching his aunt dance. His tears began to flow and he didn't bother to wipe them. She danced and he wept. He noticed that one of the guitar players was also crying. Several of the women were crying, but most of them had smiles on their faces. When the song ended, Tía Estrella sat down and cradled the baby in her lap. She wrapped the little girl in her long black scarf and listened to the music as it came though the front door.

The trio began to repeat the song, but more softly this time.

Solamente una vez...

The church was packed. Carlos sat behind the family. Just before the Mass began, Ann and her mother came in and sat next to Carlos. He was not surprised to see them. Ann took his hand for a moment and gave him a light kiss on the cheek, but said nothing.

The priest was well-known to the family. When he started his homily, he came down from the altar and stood next to the coffin. With his left hand on the wooden box for balance, he began to speak.

"It's appropriate that I've come down here to talk to you about our friend here, because what I have to tell you makes sense only if I am touching him. You see, this man was a man in the truest sense of the word, and he was never afraid to touch people. Of course he touched his family. It was obvious when you saw him and Estrella that they were always touching, if not physically, then by eyesight. They were inseparable, as their marriage meant them to be. But he touched all of us, too. His kindness, his willingness to work hard, and his honesty put many of us to shame."

Carlos listened closely, knowing that the priest had indeed known his uncle very well. Looking down, he realized that Ann had taken his hand again. She had intertwined her fingers into his and leaned her head against his shoulder. He could smell the freshness of her hair.

Carlos then returned his attention to the priest, who was still resting his hand on the coffin. "...the duty of we the living, is to honor our friend's memory by following his example: the love he showed for his God, for his church, for his family, and for his fellow man." The priest paused for several moments, gathering his thoughts and allowing the congregants to consider what he'd said. Those who'd had their heads down looked up, wondering why the priest has stopped talking. Then he went on. "Many of you think you're here to pray for our brother, but that is only part of why we're here. Our faith tells us that his soul has been taken care of. But we're also here to pray for our own souls, because we're still here and can still make peace with our brothers and with ourselves. If we can do that, then we will truly be honoring Francisco Baca." The priest turned toward the coffin, made the sign of the cross over it, patted it affectionately, and returned to the altar, a gentle smile on his face.

The rest of the Mass went quickly. Afterward, the church patio was crowded. Some of the women were crying, but there was also an atmosphere of happiness as people were renewing acquaintances. Death was indeed sad, especially for this poor, close-knit family and their friends, but their faith gave them hope for a better life within the greatest mystery of all.

Back at the house, friends and neighbors gathered again. Food and drinks appeared; children ran about, giggling and shouting. The men resumed their card game in the back yard. The three musicians returned with their guitars and started to play again.

Carlos and the rest of the family had just arrived from the brief service at the cemetery. Tía Estrella went straight to the kitchen and began to prepare food for the guests. Ann and her mother waited in the front yard. Julie Ferranti was watching two little girls show off their hand-clapping game.

"Carlos, Mom is leaving," called Ann. "If you like, I can stay here and go back south with you. I'd like to help out if I can."

"Well, I'm not too sure when I'll be leaving, but it would be nice if you stayed." Carlos, observing all the people and activity around the house, knew that for the next day or so, his aunt would not be alone. "Let's get something to eat," he said, taking Ann by the hand. He led her into the crowded kitchen.

As they drove back in silence, each with their own thoughts, they felt the summer heat which was tempered by the setting sun. Nearing the San Fernando Valley, Carlos asked, "Would you like me to take you home?"

"No, let's go to your place first."

Chapter 56
Equal Justice?

"Hey, Doc! This is Johnny. How ya doing?" Johnny Cruz was calling from the Agri Workers of America headquarters. A young man and woman were listening to the conversation, which Johnny had set up on a speaker. The woman was reading a document and the man was leaning against the door drinking a soda.

Carlos was still in bed. "Who is this?" he asked, yawning.

"Hey buddy! Sorry if I woke you. This is Johnny from the AWA. Listen, we're sorry to hear about your Uncle. We understand he was a fine man."

"Yes he was; he was a nice man. What did you call about?"

"We wanted to talk to you about your uncle's autopsy report," replied Johnny.

Carlos found his use of the word "we" a bit odd, but let it go. "I really don't know anything about it. I don't think it's done yet," he replied.

"You haven't seen it or even heard about it? Really! I'm surprised! One of his sons said he was going to talk to you." Cruz frowned at the two others in the room, he motioned to the girl to hand him the coroner's report she'd been reviewing. "Here, let me find the place. Uh, basically it says that your uncle died of an injury to his brain, a slow leak of blood caused by a blow to the head. It appeared to have been bleeding slowly for several weeks at the time of his death. That would have made it about the time the Grady kid knocked your uncle off the ladder."

Carlos was now awake but said nothing for a long while. He was trying to figure out the real reason the union organizer was calling. He took a deep breath. "I don't understand. Why you are telling me this?"

"Well, if your uncle died because of a head injury caused when that kid, Jeffrey Grady ran into him, then that's murder or manslaughter or something. I'm not a lawyer, but an attorney friend of ours tells us that this seems to now be a serious crime that should be prosecuted." As he spoke, Cruz checked off points he had previously written on yellow note pad.

Again Carlos was cautious and slow to answer, "Okay, so it's some kind of a crime. What's it got to do with me and what's it got to do with you?"

Johnny smiled at the other two and raised his thumb to them. "Well, frankly we're concerned for all farm workers. It's just not right that some damned rich kid can knock an old man off a ladder and kill him and have nothing happen to him. The spoiled brat is getting away with it. We don't think that's right. He continued, "And we know you're concerned too, because you were so close to the victim."

"Well, I'm concerned about my uncle and my aunt, too, but it seems to me that you need to go to the police. If there's a crime, I'm sure they'll look into it," said Carlos, his mind swimming with the new development.

"We've already done that, but they don't seem too anxious to look into this. We thought you could help us," said Cruz.

"Okay, how can I help?" asked Carlos cautiously, trying to figure out where the conversation was going.

"We thought you could call your friend, Detective Alonzo and ask her what's going on," said Johnny.

"You know Johnny, you should be talking to Chuy, my cousin. He's now the head of the family. Is he aware of any of this?"

"I don't think so. My hunch is that the coroner isn't going to bother to send him a report," said Cruz.

"Okay. I'll give her a call, but you need to let Chuy know what's going on. I'm not going to do anything that he's not in agreement with."

"Great! We'll go see Chuy this afternoon. Will you call us and let us know what Alonzo says?"

"Yeah, I have your number. I'll get back to you." Carlos hung up the phone and headed to the refrigerator. He drank some orange juice from a carton, and stared at it, his thoughts occupied. It was obvious that the

AWA wanted to use his uncle's death for their own benefit. Yet if the Grady kid's action had contributed to Tió Francisco's death, it wouldn't be right if there were no consequences for the young man. Realistically though, the Grady's were one of the most powerful families in the county. The chances of the boy suffering any legal consequences were slim to none. "Where is justice?" he wondered.

Carlos had no particular interest in the union. He was off the farm and his future life would no longer have any farm connections, with the exception of his relatives. Yet he knew he could do nothing without Cousin Chuy's permission.

Chuy had taken some days off, so he was home and answered Carlos's call.

"Chuy, how're you doing, *primo?*" asked Carlos.

"Carlos! I'm glad you called. I was just looking for your phone number to call you."

"What's up?"

"I just got a call from Johnny from the AWA. He told me that dad's death was the direct result of the accident… and that we ought to do something about it." Chuy sounded uncertain. "What do you think?"

"I don't know, *primo*. The guy called me this morning. He told me the same thing. He did suggest that we talk with Detective Alonzo to see what the police are going to do about it, if anything. But whatever needs to be done, you need to be the one who decides. We can talk it over, but I'll do whatever you ask."

"Thanks Carlos; I appreciate that. I know the union just wants to use Dad's death for their purposes, but if Jeffrey Grady killed my dad, he should face some kind of consequence." Chuy paused, "Do you think it would help to meet with your friend?"

"I don't think it would hurt. I'll arrange a meeting, if you want me to."

"Go ahead and do that. I still have a few more days off, so anytime this week is fine with me." Chuy sounded relieved.

Later that same day, Carlos entered a small Mexican restaurant on the outskirts of Camarillo. He paused by the cash register to let his eyes adjust to the darkness. It was midafternoon and the place was nearly empty. In the back he saw his cousin and Connie. They were just sitting there, toying aimlessly with their water glasses.

"Hey Connie, Chuy! Sorry I'm so late. There was an accident on the 101." Carlos turned to his cousin. *"Primo,* how are you doing?"

Chuy did not answer, but got up and hugged Carlos. He smiled a greeting to Connie.

"Have you guys eaten? I haven't had anything to eat all day!" He turned to Connie, "Connie it's good to see you. Thanks for coming right away to meet with us."

"Carlos, I'm so sorry your uncle passed away. You both must miss him so much. Tell me, what was he like?"

Carlos and Chuy shared memories of the old man and Connie nodded in appreciation. Bringing more chips and salsa, their waitress arrived to take their lunch orders. They ordered, Carlos going last as he quickly decided what he'd have. The waitress left and they returned to a story that Chuy had been sharing when the waitress came. The detective nodded and smiled a bit but said nothing.

"Connie," began Carlos, now ready to come to the main point of the meeting. "We want to be frank with you. We hope you will be straight with us too, because we honestly don't know what to do." The waitress returned with their lunch platters. Despite the seriousness of the moment, Connie and Chuy dug in with enthusiasm as Carlos continued. "This morning, both of us got a call from the AWA fellow. He told us that my uncle's autopsy report showed that he died of a brain injury caused by the fall when the Grady kid hit my uncle's ladder. He wanted to know what we were going to do about it."

Connie's brows knit in concentration. "Hmmmm," she murmured, looking down in thought. "What did you tell him?"

"Frankly," continued Carlos, "I told him that it was up to the sheriffs to decide. That's why we asked you to meet with us: to find out from you what action your people are going to take."

"And you?" she looked to Chuy.

"Same thing. I wanted to talk to Carlos before doing anything with those guys. They seem to have things all figured out, but I'm not sure I trust them."

Avoiding Carlos's eyes, Connie looked at Chuy and started to speak.

"First, let me say that, though this is an informal meeting, I'm glad to meet with you to share any information that I can." She pulled out a paper and handed it to Chuy. "This is a copy of the autopsy report that was sent to us. It does say that the fall might have led to your father's death." Carlos could see that she was choosing her words carefully. "We also received this report a couple of days ago. We're still reviewing it to see if there's any further action we need to undertake." She cleared her throat. "It's not an easy case, since there was no obvious intention to…"

Chuy had been very quiet, but at this point, he interrupted her. "Tell me, Detective, what would happen if I had been driving the car and Jeffrey Grady had been on that ladder? What would happen then?"

Surprised at his question, Carlos looked from his cousin to Connie, waiting for her reply.

Connie took a moment before responding. "I don't understand your question."

"It's just a simple question. Let's turn the situation around. What would happen to me if I drove a car, then knocked the Grady kid off a ladder, and he died?" Chuy held Connie's gaze. There was a challenge in his manner.

"Are you suggesting that we would treat the case differently just because this kid's last name is Grady?"

"That's *exactly* what I'm wondering," said Chuy.

Connie's face was very serious, "Do you think that I would act differently toward a person just because of who his family is?"

"I'm not wondering about *you* specifically, but in general. How would your department act because of his family's name?" Chuy asked quietly.

Connie opened her mouth to answer but stopped herself. She was in a difficult situation. Speaking to both men now, Connie brought the meeting to an end. "I need to get going, but first let me say how sorry I am about your father and uncle. I don't yet know if there actually was any criminal action in this case. But there might be some civil action your family could take. Here's a card from a friend of mine who can give you some advice. She handed a business card to Chuy and started to place several bills on the table to cover her tab.

Carlos stopped her. "I asked you to come as a favor. The bill is my responsibility." Thanking him, Connie closed her purse and looked up as he asked, "Can I call you later?"

"Please do." Her voice sounded a bit too formal.

On their way out, Chuy asked, "Well *primo*, what do you think?"

"I think you pissed her off with your question," answered Carlos with a wry grin. He put his arm around his cousin as they walked to their trucks.

Sergeant Teal glanced at his partner. Connie had been sitting at her desk all morning, reviewing various documents and staring at her computer, but saying almost nothing. Teal carefully tossed a paper clip. It bounced off her keyboard. His partner turned around, looking puzzled.

"You want to tell me what's wrong?" he asked.

"What do you mean?"

"A simple question. What's wrong? You've been pretty quiet today." He rose to refill his coffee cup.

She said, "Let me ask *you* a simple question. What would happen if the Grady boy had been on the ladder and one of the pickers had hit it with a car, knocked him down, and later on, the kid died?"

"What kind of question is that?"

"It's just a question that I was asked yesterday. What exactly would we do if that were the case?" Teal noticed that she was very serious and deliberate in her question.

"Well, we would definitely have the person in this office, question him, and try to determine intent. If we thought the person did it deliberately, or even recklessly, we'd probably charge him," said Teal.

"Then why haven't we brought the Grady kid in?"

"We can't do that."

"And why not? It's exactly what happened, but with Mr. Baca as the victim. The Grady kid hit his ladder with his car, knocked him down, and later, he died. The autopsy report says Francisco Baca died of an injury to his head from the fall. Why haven't we brought the kid in for questioning? What if we thought he did it deliberately... or even recklessly? Would we charge him?" Connie asked the questions slowly, never letting her eyes leave Teal's face.

"That's different," said Teal, somewhat irritated. "Grady's old man owns the ranch and he's well-known in the community. We just can't go around bothering the family."

"So, you're saying that it's okay for the Grady kid to hit a picker, but it's not okay for a picker to hit the Grady kid?" In her intensity, Connie had moved to the edge of her chair.

"Now that's not what I'm saying... I mean, there's a difference... The Grady kid..." Teal's voice faded and he looked at his partner intently. "Who asked you the question?"

"Chuy, the old man's son."

"Oh shit; I see what you mean. When did you see the son?"

"Yesterday. He asked to meet with me. As near as I can determine, the AWA has some scheme to make the old man's death part of their campaign. They're urging Chuy to take some action. From what I hear about that group, they could make a real pissing contest out of this." Connie seemed to relax now that she shared the burden with her partner.

"Anybody else at the meeting?"

"Yes, Carlos Reynoso. He was the one who asked me to meet with them, but it was Chuy who asked me that question," she explained. "During our conversation, they told me the union people were behind the idea. That activist, Johnny Cruz phoned each of them."

"What'd you tell them?"

"Well, I fumbled the answer just like you did. I did suggest that if there was no criminal action taken, they might have something for a civil action." She shrugged her shoulders and chuckled for the first time.

"Well I'm sure glad they came to you first. That gives us a heads-up. Listen, I'm pretty free this afternoon. Let's try to set up a meeting with the commander and one of the DA's boys. Hell, let's share the fun with them!"

Chapter 57
Consultation

THE DETECTIVE BUREAU'S COMMANDER was a stocky blonde of about 50. She greeted Ron and Connie with a generous smile. Dressed in a crisp department uniform, Commander June Schaeffer rocked back in her chair.

The neatly-dressed Assistant District Attorney was a young Korean American who sat quietly, waiting for the meeting to begin. He had arranged a yellow pad and a pen on the table. He read the two-page coroner's report that Connie had provided for those present. He underlined a few items, circled others, and made notes on his pad.

Commander Schaeffer quickly skimmed the report. Then she reread it very deliberately, laid it down, and waited. She made no notes.

Seeing they were ready, Teal addressed them. "Thanks for making time for us on such short notice. I realize you're both busy, but as you'll see, we need some input from you on this case as soon as possible. I'll let Detective Alonzo give you a brief overview." With a nod, he passed their attention to Connie.

"The facts are pretty straightforward. Apparently young Grady was racing a company car in the orchard. Then he drove by some pickers and hit a ladder. Francisco Baca, an older man who worked and lived on the Grady Ranch, was on that ladder and fell. The fall broke his hip. He also hit his head, which apparently led to his death a few weeks later. As you can see, the coroner has concluded that Mr. Baca very likely died as a result of the head injury he sustained at that time." Connie spoke very deliberately. Her words were a bit more formal, as they would have to be, should this case end up in court. She waited a moment for the information to be absorbed before continuing.

"I was asked by a family member what action we were going to take against the Grady boy, since the death was probably caused by Jeffrey Grady, the boy who drove the car that hit the ladder. I also should add that the Agri Workers of America Union has been doing some labor organizing in the area. They apparently see an opportunity to make Mr. Baca's death a unifying cause for their movement." DA Kim jotted down a few words. "Baca's son specifically asked me what would happen if the situation were reversed. That is, if the Grady boy had been on the ladder and one of the pickers had hit him with a vehicle and Jeffrey Grady had died." She ended her comments in a very low voice.

"The implication of the question was that, just because it was the ranch owner's son, we would treat the case differently?" asked the commander.

"That's exactly the implication," said Teal.

"And are we treating him differently?" asked the DA.

"Well, actually I suppose so, because until we got the query from the family, we assumed the case was closed," said Teal.

"Wow," breathed the commander, running her fingers through her short hair. "The Grady family is one of the richest and most powerful in the county. If we pick up the son, there will be hell to pay."

"And if we do nothing, the AWA will splash the whole thing through the media, and there will be hell to pay," said Teal.

Commander Schaeffer turned to Lee Kim. "What's your legal opinion of what we can do this situation?" she asked.

"If I were looking at this as just another John Doe, there could be some actionable items, at least some kind of misdemeanor," he said, scribbling a note on his yellow pad.

"What about the victim's son? What can we expect from him?" asked the commander.

"He's seems a like a nice, quiet, and decent fellow," answered Connie. "He's picker who also lives on the Grady ranch. I'm pretty sure he'd just like to be left alone so he can work. But of course, the AWA's pressuring him. I suppose he sees some inequities in the system now and is surely wondering about why they exist. It also didn't do any good that Grady's attorney threatened to evict the Bacas shortly after the accident."

"There's another factor we should consider," broke in the DA. "The Civil Division of the U.S. Attorney's Office has recently been looking at cases of civil rights inequities. If they were to catch wind of this, or be forced to take action in this case, our lives would be hell for a long, long time." The young Korean attorney dragged out the last words slowly.

The group sat quietly, saying nothing, each in their own thoughts. The attorney continued to make notes on his yellow pad.

After a few moments, Commander Schaeffer spoke. "There is perhaps another way," she suggested. I know the Grady's new attorney; we attend the same church. Maybe I can speak with him, tell him about the overall situation, beyond just the Grady's viewpoint. Then I'll see how he reacts."

"That still sounds like we are giving the boy special treatment," warned Teal.

"In a way that's true, but the reality is that our department has been known to show courtesy to lots of people. Why shouldn't we take an extra step, at least informally?" The commander paused then continued. "I'd like the time to inform the County Sheriff about our conversation, so he doesn't feel blindsided. She directed her gaze to the attorney. "Lee, perhaps you should inform your boss, so he isn't blindsided either."

After the meeting, Teal and Connie drove back to the office together. "I'm glad we brought them into the situation," said Teal. "At least the higher-ups know what's going on. By the way, you said your doctor friend, Carlos was involved. What's his part in this deal? Have you seen him lately?"

"Not really. I haven't seen him for a while, except at the meeting with his cousin. I got the impression that he's following Chuy's lead. I guess it might be a good idea to talk to him when he's by himself," she added.

"It might at that… if you just happened to run into him," grinned Teal

The rest of the way back, Connie tried to figure out what she could and couldn't say when she spoke with Carlos. Their relationship had become very complex.

Chapter 58
Questions

CARLOS DROVE BACK TO HIS OFFICE, but he felt confused. His uncle was dead; his aunt would never be the same, and it seemed that other people wanted to take over his uncle's memory for their own benefit. Yet even if the union wanted to improve the lot of the humble farm workers, the whole idea felt like a moral hijacking of his uncle's life and memory. Still, if his uncle's life and death were used for the betterment of others, was that such a bad thing? Would his aunt's life be more comfortable if she had additional money? He really didn't know her financial circumstances. Perhaps she would need more money to insure her independence. Would it be wrong if farm workers' lives improved as a result of his uncle's death? What would Tió Francisco think?

The questions raced though his mind. He replayed them over and over, but he got no answers. He could come only up with more questions. Carlos drove into the medical center's parking lot. A blast of hot air from the summer heat quickly pushed these thoughts aside. Before he knew it, he was inside, and the demands of seeing patients overcame the nagging questions... for the time being.

It was late when he entered his apartment. He was just in time to answer the phone. It was Ann.

"Doctor? This is your favorite patient. I need a consultation with you."

"Is that so? What seems to be the trouble?"

"There seems to be a strange feeling in my stomach."

Carlos knew the ruse. "Perhaps, you should try eating," he suggested, his smile carrying through his voice.

"Good idea! Your place or mine?"

"Your place, definitely! The only thing you'll get here is orange juice or beer," admitted Carlos.

"Great! Come on over. I'll have something ready by the time you get here. Oh, make sure to bring your swim trunks. It's still pretty warm out here."

Ann noticed Carlos's distraction. After dinner they sat by the pool in the still-warm evening. "What's the problem?"

Without more prompting he told her everything about the meeting with Chuy and Connie, his thoughts and his concerns. He spoke for a long time, but unlike her usual chatty self, Ann said nothing. She just held his hand.

After a long silence she said, "I wonder if I will be as lucky as your aunt was, to have a great love affair for such a long time, with a good man like your uncle."

"Their life wasn't always easy," said Carlos.

"I'm sure it wasn't, but genuine love sure smoothes out lots of bumps." It was time to take his mind off the family situation. "So, how are things at work?" she asked.

"Great! Better than I ever dreamed, but even there you get some bumps now and then." He told her about the encounter with Mr. Spencer, the man that wouldn't let a 'Mexican' examine him.

"Oh, Carlos! I'm so sorry! You're so innocent; people like that idiot are everywhere," she sighed. "Some people have such a disgusting attitude!"

"I don't know. When I was picking lemons, life seemed so much simpler. You work hard all day, have a cold beer or two, take a long, hot shower, eat some beans and tortillas, and sleep like a baby all night..." said Carlos wistfully.

"You mean there are no idiot lemon pickers?" she asked.

After a few seconds he started to laugh. "I guess I do know one or two, now that you mention it." His laugh continued, "In fact, I can think of several who would be just as bad as that guy in the office." Suddenly his mood changed, he put his around Ann, "Where are you going to look for this great love affair?"

"Oh, I guess sometime I'll just get on a bus on a dark night in a strange country, go to sleep, and then wake up next to some fellow who'll sweep me off my feet!"

"What a dreamer you are!" smiled Carlos, who soon fell asleep on the lounge.

When he woke up, Carlos went into the kitchen. Ann and her mother were having ice cream. "Well, Carlos! How was your nap?" asked Julie.

Carlos was a little embarrassed, "I'm sorry; I guess I must have been tired. Did I miss anything?"

"Not much. Ann was just telling me about your experiences lately. I've got just the medicine for you." She served him a dish of ice cream.

"Thanks!" he said. "Your daughter is a wonder! She made me realize that there are idiots everywhere. Just as, I suppose, there are good people everywhere from all walks of life."

My bright daughter is wise beyond her years at times… even though at times, she can be a dreamer."

"I don't know how wise she is," he joked, "but she certainly is a dreamer!" He turned to wink at Ann. She reached over and pinched his arm, "Ouch! Why'd you do that?"

"Just a pinch from a dreamer to a hard-headed one," smiled Ann.

Chapter 59
Service

" "CARLOS, THIS IS ADRIANA. HOW HAVE YOU BEEN?" This time Carlos connected the voice to the surgeon more quickly.

"I'm fine Dr. Colson," he replied.

"As I mentioned, I was very impressed with the work you do at the clinic. I have some extra supplies for you from here and some more that I conned out of some of our suppliers. I want to make arrangements to get them to you," Colson's voice was very businesslike.

"Thank you very much! I'm sure that Luz and I can use whatever you have. What do I need to do to get them?"

"Well I thought that if you were free this evening, maybe you could drop by my office at the hospital. You can pick it all up and then…" She paused a second,"…then I'd like to buy you dinner. I'd like to discuss a few ideas with you."

"It will be close to 7:00 p.m. before I can finish up here," said Carlos.

"Perfect! I'll be waiting for you."

"Let's walk," suggested Colson, as they finished placing the boxes in Carlos's truck. Carlos thanked her profusely for the large quantity of useful supplies she had donated to the downtown clinic.

"There's a little restaurant around the corner. They have good food and it's a good place to talk," said Colson. She linked arms with Carlos as they walked. The restaurant was busy, but being only a party of two, the head waiter seated them immediately at a little table off to one side. The Italian food smelled wonderful. Carlos took Adriana's advice and ordered the Chicken Alfredo.

"How has your work been going?" he asked. As he expected, she had been very busy, working long hours, since so many people needed her skills and there were still so few doctors trained in her field.

"So, how are things going with you, Carlos?" she asked, turning the focus to him.

"Things are fine, except it gets hectic at times, of course. All in all, it's been a very positive experience at Angelus Medical Center. I was very fortunate to have become associated with Dr. Pilabos. He has made it a real learning experience... It's much different from picking lemons!"

"Carlos, I'll get right to it. The University, working with a special government program, is recruiting bilingual physicians for our Organ Transplant Program. We think that a large part of the population that needs our help is underserved, just because those people are unaware of what's available. We think having the right doctors is the key to solving the problem." She took a bite, giving Carlos time to think, and continued. "I wonder... have you considered doing this kind of work full-time?"

Carlos was quiet for a while. "I never really thought about it. I just haven't had time. Things have happened so fast over the last several months. Then of course, Dr. Pilabos has been very kind to me. I would hate to leave him."

"I understand. Actually, you wouldn't have to." As Colson continued, she leaned forward earnestly. "The way I have it worked out, your transplant work would be in conjunction with the downtown clinic, as well as with Angelus Medical Center, since you see many of the type of patients we want to target. We would want Pilabos onboard with this. In the long run, it could be complementary to your work at the clinic."

"I guess my next question is, how can you be sure that I have the talent to perform this kind of surgery?"

"I don't, but I have a pretty good hunch. We would have to spend quite a bit of time together in a short period to make that determination. I'll be very frank. If I don't think you have the talent or the inclination, I will not waste your time or mine."

"That sounds fair," he said. "Shall I tell Dr. Pilabos?"

"No, let me call him," she replied, a pleased smile crossing her face. "Now let's consider dessert!"

"Hey, Doc! How are you?" asked the attendant, as Carlos entered the parking lot. In the bed of the pickup were several boxes. They contained a variety of medical supplies from Dr. Colson. Carlos and Luz each picked up a box and headed for the clinic.

"We're fine; how about you? How are you doing?" asked Carlos. Is there any chance you can bring in the other boxes when you have a minute?"

"Sure, Doc! I'll have them over there in a few minutes. I also have some more doughnuts for you and the kids." He was eating one of them himself. He tuned and spoke to a couple of men he'd been talking with when Carlos pulled in. They reached into the truck and carried the boxes to the clinic.

"What did you have to do to get all this stuff?" Luz asked Carlos.

"Not a thing. Dr. Colson had a lot of this stuff, mostly samples. It was just cluttering up her office, so I helped take them off her hands." He set a box next to the orange-haired receptionist. "Angel's bringing more stuff in a second. Would you please sort it out so we can get an idea what we have?"

"Sure! As long as he brings some doughnuts!" she replied, bending her brilliant red lips into a crooked smile. The effect was comical, but Carlos and Luz were careful not to laugh.

"Well, we'll certainly have to send her a nice thank you note," said Luz, "unless you've already thanked her personally."

"I *did* thank her personally, but it would especially be nice if you sent her a card. Your English is better than mine," winked Carlos.

"Okay!"

Clinic day was hectic, as it always was. Carlos and Luz saw the usual: an assortment of scrapes, too little food, and too much alcohol. The summer heat affected personal hygiene and made people seem a bit crankier. It occurred to Carlos that a shower and barber shop might be even more beneficial than the medicine they were distributing. That thought stayed with him all day, and once he'd seen the last patient, he knew he was right.

On the way home he asked Luz, "What do you think the chances are of our expanding the clinic to include a shower? Then, we could also invite a barber or a hair stylist to help these people out. What do you think?"

Luz looked at him in amazement. She said nothing as she considered the idea for a few minutes. "Carlos, that would be a godsend for some of these people, but it sounds impossible! It would be too difficult to set up. Then, how would we supervise it? Oh no, Carlos it's too far-fetched."

"And you are thinking of being a nun so you can help people?"Carlos kidded his companion. "Heck, it won't hurt just to ask a few people. Perhaps a miracle will happen."

On Wednesday of the following week, Luz caught up with Carlos in the hall of the medical center.

"Guess what? I talked to my cousin Maggie. She's a teacher at a beauty college downtown. She said she and some of her students would come to the clinic next Saturday. They can cut hair and even wash hair, just for the practice. She told me they even have a portable water system so they can wash hair outside."

"Wonderful!" responded Carlos, very pleased.

"There's also a company that rents linens, and they're willing to give us some of their old washcloths and hand towels. We can wet them, so people can take kind of a sponge bath, not a real shower, but considering the situation, it could help."

"Wow, you sure have this all worked out! Our patients will be very surprised!"

The following Saturday, Maggie showed up with several students even before Carlos and Luz arrived. The clinic was not yet open, but they'd already set up their portable chairs and sinks, hung mirrors on the wooden fence along the alley, and already had people in line, getting cleaned up.

Maggie called out, "Luz! Good to see you!"

"Hiya, Mags! You're sure busy for such an early hour!" Turning to Carlos, she continued. "This is Dr. Reynoso."

"Nice to meet you, Doc! Since it's such a nice day, we set up in the alley. I hope that's not a problem," said Maggie.

Luz looked to Carlos for an answer. "What do you think?"

"As she says, it's a nice day. Why not?" Carlos shook hands with Maggie, who then turned to continue cutting the hair of a teenage girl.

Later that morning, Carlos heard a loud commotion outside. He saw two police squad cars were parked in front. Four police officers were arguing with Maggie. Carlos walked up to them. "What's going on?" he asked.

"Dr. Reynoso," said Maggie, "these cops are hassling us and our clientele."

The doctor's lab coat had an effect. One of the police officers turned immediately to him. "Sir, you can't have a barber shop out on the street… or even in the alley for that matter. You don't have a permit," he explained. The officer was a short man. His black shirt stretched taut across his ample belly and over his armored vest.

Calmly, Carlos asked, "Why is it a problem? No one's being hurt. Our patients need to be able to clean up. It helps us when they come in for medical attention."

"Now, Doctor, I know you're running a medical clinic, but this out here is a barber shop!" said the cop.

"Well, yes and no," replied Carlos. As their doctor, I am actually prescribing this personal hygiene. It is part of the medical treatment. As you probably know, a simple thing like getting rid of lice and getting cleaned up helps wounds heal and prevents infections. It's a huge help to me when I examine them, not to mention how much this helps the person's self-esteem."

"Yeah, but you can't do this out here in the open."

"What's the harm? No one's being bothered. Some of these folks are getting cleaned up for the first time in weeks," Carlos continued. "It's a clean operation. When you think about it, people piss in the streets here all the time, but nobody stops them. I suppose that's not permitted, is it?"

"Of course it's not permitted. It's against the law," said the officer.

"Then I guess you should arrest them, because it's a more serious health problem, right?" continued Carlos calmly.

"We can't do that! If we did, the jails would be full," responded the officer.

"You mean you won't arrest people for pissing in the street, but you will if they get a haircut and wash their face?" asked Carlos innocently. "Look over there officer. See that fellow in the red plaid shirt over there?" urged Carlos. He pointed out a middle-aged man who wore dirty, scruffy clothes and unmatched shoes. He held a plastic bag with some clothes in it. "Just look at him from the neck up." The man's neatly trimmed hair gleamed. He was patting shaving lotion on his freshly shaven face. He inspected himself in a small mirror, grinning. "Now Sir, isn't that smile worth more than a hundred men pissing in the streets?"

The policeman looked at the strange sight. The man's head seemed to belong to an entirely different body. The incongruity made the officer smile. He waved his hand at Carlos, dismissing him. "Okay, Doc, you got me there. Have a nice day!" He and the other officers got into their squad cars and left.

The clinic itself was less hectic than usual this time. It was as if the hair washing and grooming had washed away some of their ailments. One homeless man had a portable radio tuned to a station with a heavy beat. The music and the buzz of hair clippers lent its rhythm to the sidewalk barber shop.

Later that day, Luz and Carlos stepped out to watch the activities for a minutes. Luz said, "Oh Carlos! Wouldn't it be great to have a hot shower? And how about a washing machine and dryer to wash their clothes? Then they would be clean all over!"

"I'm very proud of you Luz," smiled Carlos.

Chapter 60
Equality

COMMANDER JUNE SCHAEFFER LOOKED at the people around the table in the Sheriff's Department meeting room. The young DA had arranged his yellow pad and pen, Connie had set out a short stack of three-by-fives rubber-banded in groups, and Teal rocked back in his chair, fingers locked behind his head.

"I saw Grady's attorney at church Sunday," she began. "I briefly outlined the situation for him. I got the feeling he was not surprised about our conversation. In fact, he seemed to have been expecting my comments. He told me Grady had already made a generous offer to the family. Furthermore, he was willing to even increase it, if he knew what it would take to resolve the issue. He also inferred that he was willing to have the boy accept some minor slap on the hands, but that was it. He even warned me that if anyone tried to make an issue of this, there would be hell to pay."

DA Kim made a note on his yellow pad before speaking. "My boss just happened to come by my office yesterday," he said. After we talked about last night's ballgame, he casually mentioned that, since this accident happened in the workplace, this was actually a Worker's Compensation claim. He told me that the law was designed especially to take care of these kinds of things. Worker's Comp. pays all medical costs and provides a death benefit in the case of a death. This is all very straightforward, according to employment law."

Connie glanced at Teal and picked up one of her cards. "Are we, as law enforcement officials, to ignore a similar such incident, if it were to happen tomorrow?" she asked.

"Well, that depends on the circumstances," hedged the commander.

"Would the circumstances be that, if the accused is the son of a prominent citizen, then leniency is okay?" Connie asked coolly. No one answered her, of course, so she continued. "I guess you all know that the AWA will use this to whip us about. All we will have to back up our inaction is some lame excuse. I've met some of their organizers, and something tells me they've been waiting for something just like this to happen. These fellows are not lemon pickers. They are smart, well-trained people. I bet they've been praying for something like this to come along, and we're handing it to them on a plate."

"I'm sure that the Gradys have factored all of this into the equation," said Commander Schaeffer. It looks to me that the Grady boy will not be touched. If asked, we will refer people to the Worker's Compensation Board. We'll let them take care of it... Understood?" Schaeffer eyed each one as they nodded their understanding.

Teal looked at the others, and in a quiet voice said, "I just want to clarify what Connie was getting at. When this gets out, and it will... we'll have egg on our faces. We'll all be running for cover. I'd like it to be on the record that even though we will do as you have asked, Connie and I believe that at the very least, we should investigate the situation further." Slowly, Teal eyed the commander and the DA, not breaking eye contact until they had acknowledged his comments.

Commander Schaeffer and Assistant DA Kim rose to leave and all said their polite farewells.

Connie wrote something on one of her cards and turned it over. When the pair had left, she turned toward Teal and said, "Hey, thanks for backing me up there at the end, Ron. So, who's going to tell the family that we're dropping the case?"

"I suppose you are," Teal smiled. "Connie, I know this stinks, but in this world, some folks are more important than others. What the AWA does is not our business."

Connie riffled through her cards and said sadly, "I'm not *that* naive, but you know, tomorrow the very same thing will happen to some Mexican kid, and we'll hang him. In fact, we already have a jail full of them just for stealing a six-pack of sodas. But Ron, let me tell you: the AWA will definitely use this incident to make us look like blithering idiots."

"Connie, when you tell Carlos or the Baca's son, just give them the basics; don't elaborate," advised Teal.

"I think I'll call Carlos right now." She picked up the phone. "Dr. Reynoso please; this is Detective Alonzo calling." As she waited, she chose several cards. "Carlos? This is Connie. Listen, we just had a meeting with our superiors. Frankly, your uncle's accident falls under the State Worker's Compensation program, and as I understand it, they have jurisdiction over all aspects of this case." She listened a moment. "Sure, I understand... Sure, give me a call when you come into town."

Teal waited for a few seconds, "How'd it go?"

"He was very proper and polite, as you'd expect a physician to be, but his voice could freeze a person... He was *not* impressed."

"Shit, I don't blame him! I'm not impressed with us either!"

"So much for equality of justice," said Connie, putting away her cards.

Chapter 61
A Demonstration

THE MAN WITH THE NEATLY TRIMMED BEARD SAT quietly as he listened to three young men and a woman reporting to him about recent union activities in the county. He was particularly interested when Johnny Cruz reported on the death of an old man at the Grady ranch. He took some notes and listened as each person had their turn to speak. Rubin Goldberg was a small man. He wore a red tee shirt with the union's Aztec-style black sunburst on the back, some well-worn jeans cut off at mid-thigh and bare, sandaled feet. His thinning hair was pulled back tightly in a skinny pony tail, held by a strip of leather.

After each speaker had finished, Goldberg turned to Johnny Cruz. "Why don't you review for me exactly what happened at the Grady ranch and why the old man died," he suggested.

Cruz handed the small man a file holding copies of the coroner's report and his notes. "Briefly, Jeffrey Grady's about sixteen. He was hot rodding in a lemon orchard. He hit the ladder on which Mr. Baca was standing. Baca was up near the top of the tree. He fell and broke his hip. He had surgery to fix the hip, but a few weeks later, he suddenly died. The autopsy report, which you're looking at now," noted Cruz, "says that he also hit his head when he fell, and that he probably died of complications from that injury. The family asked the County Sheriff to investigate." He smiled and continued. "The cops said that since this was a Worker's Comp. case, they would beg off. We believe that pressure has been put on both the DA and the Sheriff to drop the case."

Goldberg rose and walked around, rubbing his hands and smiling with satisfaction. "We've been fishing in this county for months without a bite and suddenly, a big fish jumps right into our boat! Wow!" He removed several papers from his briefcase and passed them around. "Okay, this is a list of what we need to do. How soon can we get a bunch of people at the entrance to the ranch, or maybe at the Baca's house?" A hand rose and a young man volunteered to organize the gathering.

"Thanks. We can probably get a good crowd tomorrow," continued Cruz. It's Saturday, so school will be out and the weather looks nice. I guess we should focus on the ranch entrance. The entrance is well-known, plus it will be great for the media shots. Okay... next on the list is getting this out to the media. We need all the media coverage we can get.

"I'll take care of contacting the media in the area," offered the woman. "Should I include the Los Angeles area, too?"

"Not right away, but be prepared to do so if I ask. Okay?" She nodded in agreement. "We should have plenty of fliers and flags, both Union and American. It makes a better impression. Let's see if we can get a photo of the old man. Here are samples of some fliers we've used in the past," continued Cruz.

"I'll take the flags and fliers, and I'll look into getting a photo of Mr. Baca," offered another.

"I can see that we'd better call in some of our volunteers," said Johnny Cruz. "We'll be working all night. We need some locals in for the overnight work. Manny, can you do that? Oh, and also call our contacts in the Valley and get a couple of carloads of our organizers here tomorrow morning." Manny nodded and headed immediately for the phone.

"Manny?" added Goldberg. "Will you also make sure to notify the Sheriff's Office? I'll bet we can get quite a reaction from them! All right everybody, let's get moving!" urged Goldberg. His energy and enthusiasm for the cause was contagious.

Turning to Cruz, Goldberg spoke with great intensity. "Johnny, you'd better get to the family right now. Tell them how irate people are that their father and husband was *murdered* and that *nothing* is going to happen to the *killer*. Use those same words. Tell them about the arrangements we are making. Tell them we're doing all this in honor of Mr. Baca's memory. Tell them it would be great if his entire family and friends would join us at the gate. If necessary, tell them we're starting a scholarship program in his name. Say whatever you have to, but get them there! You understand? This is very important! You *must* succeed with the family!" He paused then mused aloud, "What are the chances of getting the old man's widow to come out...?"

"I understand; I'm on my way," replied Cruz. He headed out to his car.

By late morning it was warm and people were in a festive mood. Children played in the street. Music played as loudly as possible from a large portable radio. A little boy handed out union buttons from a box, accepting donations for them when people offered them. Several people carried the AWA's distinctive red flags with the black sunburst emblem. One pair held a AWA banner aloft. Others distributed fliers with a photo of Francisco Baca on the front, and bold lettering that read:

"He worked his entire life for the company that killed him!"

The crowd gathered at the ranch entrance. Employees and others had to slow down to enter the property. Two vans parked off to the side of the road. Their tall TV antennas were soon raised to transmit. Cameramen and local correspondents prepared their equipment for live interviews. A newspaper reporter interviewed a local fellow, making notes. A chunky camera hung from his neck.

Within half an hour, a deputy sheriff drove up. Everyone but the children quieted down, but continued to mill around the entrance. Deputy Sheriff Larry Nelson asked no one in particular, "What's goin' on here?" No one answered him. Eventually he noticed Johnny Cruz. "Hey, Johnny! What's with the big crowd?"

"We're picketing the Grady ranch. The family of the old man who was killed is concerned that the old man died and no one has been arrested. Many workers here have signed union cards. They want us to organize the ranch so they can have justice." Cruz's manner was friendly. He'd gotten to know Larry through various similar encounters and they had established a mutually respectful working relationship.

"I don't suppose ya have a permit to assemble, do ya?" asked Larry. "We got a complaint that yer impedin' workers and trucks from enterin' the property. Ya know ya cain't do that."

"Of course I know that. We're not stopping anyone. We notified your office so your people are aware of what we're doing. If anyone wants to enter the ranch, these people part like the Red Sea," Cruz laughed at his joke. "All we're doing is giving people some fliers and telling them what the company did to the old man." He handed one to the deputy, who folded it and put it in his pocket.

Just then, one of the company foremen honked his horn and slowly turned onto the company road. Several people started to holler to get his attention. Someone else put a flyer on his windshield wiper. Others drummed on the truck as it drove through. The driver of the pickup appeared terrified, especially when people pounded on his truck. However, true to their leader's word, the demonstrators did part and allow him to pass.

Several minutes later, another patrol car arrived and two deputies got out. Grabbing their face protection and shields, they were soon in full riot gear. The senior officer also carried a megaphone. They pushed their way roughly through the crowd to reach Deputy Nelson. A few people complained about being pushed back. Then two more cars arrived and more riot-geared officers arrived. Everyone seemed surprised at the large number of officers. The crowd grew quiet. Even Nelson was surprised, "What's the problem?" he asked one of the officers. "I didn't call for back up."

"One of the foremen phoned. He said he was attacked when he drove through the gate a few minutes ago," he answered.

"Whaddya mean attacked? I was raht here when he drove through. Dang it! Nobody attacked 'im," said Larry indignantly.

"He said he was attacked, Deputy Nelson. We have orders to disperse the attackers and to arrest anyone who will not leave." His face was red and he trembled a bit as he spoke into his megaphone. "You are hereby ordered to disperse!" he commanded.

"Come on Larry! Talk to your people!" urged Cruz. "We don't want any trouble. You saw what happened. We have a right to demonstrate peacefully, and that's all we're doing."

The reporters had seen all the officers arrive. The newspaperman took some quick shots and jotted notes. The TV reporters alerted their cameramen to begin taping. One walked closer and aimed her microphone at the officers and Johnny. She picked up the AWA organizer as he said, "Look, most of the people here are women, children, and a few old men. Do they look like attackers?"

A little girl came up to Johnny. She put her arms around his waist and started to cry. Cruz hugged her. "It's all right, Honey. It's all right," he said, patting her back. Cruz looked back up at the officers and pleaded, "Look, guys. We're doing nothing wrong. We have the right to…" But before he could finish his sentence, an officer cracked Cruz on the head with his baton. He swung again as Cruz was falling, but the baton hit the girl solidly on the forehead. Her face exploded in blood as the two fell to the ground. Cruz rolled over the girl to protect her. The deputy struck him three more times on the back.

Shocked at what had just happened in front of him, Deputy Nelson jumped in front of the officer and pinned him with a bear hug. He yelled, "Gol darn it! What the haill's the matter with you…?! You nuts?"

The crowd was stunned, and for a second time, there was silence. Even the other officers were taken aback. Then the girl stood back up. Tears joined the blood which streamed down her face and onto her white t-shirt. "Mommy!" she wailed. Seeing her bloody hands, she cried out in terror, "Mommy! I'm going to die… Oh please, Mommy! Mommy… I don't want to die! Don't let me die!"

Larry Nelson called to one of the other officers, "Get this dumb shit away from 'ere!" Pointing to one, he ordered, "Call an ambulance!" and to another, "Bring a first aid kit, and step on it!" Two other officers grabbed the man, pulled him away and stuffed him into the back seat of a squad car.

Someone had brought out a white towel to stem the bleeding. Within seconds, the towel was deep red and the little girl's face looked ashen. Her mother knelt beside her, her face creased with worry. Larry sat her down to the side of the road. He noticed that Cruz was also bleeding from over his right eye. Cruz sat next to the stunned girl and they both shared the towel. One TV cameraman was less than ten feet from the two, filming nonstop. The blood-soaked towel lay in the girl's lap. Her little face was etched in terror and her body shook uncontrollably.

Deputy Larry picked up the megaphone. In a soothing tone, he spoke. "Okay now, folks. We got an ambulance on the way. Let's all move on over to one side so they can git in here." He waved his hand to the left of the entrance road. "I know you don' wanna make this any worse than it's already been…"

Like a slow wave, the muted crowd flowed quietly off to the side.

Meanwhile, the Baca family had just begun to approach the scene from inside the ranch. Fortunately, an alert, bilingual newspaperman scurried over to interview them. He hadn't been able to break through the crowd to get the story of the day, but what he heard gave him a great human interest story with many details. It did not make the front page… but it interested many readers. In fact, as it turned out later, his story filled in many details prosecutors would find helpful.

"I can't believe it! I can not believe it! I damned well can't *believe* it!" crowed Goldberg as he watched the scene on the TV. He smiled gleefully and danced about as he drank a soda. "I damned well just cannot believe it! Oh, I could kiss that dumb son-of-a-bitch cop in the ass! I couldn't have planned it better myself!"

The local channel's story opened with an overall scene of the crowd, their flags, and the little boy and his AWA buttons. There was a close-up of the officer in black riot gear striking Cruz and then the little girl. The blow to the little girl was a tight shot. There terror in the girl's face was unmistakable as her blood spurted out, instantly staining her shirt. This part of the film was shown several times at regular speed, then in slow motion. Then, frame-by-frame, it showed the terror on the girl's face, then the baton hitting her face, then the blood spurting toward the camera. Subsequent shots showed the officer in black riot gear, his face straining grotesquely, twisted with hate. The reporter's voice matched the shock and terror of the film. Then it showed the officer sitting in the squad car, his wild-eyed face visible through the window.

A long-range shot showed most of the crowd kneeling and quietly praying the Rosary. The girl sat holding the blood-stained towel to her face, sobbing. The story closed with the wailing of the ambulance as it arrived.

By the evening news, CNN had picked up the story. Within hours, the short clip had circulated all around the world. Within an hour, the Governor, a farmer with strong support in the agriculture community, also appeared on TV, saying that he was forming a task force to investigate the incident. Additionally, he was flying into the Ventura County personally to get a first-hand view of the situation.

The following day, the Buenaventura Examiner and the L.A. City Register had a color photo on the front page and several black-and-whites inside. The color photo above the fold, showed the little girl's terrified, bloody face. Other shots showed the hate-filled face of the officer in riot gear, his baton raised, about to strike the girl. Goldberg had several copies of newspaper on the table. The phones in the office rang continuously.

In Asia, they showed the terrified girl's bloody face alongside a well-known old photo of a young naked Vietnamese girl who had just been napalmed, the American flag flying in the background. In other areas, the beating of the girl was described as an everyday occurrence in the United States. The commentary from one European journalist was that since the Americans felt no compulsion beating their own innocent citizens, what could other foreigners expect from such a violent country.

Over the next few days, the story spread across America and then to other nations. Goldberg watched as the President of the United States came on camera. A somber President looked at the cameras and stated that he was forming a bipartisan task force, led by the Attorney General to investigate, "...the brutality inflicted upon innocent people and especially this little girl." The President was obviously uncomfortable as he spoke.

The President of Mexico immediately called for the World Court at The Hague and the United Nations Security Forces to investigate the beating. He charged the United States with exploiting its citizens. The Mexican government asked specifically that the Ventura County Sheriff's Department be charged with criminal action.

"Shit! I just can't believe it!" Goldberg repeated, looking at Cruz. "Johnny, you were great, just great, just fucking great!"

Johnny Cruz sat at the table watching the news program repeat, each time with added bits as reporters came in with details. Johnny had a black eye and a bandage over his right one. "I don't feel great," he said with a grimace. "I thought the riot squad had been through training to avoid this kind of shit. That nut must have been asleep during that part of the class."

"I wish I knew who that cop was so I could thank him. I'd even kiss his ass!" said Goldberg gleefully.

"You know, I think you actually would," chuckled Cruz. He grew serious. "What about the girl," he asked. "How is she doing?"

"I think she's fine. We already have the California Rural Legal Aid working with a private attorney preparing to sue Grady, the county, and the state, all on her behalf. That should be a slam dunk," he said. "We've already made an arrangement with CNN for an exclusive interview tomorrow, when she's released from the hospital." Goldberg started to sing softly, "Happy days are here again..."

Ron Teal and Connie Alonzo watched the news on a large TV in the main office. They glanced at each other and shook their heads in mutual disgust. "I've seen that little girl playing on the ranch," said Connie. Watching the officer as he was shoved into the patrol car, she added, "Where did we get *that* asshole?"

The station's main office was large and held about twenty desks for officers, clerks and their supervisors. Though most of the desks were filled, the room was silent, as people watched in disbelief at the scene replaying time after time. A few actually turned their heads aside as the deputy struck the girl in slow motion. Several moaned as her blood spurted out toward the camera.

Teal shook his head. "God knows! One thing I do know however, is that no matter what our Commander and the District Attorney say, we're back on the case with young Grady. When the Feds and the boys from Sacramento come here, crawling all over the place, they'll want to know everything. And they'll want to see some follow-up."

Connie smiled, "I'll bet you a beer that our fine Detective Commander and the DA won't tell them they pulled us off the case."

"No bet there! But that being the case, we'd better move fast to make our leaders look good," said Teal with a wry smile.

Carlos was sitting with Ann, watching the news at his place. "Oh my God!" he said. "I know that little girl! She lives a couple of houses down from my aunt, on the ranch." The two sat mesmerized as the scenes unfolded again and again. The newscast switched to show a still shot of the terrified, bloodied little girl, crying for her mother. It was the teaser shot for a segment, featuring talking-heads from various backgrounds, analyzing and commenting on the incident. Religious leaders commented on issues of morality. Union leaders spoke about working conditions on the farms. Social scientists considered what might have made the officer go off the deep end. Elected officials stumbled all over themselves to be the first to condemn the actions of law enforcement.

An enterprising reporter got wind of the old man's death and actually connected his death to the demonstration of protest and little girl's beating. By the following day, the new coverage delved deeply into all phases of farm work and the living conditions of farm workers. Reporters bombarded the County Sheriff with questions about his department's negligence and the offending officer's brutality. He asked specifically about his unwillingness to investigate the young Grady boy's role in the event that had led to the tragic death of the old man. The Sheriff only said that he could not comment, because his department had an ongoing investigation in the matter.

Carlos was mesmerized by the flood of attention devoted to this event by the news media. He saw familiar faces in newscast, and in the morning newspaper. He had the sense that he had been missing out on something very important.

Epilogue

"Carlos, with your potential and background you would do well to specialize in thoracic surgery. I know it would take a few more years, but it would be more than worthwhile. I can help with some of the admissions… and even some of the finances in the short term." The surgeon poured some more coffee for Carlos, who listened intently to the small woman. "In the meanwhile, you can work for our clinic and help us develop our program, especially for the Hispanic community which is so underserved."

"Why do you think I would be good working in the chest?"

"Well, I've seen your work. When you stitch up a wound, it's very neat, and you seem to be able to do it rapidly. You're able to anticipate problems, all traits which are needed when one is working in the chest."

Carlos picked up the coffee mug and walked over to the window. Several blocks away he could see the Highway 101, busy with cars going in both directions. Where were they all going? Where was he going? He held the cup in both hands and took a slow sip as he considered this. Finally, he turned to the surgeon and then looked pensively back into the deep, black liquid in the cup.

"I very much appreciate your comments and offer, and I'll give it some thought… but while I know some of my people require specialized treatment, they are also in desperate need of basic medical care. I know people suffer and die from heart problems, but they also suffer and die from neglect, abuse, and ignorance. And there's a lot more of that around." He turned back toward the freeway and watched the cars for a few more moments. "It just seems to me that my best efforts should be on the frontlines, working on the basics." He raised his eyes to look across the freeway to the Encino foothills. "And…," he continued, almost to himself, "I think it would also be better for me, personally."

About the Author

Alfonso (Al) Guilin has been a lifetime participant in and observer of agricultural production in California. This dynamic industry has local and worldwide influence on the lives of producers as well as consumers. Those people responsible for the cultivation, management, and harvesting are part of Al's background and family legacy. He spent his youth on the family farm, working alongside the farm workers. Al is active in the Roman Catholic Church and is an Ordained Deacon in the Archdiocese of Los Angeles.

The Lemon Thorn is based upon a lifetime of observations and experiences in California agriculture and among the types of people, scenes, and landscapes represented within its pages.